The Curse of the Fallen:

BATTLE AT THE CROSSROADS

Dr. L. Brooks Walker

ARCHWAY
PUBLISHING

Archway Publishing books may be ordered through booksellers or by contacting:

Archway Publishing
1663 Liberty Drive
Bloomington, IN 47403
www.archwaypublishing.com
1 (888) 242-5904

ISBN: 978-1-4808-6499-3 (sc)
ISBN: 978-1-4808-6500-6 (e)

Library of Congress Control Number: 2018949853

Print information available on the last page.

Archway Publishing rev. date: 07/10/2018

Contents

Preface

The story presented here began as a series of thoughts on human nature. Over the years in ministry and education, I have been puzzled by my experiences and observations of human behavior. During this time I have been both pleasantly surprised and disappointed by what I have seen, and I've found myself pondering the questions of good and evil. I began to write about these thoughts on various situations and events, and over the years I created a dialogue with myself as I sought to understand people's motivations and actions.

As the writings grew the questions continued, but the answers were harder to come by—until I realized that there was an obvious answer right before my eyes. I decided to bring the elements of my observations and explanation together in a story. Fearing that a theological or psycho-sociological treatise would be too boring, I decided to combine these academic interests with my love of history and storytelling, and this novel was born. Borrowing from historical events and personal experiences, I have written this story in a way that I hope will entertain and stimulate readers to look at the world around them and perhaps better understand, or at the least ask similar questions to those I have asked. Where does good and evil originate in humanity, and how does it seemingly co-exist within us? Is there a single environmental, genetic, or spiritual explanation for human behavior, or is it a compilation of all three? Most people say that it is all three, but the moment you think you have an answer, someone comes along and exhibits behavior that doesn't fit what was expected. You then realize that the three explanations are variables, which are continually shaping, enhancing, and canceling one another out. If that observation is true, then why are some able to maintain a certain consistency of thought and actions and some sociopathic? The answer may seem simple to some and baffling to others, but over the course of a lifetime I have found that all people seem to be locked in their private struggles with good and evil.

This story is inspired by incidents and people I have observed over the course of my life. I have taken liberties for the sake of plot, but overall, everything you will read has been observed in some form. The conversations with the fallen are based on personal speculation and some actual comments from people as opposed to supernatural entities. Names of people and places have been changed, except for information about the battle at Buford's Crossroads in Lancaster, South Carolina. All references to that historical event are based on research and accounts of the battle. You might say it was this battle that inspired me to write this novel. The events that took place there served as a historical example of the potential for evil and good in humanity. The battlefield marker has a quote that is listed as a confession from a British historian who haunts the location today. He wrote, describing the battle, "The virtue of humanity was totally forgot."

When accounts of the battle are studied, they reveal the horror and brutality of that day. Colonial soldiers were hacked and dismembered as they lay on the ground dying, after having tried to surrender. The bodies of the dead displayed multiple wounds, with survivors noting that the British seemed to take joy in Stabbing and slashing those already dead. The few survivors who fled the battle or were taken prisoner would later describe in letters how they were set upon by British troops and assaulted repeatedly with bayonet thrusts and sword attacks. One colonial captain lay near death and asked only to be moved so he could die beside an officer nearby, but instead he was bayoneted four times and then refused comfort by the British company surgeon. Sometimes we dismiss these events as the horrors of war, but how do we explain such behavior? What causes people to forget the virtue of humanity from time to time?

I wrote this novel as part of my own search to understand why civility is too often a victim of society. The death of civility is a crime that goes unpunished in the name of freedom and expression or even culture, but what happens to a culture when evil is adopted as a norm and ends justify means? History is the stage on which the presentation of man's struggle is performed. Biology seeks answers in the human genome, while psychology points at man's inward struggle with the mind and morality. Theology tells us that it is the influence of an outward source of evil, such as Satan and demons—or as I call them, the fallen ones. I believe that the evil displayed at the Battle of the Crossroads had its source in demonic influence, and that same demonic force is at work in the present day. The names and situations change, but the desire for death and destruction are the demons' primary goal. They are with us and walk among us, seeking to guide, influence, and possess anyone willing to listen and accept their presence. When it comes to good and evil behavior, the question is, do we join them or resist them? We all have choices, and these choices form the crossroads of our lives.

Prologue

In October of 1780, a decisive battle occurred at Kings Mountain, in western North Carolina. General Cornwallis, fresh from his victories in Charleston and Camden, South Carolina, was marching his army north to capture Charlotte and the rest of North Carolina, in order to cripple the revolution in the South. This would lead to a unification of the northern and southern British forces in Virginia or Maryland and end the revolution by crushing the northern forces of General Washington. Cornwallis had sent a force west to confront and secure colonial weapons and militia. The British force sent by Cornwallis and commanded by Colonel Ferguson soon found itself in a predicament. The colonial mountain militias had come down and were rallied, and when they heard Ferguson was near, they moved to intercept him at Kings Mountain. Soon Ferguson received word that a force larger than expected was advancing on his position, so he decided to make a stand on top of Kings Mountain, near Shelby, North Carolina.

Each side had over a thousand men, but Ferguson controlled the high ground. He was in a good position to withstand the colonial assault, but he could not anticipate the ferocity of the colonials. Ferguson would rely on his Tory regiment to fend off the advancing colonials, but little did he know that this would be like throwing fuel on the fire of rage that burned in the hearts of the colonials. Many of these men had come with the single desire and drive to crush all Tory units of the British army. The Tories were British sympathizers, many from the north who had come to join the large Tory contingent of the south. These Tories had made a reputation for themselves with their cruelty and brutality. The battle began, and the shouts of "Give 'em Tarleton's quarter!" or "Give 'em Buford's play!" were heard all over the battlefield. Perhaps Ferguson and the British provincial corps were unaware of what these cries meant; the colonials had come to this battle with a single-minded goal. They sought revenge on the Tory forces that, under the command of Colonel Banastre Tarleton, had massacred a Virginian force under the command of Colonel Abraham Buford in May of that same year, at a crossroads in the Waxhaw's area.

The colonials attacked the British on the crest of the hill, but the British drove them back into the wooded area repeatedly, until the militias finally encircled the Tory regiment. Ferguson had been killed in a colonial volley, so there was no one to offer surrender. The Tories huddled in a mass at the top of the hill. They dropped their weapons, but the colonials were there to give them "Buford's play." At the battle in the Waxhaw's area, Colonel Buford and the Virginians had tried to surrender, only to be decimated by the Tory murderers. Now was the time of revenge. The slaughter on the hill was short lived, and many say it should be labeled as much a massacre as the one Colonel Buford's forces suffered. Even after the battle, the colonials went on to hang ten of the captured Tories. But now the colonials' bloodlust was assuaged, and hopefully this act had quieted the blood of Buford's men who had cried up from the ground for revenge.

The battle lasted just over an hour. The casualty reports were chilling when compared to the reports of the enemy strength of 1,125 men. The losses for the British Provincial Corps were nineteen killed, thirty-five wounded, and sixty-eight prisoners—totaling 122. But it was the Tory losses that surprised many. Tory losses were reported as 206 killed, 128 wounded, and 648 prisoners—a total of 982. No one escaped. The British leader, Colonel Ferguson, was killed, along with a Provincial Corp captain, but among the Tories, two colonels and three captains died, and one major was wounded. The losses in the patriot army were small in comparison, with twenty-eight killed and sixty-two wounded. Ironically, it was another Virginia regiment that suffered the heaviest losses. The Virginian leader was Colonel Campbell, and his command had thirteen officers killed or mortally wounded. The weapons and supplies captured from the British included seventeen baggage wagons and twelve hundred weapons.

After the Battle of Kings Mountain, Cornwallis would try to destroy another group of colonials at Cowpens and suffer heavy losses again. Kings Mountain was a defeat, and Cowpens, while called a victory, was costly. Cornwallis decided to move north to Virginia and later to Yorktown. It was at Yorktown that Cornwallis surrendered to Washington, thereby ending the Revolutionary War. The victory at Yorktown can be traced back to Cowpens and then Kings Mountain. These victories may be the result of the anger aroused from the little battle of Waxhaw's, which today bears the title Buford's Crossroads. At this battle, Colonel Abraham Buford's command faced three columns of British Tory cavalry, led by Banastre Tarleton. Buford tried to surrender, but when the colonials dropped their muskets and raised their hands, the British attacked. What followed was a brutal and merciless slaughter. Today there is just a quiet spot with a mass grave in Lancaster County, South Carolina, but for a short while, on May 29, 1780, the site was filled with the screams of mutilated and dying men. One British historian described it as a battle where "the virtue of humanity was totally lost."

Chapter 1

Evil is that which we turn away from and try to avoid. Yet at the same time we are drawn to and seduced by its alluring but often hideously monstrous, visage. The question we may ask is this: Is the evil we experience born in humanity, or does it infect humanity from an external source? In times of war, evil becomes an object of interpretation and perspective. The death of a man may be a tragedy to some, but to those who oppose that man his death may be a cause to celebrate. Wars are fought in a spirit of hatred, so perhaps evil is born in hate. If this is true, then evil exists wherever hatred is allowed to be nurtured and grown. However, evil may not need a war to nurture its seed in the cold earth of hate and envy. All that is needed is a willing participant, someone who has the power to disguise and rationalize his or her acts of evil into perceived acts of noble heroics. It is often a choice that person makes.

Scene 1

The crossroads near Waxhaw's, May 29, 1780

The British soldiers formed three columns before the Virginia troops, but another force was present; it was made up of unseen specters weaving in and out of the lines on both sides. On the colonial side they sowed the seeds of fear and anguish, while in the minds of the British they whispered murder and hate. Like dark and deadly diseases, they infected their hearts and minds until rage erupted on the cowering colonials. Spirit voices now gave the orders to cut, slash, and stab, as Buford's men fell under the onslaught of bayonets and sabers raking over their bodies. Every wounded and dead man would suffer multiple wounds that day as the British raged like demons down on the helpless victims—for in fact, that was the source of their hatred: the demonic host allied with the British troops for a feast of flesh and destruction.

As the battle came to an end, a voice was heard in the world of spirits, whining out over the scene. "They are escaping, Murmus. Let us stop them and make a complete massacre of the day."

"No, Lerajie. We have done all that is needed here. Assemble the host and send some forth to the next battle. Let them remind the colonials of this event, and we will see the redcoats suffer as these colonials have here today. I will follow this leader and inspire him to greater acts of cruelty in Camden. Before you go, lead some of these to the south a short way, where you will find a wounded boy. Encourage them to make sport of his pain and torture him a little before he dies."

"But for what purpose, if he is but one boy alone, Lord Murmus?"

"Let's just say I am planting a seed for the future. For you, my friend, it will be unsanctified ground, your new home."

Lerajie did as he was instructed. The British found the young boy wounded and dying, but they did not give him peace. Urged on by the malevolent spirit, the British tortured the boy. The torture seemed like hours, but it was only a short while. They tied his arms and legs to their horses' saddles and pulled his beaten body until the bones were out of joint, and then they almost mercifully bashed his skull in with a rifle butt to end his pain, leaving his body twisted and mangled in the mud. He would lie there in a small depression in the ground, unnoticed and unburied for years, until his body sank into the mud and all that was left was his bones to mark the spot of his suffering. His only monument would be the barn that would be erected someday over his bones—the future haunt of the demon known as Lerajie.

Scene 2

Evening near the Buford battlefield, over two hundred years later

A late-summer breeze moved through the forest shadows, swirling in places as if it were clinging to a form and then moving on to be swallowed up by the coming darkness. The dark shadows seemed to take the shape of a thing or perhaps a person. The dried dead leaves of several autumns past whirled up like crackling bones of a summer dust devil, rustling with invisible steps. The evening had an unseasonable chill to it, as if fall were giving warning of its approach. However, there was still a slight warm feel to the air as fall and summer waged a silent battle over the landscape. The sun had slipped just below the horizon, and the evening sky was being painted with burnt-orange hues that in any other circumstance would have been considered beautiful. As the shadows stretched and lengthened eastward, the lights of a nearby farmhouse grew brighter, offering an oasis of warmth and welcome. But the warmth would soon be overcome by a cold breath of fear gliding slowly up the gravel drive. Why here, and why now?

In the kitchen of the ruddy-colored three-bedroom ranch house, a young woman was heating up food left over from Sunday lunch. She only stopped long enough to open the back door and shout for her daughter Amber to come in from the barn, where she had been feeding her dog. Her chubby chocolate Lab, named Becca, had had puppies a few days earlier, and the little girl could hardly tear herself away from their side, even to go to school. Amber was a tiny little girl, with eyes that seemed too big for her face and a bright, contagious smile. Amber liked her school and was excited about the beginning of a new year. She had new classes and teachers as well as the pleasure of seeing all her friends again, but the puppies were filling her mind now. Back inside the kitchen, a few moments passed as the bean pot began to boil, but her mother wasn't paying attention. Karen was lost deep in thought, staring out the window, looking for a sign of her husband's return. She noticed that it was getting dark, and he was late again; they must be working him so hard at the mill. When he did get home, his mind seemed miles away, preoccupied with unspoken thoughts. As the mother reached to turn the heat down under the beans, she shuddered as the wind moved past the kitchen window and gently rattled the pane. The sound pulled her attention away from the stove, and an odd feeling of dread edged its way up her back. Why wasn't her husband home yet? He was taking longer and longer to get home, and when he did arrive, it was just to eat and watch TV until he fell asleep. Sometime in the predawn hours he would stagger into bed and lay staring at the ceiling until the alarm signaled it was time to begin his routine again.

Just as the window rattle had nudged her thoughts in a new direction, now the barking of the dog broke her train of thought. This was followed by a sudden silence that aroused her curiosity. As she moved toward the back door, she listened for the dog again, but there was no sound, just an eerie silence—not even the stirring of the wind. The yard was almost enclosed in darkness now, and the old barn looked imposing in the low light. There were no lights coming from the open door where her daughter had entered earlier, and the opening created a dreaded cavernous look; it seemed to swallow the outside light. She called to her daughter, but there was no answer. She moved out onto the back porch and out into the cool evening air. As she made her way across the yard, she glanced down the drive, hoping to see some familiar headlights, but it was empty and dark. The wind blew up behind her and moved over her bare arms, causing little bumps to rise on her skin. She called toward the barn again, but still no answer came. Her thoughts moved from leftovers, car lights, dogs, and barns, to her daughter; now little Amber was the only thing on her mind. She hadn't heard from her daughter since she'd left the house, and her imagination was starting to paint ugly pictures in her head.

She quickened her steps across the yard and slowed down as she came to the darkened doorway of the barn. She called for Amber, but her voice could only make a whisper. She swallowed hard and called out again— nothing. She stood in the doorway, frozen in place, and listened for any sound of movement. All she heard was a rhythmic rustling in the hay toward the back of the barn, where the puppies had been born. As she cautiously made her way deeper into the darkness, the noise grew louder and louder, matched only by her own voice quietly saying her daughter's name, seeking some reassurance that everything was all right. Feeling her way through the shadows, she turned the corner to see a small beam of light from the evening sky shining like a friendly face in a room full of strangers. The low light allowed her to see her daughter's foot moving back and forth nervously.

"Honey what is it?" she whispered, and then her face froze in a grimace of confusion as she tried to take in the scene. The mother dog was nowhere to be seen, and the puppies were cuddled up in a corner, except for the little runt of the litter, which was nuzzling around in her daughters' lap. but as her eyes adjusted to the darkness, her confusion turned to fear when she saw her little girl's eyes, like two large saucers, staring off into the darkness; her hair seemed lighter, and her skin was pale. There was a small line of blood drops on Ambers' face but no wound—and then she saw a small puddle of blood behind her in the straw. Karen was on the verge of panic now, but she fought to control her fear as she recognized the signs of shock on her daughter's features. She moved toward Amber's side but stopped and gave a quick nervous glance back over her shoulder. She stumbled to one knee as she looked back toward the darkness. She had seen someone standing there. She couldn't see anyone now, but an image was burned into her mind like a negative on exposed film. She could have sworn she'd seen a tall, thin figure in a green coat and hat.

She sat and stared into the dark corner of the barn, rigid with fear, until she was convinced that it was just a trick of her mind brought on by her fear. There was no one there—but she was afraid to break her stare at the dark corner. It was almost as if her gaze was holding something at bay in the shadows. The feeling of dread was growing. She quickly reached out, grabbed the tiny, rigid form, and held her close. The puppy tumbled from the girl's lap and began to make a low whimpering grunt. But there was no time for puppies; the mother turned and fled toward the sanctuary of the house. Each footstep seemed to be sinking her deeper into the ground, and she felt as if there were hands reaching at the back of her legs, trying to catch hold and pull her back into that clinging darkness of the barn. Her breath was coming in a low pant now, and her arms were starting to feel numb and aching. But she dared not stop; she forced herself on toward the sanctuary of the back porch. In her imagination she told herself that once she got through that door and onto that porch, nothing could enter after her; she would be safe. Just a few more steps!

The back-porch door became like a scene from an old Hitchcock movie that pulled further away the closer she got. Finally, she felt the wood of the steps beneath her feet and heard the familiar creak of the second step from the bottom; she almost fell up onto the porch and then into the house. Slamming the door with her foot, she rested for a moment against the wall. Exhausted and panting for breath, she reached a sweating hand for the wall phone hanging nearby. Her mouth was dry, and her breath felt cold moving across her teeth. She had to swallow hard to moisten the dryness in her throat, as she balanced the little girl with one hand and dialed 911 with the other. The sound of a drum beating in the distance turned out to be her heartbeat as it pushed against her chest walls. It felt as if it would force its way through her rib cage at any minute. The operator answered, and the young mother mumbled something about needing an ambulance, how someone had attacked her little girl in the barn, and she feared they might still be around.

"What?" she said. "Uh … I'm Karen Hedrick, yeah, I live on Rocky River Road, or 522, whatever you want to call it, just down from the crossroads at number 9. Huh? Oh, she's eight." There was a pause for the next question. "Her name is Amber … okay, I'll be looking for the car—please send that ambulance right away. No, I don't see any cuts or anything yet."

She was starting to cry now. She heard a sympathetic voice on the other end of the line ask if she would like her to stay on the line until the deputy arrived. All she could muster now was a heavy "Uh huh, please."

It only took a few moments for the sheriff to arrive, and an ambulance soon followed. After a quick check, the paramedics loaded up the mother and daughter to take them to the hospital. The customary questions and confusion had added a buzzing vocal soundtrack to the surreal setting of what had been a quiet country farmhouse just a few hours earlier. It was now the scene of a criminal investigation. The sheriff was barking orders to his deputies, and his eyes scanned the setting as his mind struggled to find out just what kind of crime had been committed. He began to piece together some sort of scenario of events. The night air seemed to be getting warmer, and the darkness was giving way to moonlight as a warm gold moon crested the horizon and began to rise higher in the sky. The deputies walked all over the property and roped off the barn, then slowly began to disperse until it was just the sheriff and one deputy standing in the barnyard. The squad cars were pulling out onto the highway, and the ambulance that had taken the little girl and her mother to the hospital had probably arrived in town by now. The sheriff called over to the deputy and asked if he could handle things around the farmhouse.

"No prob', chief. I'll rap this up tighter'n a Christmas package," he whined back with his siren-like voice and slow southern drawl. The sheriff slid into his cruiser, and the deputy watched the car disappear around the corner of the drive. Then he turned to look around the scene once more. The deputy stepped over to his car and stood alone by his open door, taking one last look around the farmyard. He was listening, as if some voice might come on the wind with an answer to all his questions. What really had happened here? Where was the dad? Where was the dog? What had scared that little girl? All he had were a lot of questions with no answers.

As the deputy pondered the questions, another silent conversation was occurring at the battlefield just up the road. The voices were not heard by the people on the farm, and the speakers were not seen, but the speakers saw everything, even events down the road.

"He's done it again! He made another appearance at the old barn." There was anger and frustration in the tone. "Why do you allow this?"

"Leave him. He causes no problems, and in a way his appearances may work to serve us. Besides, he takes such joy in them."

"But he is acting on his own, and this is an insult to you!"

"Enough! I have told you that it is not a problem. If I deem it an insult, I will deal with him. He is like a child at play." The tone was loud and clear in its message that the conversation and complaint were over. The shadows seemed to engulf the two, and all that was left was the rustle of the wind through the trees.

Scene 3

Tuesday morning, at the sheriff's office

The next morning, Sheriff Croften was reading over his initial report when Deputy Jackson came into his office. "What have we got here, Riley?" the sheriff asked in his deep-baritone business voice.

"Heck if I know, chief," he answered with his patented shoulder shrug. "I went by the emergency room last night after I wrapped things up out at the farmhouse. I spoke with the mom a little, but she was too confused and worried about the little girl to say much. The hospital says the little girl is suffering from some sort of shock and trauma—no real injuries, but she's one hair away from being in coma or something, so as yet we don't have the first clue as to who or what scared her."

"Have you spoken to the father yet?" The sheriff spoke in an almost agitated tone.

Riley looked at his notebook as if reading from a report and spoke in a methodical tone: "David Hedrick, mill worker, lived here all his life, married nine years and just moved out here from the Lancaster town area. We got a probable ID on his car; it was seen parked on the other side of the woods, across from his house. The neighbor said it wasn't the first time she had seen the car parked there; she had seen it there a couple of times before, almost like he had been watching his own house for something. She said she had noticed it sitting out there several evenings over the past few weeks. I thought maybe he was checking to see if his wife was cheating on him or something. I asked the wife where her husband was, and she said he'd been coming home late from work, so I called the mill to see if he was there. But when I spoke with his boss this morning, he said the fella had left earlier that day. It turns out he had been leaving work early a couple of days each week for the past two weeks. It looks like he was checking up on his wife, but I'm just not sure why, because she seems to be as clean as a snowbank in December."

"You check out the snow queen later, Riley; right now, I want to know where that father's at. What have you got for me on his whereabouts?"

Riley shrugged his shoulders again and smiled innocently, like a kid who was looking at a teacher when he didn't have his homework. "Just add one more to that list of unanswered questions, chief. That fella's nowhere to be found … as yet."

"So, let me see," said the sheriff, his eyes scanning the empty wall, almost as if he were reading the story off the green-painted plaster walls. "What you're telling me is that this guy is watching his own house … and sees his daughter go out to the barn … as he watches his wife through the kitchen window? But why is he trying to check up on his wife if he knows his daughter is at home? And if he was watching and saw someone go into the barn after his daughter, why didn't he come to protect his little girl? And if that's the case, why did he leave the scene?" The tone of the sheriff's voice was rising slightly higher and louder with each unanswered question.

"Maybe he saw the guy leave and took off after him. If he caught him, we might have another crime scene waiting for us somewhere. Or, what if some guy was already out in the barn before the dad got into his observation position? If the person was already in the barn, the dad wouldn't have seen anybody go in the barn, and then maybe the little girl stumbled on the intruder, or vice versa," Riley added, seemingly joining the sheriff in his reading of the invisible text on the wall. "And of course, he could have just left when he saw the little girl was home—but where did he go?"

The sheriff picked up his pencil as if to write something but only tapped the eraser on his desk. "Riley, check to see if the little girl came home early from school."

Riley made a note in his notebook and looked up at the sheriff. "You thinkin' Amber surprised her momma and a boyfriend, and the boyfriend went to hide in the barn? That would mean that Mom's got a boyfriend who's either unemployed or a shift worker somewhere, and we can check that out. So, maybe this day the boyfriend's visiting and gets caught by the little girl, and the dog starts barking when he tries to hurt the girl, and the dog attacks, and then the boyfriend kills the dog and shocks little girl into 'veggieville.' Meanwhile, Mom is now forced to cover for her boyfriend ..."

The sheriff lowered his head and spoke to his marked-up desk calendar, "That's a mouthful, and it's weak, Riley. If what you say is true, it makes Mom out to be pretty nasty, and it still doesn't explain where the dad is—unless Daddy tried to get the boyfriend and got himself hurt. But why hide in the barn, if you got a car somewhere? Our only real witness is the little girl, who is now incapacitated. How did the boyfriend get away? Where was his car?"

There was a quiet pause as Riley watched the sheriff weigh these things in his head. "He's panicking ... he realizes the mom is going to be really upset with him for spooking her little girl." The sheriff paused again and then looked at the eager deputy. "It's awfully weak, Riley; we're grabbing at some mighty thin invisible straws here."

"Well, looks like we need to figure just who all—how many people—was in that barn last night, chief. I think I'll go out there and see if any of those invisible straws came out of that particular hayloft. I'll look for some car tracks, or footprints, or somethin'. You know, we're forgetting that the mom could have driven our mystery man to her house and then he went to hide in the barn and then the little girl came home unexpectedly. Meanwhile, Daddy was watching, went to get the guy in the barn, and bit off more than he could chew. The next thing you know, the fella does the dog and daddy in, right there in front of the little girl—that could explain her condition—and then he'd have to dump 'em somewhere. If the mom were in on it, they wouldn't have had to hurry. He could have gone out and found the dad's car parked in the woods, drove up to the barn, tossed 'em in the trunk, and then taken them both off and buried them under some leaves or something."

"Okay, Riley. Check it out, but it sounds like a lot of ifs and could'ves.

Maybe you been watching too much TV. Oh, and while you're at it, you may as well check that school bus thing to see if the little girl got home early; it'll help your theory out. You might want to ask around to see if any of the other neighbors saw anybody coming or going during the day. We also need to see if we can get an idea of what this mom does during the day: work, friends, church group, etc. Oh, and get Jason to take the K-9 unit out there and see if they get a scent on anything."

"I can, chief, but I doubt it will do any good. We don't have anything to get the dogs started."

Scene 4

Tuesday afternoon, back at the farmhouse

That afternoon, Riley and Jason were back at the barn, looking around. Jason was Riley's son; he was following in his dad's footsteps and was now in charge of the K-9 unit. The father-and-son law-enforcement team were more than family; they were friends. Working together was a treat to Riley, but he didn't let on. Jason might be a detective someday; he had a good nose for things and paid careful attention to details, just as his dogs did. Riley asked him to look around and give an opinion. After a few minutes, Jason looked at his dad and said it didn't look as if anything had happened. He was right; there was practically nothing to suggest a struggle between two people or movement around the barn. It had just been an empty building that morning. The dogs were useless, as Riley had expected. They had given them the dad's scent from a shirt, but they hadn't hit on anything. The only odd thing was that when they'd started to go into the barn, the dogs had growled and fought against the leashes.

Jason loaded the dogs up and told his dad he was sorry he couldn't be any more help. Riley was left alone again outside the barn, trying to piece together a puzzle with no clues. There were no footprints except for the mom's and little girl's going into the barn and nothing around the back, except for one shoe print. It could have been headed back to where the dad's car was parked, but it was too smudged for anyone to be sure. To make matters worse, the woods in back of the house were totally clean. It looked as if no one had been back there in ages. There were no car or foot tracks and no bodies. So much for the theory. The disappointments kept coming.

Later that morning, the school reported a regular bus schedule on Monday, no early buses. The mother had an airtight alibi: she hadn't even been home until about three o'clock. She volunteered her time to sit with local shut-ins. Now all they had was a catatonic girl, a missing father and dog, and a mother who wanted some explanations. But there were no explanations.

Scene 5

Sheriff's office, Thursday morning

When Riley walked into the office, the sheriff called him back to his desk. "Got some news on that missing dad, Riley; I knew you'd want to know. But hold on to your hat for this one. It seems they found the dad up at Duke University a couple of nights ago."

Riley's head jerked up. "What did he have to say for himself?"

The sheriff swallowed hard and made a guttural sound of disgust as he spoke. "He didn't have anything to say for himself. He was found dead in a parking lot near some girls' dorms, with binoculars around his neck and—get this now—a dead dog in the trunk. The prelim looks like an overdose."

Riley started to scratch his head. "A dog overdosing on drugs ..."

"Very funny, wise guy!" The sheriff gave Riley that *not-now* look. "He must have been pretty mad at that dog and went into some sort of rage, because they found the dog in the trunk in pieces. Which don't really surprise me too much when you consider that the dad had enough crank in him to put down a Clydesdale."

"So he killed his own dog and chopped it up, huh? Wow, that's a strange one." Then Riley looked up, with a puzzled grimace on his Irish-etched face. "Ya know, no one has said anything about a drug problem with these folks. Are they sure that's what killed him?"

"Those fellows up in Chapel Hill know what an OD case looks like," the sheriff stated in a matter-of-fact way. "You might want to go by the hospital and talk to the wife again. I hear the little girl is coming out of it, and she may be ready to tell us what happened."

"Does the wife know about her husband ... err ... ex-husband?" Riley asked sheepishly.

"Yeah, she had to go up and do the positive ID yesterday evening. She called and said that she would be at the hospital if we needed to talk to her about anything. I think we need some more answers now and less jokes, don't you agree, Deputy Funny—I mean Riley?"

"Yep, chief, I want to know a little more about this dad." Riley spoke while adjusting his holster belt. "Hey, speakin' of jokes, did ya hear the one about the lady who called to report her husband was dead in the kitchen floor? They asked her if he had said anything before he died, and she said, 'Yes, he said, "Please don't pull that trigger, honey."'"

The sheriff smiled and rolled his eyes as he pointed to the door. "Don't quit your day job, Riley"; he was trying to come up with something humorous to say. Riley smiled courteously but was thinking how humor just didn't fit well on Croften. It was like forcing a slipper on a cow; it might go on, but it just wouldn't fit.

Scene 6

Visiting the hospital

On the ride to the hospital, Riley tried to clear his mind of jokes and speculations and just weigh the evidence. The sun was warm as it shone into the cruiser, and he was thinking of a weekend at the river or maybe Myrtle Beach. But now it was time to stop dreaming and formulate some questions. Should he hit Mrs. Hedrick with the drug questions or wait and see how she was taking the death and then try to draw some conclusions from her reactions? He would play it the way he played checkers: wait for her to make a move and see what she wanted to talk about. He'd just see what came up. Maybe she'd known her husband had a problem and was covering up for him, or maybe she hadn't known about the drugs. In that case, she would be shocked at the drug news and should show some sort of reaction.

When he arrived at the hospital, he found out the room number and headed right up to the fifth floor. Getting off the elevator, he fell in behind a doctor walking down the hall. The situation was a bit awkward, as they both arrived at room 510 together. Riley didn't speak. He just quietly followed the doctor into the room.

"Well, so the little princess is awake at last and wanting to speak. That's just great! Sit up here, dear, and let me take a look in those pretty eyes of yours." The doctor was being as gentle as he could, but the little girl was holding tightly to her mother's waist. Only after some motherly coaxing would she let the doctor shine his light and look deeply into her eyes. They were smaller and more normal looking than the first time Riley had seen them. They were still filled with fear, but at least now they were blinking and even welling up with a tear or two. Riley nodded to the mom, and she responded with a polite smile and nod.

"Has she said anything?" the doctor asked, with a glance up at the mother.

There was an odd pause as the mother looked away from the doctor and toward the deputy standing at the foot of the bed. Riley saw the look as their eyes met. Was she hesitating because the doctor was in the room? The doctor was asking the question, but she was directing the answer toward the deputy.

"All she has said so far is ... Daddy." The mom choked the words out as she turned back to stroke the little girl's pale brow. Riley wondered how she was going to explain her daddy's death to the little girl.

The doctor's exam lasted a few more minutes, concluding with the usual speech: "I think she's doing fine, but we'll need to run some more tests." It was the speech doctors used when they weren't sure what would happen next. Then he was out the door. With him gone, Riley turned back to the mother, who was gently rocking her daughter in her arms. After a moment of silence, Riley breathed a heavy sigh and sat down as if he were going to stay for a while.

"How you doin' with all of this, ma'am?" he asked, hoping to open the door to a conversation during which she would volunteer some information without his digging for the answers.

"Please call me Karen," she said with a forced smile. "I'm still a little confused, my daughter's in shock, and my Dave is …" She struggled to find a word that wouldn't shock her daughter further. "Well, you get the idea. What is going on? One day we were a near-perfect family, with plans and dreams, and then overnight it's all gone, and there's just no explanation."

Riley asked her to step over near the door so the little girl couldn't hear what they were saying. "Were you aware of your husband having any kind of problems at work, or with any friends or family?" He spoke softly, but he realized he was rushing her as he heard the words come out of his mouth. He thought to himself, *So much for being subtle.* He went back to trying to get information.

"Nothing that he shared with me, Deputy." Karen had a puzzled look on her face.

Riley continued, but he wasn't sure where to take his questions from there. "Did your husband have any problems with, uh …?" Riley hesitated. "Well, ma'am, let me just be blunt. Did he have any kind of a drug problem?" He had been planning to save that info, but Riley was way off the game plan now, and the drug death needed some explanation.

The woman's muscles tightened as if she were fighting back her anger, and she stared at Riley when said, "Drug problem?" almost in a whisper, as if to keep the words from her daughter just a few feet away. "There was no kinda problem like that. He didn't even like to take Aspirin. He had an occasional beer, but never anything like hard liquor, ya know what I mean? I could probably count how many beers he had a month on my fingers. I've never seen him, or even heard of him being …" She paused, looking through a mental thesaurus for a word besides *drunk*, "You know … intoxicated. Now, you explain to me what he was doing at Duke, in that condition and, and …" She stopped short of saying *dead*, but her voice was rising in volume and inflection, and Riley began to feel that she was sincere. At least she was convincing him.

Riley pressed on with another question. "Why do you think he was watching the house?"

She looked back at Riley with a puzzled look, and he suddenly realized that she knew nothing about their suspicions of the man watching the house. He realized too that he had not gone into detail about someone seeing the car across the road in the woods.

"What … when …? What are you talking about?" Her voice took on a hint of agitation. "What are you talking about, Deputy? Who was watching what house?"

Riley cautiously answered. "You see ma'am—uh, Karen—we have a witness that says that the car was across the road in the woods on a couple of occasions. It appears that your husband had been leaving work a couple of days a week for the past couple of weeks to park out there in those woods. We just assumed he was watching his house with those high-powered binoculars."

"What binoculars! You mean the ones they tried to give me in Chapel Hill were his?" Her voice was getting that confused tone again. "I never knew he had any binoculars. This doesn't make any sense." She dropped her head as her voice began to show signs of exhaustion. Riley thought it was time to give her a break and take in all this new information. He had just one more question before he left, but this was the question he had been working up to asking. He must be careful to catch every nuance of her reaction.

"Ya know, ma'am, we do have someone who saw the car in the woods that night. We have reason to believe that someone could have harmed your husband and then stolen the car and drugged him to make it look like an overdose. Was anyone at the house earlier that day before you went to sit at hospice, or did you happen to see any strangers around the barn that night?"

She looked at Riley and said, "No, there was no one there, and I was out for the better part of the day. Deputy, if someone hurt my husband, then how did he get the ..." she paused and looked back to make sure her daughter couldn't hear her, "the dog in the trunk?"

Riley smiled when he said, "Well, ma'am, I don't know, but ya know I didn't say anything about the dog being in the trunk. How did you know about that?" Thinking he might have stumbled onto something, Riley tried not to seem too eager.

"I had to explain that to the police in Raleigh. My husband wasn't the only thing I had to identify up there. It was horrible! Are you telling me that someone did that to my husband and then came over to the house and did that to Becca, too? Why? What would they want with the dog, and why even come over to the house unless they were going to hurt me and Amber too?" Her words created a new realization in her mind. Karen paused and shuddered at the thought that someone might have been there to hurt them all. "So you think there really was someone in that barn."

"What do you mean *really was*? You didn't say anything about suspecting someone in the barn when we took your statement." Riley was feeling a little silly. It was that feeling he'd had earlier of trying to work a puzzle with some of the pieces missing.

The woman looked down at the floor. Well, Deputy, I didn't actually see anyone. I think, it was just that feeling you get when someone is near, or you feel that someone is coming up behind you. It was just a feeling I had, and I figured if I couldn't explain it, why mention it? I was probably just scared; ya know how ya get in a dark place sometimes. Deputy, do you think that someone was there to hurt all of us? But if that were the case, why didn't he get me? I was right there in the barn, and there was no one around."

"What did you think you saw, ma'am?" Riley asked.

Karen looked at the floor and whispered, "It was probably nothing, but when I came to Amber lying there, I could have sworn I saw someone standing in the shadows. It was a tall, thin figure in a green coat and hat—but there was no one there. It was just creepy!"

Riley realized that the scene didn't make any sense; it was odd that she would remember something so clearly that wasn't there. Riley thought for a moment and looked at the woman. In his mind, the only answer that made any sense was that she knew who the assailant was. Whether it was a hunch or something else, he couldn't bring himself to think that this woman was involved. Things just weren't adding up.

Just as he started to ask her another question, there was a commotion in the hall. He glanced out the door and saw some orderlies wheeling a patient into the room next door. He leaned over to close the door and saw a little boy being maneuvered into the room. Two men were leaning against the wall, and he thought he recognized one of them. When the man saw Riley, he turned away quickly as if to speak to his friend. Both men were ratty looking, with long, greasy hair and beards that had not been trimmed in some time. Riley saw their type every Friday night at the sports club on the west side, usually when he was called to break up a fight. He tried not to be judgmental, but when you'd seen all he had, you couldn't help but notice certain signs in people that seemed to tell their whole life story. These boys had the look that his momma used to call just plain *triflin'*. He never really knew what triflin' meant, but he understood it to be something bad by the way his momma sort of spit the word out when she used it to describe someone worthless. Riley was either a good judge of character or he had a pretty good imagination; either way, his hunches were about 60 percent accurate when it came to determine triflin' people. He turned his attention back to Karen, telling her he would try to get some answers. He wasn't sure why, but for some reason he believed her. He didn't think she was involved or knew any more than he did about what had gone on that night. He smiled and excused himself from the room with a nod, saying," I'll be in touch."

Riley made his way down the hall to the nurses' station and leaned over the desk to read the name tag on one of the nurses. With the boyish smile that often put people at ease, he asked, "What's the story on the kid in 512, Ms-s-s-s ..." slowly drawing out the Ms as he read the name, "Ms. Watson,"

"Now, Deputy, I cannot divulge information unless you are part and parcel to an ongoing investigation in co-operation with the Department of Social Services, and you know that as well as I do. HIPAA regulations, you know. Now, are you part of such an investigation, Deputy-y-y,"—she asked, dragging out the title as Riley had done, in a semi-kidding and semi-mocking way— "Deputy Jackson?" She smiled back at Riley, and just as he started to turn away, she said, "However, Deputy, I can tell you that not all injuries consistent with child abuse are investigated by Social Services, even though the doctors must report such injuries if they suspect abuse has occurred."

"Well … I was more interested in the man in the hall than the kid in the room, if ya know what I mean. But ya say they are suspected of abusing the little fella?"

"No, Deputy Jackson, I did not say that. In fact, I have given you no *real* information at all." She was stressing the word *real*, as if to say, "I have told you as much as I could without telling you anything; now go figure it out." Riley smiled and moved toward the elevators.

Back down the hall in room 510, Karen sat rocking her child. The door was slightly ajar, and the course laughter coming from the two men in the hall was getting louder. She gently moved her daughter back onto the bed and stepped toward the door. Suddenly she felt that cold chill across her arms again, just as she had the night the whole thing had begun. She moved to the door and looked out. It was as if her glance had somehow been heard by the two men, for they turned toward her. Their laughter stopped, and their faces slid into empty, emotionless masks that stared at her. Then a wry smile began to tilt up the mouth of one of the men. The look seemed to convey a threat and a certain innuendo that made her feel very uncomfortable. Her eyes shot to the floor, and as she pushed the door closed, she heard the man say something in a guttural tone to his friend: "I'd tap that."

The comment was met with a snickering bluster from the other man, and in that moment, she felt as if unseen hands had rubbed something cold, wet, and grimy on her skin. She brushed the imagined substance from her arm and slowly moved back to her daughter. The simple incident made her feel vulnerable and scared, but now she had no one to look to for security. She fought back the urge to get angry at her now-dead husband. What had he been thinking? What had he been doing out there? Why was this happening to her? She needed him now more than ever, but he was gone. *Just deal with it, girl,* she thought to herself. *You've got your child to think about now. Get tough and stop feeling sorry for yourself.* She would need to be strong to protect herself from people like the ones right outside her door. The world was a mean place, and she would have to get just as mean to survive it.

Scene 7

A few days later

Back at the office, the sheriff told Riley to let the investigation rest for a day or two and see what happened. Sure enough, a couple of days later he received a call from the hospital. It seemed the little girl was talking now—and talking a lot.

When Riley arrived at the hospital room, he glanced down the hallway, wondering whether the little boy was still there. The room and hall were empty. He wondered what had happened to the boy and whether there really had been child abuse involved. The world was a bad place sometimes, and it seemed that it was often the innocent who had to feel the pain. As he stepped into the little girl's room, he saw a different image from a few days prior, one that cheered and warmed his heart a little. Karen was playing with Amber, and to anyone passing by, it looked like a normal family setting. He smiled as he walked through the door after giving a light knock and hearing, "Come on in," in the mom's singsong voice.

Before he said a word, little Amber looked up and said, "Are you here to bring my daddy back?" Before Riley could answer, Karen began stacking plush toys around her daughter, as if to bury her in plush, soft, cuddly friends. As Amber giggled, Karen moved over to Riley and began to lead him out into the hallway.

"I knew you would want to know what my daughter has said, what she says happened that night," she said with a concerned tone, "so I called your office. I warn you, Deputy, I still don't understand everything, but this is what Amber told me."

Riley smiled and said, "Any explanation would be better than what we've got right now."

Karen took a deep breath and began the explanation that would prove to be just as mysterious as the problem. "The other morning, Amber woke up and asked me why her daddy would hurt Becca (the dog), and I didn't know what to say, so I asked her why she would say such a thing. Then she said that her daddy had come into the barn, and when Becca growled at him, he'd grabbed a shovel and hit Becca until she stopped making a sound, and then she just woke up here in the hospital. She said it and then, just like that, she went back to playing. I thought maybe she was not good and awake, that she had been dreaming, but later I asked her again what she'd seen in the barn that night, and she told me the same thing. She added that her daddy didn't look like he felt good at the time. I haven't told her about her father yet, but she hasn't asked to see him anymore. Why would he do something like that? What was going on in his head? What happened to my husband?"

Riley just stood there silently, trying to find an answer to her questions, but there was nothing he could say. There was no explanation for this: a man changed his whole personality in the space of two weeks, from a good, hard-working father into a paranoid brute, and then he ran off to a new life of drugs. He obviously knew nothing about drugs except the way they made him feel, so he overdosed almost immediately. Was this some bizarre suicide, and if so, what had driven him to it? Why had he been watching his house? His wife had given him no reason to be suspicious, and yet that seemed to be the only explanation. It didn't add up, but if the mom wasn't involved with someone, an idea that Riley just couldn't bring himself to believe, then suicide or accidental overdose seemed the only explanation that fit the evidence. As Riley looked at the woman, he could tell that she was feeling a sense of relief. He asked her, "You comfortable with this explanation, ma'am?"

Karen sighed, "Not really comfortable, Deputy, but seeing my daughter starting to act like a normal little girl again, and at least knowing she could give me some idea of what happened that night, even if it made little sense, answered some of my questions. It may sound bad, but I am a little glad, too, that I don't have to worry about some man trying to come after me and Amber. It's like some kind of sense in a world that has been mostly confusion lately." She spoke with calmness in her voice, and Riley just couldn't imagine her as part of a murder scheme. Riley smiled as she turned to go back into the room, and he walked away. He didn't have the answers he was looking for, and it didn't seem he was going to get those answers anytime soon.

The sheriff was more easily sold on the explanation; there was a crime and a valid explanation of events. He dismissed the mystery as just another good-person-gone-bad story. There wasn't always a good reason; sometimes things just happened. For some reason, known only to himself, this guy had snapped. He had gotten hooked on drugs and would go to the woods to get high before going home. One night he had a little too much, and he got a little delusional. He saw his daughter go in the barn, he walked over, saw the dog, and in his state of mind he perceived a threat to little Amber. He then killed the dog, took it to his car, and somewhere along the way started to realize what he had done. In shame, he took off for who knows where and ended up a couple of hours away and ODed in a parking lot. Case closed, as far as the sheriff was concerned. He had a cut-and-dry way of seeing things and tying them up in neat little bundles. It did make some sort of sense, and it cleared the mom of being a bad person, a description that had never seemed to fit anyway.

Officially the case was closed, but Riley filed it away in memory and would think of it every time he had to drive by that house. It was his son who sparked his interest, when he asked why the dog was growling at the dad. Riley couldn't figure that out either.

In the following year, Karen sold the house and she and little Amber moved back closer to town. A new family bought the property and moved in. They also had a little girl. Was it a coincidence or nature's way of trying to clean up a "bad memory" on the landscape?

In the forest near the Buford battlefield, the mist swirled into the shape of two men. They stood looking toward the mass grave.

"My Lord Baraqyal, why have we spent so much time here in this meaningless place?"

Baraqyal turned his massive shape toward the voice and spoke. "You know that time has no meaning for us, and as far as place, one place is as good as the other. But there may be more to this place than one sees. I was told that there might be a victory to be had here and that I should prepare the ground for the right moment. That moment may be upon us. Our influence is strong here, and we are ready for the next step in our work. Call for Lerajie to come forth. I have a job he will enjoy."

"Why that one? He reveals too much of himself and of our work!"

"Stop, Nakir, I know your thoughts, and I have told you that I control Lerajie. He is faithful to me, and that is of utmost importance. Now call him and be ready. The time is at hand for our work to begin in earnest."

The mist swirled, and the air cleared to reveal an empty forest engulfed by the darkness.

Chapter 2

Scene 8

Two years later, up highway 522 at Buford's crossroads

Almost two years later, Riley found himself cruising up highway 522 past that same farmhouse. And just as he always did, he remembered little Amber's face when he drove by the gravel driveway leading to the ranch-style house and barn. The new owners had fixed it up a bit, and it looked real nice. But he had no time to stop now, because today he was headed up toward the crossroads to check the college research team up at the battleground. They were a group of students doing a historical survey in the area of Buford's crossroads. A Revolutionary war battle had been fought there, and the historical marker drew a couple of visitors each month, but most people just looked at the pile of stones and drove on by.

The research team had given a new life to the site, but some of the local residents didn't think it was right to have people poking around the battlefield. It was just a roadside marker and a mass grave that supposedly held the bodies of a large group of American revolutionary soldiers who'd been massacred at or near this place. Unfortunately, some of the good Christian folk now saw it as hallowed ground. It was a grave, a sacred spot, and it should be treated with a reverence and respect that didn't include poking around. They had lodged a complaint, and there had been some vandalism reported by the team, so the sheriff had a car stop in every now and then, just to keep an eye on things.

This most recent team of "experts" had come up from the university to answer questions about the massacre and try to verify the actual site of the battlefield and gravesite. The marked site had come under suspicion recently when some university historian had questioned the exact location and details of the battle. Even the grave was under suspicion, because no one knew for sure whether that was the only actual grave or they had just stacked up some stones on an approximate spot and buried most of the bodies elsewhere. Records suggested that only some of the bodies were buried there; there may have been another grave somewhere nearby that had been lost. This area seemed to have become popular with research teams, and the rumors about some odd activity a few years earlier added to the intrigue.

A family that had moved into the neighborhood a short time back had reported some sort of supernatural disturbance in their barn and sightings of a strange green-clad figure. A paranormal investigation team from Duke University had even been in the area to look into it. They had found some odd things, but very little of what happened ever came out. The team never made an official report, but there had been some conflicts among the team before they packed up and left. That bit of info had been kept pretty hush-hush until the New Day TV show did a two-minute spot on their morning broadcast. Fortunately, no one except the good ole boys who hung around the store and grill made any connections. If people had taken them seriously, this stretch of road would still be swarming with curiosity seekers. The rumors were pretty wild and sketchy, because the storytellers had no solid information. Each one liked to add his own embellishments to the ghost stories. To Riley, it seemed best just to let the rumors run wild and not to make a big deal. The mention of Duke University sparked the memory of David Hedrick, who had driven all the way to Duke just to die in a parking lot.

The new owners had invited in the paranormal team, but the family didn't want people to know who they were or where the barn was located; they were concerned that people would be all over their farm. There were rumors about ghost sightings near the battlefield, but most folks just said they were in this area to draw attention away from the real location. A few people, like Riley, knew the truth, and he even knew the barn where the sightings had occurred. That was what bothered him the most. Was it all a hoax or a coincidence that the new owners of the farm had reported seeing a ghost in that barn? The only difference this time was that the new owners and their little girl didn't seem to mind. They had said that the ghost was friendly, a regular Casper. Riley wasn't one for ghost stories; he thought the new people just sounded a little weird, talking about friendly spirits and such stuff.

The Duke team hadn't stayed very long. Some said they were asked to leave when the owner had a sudden change of heart about the ghost. The researchers had concluded that there were some electromagnetic abnormalities in the area but nothing that they could substantiate. Then something happened, and the group had some sort of argument and abruptly left. Local reporters caught wind of what was going on, and soon the story broke on national TV. Fortunately, or strangely, the story never really went very far, and now it was just something remembered whenever Halloween rolled around. The people who now owned the property refused to mention the subject at all.

As the farmhouse disappeared in his rear-view mirror, the battlefield marker was reflecting the morning sunlight. It looked like Riley had arrived at the right time, because someone had called an informal community meeting. There was Alan, the team leader, with another person, whom he didn't recognize. Beside them stood Bruce, the preacher from the local Baptist church, and Arthur. Arthur Kirtland was the point man for the geriatric cabal that silently governed, or thought they governed, every aspect of the community. Riley knew them as the unofficial information highway—spreaders of gossip—but they saw themselves as servants of the common man, keepers of the community faith, and bastions of historical traditions. To Riley that just translated as "pain-in-the-neck busybodies." Riley often thought that if they were to take a fraction of the energy they expended complaining about things and put it into doing positive things for the community, the area would be a paradise. But it never seemed to work that way. He saw the preacher and thought of how on occasion the two of them had spoken of that very thing with regards to some of the people in the congregation. Being tactful, the preacher would never use names. He would quote the statistic of how in churches almost all the work was done by only 20 percent of the people, and the rest just sat around and complained. The preacher felt that this was one of the true faces of evil in society. Riley thought that this poor preacher had never seen true evil, such as he faced weekly. Riley would often offer to let the preacher ride with him some Saturday night and see the world as he had to experience it, but as yet the preacher had not accepted his invitation.

Riley now noticed the new face in the group, someone he didn't know. It was a girl, and she sort of looked foreign or something, with dark skin. Riley pulled up and popped the siren jokingly at the group. Everyone smiled except for Arthur, who jerked his body around in alarm at the sudden shrill noise. Riley hopped out of the car, smiling, and said, "Okay, you folks, break it up, break it up. What seems to be the problem here?"

Everyone started to speak at once, with Alan and Arthur trying to shout one another down, until the deep baritone voice of the preacher cut through the din. "Same old thing, Riley," he intoned. "Somebody took off with some equipment last night and spray-painted a message on a truck tailgate."

"What did it say, Bruce?" Riley asked the preacher. He slowly looked over the faces of the assembled crowd, stopping again at the new face for a closer look.

"*Get out,*" said the preacher.

"Get out? I just got here," said Riley with a grin as he laughed at his own joke.

Everyone smiled at the deputy's little joke, except Arthur. He spoke up to say, "No, Deputy, that is what the note said: G-e-t, o-u-t— 'Get out!'—and I think they should. They are bringing riffraff and vandals into the area, and we, the concerned citizens, will not have it. They shouldn't be digging up this grave anyway. Those are our heroes down there, local boys who fought and died for their country, right here on this very spot, over two hundred years ago."

"We don't know that for sure, Mr. Kirtland," said the team leader.

"And as for local boys, most of the bodies buried were from Virginia. Heroes, yes, but they were in the process of surrendering when the massacre occurred. The only 'local' heroes are the locals who keep stealing our stuff and spray-painting our trucks. We're getting a little tired of it."

The tension was building between the two, and Riley tried to diffuse the situation by changing the subject. "Who's the little girl, Alan?" he asked, nodding toward the dark-skinned girl.

"Oh, that's Sandy. Sanchari is her real name, but she's not officially a part of our team. She's doing her own research for another group."

Alan was speaking in a staccato, almost hesitant style, and the young woman stepped up to rescue her new colleague. "I am Sanchari Prasad, Officer. I am a doctoral student at Duke, and I have come to do a little research here for my dissertation. Alan has been so gracious as to allow me to join his group for a while."

"You see there, Deputy!" It was Arthur again, puffing his way into the conversation. "You see!"

"Well, Arthur, actually I don't see." He was getting agitated at the old man. But Riley did see what Arthur was saying, even if no one else around did. Riley understood that Arthur was directing his comment to Sanchari. It was a reference to his earlier statement about riffraff, only the term was being expanded to include a touch of racism. Arthur and his crowd didn't like strangers, and this Sanchari was about the strangest one in the group. Riley sensed that there was more to Sanchari's story than she was telling, but this was not the time to ask about it.

He turned to the old man, and in his most official-sounding voice, he said, "Arthur, you need to head for home and let me do my work here. If you have nothing to add about the investigation of robbery and vandalism, I'm afraid I'll have to ask you to leave the crime scene."

The words *crime scene* had a magical power that seemed to transform the place from a squabbling ground to an official investigation site filled with unseen evidence. Arthur looked down at his feet as if looking to make sure he hadn't smudged a track or scuffed up a clue. He stared back at Riley and then the others. "Well, this ain't over yet," he stated.

As he turned to go to his car, Riley just couldn't resist the chance to say, "See ya in church Sunday, Arthur." Arthur turned with a jerk. He made a polite nod to Riley and a tip of his hat to the preacher but nothing but a cold scowl at the other two standing there.

As they watched his car drive away, the team leader said, "There goes a man in need of a hobby—or at least a Prozac."

Preacher Bruce observed that people like Arthur were just afraid, afraid of anything new and different. They were afraid that they might have to face change in their lives, and at their age change was harder than for young people. His defense was followed by a breathy sigh. "It doesn't make life easy for the rest of us, though, does it folks?"

"Amen, preacher," came the sweet, almost musical voice of the young girl standing near Riley. "They don't realize a lot of things about their actions. The greatest evil often tries to hide behind the most fervent good. Would you agree, Reverend?"

"Well, history would seem to support your presupposition, madam. Tell us, is that the focus of your dissertation? If so, this place may have a lot of information to offer about evil in the guise of good. There was enough evil performed here." Bruce was staring across the empty field as if watching something intently. The others turned to see what he was watching.

"You know the history of this place, preacher?" Alan asked.

"Just what I can read in a book, Alan. I haven't done any digging into graves lately." He said this in a tone that sounded sarcastic or as if he were voicing a gentle disapproval of the research.

Riley jumped in before the discussion went further, using his official-sounding tone of voice again. "So, what's missing this time, Alan?"

"Oh, just a couple of shovels from the truck over there." He pointed to the blue pickup near the white rocks that marked the mass grave. "The real problem is over at my tent, Deputy, a little more graffiti and someone took a copy of the diary pages that I had copied from an original document back at school. They were pages from a diary of the Wyly family of Camden. I don't know why they would have stolen these.

They're not originals, and it turns out they haven't helped us with the research here at the crossroads."

"If they were just copies, why is that the real problem, Alan?" Riley asked in a puzzled tone.

"Well, I guess it's not that the stuff was taken, it's just that it was taken from my tent. Someone came in there while I was sleeping and took something and painted on the outside. That's a little scary to me." Alan sounded frustrated that Riley did not see the obvious danger to himself and the crew. The thieves were getting bolder. It was one thing to take a shovel here and there and paint some graffiti on a truck, but this was getting close to the people. Alan had some younger female undergrads in the dig, who up to now had thought this was all very exciting, but now they were feeling a bit uneasy.

They were nearing the tent to inspect the scene when Bruce stopped and stared at the message on the tent. "Bust his head" was painted on the canvas. The group stopped to look at the words, trying to see what Bruce had found so interesting.

"What is it, Bruce?" Riley asked.

"Looks like a threat to me, Deputy," Bruce said in an almost kidding voice. "It just reminded me of something. Riley. Come by the church some afternoon; I want to show you something."

"You see, Deputy; I'm not the only one who sees the potential for violence around here." Alan spoke with an unmistakable hint of fear in his voice.

"Don't worry—I'll look after everybody, Alan." It was the voice of the beautiful young doctoral student, and she wore a flirtatious smirk.

Riley smiled at her comment and reassured Alan that the people around the area were mostly harmless; it was probably just pranksters operating on a dare. Riley was sincere in his thoughts. The boys at the sports bar on the other side of the crossing might be rascals, but they weren't killers or kidnappers. He would drop in that evening just to remind people that the law was in the area. The older members of the research team liked to walk up to the bar in the evening and sip a few suds and watch TV. For these kids, it was like summer camp with credit.

There were no real hard feelings in the area that Riley could see, except for the older folks and a few teenagers, but most of them were just people looking for something to complain about.

"Just keep a lamp burning at night and tell the kids to zip them tents from the inside, Alan. You have my cell number if there is a real emergency. I am just three minutes away, if I'm at home," Riley reassured the student leader.

Riley then turned back to the pretty young doctoral student who had piqued his curiosity earlier. "So, you are from Duke, eh? Just what kind of a doctor does research at an old battlefield? Are you into history or curing the dead folks?" Riley was trying to insert a bit of humor in his questions.

"Neither, or perhaps a little of both," Sandy answered, with a hint of a smile and just enough mystery to pique the rough old deputy's curiosity even more. Then she stopped; she was not volunteering a lot of information.

"That name of yours, is that American or ..." he paused, waiting for some assistance as he leaning toward the pretty young student.

She smiled at the deputy with a confidence that somehow hinted, *I am only permitting this audience with you as a courtesy. Don't push it!* "My mother and father were from India," she informed him. "They came to America before I was born. My father is a research scientist at Duke. I was born in Winston-Salem. Anything else you'd like to know, Officer, before you press formal charges for being different in a small town? Is that still a hanging offense here in the deep, deep South or just a misdemeanor?"

"Well, don't get too touchy Ms. *almost* Dr. Sandy. I was just curious about something you said earlier, something about doing research with another group. Is there another group coming?" Riley asked, using his most mannerly voice.

Sandy seemed to fidget a little before she said, "That wasn't what I said. Alan said it, and he was referring to a previous study done in this area that I hope to investigate. I am doing my doctorate in a similar field."

Riley scratched his head and began to recall that last group that had come down from Duke. "I do remember that other group from Duke, a year or so back, that was investigating that old barn down the road. I may have known your dad, because I was assigned to keep a check on things when the word got out that they were looking for a ghost."

Sandy's demeanor seemed to change. She looked at Riley and said, "Then you were here with that group—you probably did know my father. I would like to speak with you more about this, Deputy. Your memories may be very important to my research. Could I set up an appointment with you in the very near future? I have several questions. Perhaps tomorrow, or even this evening, if you're free. Say around seven, here at camp?"

Her sudden interest caught Riley off guard, but he found himself nodding and agreeing before he knew what he was doing. She was walking away as Bruce stepped up and asked what the conversation had been all about. Riley just shrugged, saying, "The wife ain't gonna like me spending time with that pretty young thing. She spells trouble with a capital T."

Bruce and Riley both watched the young girl move across the parking lot in front of the memorial. She was a beauty: her hair shone like a raven's wing in the sun, and she had eyes that could melt cold steel. Then there was the rest of her, small but proportionally perfect. She had a figure that was better than anything on the tool calendar back at the garage, made only too noticeable in her low-cut jeans and high-cut T-shirt. It was the fashion of the day, but some girls made it look common and others made it look like a costume on a Las Vegas showgirl. She was somewhere in between. Suddenly they realized that they were both staring at the pretty young student.

"Why do you think she's trouble, Riley? She seems like a perfectly normal, drop-dead-gorgeous college coed to me," Bruce said with a little smile across his lips.

"Preacher!" Riley said, as if shocked. "You ain't supposed to notice the pretty girls."

"Oh, I can notice Riley. I just can't let that noticing get too far in my head. Lust is born in the mind and not in the eyes," Bruce said as if reading a passage from the Bible. "But why is she trouble?"

Like you said, Preacher—lust. It may be born in the mind and carried through the eyes, but it's what happens when someone takes it to the hands that worries me. The boys over at the club ain't used to someone that good-looking hanging around here. A girl like that walks into a bar and starts with that I-am-woman-hear-me-roar attitude—that just drives a guy crazy, sort of like a challenge, ya know." The preacher just nodded as if he understood exactly what Riley was saying, and in a way he did. Riley continued, "And then boys become clumsy hound dogs, falling all over themselves and acting foolish, until somebody loses their temper. Then we got trouble, and little Ms. Sanchari is right in the middle of it. I've seen it too many times."

"Well, that's why you get the big bucks, isn't it Riley?" the preacher said with a laugh in his voice.

"Oh yeah, me and you, preacher, bringing in the big bucks." The two began to move toward their cars, with Riley wondering out loud, "Why do you think she is so interested in her dad's work? You'd think she would just ask him what he did down here. I wonder what kind of a follow-up she's doing."

"Well, save all those questions for tonight, Deputy, because you got a date with that pretty young thing." The preacher was laughing as he climbed into his car and headed back toward the church.

Riley got back in his car and headed down the same road as the preacher, traveling by the old farmhouse and barn. As he looked across the field, memories came rushing back. He wondered what it was about that old barn that kept coming into his life and leaving unanswered questions on his doorstep. He saw the new owner walking out toward the barn, and almost as if he could feel Riley's eyes, he stopped to stare at the sheriff's cruiser going by on the highway. Riley waved, but he wasn't sure whether the man could see him in his car. It didn't matter; that fellow was weird as they got. He and his wife were into some kind of meditation or something. The little girl had been talking about it at school so much that she got in trouble, and the parents had come down and tried to make a discrimination accusation against the principal. What was it they called it—*kooda-laga, kindee-lankee*? He couldn't remember. He just knew that his wife, who worked in the school cafeteria, had said they acted as if they were from another planet when the principal had tried to talk with them about their daughter and school. They'd taken her out after that and were homeschooling her now. The man worked as an office manager, and his wife stayed home and raised herbs or something. Some folks said she was a kind of witch, but if she was, that other bunch of witches over at Great Falls wouldn't have anything to do with her. There was no time to worry about that now. He had some explaining to do to his wife, Betty. She didn't like his evening patrols—especially ones that sent him out to talk with pretty young coeds on scary old battlegrounds.

Scene 9

The sheriff's office

The sun was sinking low in the sky when Riley pulled up at the sheriff's office. He gassed up the cruiser and went inside to check any orders for the night patrol. The dispatch girl handed him a list of complaints that had come in that afternoon. It would probably look like any other dispatch, he thought. He would be in the east end of the county that night, which was usually pretty quiet. That would work out; he could plan his route to be at the campsite around seven. The girl was looking at her call screen and said, "You got the east side tonight, Riley. Looks like you'll be a busy boy."

"Na-a-aw," Riley said with his thickest southern drawl. "Nothing happens in the east side. The real work is over on the south and west side, at those apartments. That's where they get the trouble."

"Haven't you heard?" she said, smiling as she looked over her glasses. "The east side has beat the rest of the county for the last three weeks. Check your sheet against the others, and you'll see that you have twice as many calls as the other areas. It's been that way for the last few nights."

Riley looked down at the call sheets and saw that, sure enough, she was right. There were almost twice as many calls as in the other areas. He saw everything from loose dogs, stolen property, vandalism, and domestic disturbances to strange men seen walking across people's backyards. It seemed the east side was now the new rough side of the county. Some of the things he read there did not surprise him, but others caught him off guard. He saw the names of people he had known most of his life who had engaged in behavior that just wasn't like them. It just confirmed what he had been saying to the preacher: "This ole world is gettin' meaner and meaner." Oddly enough, the preacher hadn't agreed as quickly as he usually did; instead he'd just looked down and mumbled something. Riley hadn't paid much attention, but maybe he should check with the preacher next time he saw him and ask just what was on his mind. No time for that now. Riley had a lot of follow-ups to do. It looked like Halloween was coming early this year with all these pranks and things going on.

Scene 10

Reverend Strong's office

As Riley made his way around the east side, another person was going over his own kind of dispatch sheet. Reverend Bruce was the pastor of Center Hill Baptist Church, and he had left the memorial to come back to his office for a little quiet time. He had gone to the battlefield after hearing that one of his members (Arthur Kirtland) was going to confront the team leaders with more complaints. He felt that it might be good idea if he were there to help calm him down if he got overly excited. It was strange to see Arthur so upset. He had known Arthur for several years and knew him to be a pleasant but quiet, private sort of guy, who everyone liked or at least understood. But it seemed he had now become a bitter person who could to do nothing but sit at home thinking up things to criticize. Bruce had been on that criticism list several times lately, and Arthur spoke to him only when it couldn't be avoided. What had happened to that nice little old man—or was this the real Arthur showing through at last?

Bruce did not want to consider any other alternative, at least not yet. He stopped thinking about it and tried to focus on the list in front of him. As he sat there in his office, staring at a prayer list that seemed to grow and grow, he wondered, Was anyone really praying these days? Then an even worse thought darted across his mind: Was there anybody *listening* to prayers these days? The prayer list was a sheet of names and situations; people in the church had requested prayer for any and all kinds of special needs. Anyone could drop a note by the office prayer box or put a slip in the offering plate on a Sunday.

Normally he and the deacons would peruse it at the weekly prayer breakfast and spend an hour or so in prayer for these needs. In the past few weeks he had taken the precaution of looking over the requests before taking the box to the breakfast. He had begun taking these cautionary actions when he'd found a note in the prayer box. It caused the same feeling of dread that had come over him when he'd seen that message on the tent. It probably wasn't a coincidence that it was the same message. The words "Bust his head" were scribbled on the ruddy paper, and that was all it said, but it was enough to give the preacher and some of the deacons a shudder. They dismissed it as a prank, but the next week there was another note that said, "Cut 'em off," and next there was "Gut him like a fish." In the following weeks, another note came that simply read "Pieces."

The preacher thought it best not to share these at the prayer time, because it was just distracting everyone from the prayer session. A few weeks before, they had been so focused on the notes that they had left with just a quick closing prayer and hardly spoken of anything else. The speculation over who was sending the notes became ugly at times. Everyone had someone in mind, from teenagers to disgruntled older members. It opened the door to discussing problems the church had had in the past and who had been the cause. This was usually followed by arguing the issues all over again. When Bruce tried to bring the

7891112151718192022

meeting back to the point, the men would begin to discuss how the notes might be symptoms of problems in the current church family. The word *family* had become almost an oxymoron in describing the congregation. Everyone seemed to be dividing up into small groups to wage war against one another. When Bruce showed up without a note, some of the men accused him of hiding something from the deacons, and no amount of assurance could change their minds. The prayer group had thinned out until just a couple of Bruce's closest friends were coming. The prayer time was now divided between talking about the notes and wondering why everyone else was not coming to prayer breakfast.

The preacher's contemplation was interrupted by a faint knock at the door. Mr. Paxton stuck his head around the corner, smiled, and queried, "Have a minute, Mr. Strong?" The Paxton family never called him Reverend, Pastor, or even Preacher. They avoided the titles and then smiled as if making a point of not recognizing the preacher's position. Bruce invited him to come in and sit down, and Mr. Paxton moved over to the small couch.

"What can I do for you, Mr. Paxton?" Bruce asked, trying to hide his tone of suspicion. The Paxton's had never been to a church service, but the preacher had visited their home on a couple of occasions and offered an invitation. Bruce had always felt that these people had an air of superiority about them, even though they were not what people would consider extremely successful or even highly educated. Mr. Paxton had an associate degree in business administration, which Bruce had noticed proudly displayed on the wall in the den.

"Please call me Oliver, Mr. Strong," he said with that smile that Bruce found hard to interpret.

"Only if you call me Bruce," the preacher responded, with his own smile.

"All right, Bruce. I wanted to speak with you about an idea I have been toying with. I understand that you are a man with progressive ideas." Paxton's tone suggested a sales pitch, but Bruce tried to be cordial. "I believe you to be a spiritual person, with a tolerant and inquisitive mind that actually seems out of place in a community like this."

"Thank you—I think—Oliver. I do try to be open minded and tolerant as much as possible without compromising my convictions. As far as being spiritual, that sort of comes with the job you might say." Bruce was trying to be polite while keeping the tension down with a little stab at humor.

"Oh no, Bruce, I think that you have a genuine spirituality about you. I can sense it in your aura. There is a light of goodness around you that comforts people and draws others into your sphere of influence. I believe that aura makes you perfect for what I wish to suggest." Oliver leaned forward in his seat with a new intensity.

"Thanks again, Oliver, for the aura reading and the compliment, but just what are you suggesting?"

Oliver sat back and smiled again, as if pulling his enthusiasm back into himself to prepare for his initial presentation. "Bruce are you aware of the benefits of yoga and meditation?"

"Somewhat. I have studied a bit of martial arts, and in the process, I found that the concentration level is similar to focused prayer. I know some like to equate prayer and meditation as equal disciplines."

"Exactly, my friend!" said Oliver, now finding it hard to control his enthusiasm. "I knew I had come to the right man. Yoga is the practice of self-control and the ultimate discipline of the body, not unlike the ascetic practices of Christianity. It also has medicinal qualities of strengthening and, in some ways, rejuvenating the body. I have studied it for many years, and I wish to teach it in this area. I have already enlisted a few people, some from your own congregation, to begin classes. If I had a larger facility and the endorsement of some of the community leaders, I could expand my reach to benefit many more in the community. The senior adults would gain so much from this type of exercise. Don't you agree?"

Bruce now understood the politeness, and even though he had nothing against exercise, there seemed to be something more in this man's offer. Perhaps it was just Bruce's suspicious nature, but something didn't feel right. Bruce was aware that transcendental meditation involved the students exhibiting a level of devotion and dedication to the guru that sometimes bordered on worship. Some had even suggested that it *was* worship. He also knew that in the early days students had been taught to use the names of Hindu gods as mantras, a practice that had forced him to stop his involvement with the world of transcendental meditation, or TM, when he was younger. For now, he would play dumb and see how much Oliver was willing to reveal. "Aren't there some religious connections to meditation?" he asked innocently.

"No," Oliver said. "Yoga is completely separate from any form of spirituality. This would be just good, fun exercise. We just need a larger space, and since your church has a gymnasium, we thought, what better place to be! You could come and join us in the morning; I'm sure you'd find it invigorating."

Bruce had one more question, and then he would try to end this discussion with the standard Baptist dodge of "I'll need to bring it before the committee." Those committees had been a blessing in times like this, when he needed to stall someone until he could get more information. But first his question: "I have heard a little about your classes. It's said you studied a particular style of yoga—it was the *konga linga* or *kunta kinta*, or something like that." He pretended not to know the proper term.

At the mention of the issue of style, the room suddenly seemed to drop a few degrees. Mr. Paxton seemed to be caught off guard.

"I am not sure what you mean, Bruce, but personally I try to approach yoga with an open mind and not get hung up on names and titles."

Bruce was definitely sensing something hidden now, but he wasn't sure what to say. So, when in doubt, defer to a committee. He looked up and, smiling, said, "I will have to get back with you on this, Oliver. The final say-so rests with the committees, ya know."

"Yes, yes, I know, Bruce. But I also know what an influential person you can be when you so desire." His comment was followed by the smile that made Bruce's skin begin to crawl, as if he had just done something dirty.

Bruce didn't like the inflection or the insinuation that he would use his influence to sway the people. In an almost involuntary reaction, he heard himself saying, "Well, between you and me, Oliver, I don't think the majority of people will share your interest in something so closely connected to Eastern mysticism."

It was as if someone had just flicked the light switch off, and in the darkened room two new people were now facing one another. Oliver's voice became low and almost mechanical, and Bruce thought he could detect a hint of accent that had not been there before. He listened closely, but he couldn't quite place the enunciations. Oliver's head now dropped, and his eyes rolled up toward his brow, with a thin line of the white showing beneath his pupils. The Japanese called it *sanpaku*, and Bruce remembered it from his days in martial arts as an aggressive and offensive posture from someone who might be unbalanced or disturbed.

"So, you will not support me in my efforts to bring this opportunity to your people." Oliver spoke almost in a growl.

"There's no need to be offended, Oliver. I just want you to be prepared for their response. This is, after all, a farming community in the upper state, not a metropolitan area where kundalini yoga would find broader acceptance." Bruce responded with his own glance that could not be mistaken by one trained in the art of combat.

"I said nothing of kundalini, Mr. Strong. I am a simple teacher of relaxation techniques that have been practiced for millennia." Paxton's voice became quicker paced and seemed off balance, as if Bruce's comment had been a blow to the stomach.

"Oh, I know, Oliver. It just came to me while we were talking. That is the form you're teaching, isn't it? Kundalini, the way of Shakti the Serpent, the mother of all styles and considered by some the most powerful yoga. Kundalini seeks to tap energy from the sleeping serpent that rests at the base of the spine, or something like that." Bruce smiled a mischievous smile. He knew that he had pulled back the covers on something that Paxton obviously had not told his students. He had wanted to see Paxton's reaction, and now that he had, it was time to go back to playing small-town preacher.

Oliver regained his composure, and with almost serpentine eyes, he smiled and said, "You are a most interesting person, Mr. Strong. You know more than you let on to folks, but like many simple people, a little knowledge can close the mind instead of opening it. I urge you not to rush to judgment. Many people benefit from this art. I see how you may be uncomfortable with the imagery of Shakti, but the energy is in all of us, just waiting to be awakened. You and I, and our teachings, are more similar than you may care to admit. Don't let your intolerance blind you to truth." Oliver was rising now and moving toward the door with a certain grace that Bruce had not noticed before.

"Oh, I just like to read a little. As far as being similar, I am aware that yoga is seen as a path to God. I am familiar with a form of yoga called Kundalini yoga, which is the path to God of love and devotion and shares many Christian ideas. So why not approach yoga from that perspective rather than Shakti, which seems to carry some very dark connotations? There was a long, quiet pause, during which Bruce realized that Paxton was not going to respond. After a moment, Bruce smiled and said, "I'll get back with you on the use of the gym, Oliver." Bruce was still smiling as Oliver moved out into the hall and toward the parking lot.

"Oh, don't bother," Mr. Strong said. He spoke without turning or stopping, as if suddenly in a hurry to leave. "You're probably right about the response. You know these people better than I do. No need stirring them up over a little exercise class. I can always convert my barn into a studio. It would be more convenient anyway."

Paxton was finishing his sentence as he walked out the door. Now Bruce was left standing in the silence, and he realized that he was relaxing. The meeting had put him on his guard and caused more tension than he'd been aware of at the time. It was just a gut feeling, but something wasn't quite kosher about Mr. Paxton.

He moved back to the solitude of his office and began to breathe deeply and to ready himself for his prayer time. Then he stopped and gently laughed to himself when he realized that he was preparing for prayer in much the same way yogis prepared for meditation. Then he thought of Shakti, the serpent. *Yes Mr. Paxton, we do have similarities*, he mused. *It's just that the serpent I deal with is something I wish to overcome, not embrace.*

Scene 11

The home of Arthur Kirtland

At that same time, another meeting was taking pace between Arthur Kirtland and two of his friends. He was relating the story of the confrontation at the battlefield. Arthur told how he had felt that they were all siding against him with regards to the group's complaint, but how the deputy had been the only one to take him seriously. He then added that he especially resented the preacher up there getting all cozy with those troublemakers. He told the group that the preacher might be spending too much time out of the office, visiting a bunch of pretty little college girls. This was followed by a detailed description of what he called the "high yeller" girl trying to pass herself off as somebody from India or something like that. Arthur insisted that she was at least a Puerto Rican. The news of a potential scandal whipped the men into a frenzy of outrage and complaints; it turned a group of loving old grandpas into a pack of angry pit bulls. After that they would sit there and stew for another hour or so and then take their news home to their wives. From there the information highway would kick into high gear. Within a day or two there was no telling what shape the story would have taken.

Scene 12

The interview at Buford and the first team

Riley was making the turn at the crossroads now, and he glanced over to the sports bar. The place was filling up. He could tell who was there by the shiny trucks parked in a neat row. This was the scene that had given America their favorite stereotype about the South. This was just a bunch of good ole boys who had pickup trucks with shotgun racks in the back windows, out drinkin' at a honky-tonk. If non-southerners only knew that most of these boys were college grads and those trucks were more expensive than a lot of the luxury cars you'd find in a big city!

As Riley turned into the memorial, he saw the lights of the research team's campsite off near the pasture. The team was just finishing their dinner while the sun behind them dropped slowly beneath the tree line. He saw the students tending to their chores, and Alan waved hello as he walked toward the study tent. That was where the group met in the evenings to discuss the day's finds, if any, and the significance of any discovery. Near the study tent was a new tent; Riley assumed it was Sandy's. He parked near the road and moved toward the tiny tent city. He saw Sandy walking toward the camp and heard her yell a welcome. Her voice was as melodic as a night bird's song, but Riley could not help but read something unsettled in her mannerism.

Sandy motioned Riley over to her quarters and held open her tent flap, inviting him inside. Her tent was a large domed structure that had two room-like areas. The one he was standing in was tall enough to stand up in the middle. This section of the tent had a cozy oriental flare. There were imitation tapestry rugs on the tent floor and cushions stacked around a low table. On the table there was a small battery-powered lamp and a laptop computer. Plastic crates held books, spare batteries, and snack food. Riley smirked and thought to himself, *why is it that the people with perfect figures seem to always be junk-food junkies?*

Sandy saw him checking out her quarters and its contents. "Would you like a chocolate cake or candy bar, Deputy, or maybe a cup of coffee?" She was opening a thermos as she spoke, and Riley smiled with a nod and sort of grunted a yes, ma'am. Sandy sat back on a stack of pillows, and Riley looked around uncomfortably for a place to sit down. Sandy reached behind a cushion and produced a small folding stool. Riley smiled and straddled the small seat near the table.

"Now, miss, what can I tell you that your father hasn't already told you?" Riley asked as if interrogating a prisoner.

But Sandy wasn't going to let Riley take control of the interview. "Wait a minute, Deputy. *I* asked *you* here, remember? I'm the one doing the research."

"Touché," Riley said. "It's a hard habit to break. What do you want to know?"

Sandy leaned forward and held her head erect as if forcing the questions out of her throat. "Well, first of all, what do you know about the team's investigation here?"

"Not too much, really. The group didn't let folks know much. My job was mainly to prevent any interference from the locals in case the story got out and caused a stir." Riley was speaking in his best business voice.

"But the story did get out, didn't it, Deputy? How did that happen?" Sandy asked.

"Well, I am not really sure. Some say it was because the little girl told a teacher about the ghost she saw in the barn, and others say it was one of the team members. Whatever the case may be, it just leaked out. But ya know, the strange thing is how the story just died and nobody seemed to care. Then the rumors started that this wasn't even the real location. I don't know how they got started, because the team was out at that barn every day. It was like somebody just tossed a sheet over the barn and people couldn't see the team's vehicles parked there each day. Your dad even spent the night a couple of times, or at least that's what I was told by the officer who had late-night patrol." Sandy sat up at the mention of her father, and a frown creased her flawless features.

"How many nights did he stay there, and who stayed with him?" she asked with renewed interest.

"I wouldn't know, missy; like I said, I was just there on my duty days to keep things safe and sound." Riley was starting to get a little curious, but he was willing to wait to ask his questions.

"Were there any incidents that involved you in your professional capacity during the team's residency here?" Sandy asked with unusual timidity.

Riley began with his customary head scratch while a low humming noise eased across his lips. "Hmmm, let me see; I think I was called one night. Yeah, it was a late-night call out to the barn. It wasn't trouble from the community or the Paxton's. There seemed to be a dispute among the team members."

"Was my father involved?" Sandy asked.

"Well, I can't really say, missy. By the time I arrived, the dust was settling and some of the members were packing up and leaving in the middle of the night. I was never sure whether the argument was about the research or if it was a personal problem between members. All I know is that the next day the whole team was packing up. When I asked for some answers, they said all they could find was some elevated electromagnetic readings. What was the final report, anyway?"

"Well, Deputy, that's hard to say, because the team never published a formal report." Sandy seemed hesitant to tell this to Riley, perhaps because she knew that this would arouse suspicions as to why she was there.

She wasn't wrong. Right on cue, Riley's eyebrows lifted, and he said, "I thought you were here to do follow-up research. If there wasn't a report, then either you're working from just your dad's notes or you're not doing a follow-up at all; you're looking for something else. Now, which is it?"

"Well maybe neither, and maybe a little of both, actually," she told him, parroting the statement she had made to Riley earlier in the day. But this time she didn't leave the deputy in suspense. "I am working from my father's notes, and I am a doctoral student at Duke, but I'm not looking for a paranormal explanation of some ghost in a barn or any other phenomenon. I'm looking for an explanation for something more personal."

"Well, I guess you know what my next question is gonna be: Why didn't you just ask your dad?" Riley now realized there was more than a dissertation going on here.

"I can't ask my father. Even if I did, he wouldn't tell me anything. He hasn't been the same since this project. He's had to take a sabbatical— well, actually, my mother placed him on sabbatical. He just quit going to work … he just sits at home. When we try to speak with him, he gets very edgy and angry. He's not the same man who came down here to do research into the paranormal. He changed, and the only thing we can attribute it to is this project. I came to see what happened to my father. I'd rather this stay between you and me, Deputy. I'm not sure if they'd allow me to be a part of this group if they knew my motivation was less professional and more of a personal nature."

Riley's mind began to wander back to another young lady—she also had needed answers about what had happened to a loved one who'd hung around that old barn. She'd never found the answers she wanted; she had just moved away. But something told him that this girl wasn't going to give up that easily. She was a research scientist, and her job was finding solutions to problems. "Did you talk to the other team members about what happened?"

She fidgeted nervously with her hands. "I tried, but the only one that would speak with me was a student aide, and he wasn't in on the final concluding meetings. The others were either angry with my father or declined to discuss it out of professional courtesy."

"Well, what did the one who *would* talk with you say?" Riley edged closer and spoke a little more softly, as if afraid someone outside might hear.

"He was of little help. It appears that Dad ran the team in a different manner than normal. You've seen the way Alan runs this project, haven't you? Everyone is over in that tent right now, discussing today's work. They brainstorm and theorize, and it helps lead to group cohesion. It really makes for a good working atmosphere."

Riley interrupted to say, "I came by in the evening and saw that same thing with your dad's group, that first night they were there."

"Yes, from what the grad assistant said, they did that for one night, but only the official researchers were in on the rest of meetings. Mark, the grad assistant, said that he thought they really had something, because those guys got real secretive and serious. The only interviews on the site were done by Dad, and his notes are sketchy. A lot of the experiments went late into the night, and then, it appears, things went bad fast. There were arguments between the staff members and overall bad karma. Mark said my dad started doing more and more work on his own. The others didn't like this and insisted on his involvement with the group process. Mark said that finally, one night, the others found my dad in the barn alone, and he just told them he was shutting down the project. There was a shouting match, and some of the folks left that night. The next day Dad reported that they had found some strong electromagnetic readings but nothing else. Dad's notes confirm that there were electromagnetic readings found in the barn, but Mark said he thought they were onto something else." Riley felt the hair on his arm begin to rise as she told her story of sudden changes in behavior and a man whose character had changed overnight.

"Just what do you think they were onto, missy? Are you trying to tell me there really is a ghost in that old barn down there?" Riley sounded like a boy scout on his first camping trip, sitting around the campfire listening to scary stories.

"Paranormal investigations are similar to the Christian exorcisms; we rule out all possible physical or man-made explanations before we involve the supernatural. Contrary to popular opinion, paranormal investigators are not psychics, mediums, or even ghost hunters. We are scientists seeking an understanding of forces that have thus far defied normal and contemporary explanation. There are natural occurrences, such as electromagnetic fields, gaseous anomalies, and spontaneous discharging of static electricity, just to name a few. The majority of researchers avoid the supernatural realm completely, if possible." Sandy was simplifying things as much as possible for the sheriff's deputy.

Riley smiled at the young researcher and did his own simplification. "So you're telling me there ain't no such things as ghosts. Well, that suits me just fine, but how do you explain all the stories and sightings we read about and see on TV?"

"Mostly it's just wishful thinking. People are fascinated with the supernatural and spiritual world. It is the basis of our myths and religious developments. People have always wanted to contact dead relatives. This is usually based on a desire to keep the relationship that is lost, as well as assure them that these departed loved ones still exist in some form. In ancient cultures, and even in some oriental systems, ancestor worship is the communication with dead relatives through various spiritual methodologies or rituals. Prayers, offerings, or adherence to certain moral codes are often related to a desire to appease dead ancestors who are constantly observing us from some alternate dimension." Sandy paused to allow her impromptu lecture to take root in Riley's mind.

Before she could begin again, Riley put in, "Excuse me, missy. This is all fascinating and everything, and you just about got me ready to not be afraid of the dark, but let's get back to your dad and his research. I know I may have sidetracked you with the whole ghost question, but if your dad said there were no ghosts, and it was just some electro-whatchamacallit, how does this connect up with what your dad was doing?"

"Well, as I said, Deputy, my father's notes confirmed the presence of electromagnetic activity; however, the readings in the notes were nothing unusual. The levels he recorded were within what we consider a normal range—with the exception of the last night." Sandy's voice had a hint of anxiety.

"Seems to me that would confirm that there was nothin' there and case closed." Riley caught himself sounding like Sheriff Croften, and he wondered if it was as frustrating to Sandy as Croften was to him at times.

"No, Deputy!" Sandy voiced a stronger sound of frustration than Riley had ever used with Croften. "That's just my point! The case was most definitely not closed. If anything, it was just beginning to open when my father shut it down. They had run no other tests or even held in-depth interviews with participants in the phenomenon. It's like they started fishing and at the first nibble they reeled in and declared there were no fish in the water."

Riley could understand the fishing analogy, and a scowl inched across his forehead. "So, you're telling me there is a ghost in that barn?"

Now Sandy was even more frustrated with the deputy. "No, Deputy! I'm telling you that my father was a loving, kind family man, not to mention a highly respected and motivated research scientist. He put together a team of specialists, came to this place, did a few days of what we would call freshman-level testing—and came home a completely different person. And I want to know just what the hell happened here!

I want my father back. The last time anyone saw the man who resembled my dad was down there in that barn. Now, can you help get me some answers or not?"

Riley was daydreaming. Her words were bringing back memories of the other little girl who had thought he could help bring her daddy back and the young mother who desperately needed to know what had happened to her husband.

"Well, Deputy, I didn't mean to bore you. Obviously, you're not interested enough to help me. I'm sorry to have troubled you tonight." Sandy looked sad, but she was far from tears.

"No, it's n-not that, missy." Riley stuttered slightly as he regained his composure. He felt he had just returned from a trip. "It's just that your story is sort of familiar to another missing person report I dealt with once, and I just got to thinking about it. I'd like to help you all I can, but I'm not sure just what we are looking for. Your dad made a sudden change and sort of snapped; that is how a lot of people would see it." He was sounding like Croften again, and he didn't like it. He was sure it wasn't what Sandy wanted to hear. "A lot of people would say that, but not me. I, for one, have a hard time accepting that people just do a 360-degree turn in one day."

"That would be a 180, Deputy." Sandy spoke with a softer tone and a hint of a smile across her lips.

"Uh, oh yeah—360, 180, whatever. The guy made a turnaround, and I'll try to help you figure it out, missy." Riley's little math slipup was just enough to break the tension, and they both sat there laughing. Riley was making a pledge to help this person because he had always felt he had left the first occupants of that house, Karen and Amber, on their own, with no resolution. He had never been comfortable with that, and this was a chance to make some amends. "I want to help, missy, but I wasn't closely involved with what your dad was doing, so I need your assistance. I can't start an official investigation into mood changes. I need a crime or a victim. We don't have anything like that here. So, give me an idea of what exactly you want me to do."

"I think the first thing to do is to start my own investigation into that barn. But the Paxton's said they didn't want to draw attention to themselves, and they denied my request." Sandy was becoming frustrated again.

"Maybe you just need a contact person who can influence them." Riley was running an imaginary list of names and faces through his mind, trying to find a friend of the Paxton's. "Preacher Bruce, he might be able to talk them into letting you look around a little. I'll give him a call and see what he says."

"Thank you, Deputy. That would be a great help." She paused and almost reluctantly spoke, "Just one more thing, Deputy. I'm not even sure it is of any importance, but in the margin of my father's notes he scribbled the words 'saw the green man.' Is there a Mr. Green who lives around here that may have anything to do with his investigation, or is there any reference to the 'green man' that means anything to you?"

She was not telling him the whole story of the green man, because she didn't want to scare the deputy. There had been more in her father's notes than just this notation. She was hoping the term referred to a person in the area, because the other alternative had her concerned.

Riley thought for a moment, scratching his head. He started, "I can't think of any Greens livin' right around here off the top of my head, but—" He suddenly stopped as if he'd been hit with an electric shock. He was remembering what a young woman had said to him years ago, and he felt a chill on his skin.

"What is it, Deputy?" Sandy had noticed the sudden pause and puzzled look on Riley's face. "Deputy?" she repeated, as if trying to wake him from his stupor.

Riley smiled and stuttered a bit. "Oh … it's nothing, miss, I just had a recollection of a lady who lived at that house a while back. I seemed to recall her saying something about seeing, or thinking she saw a fella in a green coat and hat down there in that barn one night. But she was pretty confused and said she was just hallucinating or something. Nothin' ever came of it, and it turned out it was her husband, who was acting strange. It was a mess, but they been gone for two years or so now."

Sandy made a mental note and thanked the deputy again. There was a new look of hope in her eyes. Riley stood and, stretching as best he could in the confined space, made his way out into the night air. The sky was starry, and there was just a slight glow from the bright lights of the nearby gas station and sports bar. He could hear the muffled sound of music drifting across the empty field. The big tent was filled with students and the sound of Alan's voice and an occasional burst of laughter spilling out into the dark. It seemed this group was having fun at their dig in spite of everything else. The visit with Sandy had been an escape from reality, but now it was back to the cold metal casing of his car and evening patrol. He could hear the radio popping, calling him back to the real world, as he drew near the cruiser.

Scene 13

The team meeting

Sandy walked over to join the others in the study tent, to listen in on the day's finds and opinions. The large army surplus tent had its side walls rolled halfway up to allow a breeze to circulate through. As Sandy walked in, someone shouted, "There she is now! Let's ask her."

All eyes turned to her small figure in the back. Sandy gave a smile and a look of surprise; Alan was trying to calm down the frenzied crowd. Small groups were carrying on heated discussions, and Sandy's smile gave way to a questioning glance toward Alan. Alan raised his arms and flapped them like an eagle's wing as he tried to regain control of the crowd.

"All right, all right! Everybody just settle down. We will consider all the options on the table, and we will allow input from all team members—even our newest adopted member, Dr. Sandy." At that there was a round of applause and a neat little bow from Sandy. You could almost hear the heartfelt sigh from the young guys in the tent. Sandy had only been there a week or so, but she had stolen the hearts of all the male members of the team. Some of the girls were laughing at the boys' apish behavior, but there were many who did not like the competition from this stunning exotic beauty. Sandy made her way down the side aisle toward the front area. She quietly leaned toward Alan and asked, "What exactly do you need my opinion about?"

Alan spoke to Sandy but purposefully spoke loud enough for all to hear. In a mockingly British accent, as if reading a scene from Henry V, he said, "We are simple historians for the working day, but we find ourselves divided into three inquisitive camps. The question that has brought us to this division regards yonder grave out there. To dig or not to dig, that is the question."

Sandy smiled and said, "I thought you said there were three camps. What's the third question?"

"Alas, fair maid, the third group of questioners consists of yonder underclassmen." He pointed at a front row reserved for the youngest members of the group, which for this team consisted of four underclassmen. "The question they ponder day and night is … would there be any chance in this world or the next that you would go out with any one of them?" At that the boys' in question blushed crimson, and Sandy gave them a wink as the whole crowd in the tent erupted into laughter.

As the laughter began to subside, Alan turned again to Sandy and said, "Seriously, we are debating the need to look in the grave. Some say we must, to find the truth of this place. Others fear the wrath of the supernatural world, and that's where you come in. What are the paranormal ramifications of disturbing the resting place of the dead?"

Sandy stopped smiling and put a more serious look on her face, along with an almost angry tone, which caught Alan off guard. "If you are you asking for a professional opinion on the sanctity of a grave site, you need a priest. If you are asking if there are any spiritual ramifications connected with opening a grave, I would have to say …" She paused and looked at the tent full of kids. "No, the only thing you will find out there is a hole filled with bones and remnants of men who died for a cause that was obviously important enough to them to make such a sacrifice." She gave a cool smile and walked out of the tent.

The kids were silent for a moment, until one of them, who was in favor of exhuming the grave, shouted, "That's good enough for me! Let's get the shovels." No one else responded, and the speaker's enthusiasm fell dead on the cold floor. Sandy had injected a serious note into the evening with her reminder to the group that this was more than just an archeological site. It was, after all, a site filled with the bodies of brave men who had paid the ultimate price. This group of kids could be getting an education and cutting up like they were that night.

Alan raised his hands again and said, "Hold it, you guys. It's not that easy. I anticipated this move, but we still have to go into town tomorrow and see if my exhumation request has been honored. Now listen close. Do not mention this outside of camp, because we have some locals that are extremely sensitive to this possibility. If we can get the ground-piercing radar, we can get some readings. We will probably not be digging into the grave itself but just some small exploratory holes and side-approach holes. We will try to disturb as little of the actual grave as possible. Sensitivity and knowledge of the social environment is as important as expertise in your subject matter. We are guests in this town, and don't forget it. This is as true in Buford as it is in Tibet. Now, you got about an hour until lights out. Anybody going up to the store, remember to take a buddy—and the sports bar is off limits tonight. Good night!" There was a slight sigh when he mentioned the bar being off limits, but once outside, the kids began to divide up and move around camp. Some went straight to their tents, while others teamed up for a short walk up to the convenience store for their nightly soda or snack. Alan was answering questions as he made his way across the campsite. He was on his way to Sandy's tent to see if he had offended her at the meeting. Also, he didn't mind spending a little time with an attractive young professional who might share his love for research.

"Hello, inside! Are you decent?" Alan shouted through the half-opened flap.

"Yes, come in, Alan. The doors open," Sandy answered.

"I just wanted to come by and apologize if I offended you tonight, it was all in the name of a little fun," Alan began his mea culpa.

"I know, Alan; don't sweat it. That was a little bit of drama on my part. That bunch was about to get out of hand, and I felt they needed a little calming down. I just wanted to remind them that this isn't summer camp; this is serious research." Sandy was still in lecture mode, and whether she knew it or not, she was whittling Alan down to size by implying that he wasn't running the dig with enough discipline.

This air of condescension did not go unnoticed. Alan took a deep breath and exhaled audibly before countering her assault. She might be the best-looking girl he'd ever seen, but nobody was going to question his professionalism. "If you had opted to stay, instead of making that dramatic exit, you would have seen that I can string out the fun and bring it back to serious research. I know what I'm doing here, Dr. Prasad." His tone was unmistakably commanding.

Sandy fought the urge to counterpunch, because inside she was thinking, *I am a guest, and I don't want friction.* Perhaps she was overstepping her bounds as a guest. That was the thought that started coming out even as it formed in her head. "You're right, Alan. Please accept my apology. I simply get a little overzealous when I think about my work. Please forgive me—shall we call it even, then?" She held the flap of the tent open for him to exit.

If Alan had been a block of ice, he would now be a puddle of water or a cloud of steam. Her voice was like an angel's song, and it completely drained the strength out of his knees. As he stepped out into the night, the cool air seemed to slap him back into consciousness. He suddenly realized that he had left as if dismissed by the Queen of Sheba. He turned back to look at the pale-blue dome tent shining in the night like an oasis. Had he won that argument? He had gotten his point across, and she had apologized, but somehow it seemed that he was doing just what she wanted him to do. *Man, what a girl!* he thought as he smiled at the night sky.

Scene 14

A slip of the lip

The smile on Alan's face wasn't going to last long, because at that moment, in the small gas station/convenience store across the intersection, trouble was brewing. Two of the students were in line to get a drink and some chips to take back to camp, when they heard the voice of Leon Courtney saying, "There's two of them now. My granddad says they are going to dig up the bodies and put 'em on display in Columbia. It's not right." One of his friends tried to quiet him down, but the young man just shoved his friend aside, saying, "You think I give a whip about what they think? This is my home, not theirs. I'm sick of the government coming in here and taking what it wants and telling folks what they can and cannot do on their own property."

Brad Welch was a graduate history major from Charleston, and he had a particular distaste for ignorance. He turned slowly and looked at the local boy. "I think you got your story mixed up, fella."

Oscar, the other team member, whispered to him, "Just leave it alone. Let's get back to camp."

At that, Leon spoke up, "Yeah, leave it alone, grave robber. Why don't you just leave the whole thing alone and go on back to Columbia?"

Brad wasn't the kind to be intimidated, and he wasn't backing down tonight. "I don't want any trouble here; it's just that if you're going to go around saying stuff, you need to get it right. In the first place, we aren't going to put any bodies on display; we aren't even going to take them out of the grave. Number two, we're not the government. We're history students, trying to get the facts about this battle, that's all. Thirdly, that property is public property, not private, and we have as much right to it as you do."

The man behind the counter got involved now. "Both of you'uns put a lid on it. I ain't having no fights in here. Leon, you leave these boys be, or I'll be talking to your grandad in the morning." He then turned his attention back to the two guys checking out. "What did you mean when you said you weren't even going to take the bodies out of the grave and display 'em? That's not the same as saying you ain't gonna dig in the grave. Are y'all gonna start diggin' in the grave?

The two boys looked at one another, and Brad said, "If we can get the radar equipment, it's unlikely we will be actually digging in the grave."

"Yeah, we just need to do some parallel holes to be able to check the contents," Oscar chimed in, but even as he said the words, he and Brad knew these were the wrong things to say. Brad tugged at his sleeve and pulled him away from the store. As they walked out and across the well-lit gas pump area, Brad looked back to see the local boys gathering around the cash register to speak with the worker. He could just imagine what they were saying. He and Oscar quickened their pace as they both realized that they had leaked some information that Alan had specifically told them not to mention. Now the natives really would be on the warpath.

As Brad and Oscar made their way across the road and moved toward the campsite, back inside the store, Leon and the other boys began to move toward the door, only to be stopped by a huge forearm across the glass door. "Have a bite of my doughnut, fella, and stay a while." It was Buck, a local dump truck driver. Buck worked hard all day, and then he liked to hang out at the store in the evenings and talk with the clerk. The boys saw the half-eaten doughnut and followed it up the burly arm until they came to a twenty-inch bicep peeking out from under a dirty blue work-shirt sleeve. Buck was a quiet, well-liked man, but he was also an imposing figure, and no one wanted to risk rousing that sleeping giant.

One of the boys mumbled, "No thanks," and moved toward the door again, but Buck smiled and held out the doughnut.

"This is better than what you'll find out there. Ain't nothin' but trouble out there tonight." The group of boys laughed nervously and insisted that they weren't up to anything. Buck still stood by the door and held out the half-eaten doughnut. "I still think you oughta eat a doughnut; they're fresh today. They got cream and jelly in 'em. Which do you like? Me, I like 'em both the same; this is cream." It may have been just a half-eaten doughnut with the cream squeezing out, but it was also Buck's way of saying that the only way through that door was through him.

Leon looked at the doughnut and then the bicep squeezing the cream out of it, and he just nodded with a smile. "I'll get my own, Buck. Thanks anyway." Leon turned and nudged the group toward the back of the store. Whatever they had planned would have to wait for a better opportunity.

Back at camp, the boys found Alan and told him what had happened at the store. It had just been a slip of the lip, and they were very sorry. Alan, in his laid-back fashion, told them not to worry; he would handle the locals if they tried to cause problems. He sent the two off to their tent without any threat or warning. As he turned to walk to his tent, he thought that perhaps he *was* too easy on the team. Just an hour earlier he had told them not to mention the digging, but it was as if they hadn't even been present at the night's session. Now it was just a matter of seeing how fast the local grapevine would spread the word. It shouldn't take long.

The storekeeper was on the phone in a flash. He called the first person who came to mind. The phone rang at the Kirtlands' home, and Arthur, who had been asleep for about fifteen minutes, grumbled to his wife that it had better be important. He picked up the phone and gave a gruff hello. Then he fell silent as he listened to the news the store clerk had to convey. After a few moments, he mumbled a positive grunt and then thanked the clerk for the heads-up. He would see to this in the morning. His wife was half awake, and without opening her eyes, she asked what it was all about. Arthur just mumbled for her to never mind and go back to sleep.

Scene 15

The campsite

The campsite was quieting down, and lights were going out one

by one. Alan was sitting in a small camp chair outside his tent. Across
the way he saw the forms of people moving around in their tents. The
evening air was cool but not cold, and the moon was not full but still
cast a light when not obscured by clouds. The sound of an occasional
car stopping or slowing down and then passing through the intersection
cracked the silence around the battlefield. A mist was rolling across the
field from the tree line. As Alan watched the mist draw closer, he tried to
imagine the scene over two hundred years ago, when soldiers had moved
across that same space. He loved history, and this little battle was one of
history's most intriguing stories. He was trying to remain objective, but
it was hard not to draw certain conclusions. His group's official purpose
was to investigate the authenticity of the battle and this site and possibly
to find another smaller gravesite. But Alan didn't doubt that this was the
spot of the battle; the other burial site could be anywhere. He felt sure
that some of the fighting had taken place a few hundred yards to the
south, near a small knoll and a clump of trees. Even though most of the
artifacts had been found across the road near the memorial, he believed
that that was a secondary battle site, where a small band of colonials and
British and Tory cavalry had met in combat. Alan began to close his eyes
and see history stretch out before him in remembered facts.

The Loyalist and British troops had been led by the infamous
Colonel Banastre Tarleton, perhaps the most hated British soldier of the
Revolutionary War. Tarleton had been a beast in a gentleman's body, a
textbook bad guy, only about twenty-six years old at the time. His father
had been a wealthy sea trader and mayor of Liverpool, but after his father
died, he had squandered his inheritance on gambling. Banastre had been
the third of seven children and unable to do the college work required
for Oxford. He was more comfortable at sports than his schoolwork,
and when he found himself broke, he asked his mother to buy him a
commission in the army. The army was a perfect fit for this brash young
tough. He volunteered for duty in America in 1776 to help put down
the coming rebellion and perhaps become a gentleman. He won notice
by capturing General Charles Lee, which led to his promotion. Soon he
was commanding a troop of cavalry for Lord Cornwallis.

It was Cornwallis who had sent Tarleton on this venture, hoping to capture the South Carolina governor, John Rutledge, who had joined Colonel Buford as he was trying to escape the defeat of Charleston. At Camden, the group of Virginians, led by Colonel Buford, was met by a larger force, led by General Caswell, who then took over the job of escorting the governor with them to Hillsboro. Colonel Buford continued on north toward the border of the Carolinas, hoping to reach Salisbury, just north of Charlotte. But Tarleton was coming quickly up behind, unaware that his prize had eluded him. He was hoping for another prestigious capture and the rank of full colonel. The two groups met in what many called the Waxhaw's area for their date with history and destiny.

This little battle was only remotely mentioned in the records of history, but Alan felt it had played a very important part in the war for independence. However, few knew the story. In Alan's mind, it was the single lit match that set ablaze the whole of the South. Alan wrestled with whether he wanted the world to know that the fighting spirit that made America free might have been fermented right at this very spot. Of course, the British told a different version—all except the one who was quoted on the tall gray marker stone in the center of the site. His words were a chilling reminder of what had happened there: "At this place, all human virtue was lost" were his words, and they rang ominously in Alan's mind. What had really happened here? Was it the bloody massacre that some suggested, or had it been just a brief skirmish in which a few overzealous soldiers had committed acts of cruelty?

Alan closed his eyes and tried to imagine that day. It was May 29, 1780. Colonel Abraham Buford was returning after taking between 350 and 400 men to fight at Charleston, but he arrived too late to aid the Charleston defenders. When they reached Camden, they heard the news that Charleston had fallen. He turned and tried to make his way north to join with other colonials at Salisbury, North Carolina. He would escort the governor of South Carolina and then send him away secretly with another group. Meanwhile, Colonel Banastre Tarleton was sent in pursuit, with his 350 mounted infantry. Tarleton wanted the recognition for capturing the governor; it could mean another promotion in this young officer's ambitious career. Tarleton pushed his troops hard, and they covered ground faster than anyone thought possible. By the time Buford reached the crossroads near Waxhaw's, Tarleton's men were on him—before Buford even realized they were there.

Tarleton's' dragoons and mounted infantry took up position on the field in three columns, with Tarleton on the left. At this point, history becomes obscured by differing versions of events. Some say that the British were fired on under a flag of truce, and others say that Colonel Buford, thinking he was outnumbered, tried to surrender, only to be attacked after his men laid down their arms. The most probable story seems to be a compilation of the two versions. The two leaders sent messages back and forth, and under a flag of truce they sought to arrange a conference. While this was going on, Tarleton was strengthening his position and preparing his forces for an attack. This was against the etiquette of combat, but Tarleton had little use for rules of war. Perhaps he thought he was outnumbered and had to strike fast and hard, but more than likely he wanted a sure and quick victory. "Dash and slash" had been Tarleton's method since receiving command. The conference began, but it was very short, and as soon as it was over, Tarleton's bugle was heard sounding an attack. No sooner had this started than Tarleton's dragoons, in the dark-green coats worn by the Tories, or Loyalists, attacked Buford's main body. Tarleton's dragoons were advancing before Buford could organize his forces, and the Colonials were totally caught off guard. They presented their rifles but waited too late to fire. The cavalry were upon them in a flash. Tarleton would later claim that his horse had been shot from beneath him, pinning him on the ground and preventing him from stopping what happened next. Some members of the dragoons claimed they thought their leader had been fired upon under a flag of truce, and it so incensed them that they waded into the colonial ranks in a murderous rage. Regardless of the reason, the melee gained instant momentum and was in full swing.

The colonials, thinking they were surrounded and outnumbered, had no directions from their commander. Many assumed that in such a case they would surrender and seek a parole, as had been the custom of others when captured by the British. The British would often take prisoners and then allow the men to sign a promise that they would not take part in the fighting; this was called a parole. Anyone breaking parole was immediately executed. This may account for the reports that many of Buford's' men simply dropped their weapons when the cavalry charged at them. Some even knelt on the ground with their hands in the air. What followed was fifteen minutes of carnage that would give Tarleton the nicknames Bloody Ban and Ban the Butcher. His troops rode into the surrendering colonials, hacking, slashing, and stabbing at the now running and falling soldiers even as they begged for mercy. But there was no mercy or kindness at the crossroads that day. Reports say that all of the dead had at least two bayonet wounds and multiple slash and hack marks on their bodies; the Dragoons had literally hacked away at their victims in a bloody frenzy.

In one letter, a Captain Stokes, for whom Stokes County, North Carolina, would be named, miraculously survived after receiving twenty-three stab and slash wounds and a gash that opened his head from crown to eyebrow. In his letters, he wrote that even as he lay there close to death, he could see the British soldiers going over the field, stabbing and hacking at the bodies lying on the ground. Two soldiers came up to him and asked if he wished mercy; Stokes simply asked them to make his end quick. The first soldier stabbed him twice with his bayonet and the next soldier added two more bayonet thrusts to his bleeding body. Stokes would have suffered more had not a kindhearted British sergeant stopped them. He then stood watch over the young officer's body and kept the soldiers from doing further atrocities to the wounded man. When he was found still alive near the body of a British officer, a rude field surgeon stuffed rags into his wounds to stop the bleeding. It took two days before someone could safely remove the matted bandages from his head wound.

Could Tarleton have known that the Virginians were going to surrender but, not wanting to be slowed down with prisoners, held his horse on the ground and feigned being trapped until the carnage had ended? That way he would have been unable to give the order for quarter to be given. Other rumors suggest that prior to the battle Tarleton ordered that they show no quarter to the rebels. Whatever the case, mercy was in short supply that day.

One hundred and thirteen men were believed to have been hacked to death, and one hundred and fifty were so badly maimed that they couldn't be moved. Colonel Buford was said to have escaped when they sounded retreat. Tarleton took fifty-three men as prisoners and marched them back to the little town of Camden, where he displayed them like trophies of war. Tarleton was praised by some for his murderous rampage, but he was shunned by others, who found his methods appalling and unseemly for a true gentleman soldier.

When word spread to the colonial soldiers that Colonel Buford's men had been killed while trying to surrender, the phrases "Tarleton's quarter" and "Buford's play" became the rallying cries of revenge at the coming battles of Cowpens—and especially at the battle of Kings Mountain. There the colonials committed similar atrocities as they called out their battle cry of "Tarleton's quarter!" These battles would end the British attempt to subdue the South and would force Cornwallis north to winter at Yorktown, where he eventually was forced to surrender. The Colonials would ride the crest of a wave of rage and hatred into Yorktown and win their freedom.

In Alan's mind, the big battles of the south might have been fought at places like Cowpens and Kings Mountain, but the motivation and fighting spirit were born in blood at the battle of Buford's crossing. He always likened it to the cry "Remember the Alamo!" That phrase had spurred Texans on to defeat the larger and better-equipped army of Santa Anna at San Jacinto. If the fighting spirit had been born there, one could say that perhaps the seeds of freedom were sown there as well. They had been watered by the blood of martyrs, blood that seemed to rise up from the ground and shriek out for retribution.

What would have happened at Kings Mountain if there had been no Buford's crossing? Would the mountain men and colonials have had the spirit to fight, or would they have run away, as they had on other occasions? No one could know for sure, but Alan imagined that the war for independence was won right there at that little spot south of Waxhaw's. Alan sat there thinking of all he had read and discovered about this place. There were just so many odd things about that day—like the speed with which Tarleton arrived at the spot and the possible deception or confusion about him being trapped under a horse, unable to stop the slaughter even if he had wanted. There was the fear in the hearts of the colonials, which led them to unarm themselves and become victims to a group of men who were overcome with rage and had a taste for blood.

Another point of interest was the witnesses. One young boy, there that day with his mother, would try to help the wounded and victims of the carnage. Had this shaped a young man to become a ruthless warrior in his own right? He would grow to be an Indian fighter, responsible for the death and deportation of almost the entire Cherokee people in what would come to be called the Trail of Tears. This boy would take revenge against the British in the Battle of New Orleans and save the young nation in the war of 1812. Andrew Jackson was thirteen years old when he witnessed the horror and carnage as his mother helped treat the wounded soldiers Tarleton had left behind.

Many of the 150 wounded men died within a few days. Men such as Captains Stokes, Lawson, and Hoard; Lieutenants Pearson and Jamison; and Ensign Cruit were spared to tell the story of what had happened. What effect did witnessing the results of the massacre, helping treat the wounded and then burying the bodies of the dead have on young Jackson? It is believed that they buried as many as eighty-four men in the mass grave with a small two-foot-high white stone wall around it and that another twenty-five were buried somewhere nearby—or vice versa. There had been an old ARP church nearby, and there was still one grave left from that cemetery near the mass grave, but any sign of a church was gone. It was as if the place itself had been made unholy and the ground could never be sanctified. Ironically, the only grave that could be seen from the old church was that of a little girl or possibly a young boy. A little innocent child shared that bloody ground. It saddened Alan to think of who she might have been, and he imagined the dead all gathered round beneath his feet. Amid the rough and mutilated corpses of soldiers there rested the sweet innocence of a child, frightened and alone in such a place.

Alan stared toward the moon-soaked rise in the pasture nearby, where the actual battle might have taken place. The moonlight had illuminated the spot as if on cue in a play. He could almost feel the earth shake from the pounding of the horses' hooves and see them as they approached the fear-stricken men from Virginia. The air would have been heavy with the smoke and smell of gunpowder from the volley fire and perhaps a hint of leather from the cavalry saddles. Then there would have been the noise of men screaming as they realized that they were being killed. Some would have been running, only to be cut down with a second volley fire and then the aftermath of soldiers scouring the field, beating and bayoneting the wounded, until some semblance of decency crept back into the British hearts. But as the smoke cleared and the sounds of battle drifted away like an echo on the wind in the peaceful Carolina plains and forest, there would have come Banastre Tarleton, riding up to see the handiwork of his men. Then Tarleton would have felt a sense of frustration as he realized that the governor had eluded his grasp. Perhaps that is why he took prisoners then, rather than paroling this ragtag group of walking wounded.

Alan looked around again and thought that now he was there to research and find out if, in fact, there had been a massacre. Some suggested that the number of dead had been exaggerated and that there had been no hacking and slashing of bodies as survivors had reported. The battle had been just an amplified rumor by people of the area.

Could this plot of land have been the site of so much hate and anger, bloodshed, and violence? Had evil risen up from the ground, just like the night mist that now rose up around his feet? Had the evil that men committed that day created a place that could harbor that evil and for generations infect people who walked over the ground? The swirling shape of the mist flowed around the tents and trees, forming haunting shapes in the night. Alan could smell the moisture and feel the cold, and suddenly his affection for the place changed to a feeling of dread. It was as if the spirits that inhabited this space had grown tired of his presence and were telling him his audience was over. He moved to his tent and pulled the zipper down behind him to shut out some of the night air. The camp was quiet now; everyone was either asleep or would soon be. Alan dosed off, wrestling with the question of the nature of evil. The subject of evil could not be measured in his study, but it played a vital part in this battle and in his historical study. He thought of the dark side of humanity that came out in war—and particularly the darkness that engulfed this battle.

Alan would only have a few hours of sleep, for soon he would be awakened by a sound and a problem that didn't fit into his textbooks, shovels, or research technique. It would be a job more suited for someone like Sandy. The moon was just slipping below the horizon, turning the night sky into a dark stellar canvas, when a scream was heard that roused the whole camp. Alan sat up from his cot and tried to shake the confusion from his mind; it was like shaking a layer of dust that had settled on his head. By the time he was dressed and out of his tent, a few of the others were peeping out with a mix of confusion and sleep on their faces. Sandy met Alan at the small tent on the end of the campsite, near the mass grave. They heard a young man sobbing and another, with a shaking voice, trying to reassure him that everything was all right. The two young men jumped as Alan leaned in past the tent flap and shone his flashlight into the small space. "What's wrong, boys?" Alan spoke softly but with intensity.

"It's Topper. He said he saw something," Cedric said as he sat close to his friend, rubbing the blanket he had just thrown over his shoulders.

"It wasn't something, Cedric—it was a man. A man was standing right there at the tent." Topper's voice had a noticeable effeminate quiver in it, and he seemed overly emotional.

Alan looked at the two boys and asked, "Who was it, Topper? Did you recognize him?" Alan paused for an answer, but the young man just shook his head as if to say no. "Well, where was he standing, Topper? Was he actually in your tent?"

"No, I got up to go pee, and when I pulled open the flap, he was just standing there like he was getting ready to come in the tent." Topper raised his hand to point at the tent opening.

"What did he do, or say? What did he look like?" Alan was firing the questions so fast that Topper couldn't answer.

"Hold on, Alan. Get a breath and let him answer them one at a time." It was Sandy; she had moved into the tent and was sitting beside Topper, with a hand on his neck, rubbing the ever-tightening muscles. They could hear the tension easing in Topper's voice, and Alan couldn't help but envy him for a split second.

Then Topper looked at him and began to speak. "He didn't say anything, Alan. He was just standing there, and when I looked up, it scared me. I fell back into the tent, screaming, and woke up Cedric. When I looked through the door, he was suddenly over by that tree, somehow. I don't know how he got there so fast"

"That's a good way off, Topper. Maybe you scared him, and he ran over there—" Alan was interrupted by Topper, and the fear was evident in his voice again.

"No! Alan, that's just it! It was weird—he was standing right there, and then it was like he was just standing over there all of a sudden, like, ya know, just *poof* and he was here, and then *poof* he was there. He didn't run or walk or even move; he was here, and then when I looked he was there, and …"

"And what, Topper?" Alan sounded a little perturbed.

Topper swallowed hard and looked at Alan. Almost in a whisper, he said, "He was smaller."

Alan looked at the frightened boy and was almost afraid to ask his next question for fear of the answer he might get, but he asked anyway. "What do you mean, he was smaller? Are you saying he looked smaller because he was farther away?"

No, he actually *was* smaller. He was standing right over by that tree, but from the size of him he looked like he was way out in the pasture." Topper was looking around to see if anyone could understand what he was trying to say.

Alan spoke up and, smiling, said, "It was probably a distortion from the mist, and remember, you said you fell back in the tent before you looked out again. He probably ran over there and looked back to see if anyone else had seen him. Did you get a look at his face, so we can give a description to the deputy?"

Topper shuddered again and mumbled almost inaudibly, "He didn't have a face that you could see. The shadows were on his face, even when he moved out over by the tree. I couldn't see anything."

"Remember, accurate observations, Topper, that's the first rule of field research. Now think. What did you see?" Alan asked in his most professional tone. "What did you see?" Alan was trying to be professional without revealing his frustration.

"I looked up at this shape. He was tall and thin, maybe six feet. He had thin fingers, real bony looking, and he wore a hat that shaded his face. It looked like he had something in his other hand, but I couldn't really tell. Oh, and he was wearing a coat, a long coat, that looked sort of gray—or no, dark green, I think. I'm not sure." Now Topper was getting frustrated. Sandy started rubbing his neck again and softly encouraged him to relax and just try to remember. But Topper was finished; he couldn't remember another detail.

Alan moved out of the tent and into the darkness that had fallen like a curtain on the land. The mist was gone, and all seemed quiet and peaceful. He directed his light out over the field and over toward the grave but saw nothing out of the ordinary. He stepped over to the tree where Topper had said he'd seen the man and looked around. He was just a few feet from the foot of the grave. A soft touch came across his shoulder. "See anything out here?" Sandy asked.

"Nothing unusual," Alan responded with a smile as the two of them began to walk slowly back toward the camp. "How's Topper?"

"He's okay, but he says he's leaving in the morning. He's pretty shook up." Sandy had a way of making bad news sound almost acceptable.

"What do you think he saw, Sandy? Do you think it was a man or an animal, or a touch of indigestion?" Alan gave a cross between a low grumble and a laugh.

"Well, normally I'd say he saw somebody, or he had a really bad hallucination or dream. I don't think it was a real person because of that moving thing. That tree is forty feet away, and it would have taken a few seconds to cover that space. I think I'm leaning more toward the dream idea. What about that description of a man in a gray or green coat? Do you think it means anything?"

They were back at the tent, but Alan wasn't paying close attention to what Sandy had said. Then he looked at her and stated, "Well, a few moments ago I would have agreed with you about the dream thing, but now ..." Alan knelt and pointed his light down to the ground, near the tent opening where Topper had said the man had stood. There on the ground was the smeared print of a long, narrow foot. There was only one print, and Alan couldn't see others anywhere else. "Now, who do you suppose made this?"

Sandy leaned over and then looked around and said, "Where do the prints lead?"

"Print, singular. There is only one print, and it's pointed south, my dear." Alan stood up and looked south toward the empty field. He knew the 'my dear' crack would drive her crazy. "I wonder where our visitor went, and I wonder where he is now. If he had taken off south across the field, we should still be able to see him, so he must have circled back around toward the crossroads."

Sandy was walking back toward her tent, speaking as she walked. "It doesn't matter to me, as long as he's gone and not coming back."

"Hey, Sandy, do you think we should get a couple of folks to stay awake and sort of ... you know ... stand watch?" Alan had a more serious tone, and Sandy stopped and turned to look in his direction.

"Well, I guess that might not be a bad idea, but count me out. I'm exhausted." And with that she turned around and walked slowly to her tent.

By now most of the camp was awake, and Brad and Oscar came over to speak with Alan. When he told them of his guard-duty idea, they offered to take first watch. After a discussion with two others, Alan went back to his tent to try and get a couple of hours sleep before sunrise. He was afraid he would have another battle to fight in the morning.

The night passed without any other disturbance, but Alan still could get no sleep. He would call Deputy Riley first thing in the morning and report an intruder. He just wasn't sure how to describe the intruder. Was he a one-legged man or a guy who could hop really well? Maybe he would just say that one of the locals was in camp harassing the kids.

In another tent, someone else was awake and also thinking about the visitor. Sandy had not wanted to stand guard because she wanted to go back over her father's notes. Something about this seemed odd and yet familiar. She had a low light so as not to attract attention as she thumbed through some handwritten notes of her father's. He had kept a log in his notebook but had never transferred the data to his computer. She found what she was looking for; it was the notes from the first interview with residents. In the margin was written, "Saw the Green man." Some of the residents claimed to have seen a tall figure, with bony hands and a hat and green coat, standing in or around the barn, looking north toward the battlefield. The residents of the house had also seen this, but her father had noted that they were not afraid. There was no mention of attempted communication until later in the book, when her father mentioned he was going to try to make contact with the apparition. But then it stopped. There was no further mention of an entity or any attempt to make contact, just a few frequency settings for some of her father's machinery. That word *apparition* bothered her; it didn't sound like her father. Usually he would say that he was going to probe, study, and take readings from an energy source. The phrases *apparition* and *trying to make contact* suggested something different. There were no further entries, but there it was—the same description that Topper had given tonight. Was this just a coincidence, or could it have been a real sighting?

She hadn't wanted to frighten the others, but Alan had missed an obvious point when looking for a trace of the intruder. Alan had said that the intruder had gone south toward the pasture, but to do so he would have had to pass right by the grave, and the ground around the grave was two inches deep in dried oak leaves. Anyone running through there would have sounded like a bonfire at a popcorn factory, plus they would have left a trail that a blind man could follow. Sandy had seen nothing, and no one had said anything about hearing anything moving away from the camp. The only route away without making noise would go right through camp or over by the highway, but that's not what the kid had seen. Whoever or whatever it was, there was some connection between what her father had experienced at that barn and what Topper had experienced here tonight. Then there was the Paxton family. She had to talk with that family again and get into that barn.

Scene 16

Quick thinking

The next morning was uncommonly quiet compared to the night before. Alan had waited around the camp, expecting trouble in the form of a visit from Mr. Kirtland, but no one had been around. Maybe they had dodged a bullet, he thought to himself. He called Riley to report the intruder, and Riley said that unless there was an immediate need, he would be on duty that evening, and he would come by the camp then. Alan agreed that he would see him later that day. He then spoke with some of the older kids in the group, to inform them he was going into town to check into the digging permit and find out whether they could use the ground-piercing radar.

When he returned with the permits, he came to a totally different world. There were people everywhere. He saw locals with signs that said Stop the Ghouls, Save Buford, and Protect the Battlefield. Out in front were Arthur Kirtland and his crew, and off to the left he saw a group of teenagers and younger boys and girls. He had expected these groups, but what he hadn't expected was the television truck that was setting up for a live broadcast. It seemed that Arthur was a little more industrious than he had imagined. There were a few sheriff's cars, and in the middle, near the gravesite, was his own group, looking like the Spartans at Thermopylae.

As Alan pulled his car up, he heard someone say, "There he is!" and watched as people came running over to his car. The sign carriers and a TV reporter were followed by a deputy, and in back was Arthur, looking smug as a general moving his troops on the battlefield. The moment seemed to freeze in time as Alan's mind moved back to another day when forces had converged on this place, forces filled with hatred, shouting, and screaming. Was this even remotely similar to what Colonel Buford had felt as he watched the enemy converge on his band of outnumbered soldiers? Alan snapped back to reality and told himself that there would not be another massacre at Buford's crossroads today. As the tide of people washed over him, he saw Sandy in the distance, standing in the door of her tent. She was wisely staying out of the fray. There were screaming voices and a microphone shoved in his face, but a deputy pulled them back as the crowd surrounded Alan. Alan made his way through the crowd to where his band of students stood defiantly in front of the gravesite. As the reporter screamed his question, Alan turned, and the crowd began to quiet down. The reporter repeated the question. "Is it true that you are going to exhume the bodies and display the corpses?"

Alan stood up tall and looked over the crowd. "Everyone listen up. Let me make this perfectly clear. There will be no exhumation of bodies at this site."

The reporter smiled and asked, "Isn't it true that you just today received a permit to dig in that grave?"

Alan smiled again and spoke even louder to the crowd. "What I received today was the permission to use our non-invasive—and I stress *non-invasive*—ground radar. If need be we will dig an exploratory hole beside the grave and not—I repeat *not*—into the grave itself. We will make a small hole beside the grave and insert fiber-optic cameras to investigate the interior. No hands will touch the remains inside, and none of the bodies will be disturbed. Many of you here today have been the victims of malicious rumors, started by people who seek to halt the search for truth. We are not your enemies; we are students seeking to confirm the brave actions of the men who gave their lives in defense of their homes, families, and freedom. These men died to give us the freedoms that you are all exercising here today. I will be glad to take any questions, and if you would be willing to gather in groups of four or five, my team will be more than happy to escort you around the dig site and share the information we have discovered thus far." Alan could feel the eyes of his team members burning a hole through the back of his head. He just hoped that they were masking their surprise. He was pulling a monumental bluff to give the impression that he had planned this event. It was a masterful stroke to steal the momentum of the moment away from Arthur Kirtland. If Alan were playing the role of Colonel Buford to Arthur's Colonel Tarleton, the tide of the modern-day battle was about to shift, he hoped.

The reporter just looked at his cameraman in dismay as he saw his story disappearing on the wind. The protesters were mumbling among themselves, with some staring over toward Arthur as if looking for instructions. It looked as if Alan had pulled off a major upset.

Suddenly Leon Courtney spoke up. "Are we gonna let these bunch of know-it-alls tell us what to do? Who you gonna believe—this bunch of college potheads or people you know? I say send 'em back to school. Back to school! Back to school! Back to school!"

Leon kept chanting until his friends joined in, and Alan saw the momentum begin to shift back to Arthur's side. The only satisfaction was that the reporters were now filming the crowd and not asking him questions. They were getting some footage for the news, but Alan sensed they had the entire story they were looking for. The battle was turning into a draw. The locals would continue complaining, and the team would keep working, but that was about all that would happen. The chanting lasted a while longer, but soon the energy died down. No one wanted a tour of the site, and when the TV truck left, it took with it most of the enthusiasm. If there was any kind of victory for Alan, it came when he saw the look of disappointment on Arthur Kirtland's face to see his plan fall short of his goal of shutting down the dig.

By evening it was over, the people were gone, and the campsite was getting back to normal. A few people complimented Alan for his incredibly cool-headed speech, not to mention the bluff in front of the TV crew. Now, as the sun highlighted the clouds over his head, Alan was finally breathing a sigh of relief. There was a feeling in the air; it reminded him of when his mom would change the sheets on his bed. When she stretched a clean, crisp sheet over his bed, it would feel so good and smell like springtime. His bed was calling him to come and rest his head on that sweet-smelling linen, even though it would be his same old sleeping bag that hadn't been washed in weeks. Still, it was strange how the feeling in the place had changed from this afternoon. There had been tension all around, as if someone were twisting his collar tighter around his throat. Maybe it was the heat of that early fall afternoon now being eased by the coming of the cool night air. Whatever it was, he was glad to feel a change. He'd had a sense of fear that day that had almost choked him when he tried to speak. He hadn't been afraid of the cameras, or Kirtland, or even the crowd. It had been as if there were a fourth dynamic present in the camp, something that was fueling and feeding on the anger. He'd really felt it when the kids had started chanting. The rhythm of their voices had been like the distant pounding of a machine or an engine beating to a slow and steady pulse, pumping hatred up out of the very ground they were standing on. Was this project really worth all the hassle? He wanted to lie down, but he had responsibilities to see to before the sun set on the camp.

When Riley pulled his sheriff's cruiser into the campsite that evening, all was quiet. Alan and Riley sat by the cooking area, finishing off a pot of coffee and talking about the day's events. The digging in the grave that everyone was so worried about had not happened that day, and that was just as well, because the scope and camera equipment hadn't even arrived. The two sat there comparing notes about Arthur Kirtland, until Sandy came over and asked to speak with Riley before he left the camp. Riley said that he would be going soon, so they had better talk right away. Riley followed Sandy to her tent again and sat down on the small camp stool. Sandy wanted to ask some more questions about the farmhouse, particularly about the previous owners and what had happened to them. Riley had told her just enough to pique her curiosity about the man who'd lived there and had a sudden change in personality. Over the course of the next twenty minutes, Riley told her the story of the Hedrick family and what Mr. Hedrick had done. This was not what she'd wanted to hear just then, but when Riley finished the story, she went immediately into research mode and began to tell Riley a thing or two.

"We got a problem here, Sheriff, and I'm not sure how to address it, or even who I should be speaking with about this problem." Sandy spoke with strength, but Riley could tell this was taking its toll on her, emotionally if not physically. She told Riley of the apparent similarities between her father's behavior and that of Mr. Hedrick. All Riley could say was he that didn't know what to think. Sandy was trying to explain that, based on what her father had written and his current behavior, coupled with the information about Mr. Hedrick, she feared they might be dealing with something beyond the scope of normal explanation. She was considering requesting another research team, but that wouldn't happen without the permission of the current occupants of the property. But the Paxtons had not been very cooperative. Alan might have something strange going on here at the battlefield, and if her hunch were right, the two might be closely related. She just couldn't make a connection that made any sense.

Riley stopped her and said, "Missy, are you trying to tell me that we got ghost problems? Because if you are, I am going to be very sad. I went away from our last meeting feeling pretty good about that whole ghost-story thing, and now you're gettin' me worried again."

"I am not saying *ghost*, deputy. I am saying we have two choices here. One is that there is some type of energy that is affecting the conscious level of reason and behavior in the people around this area. The second is that there are people trying to perpetrate a hoax and masking it as a supernatural occurrence." She stared at the deputy as if to say, Now it's your move.

Riley began to process the information he had just heard, and it sounded to him like a loud and clear call to action. But this was action that he could not report to his superiors until he had some evidence. He looked back at the little girl and said, "Looks like you want me to start the external investigation based on nothing much more than a bit of pilfering and some graffiti, while you start looking into the world beyond. Is that about it, missy?"

"That's sounds like a plan, or at least a start, Deputy. I know that you have already filed your initial complaint, but we both know that unless someone tips you off, or you get real lucky, you're not going to find out anything about our mystery intruder. As for me, I've got to talk to Alan about running some research without alarming the team." Sandy sounded a bit apprehensive about bringing Alan into their plans, but Riley reassured her that Alan needed to know so that he could be prepared for whatever they found.

Riley was thinking out loud again when he said, "You know there's someone else that might be a help in this ... Preacher Strong has got his ear to the ground on a lot of things around here, and he's a pretty smart guy when it comes to figurin' things out."

Sandy was still unsure whether the clergy could be objective in matters such as this, so she was in no hurry to bring the preacher in on their investigation. Riley said, "Well, you use your sources, and I'll use mine. Besides, I still think he might could get you a conversation with the Paxton family, and that is what you are wanting, isn't it?"

Sandy nodded her head in a sheepish way, realizing the deputy was right.

"Don't worry," Riley said, "I'll talk to him for ya. He wanted to see me about somethin' anyway. I'll just let it slip out in the conversation that you wanted his help in a certain matter."

Sandy smiled at Riley and told him, "You can mention it, but if things go well tonight, I may not need any help with the Paxton's. They don't know it yet, but they just invited me back to their house." Her smile turned into a full-fledged grin as she tossed a small flyer at the deputy. He read, "Yoga Classes, 7 P.M." and the address of the Paxton farm. Sandy was packing a gym bag as Riley made his way back to his car.

"You better hurry or you'll be late. It's almost seven now, missy," he shouted back as he ducked into his cruiser.

It seemed odd to Riley that the paranormal scientific folks and the religious spiritual folks could never seem to get their heads together. In his mind, they were in the same field. What he didn't stop to consider was that one group spent their whole lives trying to get people to accept a supernatural world, while the other tried to prove that there was nothing super about the supernatural world. He turned in at the parsonage and called the dispatcher to tell her he would be out of his vehicle again.

Chapter 3

Scene 17

The Kirtland plan

Not far from the parsonage lived Arthur and Bea Kirtland. They had lived in that community for most all their lives and had been friends in school. Some said they were childhood sweethearts until Arthur went off to the Agricultural College and married Amelia. She was his first wife, and when they returned to the old home place Arthur had inherited and planned to farm, just as his father had done, people said something wasn't quite right. Amelia never really took to country living. She was a college grad stuck out in the middle of nowhere. After they had been married only a few years, she was diagnosed with cancer. She died around their fifth anniversary, but no one seemed to miss her. She had been an outsider and had never really been made to feel welcome. It came as no surprise when Arthur and Bea started dating and within a year they were engaged. Most people were happy for them, because they felt that it was the way things were supposed to have been in the first place.

Bea was always Arthur's strongest supporter, no matter what the cause. She had the man of her dreams and seemed happy as could be. Yet Arthur never seemed happy. He was always buried in some project that took most of his time and passion. No one knew it, but Arthur was a man of dreams and vision. He had wanted to come back and farm the old place until he could start his own business. He'd planned that in a few years he and Amelia would retire early and travel the globe. What he found instead was a wife who was impatient with the small-farming folks around Buford and a community that did not accept his fine young wife. He felt trapped by his unfulfilled dreams and the expectations of the community. He was trying to make everybody happy, including himself, but it seemed that the more he tried, the less satisfied people were. No one was ever truly happy. Arthur looked in the mirror every morning and saw an old man who was stuck in one place. He secretly longed for someone like Amelia to come along and put life back into his dreams. She had been his muse, as she liked to call herself—in fact, she *had* been his inspiration. She'd inspired him to do something different with his life. But God had let her die, and no amount of prayers and kind words could change that. He attended church but usually it was just to find fault and look for better ways to do things. He hadn't been able to save Amelia, so he tried to save everything and everybody else, by telling them how they should live.

Then there was Bea, sweet innocent Bea. He had married her out of emptiness but had found himself starting to loathe the sound of her voice. She never challenged him or questioned him about anything. It was as if she couldn't do anything but cook, clean, and can beans with her precious pressure cooker. He was tired of farming and had almost stopped the business, but he still worked a few acres, so she could have her precious vegetable garden. He did all the work, and she sat around on her backside, telling everybody how much they liked to plant and grow beans and corn and whatever else she would throw in the ground.

Late in the evening, after Bea had gone to sleep, Arthur would put on the recording that he and Amelia had called their song and then thumb through old copies of *Nations Geography* and some travel books, with names of places circled. He remembered when he and Amelia had planned all those trips to Europe and the Middle East. Her enthusiasm had energized his mind and made him want to do more to make their dreams come true. One day Bea had seen the magazines and suggested they take a trip to some of those places he had circled, but Arthur took offense, saying what a stupid idea that was at their age. The truth was that he resented Bea trying to steal her way into the dream he'd had with someone else. Besides, she was no traveler. She got carsick going to the beach for a vacation and complained the whole time they were there: The sun was too hot, the surf was too rough, the water tasted funny, and the food was all some sort of fish. He remembered angrily leaving a restaurant one night and finding a grill, after another round of complaints about seafood. He had said to Bea, "For God's sake, woman, what do you expect to be on the menu? We're at the beach, not out in some desert." She'd had the oddest look on her face, and he realized she hadn't understand his mood at all. But she was good company when no one else would come around, and he was so lonely out on that farm. When he was tired of her, there was always something that required his attention.

Recently Arthur had decided to launch a one-man assault committee on the denigrators of their hallowed ground around the Buford battlefield. His plan to bring the local media in had been overcome by the TV crew's own incompetence—and Alan, his worthy adversary. However, that young man didn't know who he was dealing with. Arthur had just been in contact with the person he had been trying to call all evening; he would be his ace in the hole. Arthur felt the best strategy to end the investigation would be to get too much media exposure in the area. He knew that his plan might sound like just the opposite of what the local people wanted, but Arthur was using reverse psychology. Rather than try to run everyone away from the site, he would try to get more people to come there. He would flood the site with visitors for a while, at least until the winter months could set in, and it was going to start getting cold at night in a few weeks. That would make it nearly impossible for the team to work, and they would be forced to give up and go home. To accomplish this, he needed some type of celebrity exposure. The local media exposure didn't seem to be working, so he needed a plan B.

John Criton was just the man for the job. He was a bestselling author on the topic of communication with the dead. If Criton would come and speak to the dead here and get a message in which the dead were requesting to be left alone, Arthur could win public support and flood the area with curiosity seekers. Criton had been an advocate of civil rights for the dearly departed, a cause that Arthur thought sounded as crazy as speaking to the dead, but Arthur considered himself a pragmatic man and had no problem with the phrase "the ends justify the means." He would get those people out of there to protect the grave, even if it meant destroying the site in the process. This was no longer about saving the sanctity of a piece of ground (if it ever had been). This was about winning, and Arthur felt the world owed him the satisfaction of getting things the way he wanted for once. But in his zeal, Arthur had become like the crusader who cared nothing for his cause, only what he could gain from the struggle. Some would call him passionate, but others would feel the true depth of the coldness of his heart, which he himself had only recently realized.

A voice broke his concentration as Bea shouted from the kitchen, "My ride's here, Arty. I'll be back after a while. Don't worry none, I'm just going up the road a piece with Shirley. Arty, Arty? Did you hear me? Love ya."

Arthur grunted a loud uh huh as his approval to Bea, and she scooted out the door. He couldn't care less where she was going or with whom she was riding. He had important matters to attend to. Let her go and do whatever it was she did in the evenings.

Scene 18

The parsonage

Riley had pulled up to the parsonage and was headed for the back door when he saw the preacher in his backyard. He was just staring into the evening sky, spread out over their heads, loaded with stars. "See any UFOs, preacher?" Riley cracked his neck and smiled at the preacher.

"No, not really. Just doin' some looking at the western skyline; you can see Venus and Jupiter, ya know."

"No, all I ever saw was falling stars, and I haven't watched for them since I was courtin' my wife." Riley spoke with a smile in his voice. "And even then, I wasn't all that interested in the stars."

"So, stars weren't the only thing that fell." Bruce smiled and thought he saw the deputy blush a little.

Riley adjusted his holster and said with a grin, "Yep, we both fell pretty quick, and she's been a good woman for a lot of years. She has to be to put up with me, and that says a bunch." The two laughed and turned toward the house. As they walked up to the back porch of the parsonage Riley looked at the middle-aged pastor and silently wondered why he was single. He was a nice fellow, with a good job and a good education. He was tempted to ask, but tonight there was another topic on his mind. "We got ourselves a situation this time, don't we, preacher?"

"Maybe, Riley, but between you and me, I think we may have a couple of situations going on. I'm trying to figure out how many of them are related or may be the same situation."

Riley took note of the preacher's worried look and just nodded his agreement. "I know about the campsite and Arthur Kirtland. Is there something else I don't know about?"

The preacher cleared his throat and said, "That's one of the reasons I wanted you to stop by, Riley. It may be nothing to worry about, or ..." He paused to look at the deputy and then reached into his pocket. "Here, Riley, take a look at this and you tell me what you think—connection, coincidence, or nothing to worry about?"

The deputy unfolded the now-well-worn note that the preacher had been carrying around with him. As he looked over the words, he sighed and looked up at the preacher. "This sure makes things a little more interesting, now don't it?" The words on the note were the same he had seen at the campsite. "When did you get this preacher?"

"A few weeks back ... but there are others. We have averaged about one a week in the church prayer-request box. I wasn't sure how seriously to take them, until I saw the same thing on that tent at the kids' campground. It must be the same person, and that means that it's someone in the church." The words were hard for the preacher to say. He didn't like to think that any of their members would take to vandalism.

Riley smiled and said, "It's obviously connected, but I wouldn't worry too much, preacher. It's more than likely some kids playing a trick. When they tried it at Buford they couldn't think of anything else to say, so they just put this on the tent. At any rate, we have very little to go on with just this. Let me see the other notes. If you don't mind, I'll show them to Alan and see if they have had other messages that he may have forgot about. You let me know if you have any hunches as to who our new editor might be."

"I hate to think of any of our folks hurting someone. These notes don't sound like any of our folks." The preacher looked at Riley as if asking him to confirm again that there was nothing to fear, but even as the preacher spoke he knew that there was reason to be concerned. He had seen the face of evil many times, and comments like this had the feel of evil and violence.

"Not to change the subject, preacher, but I got another little favor to ask on behalf of that pretty little girl up at the battleground," Riley asked with a mischievous grin. "Ya know she is single and you're single. I could fix you two up, if ya like. She ain't that hard to look at, ya know?"

The preacher laughed and said, "You don't have to remind me, but you told me up at the campground that I wasn't supposed to be looking. I think that rule applies double to you, Mr. happily married man."

"I am a happily married man; I just want to share the joy with you. You haven't seemed interested in any of the local girls. I just thought you might be interested in an outsider. Sandy is definitely an outsider."

"Enough of this matchmaking, Riley. What's the favor?" the preacher said. He was starting to feel a little uncomfortable with the subject matter.

"Well, it seems she wants to look around the farm and speak with the Paxton family, but they haven't been too willing to let her on the place. I told her that you were as close a friend with them folks as anybody."

"I'm not sure if I can be of any help to her, Riley. It seems that Mr. Paxton and I were on a first-name basis for about twenty minutes the other day, but unfortunately it ended rather abruptly." The preacher didn't want to go into too great a detail with Riley; it was just another of the many things that his position required him to keep in confidence. "Has she spoken with them before, Riley?"

"I think so, but for some reason they don't want her comin' around anymore."

"You know that's really odd, Riley, given Oliver Paxton's interest in kundalini yoga. I would think that he and Sanchari would have a lot in common, what with her being Hindu and all."

"*Kunda-whata?*" Riley asked, with a look of astonishment that the preacher knew the terminology.

"It's what he wants to teach at his barn. He says that he has some students from church already." This information sent a shudder through Riley when he thought of that barn. "But isn't it odd that Paxton is willing to open his barn to a group of locals to study yoga, but he is not willing to let one young girl in to look around and just talk? What's she looking for, Riley?"

Riley explained Sandy's interest in the Paxton farm and her desire to find out what had happened to her dad. Then he asked that the information remain between the two of them. He explained to the preacher that Sandy was not quite ready for the team at the battlefield to know what she was up to. The preacher was only half listening to Riley as he considered that maybe he should visit with Sandy and discuss these things further.

Scene 19

Yoga class

As one meeting was being held at the parsonage, another group of people was meeting at the Paxton farm. The group was as odd a mix of people as one could find anywhere. There were teenagers from the local high school, a couple of men and women from Oliver's office, and even some local curiosity seekers who had seen the flyers at the grill and store. The oddest members were the senior adults from the church. They were there because they had heard on the morning show that yoga could slow the aging process and create an overall sense of well-being. They were like little girls at their first high school sock hop.

The ladies of the senior sewing circle had heard that some of the women at the Spoon Valley Church were going to take the class, and so they'd joined as quickly as they could. The class totaled twelve people besides the one who was trying to stay toward the back and remain unnoticed. Oliver and his wife entered the barn with big smiles and words of welcome to all—until they saw a small demure form skulking in the back of the group. Oliver's face almost betrayed his concern, but he quickly recovered. He turned toward the group, made his introductions, and declared, "Let's get started." He started soft music playing over a small portable CD player as he began to demonstrate some simple stretching exercises. The group attitude was like that of a party, but as the evening wore on, the Paxton's' patience seemed to be wearing thin. They were struggling to contain feelings of contempt toward these new initiates. They knew they must reserve their emotion until the new disciples could come to fully appreciate the beauty of Shakti. After an hour and a half of stretching and lecture, the class was dismissed.

As the group was making their way out of the barn, Oliver moved over to the beautiful young girl who had tried to stay hidden in the back of the class. "Ms. Prasad, I was a bit surprised to see you here. I wouldn't think you would have the time for our little class, or the need. With your background, surely you are familiar with the yoga exercises we teach." Oliver spoke with a mix of part irritation but mostly awe in his tone. It was hard to hide his interest, and he almost blushed as his tone of voice took on a languid texture, like sticky syrup slipping over his lips. This was like a clumsy type of flirtation that reminded Sanchari of a snake slipping over a wet surface. His conversation did not go unnoticed by his wife and two of the ladies from the church.

Sandy spoke with confidence to hide her discomfort. "I can always use the practice, and I saw the flyers at the store—"

Oliver interrupted her, saying, "Yes, but I failed to mention on the flyers that the enrollment would be limited due to space constraints here in the barn. I am sorry, but all the others had made arrangements, and we are only accepting twelve members in this class." Oliver's smile made Sandy feel that the words were spraying slime on her shirt.

"It's a large barn, and I am a small person. Perhaps I could help teach—"

Oliver interrupted again. "I am sorry, but we are limiting the class to thirteen—"

Now it was Sandy who interrupted Oliver. "But Mr. Paxton, you have fourteen, counting your wife. Surely one more couldn't hurt?"

"My wife was just sitting in tonight for the introduction. I will be the instructor and have my twelve dis—" he stopped short of saying *disciples* and instead said, "students in my class. Perhaps we could work out a time for private lessons or sessions." Paxton had a look of embarrassment and anticipation on his face, and Sandy could only imagine what images were playing out in his skinny balding head.

"The class schedule really works best for me. I don't think I would have time for any private sessions," Sandy quickly interjected. She continued her protest, even offering again to assist in teaching the class, but Paxton was now more adamant about rejecting her. His kindness was lost behind a firmer tone of voice. Sandy feared that if she agitated him further she would never get another look at that barn. Her eyes scanned the area as she walked out the door, trying to take in as much of the scene as she could with her last glance. She had been looking around the barn all during the class but had seen nothing out of the ordinary, except for the makeshift altar Paxton had erected, with a picture of his teacher, and a few boards in the floor that looked like new wood where a door or opening had been. She walked away from the barn, frustrated. Once outside, she stood by her car and tried to imagine what her father had found at this place that could have brought about such a change in him.

Sandy also noted the names of some of the people in the class. Perhaps she could get information in a second-hand manner. Suddenly she saw movement at the side of the barn and flash of green. The others were finishing their class and standing around chatting, so Sandy ran toward the corner to get a glimpse of the figure. She heard a shuffle as she neared the dark side of the structure. She slowly peeked around the edge and again saw a hint of green; it moved around the next corner of the building. Was it playing with her, teasing her to follow? She glanced back at the group making their way out into the evening. She had to move quickly or get back to her car. She would be cut off from her car on the other side of the barn, and Paxton might see her, but she had to follow this evidence. She took a deep breath and moved on into the darkness. Halfway down the wall, she heard a rustle behind her, and as she turned, she heard a sound in front. She pressed her back against the barn wall and turned to see a small figure standing almost within reach. Then she heard a voice. Heart racing, she turned her head toward a thin figure and a flash of green moving quickly toward her. She froze, and then a thin face and bony arm wrapped in a green sweater, with a dangling skinny hand, reached out and grabbed her wrist.

"What are you doing snoopin' around here?" Anna Paxton's voice was a guttural growl as she pulled Sandy away from the wall and moved herself between Sandy and her daughter, Willow.

"I was just ... I thought I saw ... someone ... uh ... I'm sorry, I should be going." Sandy was backing away and trying to say something, but she was fumbling her words as she realized she had been so interested in the paranormal that she hadn't even considered what she would do if she was caught by a real person. She calmed herself and regained her composure.

"I am really very sorry, and I didn't mean to be snooping. but I really thought I saw someone creeping around your barn." Sandy was calmer now and began to back away to the corner, only to be stopped by a hand slipping around her waist and pulling her back. It was Paxton, gripping her waistline and leaning into her face as she turned.

"What do we have here?" He spoke with an acerbic, almost reptilian tone that made her skin crawl.

Sandy pulled away and shoved past Paxton as she walked quickly to her car. When she looked back, she saw the mother and daughter scowling and Paxton grinning like a child who had just gotten away with something.

Two ladies who had noticed her walking by were still standing at their car, looking at her with a strange wariness. Their lips were moving, but Sandy couldn't hear their comments, and she didn't wish to stare. Bea was the one doing most of the talking. "That's her," she said, trying to hide her glance at Sandy. "My Arthur told me that someone told him that the preacher had been spending a lot of time up at the battlefield with a certain young lady of uncertain ethnicity, and I believe that she is the one."

"Well, she is awfully pretty, Bea, and he is a single man. I would think it strange if he weren't attracted to such a pretty little thing." Shirley spoke as they sat down in the car, but a quick glance from Bea sent the message of shock and scandal that Shirley understood all too well. "Well, I suppose she is a little young for the preacher, and some folks would not take to him dating a ..." She paused as if trying to think of a term. "What is she anyway, Bea, some sort of Catawba or Lumbee Indian or something?"

"Heavens no, Shirley, My Arthur told me that she was a Puerto Rican negress trying to pass herself off as just plain Puerto Rican, you know, like that baseball player the fellows all liked so much."

"What is the difference between the two, Bea?" Shirley asked, trying to look at Sandy once more to see if there were any discernable features to reveal her true bloodline.

"Oh, I don't know for sure, Shirley, but I know that the preacher has no business goin' around her so much. It's not right, and it could get people to talking, and we don't need that around here. I intend to tell folks that!" Shirley pulled her car cautiously around the barnyard and down the long drive toward 522.

Sandy watched them drive away. When she turned back, she noticed the Paxton family still motionless and staring. Sandy got in her car, drove down the winding drive, and turned her car out onto the highway. But she wasn't going back toward the battlefield. She was following the lights of the last car she had seen drive away. Luckily for her, the two ladies were moving slowly down the road. She caught up with them quickly. She followed at a distance, and when the car pulled into a driveway she slowed down to read the name on the box. Unfortunately, it wasn't very clear, so she drove a little further down the road and pulled off onto the shoulder. Just as she'd suspected, the driver was dropping off her friend, and in a moment the car slowly pulled back out onto the highway. Sandy felt a new tingle of excitement as she thought, *I am actually following someone!* The fear she'd felt at the farm had passed, and now she was like a little girl playing hide-and-seek again, just as she had done with her father when she was a little girl. The car drove by, and Sandy waited a second or two before pulling out behind it. Shirley went a little further down the road and turned into a short driveway. Again, Sandy strained her eyes to read the name on the box, but there was no name. *Does no one put their names on mailboxes anymore?* she wondered to herself. She made a mental note of the location of the two houses and turned to drive back to the battlefield. As she passed the Paxton farm, her fear had been replaced with anger, anger at the family and at herself for letting them intimidate her. A crazy idea began to ferment in her mind. She was already following cars around—why not do a little more unannounced investigation? The words *breaking and entering* began to echo in her mind, but she thought to herself that it was time to pull in the mental reins and get back to the research discipline. Her excitement was making her forget that research involved patience.

In the farmhouse, as their daughter was retreating to her bedroom, the Paxton's were beginning one of their nightly arguments. Tonight, it would be about the class. Anna Paxton accused her husband of spending too much time and attention watching the young and beautiful Hindu student at the back of the class and then not being able to keep his hands off. Oliver Paxton countered with the fact that he had asked her not to come back, but his wife was not listening. In her insecurity, she kept saying how he would probably like to have a younger, suppler body beside him, especially one that had the look of the Indian subcontinent. It ended with a dramatic slam of the door and her retreating to her bedroom mirror to gaze at her gaunt and sagging figure. It seemed that no amount of stretching and exercise could remove the scars of childbirth. Her mind raced to thoughts like why shouldn't her husband want someone else? She looked like a scarecrow, with skin dragging the ground. Her inner rage grew even hotter. He was fit and firm. All the workouts had made him look younger, and his confidence level was at an all-time high. Ever since he had begun the discipline of yoga, he had become a changed person.

Coming to this place had not given them time together or brought them closer, as she had hoped it would, because he had opened their world to outsiders. Her daughter was on no one's side, and she found herself all alone here in the country, with no one to share her sorrows and worries. She only had her herbs and her reading. When she burned inside, she would utter her prayers to the earth and sky and call on the goddess. The one consolation was that in this space she had felt a closer spiritual connection with the wisdom of the mother spirit. The belief in the mother goddess had led her to see motherhood and the creation of life as the highest achievement in a woman's life, and this belief had resulted in them having a daughter. But now she saw her daughter as one of the other women who was stealing her husband's time and energy. Besides, the little girl seemed so slow; she couldn't understand the ways of wisdom. She had been perverted by the world and by these selfish people. Anna and Oliver had taken her away from school and tried to purge from her head all the ideas she had been exposed to in the elementary classes. However, her relationship with her mother was still cool, and her father still had little time for her. Why didn't he do the teaching in the home-school curriculum? Why did the little girl give her mother so little attention?

She felt her tension begin to rise as she prayed for the wisdom of Sophia, the first female spirit of earth, to help calm her spirit. She lit her scented candles and fell back on her empty bed, mumbling her prayers under her breath. Every night she lay there while her husband read his books and spoke with others in the yoga chat rooms on the internet. Then there were the times he would go out into the barn and practice his art late into the evening. At times she had tried to get him to come to bed, but he'd barked at her, saying that the needs of the body must be overcome. He felt that Shakti would strengthen him and cleanse him. He practiced his breathing techniques for hours, trying to slow his pulse and respiration down to nearly the stopping point. She admired his discipline, but she felt that he was being transformed into someone or something else. When she confronted him, he would just smile his arrogant smile and say that she had no idea how close he was to the ultimate joining. Her mind was still racing as she continued to mumble her prayers and finally talked herself to sleep.

The house was quiet now; each member of the Paxton family had retreated to his or her own corner of the world. Mr. Paxton was doing more of his breathing exercises as he waited for his friends to log onto his favorite chat room. In the room down the hall, Willow was playing with her dolls in a scene that looked similar to one played out in any little girl's room. But Willow was not like other little girls. She lifted the girl doll, held her lovingly in her arms, and then placed the boy doll on the floor in front of her. She whispered to her dolly, "Bust his head."

In the corner of the barn, Nakir spoke softly to his master and asked what was going to happen next. Baraqyal smiled and said, "I have spoken with Murmus, and he will bring him here soon. Tell Lerajie to prepare his host, and I will speak to my friends."

"As you wish, Lord Baraqyal."

Chapter 4

Scene 20

Upstate New York

    John Criton sat in a big leather easy chair in his comfortable upstate New York home. Being surrounded by the sweet, musty smell and feel of leather always reminded him of how far he had come and how fast. Success had washed over him like a warm, gentle wave and left him feeling refreshed and free of his past life. No more macaroni and cheese dinners from the box and scraping together pennies just to go to the movies. Now he had a media room and gourmet kitchen. Most of all, there were no more whining relatives telling him how odd he was and trying to get him to be like everyone else. He was alone in his house, in his chair, in his den, and in his world. All the other things and people were back there in the land of the lost and ignorant. He breathed a long, slow sigh as if to blow away the dusty memories that had clouded his vision and dirtied up the bookshelf that had been his whole world. He had hidden himself for the better part of his life on that imagined shelf in the top of his mind, where no one could reach up and touch him. He could rise above the clutter of the place he was forced to call home and live in imagined seclusion and protection. The air was cool and filtered in his new home, and there was no telltale stench of leftover cigarette smoke to yellow the drapes as if someone had used them for a urinal. The stained carpet that looked like someone had parked a car with a bad oil leak over it and well-worn spots of the cheapest pile on the market had been replaced with imported handwoven tapestry rugs over a glass-like hardwood floor. Soft lights and soothing music, too, now helped erase the mental echoes of lamps with broken or absent shades and the sound of blaring rock, country, and rap bleeding through the cheap walls from all-too-close neighbors. The memories made him want to shower, but the smooth feel of the leather and the bouquet of the nearby Chablis carried him safely away and back to the stack of letters sitting on his ottoman.

Criton was going through his personal mail and checking his gold brocade date book. He had a personal appearance in Chicago on a morning talk show in a few weeks and an open-forum discussion at the local university. He also had the taping schedule for his television show to consider. There were stacks and stacks of requests from families and individuals all over the world. Ever since his first book had made the bestseller list, his publisher and agent had been so busy they had had to hire extra staff. He had moved quickly from being the latest sensation to being the authority, but there were signs that the excitement was reaching its apex. There had been several copycat books published, and those authors were experiencing some measure of the success that should be solely his. One in particular, that young, good-looking fellow in Los Angeles, had developed quite a following within the movie-star circuit. Criton felt that tingling sensation in the back of his head that always accompanied a rise in blood pressure. He didn't like feeling this way, but it was so hard not to get stressed when he saw someone capitalizing on their gift. If they were genuinely gifted, as he felt he was, they would not cheapen their talent by making it a spectacle. However, he dared not criticize his contemporaries openly, for it would only cause the public to doubt everyone involved in his field. Even as he thought of his rival, he remembered all the others who claimed to communicate with spirits of the departed. They were mediums and spiritualists, and he didn't like being grouped with their sort. They were like gypsy fortune tellers and parlor frauds, holding séances that caused tables to rise and trumpets to float through the air. But he was real—he heard the voice from the other realm.

Criton remembered how as a child he'd constantly had the

high-pitched buzzing in his ear. When he'd described it to his grandmother, she had poured castor oil in his ear and told him he had "the earache," even though his ear wasn't hurting. It was his grandfather who first told him to try to listen and make some sense out of the noise. It was the echoes of old souls, he would say, trying to contact him with an important message from beyond the grave. And when his grandfather died, he sought his voice out, but it was elusive to him. Then one voice came to him and relayed messages from the only relative he really missed. As the years passed, he became more and more aware of the voice and could discern the words and phrases being spoken to him by the spirit. It became his task to unite the spirit with the person for whom the message was intended. With the help of the one spirit who guided his mind, communication became clearer. He could hear the voices of others, but his main line of communication was with the one voice. The task became easier, and his popularity began to spread. People came to him, and when they were in his presence, their departed loved ones would send words or phrases that meant nothing to Criton but could be easily recognized by the loved one. Once contact was confirmed, Criton could focus his energy on the one spirit and on the person's relative or friend and the one they wished to receive the message. His goal was to make people happy, and he felt that he had been successful in that goal. He had connected the two planes of existence in a way that was beneficial for both sides.

All the years he had suffered as a scorned child with no friends except for his grandfather were now just painful memories. He had a purpose and a mission in life. Perhaps his early life had been that way as part of some plan to shape him as a tool for his and role in life. He was not like the other children, and now that he knew why, he was glad. He was special, and he took pride in his abilities. As a child, he had gone to church thinking that if his gift was from God, then perhaps God would wish to give direction to his life. But the priest had only scolded and warned against communication with the dead. However, it had now been revealed to him how petty and foolish most of the members of the priesthood truly were. They didn't understand, and they didn't wish to understand. He left the church with its gilded altars and ostentatious, tedious rituals when he realized that the institution was only interested in its power to control the lives of the people.

Leaving the Church had been a struggle at first, but his growing apathy and the general need to find something different in life had helped in his decision. The truth of what he felt and had done was later confirmed by the spirits, and he had no more regrets. The one spirit that had become more and more helpful to him was the spirit of an ancient holy man. He revealed that he had sensed Criton's abilities and wanted to help him with his understanding. This holy man had become more and more prevalent in his sessions; he would block out the plethora of voices and allow Criton to hear only specific spirits. He had said his name was Murmus, and he was an ancient priest of Persia. Criton saw him as one who pointed out the direction at the intersection of the two worlds. Some would have compared Criton to a typical medium, with his spirit guide, but Criton did not like that comparison. He was different than anything or anyone that had ever possessed such a gift. The holy man had confirmed that as well and had said that he would soon be allowed to speak to the Nameless One, the holiest of spirits. Criton had been told that of all the people practicing contact with the spirit world, less than a handful were genuine. The others were like carnival shows, and none had ever had audience with the Nameless One. That is why he had coined the phrase *spiritual liaison*. He was no medium or channel; he was a liaison, or ambassador, with special connections from this realm to the next. The Nameless One could only be a reference to the ancient Hebrew God who was spoken of but never named in Judaism and the Bible. It made sense to Criton after he read the books of Esther and Daniel and learned how the rulers of Persia had favored the God of the Hebrews at different times. Murmus must have converted or allied himself with Judaism many centuries earlier, and Criton was nearing the relationship that only the greatest of prophets had known. He would speak directly to God!

As his attention returned to his schedule and his stack of mail, he held one letter to his lips and breathed across it as if speaking to the writer through the envelope. He was not yet sure why this letter was so important; he only knew that his contact with Murmus had been increasing in the past few weeks. It had started with the arrival of this request for a sitting. The messages he had been receiving began to make sense. Even before the request came in, the holy man had said that he needed to speak for those seeking "pieces and rest." The single word *pieces* kept echoing through his mind—and then he realized that it wasn't *pieces*, but *peace*, with a crude plural insistence that sounded like "peace's" to imply the peace of many people. As soon as he read Arthur Kirtland's letter, he understood, and it had been confirmed by Murmus. Murmus could have told him the answer, but it was always better for him to figure these things out. Now his secretary had told him that everything had been confirmed with Mr. Kirtland; he had rearranged his schedule, so he could visit this place where the dead were being disturbed. He would save them in their slumber and perhaps upstage that charlatan in LA once and for all. He thanked the powers for this opportunity, especially his friend and aide Murmus, the ancient holy one. He sensed the coming of Murmus, and he prepared himself by taking deep breathes and speaking only to the Nameless One.

His contact with the other side was having less to do with delivering messages and more to do with receiving the teachings than ever before. He was prepared and ready for his encounter. "Come, my friend, and show me the will of the Nameless One, who walked these places before time began."

Scene 21

Back at Arthur's house

Arthur Kirtland was watching the evening news to see how the reporters mentioned the scene from the battlefield that day, and it was just as he had feared. They were incompetent. They flashed the name of the area up on the screen and spelled it Beaufort instead of Buford. "Dern fools, they'll have people driving all the way down to the low country.

Can't they get nothin' right?" And then there were the interviews. They made Kirtland look like a dumb redneck leading an army of dumb rednecks. That Leon Courtney boy came in handy, but he looked stupid on TV, with his mouth bigger'n a badger's head. No, he couldn't rely on local media; he needed the big boys from the networks and cable outlets, and the only way to draw national attention was with a celebrity endorsement. John Criton was just the man for the job. Criton was eager to establish his place as premier spokesperson for the spirit realm, and Arthur Kirtland was just as eager to have Criton come and speak to the soldiers in that grave.

He didn't really believe in spiritualism of any kind, other than good ole Southern Baptist Holy Spirit spiritualism, but this was a fight that required strange alliances. Arthur was fighting to have his way by any means possible, and John Criton seemed eager to help him. All the better! In his letter, he had enticed Criton with the promise of a mass liaison with at least a hundred spirits on the site. Kirtland was overwhelmed by the response; Criton's secretary had called to say that he had read the story of the battle and spoken with others and felt assured that he should be involved in this opportunity to right a terrible wrong. He'd even said he would alert the press that a spiritual conflagration was about to occur if he did not intercede on behalf of those brave souls being accosted in their eternal rest. It was more than Arthur could have hoped for—it might even lead to a run for county commissioner. He could rid the area of those nuisances and attract some tourism dollars at the same time!

Suddenly the door burst open, and Bea walked in, talking a mile a minute. "Arty, you will not believe the evening I had! We did yoga at the Paxton place, and Shirley and I saw that pretty little Negro girl you were talking about, and I think we were followed home. I've got to call Shirley and see if she is safe. Who would follow us home, and why? I wonder what that Negro girl was doing talking to Mr. Paxton so late after class. I don't think his wife liked it one bit! They say she's a witch, you know."

"Woman, what in the name of Daniel's drawers are you talking

about! Yoga and Negros, someone following you, witches and Shirley—?"
But it was too late. Bea had already dialed Shirley, and the talk was on.

"Shirley, are you all right? Were they there waiting for you, like
you thought?" There was a pause and a couple of soft uh-huhs as Bea
listened intently, agreeing with her friend at the other end of the line.
Then there were the occasional exasperated responses: "Oh no! You don't
mean that." Arthur knew the routine well by now, and he knew that
his questions would go unanswered for some time as the two friends
rehashed everything that had happened just a short time ago. He shook
his head and turned back toward the TV news. He sat there planning
and imagining the scene when all the media people came around and
he and Criton were seen together saving a national monument. He
could just imagine the headlines: "Local Crusader Stops Outsiders," and
"Kirtland Credited with Winning the Second Battle of Buford." Yeah,
that was the one; that was just what he hoped they would say: "Arthur
Credited with Winning the Second Battle of Buford." *I wish Amelia
could have seen this*, he thought as he sat there trying to block out the
cackle from the phone conversation nearby. Bea had distracted him, but
still he would like to know what that Prasad girl had been doing at the
Paxton's'.

Scene 22

Disturbing the dead

The next few days, things were relatively quiet around the battlefield,
which made Alan and Riley happy. Alan had spoken with Topper and
Cedric and convinced them to stay on, at least for a few more days.
They seemed okay with things, especially since the days had been quiet.
Sandy had buried herself in her father's notes, and Preacher Strong had
been tied up with hospital visitation. There was time to get a little work
done before the cold weather started to set in. The researchers would be
leaving soon, and the people and place could get back to normal. The

student helpers were going to have to return to their regular schedule, and Alan had to start writing up his conclusions. The only problem was that, with all the distractions, there were few conclusions but a lot of questions. There was the grave itself, which had not yet yielded its secrets. Then there was the child's grave near the others; Alan wasn't sure what to make of its location. Where had the old ARP church stood, and why was there only one child's grave in the cemetery? The other thing on the site that had him curious was the spiral of stones over near the grave. They were the same kind of stones that had been used to build the wall around the grave. Was there any significance to their placement, and had they even been placed during the same period? Some suggested they were a prank that no one understood, and others thought they were just old campfire stones. He was having trouble finding any records that definitively mentioned the stones.

The ground radar had confirmed objects in a relatively shallow grave, which would allow for clear images when they used the cameras. The camera equipment had arrived, and the drill team had finished the preparations; they were ready to look inside. There were no protesters this time, however, and it appeared that no one even knew they had been drilling. Alan wanted to drill the pilot holes as quickly as possible and get the heavy equipment out of there before anyone noticed. The drill team had set up and done their work in a short time, and Alan briefed the team on how to use the camera equipment and just what they were expecting to find. Soon the holes were drilled, and the fiber-optic cameras were inserted.

Alan looked over his shoulder as if expecting to see Arthur Kirtland sneaking up behind him at any moment—but no Arthur, no crowd, nothing. "Well, boys and girls, it's show time." Alan smiled as he flipped the power switch and adjusted the dials. "Lights, camera, action—or inaction, as the case may be. Let's see what's down there."

The slow, probing camera and light attachment pushed through the soil like a snake through a burrow, passing through rock and dirt; then they stopped. To everyone's surprise, they had reached a small open spot.

"Looks like an air pocket. Are we in the grave?" someone asked over his shoulder.

"I'm not sure yet. Maybe it's just a pocket created by the drill," Alan answered the unseen voice. "No, I'd say we're in. Do you see that, kids? It looks like a piece of a tattered uniform or burial clothe."

"Where's the coffin walls?" someone asked.

Alan, still staring at the screen, said, "They probably didn't put them in coffins. It depends on who did the burying. In all likelihood, the colonials were so badly hacked and wounded they couldn't form a proper burial party, and maybe even some of the British buried some of the bodies. We do know that some of the local folks buried some of the dead, and they also tried to help treat the wounded. So they may have not buried all the casualties at the same time. But still, there were 113 dead men lying on the ground. What was the date?"

Someone shouted, "May 29, 1780."

"That's right," Alan answered back. "Now, what time of day was it, and what was the weather probably like?" Alan waited for an answer, but the students were hesitant to respond. "Come on, guys, It's late May 1780; what is the weather like around here in late May?"

Brad spoke up. "It was probably hot, and it was probably *real* hot because it was late afternoon." Brad seemed almost embarrassed to be providing so much information without consulting his notes.

"Excellent, Brad. Now, what can we speculate about the burial scene, knowing these simple facts?" Again, Alan waited for an answer. "It's a hot afternoon in early summer, and you've got 113 dead bodies on your hands. What's going to happen to them in the heat of the day?"

"They're gonna ripen like a bruised banana before ya know it." It was Oscar adding his comments to Brad's, and a riffle of laughter spread through the crowd.

"Right. Now keep going. What do you think they did?" Alan was pushing the thought process further to get the students to analyze and theorize on this scene that had taken place over two hundred years earlier. "They need to get these bodies in the ground before sundown, don't they?" The crowd responded with a collective affirmative grunt. "Would they take time to dig deep and build coffins?"

In unison, "No" rang out from the crowd.

"Who did the digging?" Alan paused for an answer again. "The British, the few healthy colonial soldiers, or some local farmers, perhaps?" Another long pause as some began to shout guesses to their teacher. "The answer is …" Alan paused again and then began to smile. "We don't know for sure who did the digging." Everyone began to mumble their own theories as to who had done the digging, and Alan spoke up again. "Be careful that your speculation doesn't become full-blown fabrication of history. There is no crime in saying we are not sure in matters such as this, where the records are not complete."

Alan turned back toward the screen as he maneuvered the camera further into the lateral shaft that had been dug, and then they saw it. There before them was the first real glimpse of actual human remains. A bone fragment was now visible on the screen. "It looks like a wrist or forearm," Alan said as he continued moving the camera down the length of the bone. "This may be as far as we go, guys; the sediment is pretty tightly packed. Remember, we are trying to access the grave with as little disturbance as possible. Now, what have we learned thus far?"

There was silence from the crowd, until Brad spoke up again. "Well, we have confirmed the presence of bodies, or at least a body, and that it was not buried in a traditional manner with a coffin. But how do we know that this is the site of a mass grave? Shouldn't there be more human material?"

"True, Brad, and I am going to try and move above and below this spot, to see if we can see any other similar material. But it's going to be difficult without damaging the grave itself. Remember, in cases like this you want to be sensitive to the actual site and remember it is a grave, not just a hole in the ground. It's time to do a little more speculating, class. We have a body count of eighty-four and yet a grave that appears to be only large enough for maybe twenty people packed close together. Do you think that all eighty-four bodies are in there, or did more than the suspected twenty-five get moved and buried elsewhere?"

"What about the idea of stacking? You said you were looking above and below, so obviously you think they stacked the bodies in a mass grave, don't you, Alan?" It was Oscar's voice coming from beside Brad.

Alan looked back at Brad and Oscar with another smile. "Yes, I am expecting to find evidence of layers of bodies, maybe bodies piled five high in this grave. Here we have a shallow grave with bodies stacked on top of one another, which may account for eighty-four of the bodies in this small grave. But remember, we still have twenty-five soldiers buried somewhere nearby, to account for the total casualty list recorded on that day."

As the camera moved slowly at an angle up and then downward, one of the students shouted, "Whoa, look at that." It was a dull metallic object, and then they shouted again, "It's a ring! This dude was married man." There was an audible sigh in the group as suddenly what had been a pile of bones and research material suddenly took on a real persona. It was an actual person, perhaps with a family, or at least a wife, who never saw her husband after that battle. Did she visit the gravesite, or did she even know where her husband was buried? The tragedy of that day was suddenly hitting some of the kid's right between the eyes. The mood was somber and for some more uncomfortable than they could bear.

Suddenly one of the boys near the screen yelled out, "Did you see that?"

"What? What did you see?" Alan turned his attention back to the screen.

"It moved, man—it turned toward the camera." There was fear and excitement in his voice as others crowded near the screen to see. "It moved man—I saw it!"

Alan was looking intently at the screen now. "I don't see anything different. It was probably just nudged by the camera."

"No, no way! It moved and turned toward the camera, then turned its hand up and dropped these three fingers, and ..." The boy mimicked the motion to form the international one-finger salute known as the "bird" to some and the "gig finger" to others.

The group erupted in laughter and playful slaps at the one who had taken it upon himself to break the somber mood with a little irreverent humor. Alan was a little perturbed, but he gave a hint of a smile mixed with the unmistakable message "We will talk about this later," as he tried to restore order to the gathering.

"So, this is how you pay respect to the brave heroes who died to give us the freedoms we exercise today. Those were your words, weren't they, Professor?" It was Arthur Kirtland, flanked by an entourage of faces. Some were familiar and there were a couple of new people whom Alan seemed to recognize but couldn't place just then. "The TV cameras are gone, and you thought you were alone, and we see the respect you pay to this place and the men who lie buried here. It's just as I have been saying: You have no business here. You're just a bunch of kids on a wild party weekend, making a mockery of all that we hold dear in this place. Digging your holes and poking around with cameras, not to mention treading on the graves of the dead. You should all be ashamed of yourselves. I wish all those men down there could rise up and run you out of this place. Are you satisfied, Professor, now that you've poked your hole and touched the dead? Are you satisfied that they are all here and this is the place, or do you want to drag one of the bodies up and take a few pictures with it for the daily gossip paper? You're no scientist or historian. You're just a gold-digging grave robber, teaching children to follow in your wasted footsteps."

"Now wait a minute, you old—" Brad was advancing on Kirtland as if he would punch him out, but Alan grabbed his sleeve.

"Just hang on, kids. Mr. Kirtland has a right to his opinion of our work, even if it borders on slander. For your information, Mr. Kirtland, we have confirmed some important information here today." Alan was drawing on all his composure and professionalism now. "There was no intentional disrespect, and I am sorry for the indiscreet behavior of one of my team members. But may I remind you that I have a permit to do this research, and if anyone is going to scold my team it will be me and not some amateur observer. We have confirmed that there are multiple bodies buried in this place, and we can assume that they are the remnants of Colonel Buford's command casualties. We have not determined if they are all here, but—"

"They are all here, I can assure you, sir." It was the voice of John Criton as he stepped to the front of the fray and right past the group. He was making his way toward the grave as if being pulled by a leash. His face had an expression of pain and anguish, and his tone of voice was deep and serious as if he were narrating a horror story. He sounded like a cross between old horror movie stars Vincent Price and Boris Karloff. The crowd parted like a wave as Criton almost glided with ethereal grace on the end of his spiritual leash to the edge of the grave. "You have no idea what you are doing and have done here, do you, Professor? Do you have the slightest understanding of the forces you have disturbed?"

A low murmur swept through the crowd as some of the students recognized Criton. "That's him," someone murmured. "It's the guy from TV that talks to dead people." The students showed a mix of awe and humor. Some of them watched the show out of genuine curiosity and others simply considered it kooky entertainment.

"He speaks to the dead, and they tell him stuff that no one else could have possibly known."

Criton was in an almost trance-like state now and listening intently to the inner voice that was directing him. "They say they have visited your camp before, to offer you a warning, and you ignored them. You were worried about them … getting small. Does this mean anything to one of you? It could be the leader; I keep getting the impression that it is the top person or top-most person—no wait, it's Topper. Is there a Topper here?"

No one made a move toward Topper, and then Topper stepped up and said, "I'm Topper. What of it?"

Criton was wringing his hands as if they were on fire. "I am not sure what this means, but one of the spirits is asking me to say to you, 'This is how we move.' Does that make sense to you?"

"Yes, I know what he means. I was asking how that guy had moved so fast when he went from my tent to the tree in the blink of an eye."

Topper felt scared and embarrassed. "So, you're telling me that was a ghost just outside my tent the other night?"

"It was a messenger taking the form of an apparition. Since they cannot speak, they try to get their message across by appearing to the living in spectral form. Physically there is nothing there, and yet the energy can often manifest some physical sensations, like spiritual telekinesis. These are more commonly referred to as poltergeists. When a spirit has enough energy, it can move objects or present a semblance of a shape, as happened to you, Mr. Topper. You have over eighty spirits working in concert here, Professor. That's a great deal of energy amassed, and they are not pleased with your presence or your probing."

"Thank you, Mr. Criton. If your little show is over, now we have work to do, and I must ask you to leave our campsite." Alan could think of nothing else to say; he saw that this man's words were having an effect on his crew, Topper and Cedric in particular. "I deal in facts, present and past, and in all my research I have yet to unearth an angry spirit or anything of the sort. Now please be so kind as to take your sideshow somewhere else."

The term *sideshow* was about the worst thing he could have said to Criton. The man literally bristled at the notion that he was a fake. His face began to turn a bright crimson as the anger welled up inside like the pressure that builds before a volcanic eruption.

"How dare you suggest such a thing to me, you small-minded little fool! It's people like you that cause the hurt and suffering in this world. You fail to acknowledge what is all around you and opt instead for your empirical evidence. Well, you've had a small taste of evidence here, and you will get much more if you do not take my advice and stop what you are doing." Criton was not gliding now, he was stomping back through the tent city and toward his car. Then he stopped for one more dramatic turn, like Garbo in an old black-and-white movie, turning to pronounce his final curse for the day. "You have not heard the last from me or from them," he said, pointing a bent finger back toward the grave.

Arthur Kirtland stood silent, with a smile on his face, and then nodded to Alan as if to say "Gotcha!" He turned toward the car, where

Criton was just getting into the back seat. The car pulled away from the scene, and Alan tried to restore some order to his group, but the kids were more interested in how Criton had known so much about what had happened the other night.

"Did you tell anyone about the guy I saw the other night, Alan?" Topper asked with a shaky voice. "Did you mention what I said about the guy moving so fast and getting small and all that stuff?"

"No, Topper, I haven't spoken with anyone about the other night, except of course the deputy," Alan said in a calm, quiet tone.

"Then how did he know?" It was Cedric asking now, and his voice sounded agitated. "I have never been one to believe in guys like him, but after this, I just don't know what to think. How did he know about the weird way that thing moved and that it bothered Topper so much?"

Alan was stumped as well. He was trying to figure out just what to say to these kids to calm their fear, but he wasn't that good at making things up, and he was a little curious himself. "That thing you're referring to was a person, and I don't have a good answer for you guys, unless someone let it slip at the store, or maybe the deputy could have said something. You know how well news travels in a small community. They only need one word or phrase, and they can build a whole case around it. I am betting that's what has happened. I can speak with the sheriff in a day or so and find out for sure, if it will make you budding young scientists feel better."

"There's another explanation you are forgetting about, Alan." All heads turned toward the soft voice that came floating from the back of the crowd. So far Sandy had been a silent observer to the proceedings; she now saw her friend struggling to find an explanation that could overcome the hysteria slowly building in the imaginations of these kids.

"Hey, yeah, she would know what's going on! Sandy, how did he know so much about what happened? Are there really some powers at work here that could …?" The questions were all running together as several voices fired their fears at the young paranormal expert.

"Well, I am inclined to agree with Alan about the loose-lips theory. One word spoken in a country store can be front-page news in a place like this. Or perhaps the deputy did mention something in passing during a conversation. Or there is one other possibility." Sandy made her own dramatic pause. "The other possibility is that this Mr. Criton is correct." A mumbling rolled through the crowd, moving from the front to the back row like a tremor gliding across a desert plain, as each person heard and tried to process what Sandy had just suggested.

Alan gave a quick jerk of his head as if to say, *Whose side are you on?*

Sandy continued. "I am not saying that he was completely accurate in his assessment of what happened here. What he gave you was what we would call a layman's assessment of paranormal activities. Now, before we go calling in the ghostbusters, let's look at this from an objective and scientific viewpoint. In my field, I deal with this type of phenomenon. In one aspect, Criton may be subject to what is called veridical dreams, which give details of people's lives through dreams, details that would not normally be known any other way. The other option, which I feel is more likely, is that Criton has a high degree of what some call trans liminality, or being more prone to fantasy and claiming to experience paranormal phenomena. Now, be aware that this may not fit into your typical understanding, and Alan and I may not even completely agree, but we are scientists working within scientific parameters. People like Criton are not dealing with the evidence from a scientific perspective. As he has just told us, they work from an emotional and superstitious—or we might say mythological—perspective. The one important thing to remember is that these people are not seeking the truth. They already have the truth they want, and they are now simply trying to protect their belief. In their pride, they can never accept a logical or fact-based explanation for anything they have deemed unexplained, especially if they have already affixed a mythological explanation to the evidence. Criton has all the explanation he needs, and now all that's left is for everyone to accept his explanation. It is his profession to give answers to mysteries that have often defied conventional wisdom. This is more than a desire to shed the light of truth on something; this is his job, his livelihood. If he is wrong, then he doesn't sell books, and he has to go back to flipping burgers or something. It's no different than what occurs in your churches each week when the sheep all gather in the pen to be sheared. They want to believe the myths that the preachers tell them, and so they do. When they have no proof, they call it faith and give awards for the one with the greatest faith. In actuality they are rewarding the one who thinks the least. You are students of truth and fact and not some bunch of superstitious children telling ghost stories on a camping trip." Sandy's appeal to their professional maturity and the stab at organized religion was working on the crowd. She could see she had them thinking about the situation instead of just feeling the emotions.

Then, as if prompted to ask, Topper said, "But what was it I saw the other night, Sandy. I still don't think it was a person that moved so weird like it did."

Sandy pounced on the opportunity like a cat. "You want an explanation, Topper, Cedric, and the rest of you?" The crowd rumbled a low affirmative. She went on, "Pay attention, because here is where Alan and I may differ again somewhat in our scientific analysis. I am a paranormal investigator, but I seldom go out looking for ghosts. I am looking for the things that are outside of the realm of what we call normal. As researchers, we set parameters for our work; they are called norms. Are you still with me; is everyone agreeing that they understand what norms are?"

There was another low mumble of assent from the crowd. "These norms are our man-made and empirically defined parameters to our work. On occasion something occurs that is outside of our predetermined parameters or norms. For lack of a better term, we call this supernatural. I would prefer another term, because there is nothing 'super' about it—it is just an often unseen or unexpected variance on the natural world, or perhaps an anomalous occurrence within the natural boundaries, that occurs in a way that has not been documented up to that point in time. We live in a natural world with certain governing laws and forces."

Sandy reached over to the table, grabbed a pencil, and held it over her head, exposing the smooth brown skin of her stomach below her T-shirt, something that didn't go unnoticed by the guys in the crowd.

She had their undivided attention. Alan was smiling inside, thinking, *You go, girl! You are pulling my butt out of a tight spot.*

So much attention was directed toward Sandy that no one had noticed the arrival of another car in the parking lot. Reverend Stone had pulled up and was leaning against a tent pole at the back of the crowd, taking in every word of Sandy's impromptu lecture. As Sandy continued, she dropped the pencil from her hand. "If I drop this pencil, the norm we call gravity takes effect, and it will fall—agreed?"

A chorus of yeahs and yeses come from the crowd.

"Now, suppose I toss this pen up in the air. I am defying the laws of gravity for a few seconds and thereby creating a condition outside of our accepted area of norms, correct?"

"Yeah, but we saw you toss it, so we know that the norm has been circumvented by an external stimulus." The crowd erupted in catcalls and whistles at Cedric's impressive counter to Sandy's supposition.

"That is exactly my point, Cedric. There was something that circumvented the norm, and you correctly ascertained what that was by one of our first scientific methods, observation. You saw me toss it, and so you were able to determine that the norm of gravity had been circumvented, not in a supernatural way. But suppose you had not seem me toss it and instead just saw it pop up in the air? That would seem like a supernatural occurrence, would it not?"

"But there was nothing supernatural about it. We saw you do it, so it was completely natural," one of the students protested.

"Very true, but suppose I had held it below the table and flipped the bottom with my finger, making it rise up in the air? Then your job would have been to ascertain what had caused it to supposedly break the law of gravity. The mystery would have been in determining the energy source. If I had tossed it on the table and it had hit the eraser and bounced up, and all you saw was the bounce from the table, you would recognize that the buoyancy of the eraser had been the source of energy, or the apparent external stimuli, that had helped it appear to defy our norm of gravity."

The students laughed, and one said, "It would still be a natural occurrence. It's just the transference of energy from your hand to the eraser via contact with the table."

"Thank you. That is my point exactly. An occurrence is often deemed supernatural simply because we cannot define it within the realm of the norm, but once we have made the observations and tested our hypotheses to explain the source of energy, it becomes completely plausible, and we realize there is nothing supernatural about it. I believe what we called 'super' natural is simply the natural in its unexplained state waiting for some bright young scientist to come along and explain it to us all. Tonight, we have seen arise a question in need of a logical answer, and we do science an injustice if we simply run like frightened children into the realm of superstition. Some answers just need a little clear thinking, while others may be a mystery for centuries, but I am a firm believer that all our questions can be answered within the natural realm eventually." With that Sandy curtsied to the crowd, and the tent erupted in applause and wolf whistles.

Cedric looked over at Topper with glassy eyes. "Ya know, Topper," he said, "she had me at 'circumvent the norm.'"

But Topper was not quite as mesmerized as the others. He had seen something that night that still needed an explanation. He slowly raised his hand, like a kid in kindergarten. "Sandy, Sandy, I still have a question."

The crowd began to grow quiet as Topper asked in an almost embarrassed tone, "But what did I see that night, Sandy? What area of the norms did that thing come from?" Silence gripped the crowd as they realized that in the frenzy of the lecture they had forgotten that the original question involved seeking an explanation for a supernatural occurrence, and not the defining of what made something a supernatural occurrence.

Sandy paused and looked around at the eager faces, once again caught up in the events of the day and the night in question. "I don't have an exact explanation for you but try this on for size and see if it doesn't help you sleep better. If it were a true supernatural phenomenon, it would be called an 'apparition associated with spontaneous extrasensory perception.' Also, that 'thingy' moving so fast, which our guest attributed to 'the way they move,' could be what we call bio-PKI, which refers to psychokinetic energies. But let's save that one for the classroom. About the only thing I agree with Criton on is that there is energy involved here. In my studies of this type of event, the first thing we check for is unusual electromagnetic readings. There are magnetic fields all around us at all times, and the human body is a good conductor of such energy. If anyone saw *The Matrix*, you will remember that the machines were using people as batteries, because we people create energy within our bodies. All we need is a burger and fries, and you got yourself a dynamo."

There was mumble of recognition at the mention of the classic sci-fi movie, and one kid even said, "Yeah, that movie was awesome. They had these things in your back, and you were like wired in to the matrix, and—" He was quickly quieted down by others who were waiting for Sandy's explanation.

Sandy continued. "As I was saying, the human body can generate power, but we do not know where that power goes at the point of death. There are possibly eighty or more bodies and therefore that many potential energy sources in that grave out there." In a lowered, more ominous, voice, Sandy said, "And they're all there!" She was mocking Criton's mysterious tone, at which point her audience burst into laughter. She went on, "The point is that this energy could be a partial explanation for what we commonly refer to as a poltergeist. That, coupled with a day of focusing our thoughts on dead soldiers and a bag of barbecue chips right before bed, could create a pretty scary picture."

Sandy smiled her flirting smile at Topper, and he gave her a halfhearted grin right back. She knew that he was still troubled, but her explanation was more than enough for the others. "Let's not rule out the fact that we may be a source for psychic energy as well. I still feel that Criton could also be a source point for some of the so-called supernatural energy we may encounter, even more so than any of those men buried out there."

Sandy had finished her speech; it had worked well for everyone except Topper, who was still wondering how Criton had known so much about that night. One other person with some reservations was Reverend Strong, who had been listening intently at the back of the crowd. He watched her move through the crowd of kids, as attention turned back to the screen and Alan went back to his camera.

Scene 23

Picnic table theology

As Sandy emerged from among the students, Reverend Strong smiled and said, "That was quite a performance. The bards of science would be proud of you, but you left one little detail out of your analogy using the pencil and eraser."

Sandy paused and walked closer to the reverend. "And just what might that be, Reverend Strong?"

"Well, you proved that much of what we see and know is from observation, and just because we do not see the hand that dropped that pencil it doesn't mean that there is not a logical explanation. But tell me, who or what is responsible for all this unseen energy that seems to act with a sentient consciousness? You realize that you never really answered that kid's question. If it was some sort of random ESP or dream information, where did it get that information? Doesn't this imply a cognitive force in the universe, just as a design always suggests a designer? Doesn't a thought always suggest a thinker?"

"I know where you are going with this line of reason, Reverend Strong, but you forget that there are many minds thinking many thoughts at this very moment. Now, suppose someone like Mr. Criton there has the ability to hear these thoughts, but he thinks they are the thoughts of the dead. His work would be more like the power of suggestion than actual supernatural phenomena. He is only suggesting or telling the people what they have already thought, and thereby told him, through his seemingly mystic channels. Criton said that we do not realize what we are doing here, or something like that, but I contend that it may be Mr. Criton who is operating unawares. Unfortunately, people like him are rarely willing to undergo research and experimentation to try to determine just what power they have."

"Your speculation is feasible but still unproven, so you work in your realm, and I will explore my own realm of possibility," the preacher said, smiling down at the young girl. For a moment he looked into her dark eyes and thought about what the deputy had said. She wasn't that much younger than he was, and she was very attractive. He let his mind race for a moment as he imagined what life would be like shared with someone like her. If nothing else, it would be filled with some interesting debates. He was interrupted by her soft voice, and his dream bubble burst.

"So, do you have a theory of what we are dealing with here, Reverend Strong?" she enquired in a somewhat defiant tone, as if angered that he would not accept her possibility as the most likely one.

"Well, actually I do, miss," the preacher countered. "You deal in the realm of reality outside the bounds of current conventional wisdom, but I deal with what can only be called an entirely different dimension, the truly supernatural dimension of the spirit. In this dimension, there are sentient beings living outside of the constraints of our understanding of time and space, and what is perfectly normal for them would appear extraordinarily miraculous to those in our existence."

"But Reverend Strong, where is your proof that such a realm exists? Is it out there with my unseen force that drops pencils on erasers and creates a universe of speculation?" She was smiling like a chess player who had her opponent in check.

"Touché, Miss Prasad; you're right. I have no proof, but within my field proof is not the essential element. Instead I have faith, and faith is the substance of things hoped for and—"

Sandy interrupted him to say, "'And the evidence of things not seen.' Hebrews, I think, is it not?"

"Touché again, Miss Prasad. You never cease to surprise me."

"It's a bit of my father that has rubbed off on me. He insisted I go to various churches when I was a child, for the exposure to Western ideas, even if I didn't take part in the religious experience. My mother was a

Christian who was converted and since coming to America wanted us to experience this culture as much as possible. She shared the Hindu idea of tolerance, and she and my father wanted me to experience all ideas, including intolerance. It made for interesting Sunday lunch-table discussions. Sort of like having southern fried chicken with curry. I knew it was good, but I wasn't sure if I were eating Indian cuisine with a touch of the old South, or southern cooking with a touch of India. I was always asking myself, *What is it that draws two people with strong differences to fall so much in love? My parents seem to have such a strong wall of religion between them, and yet Mother and Father are very much in love.*"

"Oh, you're coming back into my field again, are you? Not that love is restricted to Christians alone, but it is the cornerstone of our mission as followers of Christ." The preacher was speaking, but his mind was still on her last sentence. The part about two people with a strong wall of differences between them falling in love sparked his imagination further. Was this a hint, a dropped handkerchief just waiting to be picked up? She spoke again and snapped him out of his romantic trance. He almost wished the deputy hadn't put the idea about the two of them together into his head. Looking at this beautiful young girl and thinking of his empty, quiet house, and then seeing her standing there, did stir his heart's fires for a moment.

"Love is too strange for me, Reverend; it is the greatest of paranormal mysteries. Give me a good poltergeist any day." Sandy was changing the subject, and it seemed to Reverend Strong that she did not wish to deal with anything beyond the realm of logic and reason.

"You know, Miss Prasad—" the preacher began, looking for a way to regain his concentration, when she suddenly interrupted him again.

"Why don't you call me Sandy, Reverend Strong? We don't have to be so very formal here," Sandy said with a smile. She was obviously becoming more comfortable being around this member of the clergy.

"That's great, Sandy. Please call me Bruce, but back to that point about love. You were talking about energy earlier, and I was suggesting that perhaps there was some design to these occurrences that would imply a designer, but I also wanted to ask you about one other thing."

"Fire away, Bruce; today seems to be my day for answering questions."

The preacher sensed a little awkwardness in her using his name instead of his title, and he suspected she felt it as well, but he pressed on with the subject at hand. "It is the love, or emotional element, that I think we may be overlooking in all of this."

Sandy tilted her head as if rearranging her brain in order to use another part. "What part do you think emotion plays in a scientific investigation such as this, Rev ... er, I mean Bruce?"

The two walked toward an old picnic table several yards away from the others and sat down. "Let's consider this situation, Sandy. Alan and those kids are here to do simple historical research. You are here, if you don't mind me saying, for more personal reasons than mere research. Their interest is scientific, and yours is more emotion driven. Then there are the local folks, who seem to be acting or reacting out of pure emotion. I confess that I am not sure why they are reacting the way they are. Arthur Kirtland is a bit of an enigma; he is not a mindless sodbuster, and yet he is acting like a redneck ringleader. I have seen him be stubborn before, but I have never seen such resentment and anger, and I can' tell why or where this is coming from. The emotion seems to be spreading as more and more people become interested in this project. People who have never even given this place one bit of attention in the past are now worked up as if their children were buried here. Now we have this Criton character; he seemed pretty upset with everyone. That emotional level is the dynamic that often gets overlooked in a scientific investigation. Let me ask you this simple question and stop all this rambling."

The preacher shifted in his seat as if he needed to get comfortable before firing his next salvo of thought. "Do you think that this energy you were talking about to the kids has a conscience?" She looked at him with a look that Bruce couldn't read; he wasn't sure whether it was astonishment or confusion.

Sandy had never really stopped to attribute emotion to the phenomenon; however, they did sometimes refer to an apparition as malevolent. But to ascribe emotion to an energy source didn't really make much sense to her. "No, Bruce, I don't think I would consider these energy sources to have emotions as a human would possess them."

Reverend Strong didn't wish to annoy Sandy, but he felt that this element might be the key to what they were seeing at the battlefield. "I cannot help but sense a spiritual aspect to recent goings-on here. Alan's work will soon be over, but the anger that it has triggered will last in the form of rumors and memories and resentment toward academicians. How do we account for this energy, and what is the source of its malevolence? I deal with emotions on a weekly basis, and I have seen the energy that can be generated and spent in acts of kindness. Love is a source of energy in the way that it empowers people to do good and show love to others. They do not do this simply out of a desire to gain recognition; these people really do care for one another. Yet, placed in another situation, you may have these same people acting as if the devil himself were directing their work and will. Where does this energy come from, and why is it sweet and innocent in one situation and filled with anger in another?"

"I must say that I had not given much consideration to emotion as an energy source and the effect that energy could have on individuals, such as a catalyst for behavior, but it is not beyond reason. Are you suggesting that the energy source transmits the emotion somehow, or are you thinking that it merely triggers, or inspires, a certain emotional response?"

Bruce thought for a moment and looked across the table at Sandy, who was now enjoying the aspect of the conversation. "I suppose that energy could trigger an emotional response, and the response could be the emotion that is just under the surface of a person's personality, like a latent energy."

"Fascinating, Bruce." Sandy's words had a genuine ring of warmth.

Bruce looked back at her with a look of bewilderment. What had he said or done that was so fascinating? "What do you mean, Sandy?"

Sandy beamed a smile at him that was as sweet as an early fall apple pie. "It's just fascinating to hear something like that coming from a minister. I wasn't expecting you to be so open and willing to consider any other option than the power of God in all things."

"Hold on, Sandy. I still believe in the power of God, and I still think that there are spiritual forces involved in this." Bruce was smiling on the outside, but inside he was worried that Sandy might think that he had just surrendered his belief to hers. "I'm not ready to leave the pulpit and step into a science lab; I am just trying to be objective."

"I understand, Bruce, and I apologize if it seems I was trying to convert you. It's just that I am not used to finding objectivity in the Christian world, especially coming from a member of the clergy." Sandy was almost blushing, but Bruce felt like that he was seeing her real self for the first time. She wasn't just a hard-nosed research expert; she was a human being, capable of making mistakes and not afraid of being a little vulnerable.

Bruce wanted to pursue this moment a little further and get to know the person behind the title, and so he asked her, "Why do you find my objectivity to be a shock?"

"Well, as I told you, my dad insisted I attend Christian worship for a while out of respect for my mother's beliefs, and what I saw was mostly what he called fundamentalism run amok. People were more interested in indoctrination than enlightenment, in proving they were right about everything and everyone else was wrong and going to hell. You do realize that Christians are the most intolerant of all religious sects? It left a bad taste in my mouth for the Christian belief."

"You're not the first person to say that to me. Some find it comforting, while others see me as wishy-washy and worrisome. I am objective because of my faith, and unlike some in the ministry, I am not trying to prove what I believe—I am just trying to share what I believe. You know the irony is that the same people who turned you off to Christ are the ones who are constantly at war with science, and yet they themselves follow the scientific ideas as rigidly as you do. They are constantly trying to prove everything they believe, as if by proving it they will convince everyone that they are right. They have forgotten the word *faith* doesn't come with a lab coat and jar labeled 'empirical evidence for God.' I believe in what I have not seen, and my faith is based on my hope in its substance. In a way I guess I am more fundamentalist than they are, because I will never change my belief. Some of these people seeking proof live their religious lives based on asking questions and getting answers, and if God doesn't answer them the way they want, or in the right time frame, they drop God like a hot rock and move on to something else."

"Fascinating, Bruce—you're making me want some spiced chicken again, just like Momma used to make." They both laughed as they once again breached the wall between East and West and found that behind their job titles were two people who had a lot in common.

"Thanks for the sermon, Brother Bruce."

"Yeah, all we need now is an offering plate and hymn or two, and we would be in business." They were smiling at one another and suddenly realized that they had strayed far away from the battlefield as a topic of conversation. Bruce was the first to bring them back from their mental sabbatical, because there was still something he wanted to explore with Sandy. "But back to the business at hand. I apologize for getting a little preachy on you there, Sandy. Perils of the profession, ya know. I am still intrigued about this idea of energy just sort of floating around out there. I can go with the idea that this energy may somehow trigger a latent emotional response. That would make sense in a psychological framework, and the fact that there may be some sort of transference of information could be explained by these veridical dreams or perhaps even ESP. But tell me what your research says about geographical involvement. Can certain places be weaker or stronger centers of energy?"

Sandy paused for a moment as if accessing files from her computer. "My first answer would be yes. For instance, we know that magnetic fields can be stronger and weaker and that energy sources seem to emanate out from a central core, from strong to weak, like the ripples on a pond. I'm not sure how that applies to this situation."

"Well, suppose that your energy source was located at a certain spot, and when people came into contact with that spot they were influenced by the energy, which in turn prompted them to act out latent emotions or thoughts. For instance, church cemeteries have always been viewed as spooky places, but by and large they are the most peaceful of places. Most of the emotional residue experienced there would be related to sadness or grief. Church sanctuaries or temples are other examples. We have our cultural indoctrinations that lead us to believe that these are places of peace and safety where one can experience the holy and profound. What if it were more than just cultural indoctrination? What if a place could be holy by the nature of the energy source associated with it?"

"Keep going, preacher; you've got me interested." Sandy's smile and words were like gas on a fire for Bruce.

He smiled back at her and launched back onto the track like a speeding locomotive. "I know you may not find this exactly scientific, but history is replete with instances of holy or spiritual places where people would come into contact with their deities, or as you may prefer, their energy sources. In the Bible and throughout the world we see holy men, priests and shamans, going to the high places to commune with their god. Remember Moses and his first encounter with God on the mountain? What did the voice say to him?"

"Oh, don't tell me! I know this one." Sandy was searching the archives of her early church-going days for the Bible story of Moses. "Let's see, there was Moses in the bulrushes, Moses the killer of the Egyptian, Moses saving the girls at the well, Moses seeing the burning bush, and a voice telling him to drop his staff—"

"Hold it, back up. You skipped one," Bruce interrupted, but he was enjoying her little guessing-game moment.

Sandy stopped and looked down at the table, while Bruce began to hum the *Jeopardy* tune that played as the contestants were thinking of answers. "Da da da da, da da da ..." She looked up at Bruce and said, "Okay, Trebek, time's up. What is the answer?"

"'The voice said, "Take off your shoes, Moses"' ..." And then they looked at each other as Sandy remembered the text. They looked one another in the face as they repeated the words together: "'You're on holy ground.'"

"Now the question for you to consider is this: Was it the ground that was holy or the presence of ..." he paused before saying the word *God* but then went on, "God, or that energy source you like to refer to? Now, if you are going to tell me that a place can be holy, then why can't a place equally be unholy? Have you read that inscription on the marker over there? It gives me a chill every time I read it, especially the part where it says, 'all virtue was lost.'"

That was enough for now. Bruce knew that he had planted seeds that could blossom into understanding. He didn't want to give away too much of his suspicion until he was sure that Sandy was ready to listen and at least be as objective as he was. Bruce had learned long ago that scientists often claimed total objectivity until anyone suggested anything to do with God, and then their minds became closed doors, as if Dracula were standing outside and knocking to get in. He had his suspicions about this place, but he knew that no one was ready for his input.

Sandy sat there with a puzzled look on her face. "You know, Bruce, perhaps you're onto something with this geographical connection. I am trying to determine why a certain farm building nearby seems to be the center of spectral activity. The owners have been less than willing to allow me access. I was wondering if you might be able to help by talking to the Paxton family."

"I'm not sure if I would be of any service to you there, Sandy. It seems Mr. Paxton and I do not see eye to eye on his yoga class." Bruce spoke reluctantly, hating to disappoint his new friend.

"What was your problem with the class, Bruce?" Sandy asked with renewed interest.

"It wasn't so much the class itself but rather the way it was presented to the public. He is teaching kundalini yoga to a group of farmers and a couple of businessmen, and I don't think they have the slightest idea what they are getting into."

"What do you know about yoga, Bruce?" Sandy asked with an innocent smile.

"Not really all that much. I tried transcendental meditation in college, but it seemed a little weird."

"How far did you get into the study of yoga?"

"I know that there are points in the body called chakras and that when they are aligned the patient or practitioner feels the most relaxed they have ever felt, and after that they could work on concentration and even healing," Bruce answered her.

Sandy looked toward the road as a car sped past and said, "I don't wish to burst anyone's bubble, but you may not be the only one who doesn't know a lot about yoga. I sat in on the class, and before being asked to leave and never return, I heard Paxton giving instructions that made little or no sense. You get more yoga from the morning TV shows than from Paxton."

"That is very interesting; it deserves some closer inspection." Bruce could hardly believe his ears. "To hear Paxton say it, he's studied under some eastern master all his life."

"Well, I don't know where he studied, but he doesn't know very much. I just sort of laughed him off as someone playing a role. He has great flexibility, but I don't think he knows what he's talking about when it comes to kundalini yoga. And that wife of his, what's up with her?" Sandy rolled her eyes as she recalled her encounter with Mrs. Paxton.

Bruce smiled and looked down at the table; he rubbed his hand across the rough surface of the well-worn wood. "I guess you never know people. He fooled me, and I guess he's fooling several people, but the exercise will be good for them."

Sandy said, "Don't get too comfortable with that class, Bruce. I still think there is something strange about that guy and his group. You know why he said I couldn't be a part of the class?" She gave a dramatic pause and then said, "He only wanted thirteen students. Doesn't that seem a little strange to you? Only thirteen people in a space that's as big as a … well, as big as a barn, and yet there's no room for one more."

Bruce looked up with renewed interest. "Thirteen, huh? You're right; that is rather strange. I wonder if …" Bruce began to trail off into his own thoughts. "Naw, it couldn't be that."

"If you're thinking coven, that's the first thing that popped into my head too," Sandy said. There was a little edge in her voice as if she were about to get angry.

"Maybe I had better keep a closer look on the class members who attend my church. I was worried about them getting lost in some sort of eastern mysticism, but they may be dabbling with some good old-fashioned witchcraft and not even know it."

Sandy looked at Bruce again with that questioning look. "Tell me something, Bruce. Is this place always like this?"

"Like what, Sandy?"

"Like so busy with the supernatural world. We have a ghost sighting, apparitions, a world-famous psychic, and strange messages from vandals, just to name a few. This place has become a hotbed of supernatural experience. I was just wondering if it has always been this way."

"Do you mean the battlefield or the community in general?"

Before she could answer, a voice interrupted her. It was Alan, who had noticed the conversation between the two and, his curiosity was driving him crazy, stepped up. "I'm sorry to butt in, but you two seemed so deep into something, and I heard you talking about this place, and I was just curious. Am I interrupting?

"No, not really." Sandy and Bruce spoke the words almost in unison, followed by a shared smile.

Sandy spoke with a hint of laughter. "I was just asking Bruce if this area has always been so active with ghost and psychics."

Bruce looked at the two young researchers. "It seems to have all started with the Duke team, or actually, I guess you could say it started when David Hedrick built that barn in his backyard. He was the guy who owned that house down the road before the Paxton's. It was a tragic story."

Sandy was first to jump at this bit of information. "I thought that the house and barn had been there a while."

"The house was there, but Hedrick wanted a barn for some of his equipment, and we sort of had an old-fashioned barn raising. There were folks from the church and some of the neighbors; we all just pitched in when we could, and that barn was built in a few weekends. But then there was an argument over something between Hedrick and somebody; I can't even remember who or what it was about. I just know the church involvement with the project ended, and Hedrick finished the building himself and never came back to church. They weren't actually members; they had just visited a few times, but everyone thought that since we had built his barn he would join the church. His wife did become very active in the community, helping out here and there, but all that stopped when her husband went off the deep end and died."

"What happened to the guy?" Alan asked.

"I don't know what happened, I just know that he had some sort of breakdown and took off to North Carolina and died of a drug overdose. The wife and daughter moved out after that. I haven't seen or heard from them in ages."

"Did they ever say anything about seeing something in the barn or anything like that?" Sandy asked anxiously.

"What does that have to do with this place?" Alan asked pensively.

"Oh, I don't know Alan. Sandy and I were just talking about all the strange things that seem to be going on around here. You know, the sightings, psychics, and messages and stuff."

"Yeah, it does seem a little odd, but what about the messages? I thought they were just a prank from the boys at the store."

"I hope you're right, Alan, but what I haven't told too many people is that the church has been getting the same messages, and some have been very disturbing. That's why I was concerned about you and the kids up here at ground zero."

"Did you say *messages*, Bruce, as in more than one?" Alan asked shyly.

"Yes, Alan, I have received several, with various threats of mutilation." Bruce was trying not to reveal his deeper feelings. "They speak of busting heads, and pieces, and gutting someone like a fish. Pretty sick stuff."

As Bruce was talking, Alan's demeanor was changing as he mentally arranged the pieces of the jigsaw puzzle that seemed to be spreading out before him. When Bruce finished talking, Alan looked at him with a very serious look and said, "I have some notes in my tent I want to show you."

Alan got up and walked toward his tent, his steps quickening with each stride until he was almost jogging into the small tent opening. He began to rummage through his stack of notes, until he had what he was looking for. He reread the messages that had been scribbled on tents and cars by vandals. In a moment, he went back out to the Sandy and Bruce. "Now tell me again what the messages at the church said, Bruce."

Bruce took a pen and began to scribble the words of the notes onto the paper: "Bust his head, cut 'em off, gut him like a fish, and pieces. There you go, Alan. Now, what is the big mystery? Do you think you can figure out who sent these notes?"

"I'm not sure, Bruce, but I have a hunch that what seems to be an intriguing mystery may have a perfectly logical explanation. Look at the notes and look at what we have found—or I should say *I* have found. I haven't shown these to the kids; I didn't want to stir them up with what appears to be a deliberate attempt to scare some impressionable students." Alan handed him a list of words: "Ban the murderer, get out, bust his head, Huck's quarter for you."

"The first and the last notes I didn't show to anyone; they didn't make any sense until I started putting things together. Someone wants to scare us away, someone who knows the history of this place, and they are using it against us."

"Whoa, Alan; I'm afraid you lost me somewhere. I don't get the connection. Let's all get on the same page here. Just what do you think is going on, and what is this 'Ban the murderer' and 'Huck's quarter'?" Bruce asked.

"They are references to Banastre Tarleton and a little-known incident when one of his captains, by the name of Huck, committed a grisly murder nearby under the orders of Colonel Tarleton. I hadn't really thought of this until Sandy asked her question about all this stuff going on around here, and suddenly it hit me that there *is* a lot of weird stuff going on. Some of the stuff is connected and some just your everyday weird happenings. I think someone is orchestrating some of these things deliberately to get us out of here."

"But why, Alan?" Sandy asked. "What harm are you really doing, and why would someone go to such extremes to end a project that is about to end anyway? You have done very little to disturb things around here, and most of what you have done has only been to unearth some artifacts and look for gravesites. It just doesn't make any sense."

"Since when do people have to make sense? People get a notion in their heads, and they've got too much time on their hands. They're just looking for a windmill to tilt at, and we are here. I don't know why we keep saying *someone*. I think we all know who that someone is; it's our resident troublemaker with too much time on his hands. Arthur Kirtland's behind all this." Alan spoke in a bitter tone. Alan wasn't a violent person, but the one thing that bothered him more than ignorance was someone with intelligence acting with ignorance. If Kirtland was behind this, he must have knowledge of the history of this place, and rather than use his knowledge in a positive way, he had turned it into a weapon aimed at Alan's work and crew.

"Arthur is a bit of a pain, Alan, but I just can't see him going to such lengths to perpetuate a scare like this. What would his motive be? Why go to all this trouble?" Bruce wasn't exactly defending Kirtland, but he wasn't sure Alan had anything more than circumstantial evidence.

"Who knows why people do anything like this? It may be that he actually does have too much time on his hands, or maybe he's trying to get some attention, for some reason. But who else has a motive to scare us away with these grade-school harassment techniques? And look at the connection with the church, Bruce. He obviously wants people there to know about all this; they are his peers. Why else would the notes show up at the church?"

It was beginning to make sense to Bruce. Everything pointed to someone with knowledge of the area and some level of intelligence who also wanted this crew out of there. Arthur would fit that description perfectly and be the prime suspect.

"But what about the barn? Where does it fit in with your theory, Alan?" It was Sandy, who had stayed quiet during this part of the discussion.

Alan gave her a curious look. "What barn?"

Sandy suddenly realized that she had not told Alan about why she was really there and the research she was doing concerning her father's strange transformation.

"Oh, it's nothing, really. I guess it doesn't have anything to do with this situation." Sandy looked at Bruce and saw a half frown on his face. It seemed that part of the cat had just been let out of the bag.

Alan looked back and forth at the two, saying, "Is there a part of the story that I am missing here?"

"No, not really. It's just that we were talking about all the strange goings-on around here, and we included the Duke research team that was here last year at an old barn down the road. But that's a different weird story that Sandy was interested in; it has nothing to do with the battlefield." Bruce had done a good job at shifting the conversation away from Sandy's dilemma. She gave him a smile that seemed to say, *Thanks for the assist.*

"Okay, but what about Kirtland? How do we nail this guy? We just can't let him get away with this sort of stuff." Alan was getting into his crusader mode, and the more he thought about Arthur Kirtland as the source of his worries, the madder he got.

"I'm calling Riley and getting him involved. I'll show this guy that he's not the only one who can play rough."

Bruce wasn't sure whether Sandy had noticed it, but Alan seemed to be taking things very seriously and emotionally. He was acting in a way that was out of character for this usually reserved researcher. Why this anger and rage?

"I have spoken with the sheriff about these notes, and you may want to share yours with him, Alan, but I doubt it will do any good. There is no direct link to Arthur Kirtland, and even if there were, he hasn't broken any major laws. I doubt if they would even fine him."

"They will if I can connect him to the vandalism and petty theft, and I think I can now. I'll explain it all to the sheriff when he gets here. I am tired of these backwoods people and their disrespect." Alan turned and literally stomped back toward his tent, with his cell phone up to his ear. He was calling Deputy Jackson. Alan wasn't wasting any more time; he was convinced he had the puzzle solved, and he wanted Arthur Kirtland to feel the pressure for a change.

Sandy looked at Bruce and shrugged. "Someone's had a bit too much caffeine today."

Bruce wasn't feeling as easy about it as Sandy. "I don't know, Sandy. Did you sense the sudden change in his demeanor—and that anger? What about that line, 'These backwoods people and their disrespect'? Where did that come from?"

"Afraid I missed that part, Rev, but I did catch that clever save when I spoke about the barn, thank you. I didn't think now was a good time to go into my personal interest in this area. I think Alan's plate is a little too full for more supernatural phenomena."

"I agree Alan's obviously frustrated right now. He's a scientist looking to connect the dots in a logical way, and it does make sense, but the thing that he's missing is the emotional aspect. It's weird, but I see it everywhere I go, normal people caught in a wave of irrational anger, just like Alan there. I was talking to the deputy the other evening, and he told me that there'd been an increase of calls in this area in the past month. What do you think about that?"

"Oh, let me see, how about that there were a greater number of complaints to the police department?" Sandy said with her mocking smile. Her face had a way of lighting up when she was kidding, and Bruce just smiled back and launched into his exegesis of the local events.

"Thank you, Ms. Freud, your analysis is invaluable. But I am talking about people and their behavior. Why do people do the things they do? Alan is looking at Arthur Kirtland as a grand conspirator who is going to great lengths to destroy some research that is actually not that important. No one cares what happened here or whether there are eighty bodies or twenty-five bodies. This place is never visited by anyone except the occasional high school couple looking for a make-out place. It all seems so blown out of proportion."

"You're right about that, Bruce. I think this whole battlefield scene is a little bit out of proportion. The purpose here is to teach research techniques rather than to make any significant discoveries. What I'm really interested in is this: How did a preacher get familiar with the local make-out spots?" The two began to laugh, and Bruce even blushed a little.

"A good shepherd knows all the places where his flock may get lost or fall into temptation. It comes with the territory." Bruce spoke in a deep, ethereal *ex cathedra* kind of voice. "I guess the idea of emotions and behavior comes with my job. You know I spend a lot of my time trying to get Christian people to fill their hearts with love and compassion, and yet it takes no effort at all for them to fill themselves with hatred and anger. As the old saying goes, 'It's enough to make a preacher cuss.'"

"Oh man, Bruce, I haven't heard that one in a while. My dad used to say that when he was frustrated with something." Sandy paused for moment, thinking of her dad and the change he had gone through. "Now he just cusses under his breath." Sandy's voice dropped off as thoughts of her dad begin to sadden the joy of the moment.

"Have you thought about the emotional aspect of what happened to your dad, Sandy? I mean, here is a guy who arrives as a hardworking, perfectly normal professor and next thing you know he has done a complete personality change. I used to think the world was just getting more and more evil, but it appears that in certain places that evil is moving even faster. There must be a reason for this. I have tried to analyze it scientifically, sociologically, and anthropologically, but I keep coming back to my instincts that it may be more theological than anything else. There is a spiritual paradigm shift going on around us, and I'm not sure if it's a good one. I believe that God directs people, but he doesn't force people to do his will. I also believe there is another force at work that seeks to prevent people from doing God's will, and it even directs humanity toward acts of evil."

Sandy had turned her attention back to Bruce to avoid the painful memories of her father.

"I am a little vague on this whole 'will of God' sort of thing. What do you think is the will of God for people? Is it the same for all people, or does each person have a totally unique destiny, or is it all just based on karma?"

"You're not alone with that question. I've been telling people about God's will for years, and they can't seem to get it—well, some do, but others act as if I were speaking in the original Greek. I think that some of the confusion is due to selfishness. People think that everything is about them. They're always asking what God's will is for their lives, and I try to tell them that it may be the same thing that God intended for everyone else but just geared to their individual lives."

Bruce cleared his throat and twisted a little in his seat as if about to give a sermon. "I believe that the teachings of Jesus are the key to understanding the will of God. So, what are the teachings of Jesus, you ask. Some would say that they are a lot of things: parables, Sermon on the Mount, miracles, all the gospels, etc., etc. But Jesus really taught one central truth, and that was what he wanted everyone to put into practice. He said to love God and love everybody else or put basically—love. Now, if you have a problem knowing how to love, he simplified it by saying, love them the way you would like to be loved. The only thing we are not to love is evil or the demonic. Now, is that so hard to follow?"

"Not really, but what about all the evil in the world? How do we combat it?"

Bruce sat up again. "We don't; it is like the art of fighting without fighting."

Sandy laughed and said, "Wait a minute! Didn't Bruce Lee say that in that kung fu movie?"

"Actually, it's from *The Art of War*." Bruce paused a moment and, rolling his eyes, continued with, "But yes, he did say that. I had no idea that you were a fan of old kung fu flicks."

"I'm more of a Jackie Chan fan, but the little guy, Lee, was hot." Sandy sounded like a college girl again.

"Anyway, the idea of fighting without fighting in the Christian sense is that if we love one another then we are essentially destroying evil. We are fighting, but we are not fighting; we are showing love. You know how when you turn on a light in a room, are you dispelling the darkness or just shining light in a place where there was none? Some may say dispelling darkness, but we didn't do that, the light did. We just prepared the room to receive the electricity and connected the room with the real power that was in the house. The electricity is like God's spirit flowing all through and around the house and out into the world. We're just the messengers who flick the switch and make the connection."

Sandy was listening attentively and yet with a smile on her face that was very hard to read.

"I know it sounds a little eastern, but people forget that technically Jesus had more in common with the Orient than he did with the western world. It's no surprise that the logic of the east could creep into his teachings. I think that truth is truth regardless of the source. It's just that sometimes evil uses truth to pervert the good."

"Whoa there, Rev, back up. You lost me on that one—evil uses truth?"

"I just mean that the idea of evil in scriptures is that the evil person is a deceiver, and the whole nature of deception is that you take something that people think is good and pervert it for evil, without the person you are deceiving finding out. One of the other main messages of scripture is to be watching all the time. People who are watching are less likely to be deceived. There! You have just heard the complete commentary on the Gospels by Reverend Bruce Strong. All donations are tax deductible."

Sandy was smiling again and thinking that this was a different kind of preacher. He was not like the men she'd heard as a child, who were only interested in getting her to come to church so she would bring her parents. He was speaking to her in ways she could understand, and it seemed important to him that she did understand.

Sandy jokingly spoke in a southern accent: "You impress me, Reverend Strong. If I had heard you as a child, I might today be a good Southern Baptist, bible totin', born-again believer, eatin' curried chicken and singing hymns, all while sitting in the lotus position."

"The chicken I can handle, but something about singing in the lotus position—I don't think I'm ready for that one yet."

Amid their laughter, Sandy was thinking how unusual it was that he was not pressing her to convert. They were having a relaxed conversation about a subject that most of her colleagues seemed to genuinely fear. This *was* a different kind of preacher, and she felt at ease with him. It was the same kind of peace she'd used to feel when she spoke with her father. He had a similar passion for his work as this Reverend Strong did.

Their conversation went on for another hour as they spoke of kung fu movies, curried chicken, spirituality, and philosophy. Both of them had needed a break from the world, and while battles were raging in other heads, Bruce and Sandy had found a moment's peace on an old battlefield in upstate South Carolina.

But evil wasn't resting; it never looks for peace. Even now these two did not realize that they were sitting at a picnic table beside a well-traveled road, and one of the travelers on that road was Oliver Paxton, and another was Bea Kirtland.

Scene 24

Evil rides the highways

Oliver Paxton sped past the battlefield. He was in a hurry to get home before two of his students arrived. They wanted to bring a cake as a gift for their instructor, and Paxton was thinking that he would accept their offering to him. He felt very good about growing his relationship with his class members, even if his wife did not. It was very proper that the students would come to love and respect him and even wish to bring him gifts. All these thoughts were dispelled when he saw the shapely curve of Sanchari's back where she was sitting at the table. He recognized her from the distance; her shape was unmistakable. She had only been around a couple of times, but he had memorized her features during those meetings, and he had thought of her often. She was his ideal woman, and she had the heritage he so envied. In another place and time, perhaps their parents would have arranged their marriage. As he slowed down, he noticed someone sitting across from her and saw that it was Strong. Of all the people she could be spending time with, he was the least worthy. He was a deceiver who had mocked him in his office. He was a man with a small mind who thought he was clever, but Oliver knew him for who he was. He was nothing but an arrogant, lustful creature who lacked the power to discern truth from fables, and now he was corrupting the one thing in this place that had come to represent beauty. Anger began to swell within Paxton as he sped away. He had an appointment to keep, and he would deal with Strong later in his own way.

Meanwhile, not far behind Paxton, Shirley and Bea were driving slowly down the highway, and they slowed even more as they came within sight of the battlefield. They both strained to see what was going on at the campsite, but Shirley had to keep her eyes on the road, so her glances were darting from road to campsite. Bea was the first to notice the two sitting at the picnic table near the edge of the trees.

"Oh my goodness, Shirley, did you see that? That was the preacher sitting there with that colored girl. My Arthur had said that he heard they were seeing each other, but I didn't imagine that they would be right out there in the open. And I thought he was a nice young man."

"Are you sure it was him, Bea? Maybe it just looked like him. Do you want me to turn around and go back by again?" Shirley was trying to look and keep her eyes on the road at the same time.

"No, Shirley, we can't do that. Someone would think we were being nosy or something. We can't just turn around right here, can we? No, that's just silly, but we could turn right up here and then right again at the end of the road, and that takes us back up by the Methodist church. I sort of wanted to see their flower bed around their sign; folks say it's the prettiest thing." Bea was pointing at the Hurley road up ahead as she spoke, and Shirley started signaling to turn.

"I meant to go by there the other day and see that and see if I could get some ideas for something to do around my mailbox. Every time I plant flowers there, that stupid ole mail lady drives over them and kills them. You'd think the woman could see the flowers."

In a moment or two the ladies were driving by the Methodist church, but by now they had forgotten to look as they turned right to head back toward the battlefield. Once they reached the crossroads, they had already decided that any children born to the preacher and that colored girl would be rejected by society. They turned right at the light and almost crept by the battlefield.

"Well, would you look at that! Still sittin' there as big as you please, just a laughin' up a storm. Somebody's havin' a good time today." Bea sounded like a crone when she used that tone of disapproval in her voice.

"If he's got time to sit up there and court that little colored girl, he's got time to go over to see Ms. Stallings. She's been sick with the diarrhea again, you know." Shirley chimed in with her suggestion of how the preacher should spend his day.

"Oh, I heard that she had that two weeks ago, but I didn't go by there." Bea spoke with her sincerest tone of concern. "You know she hates it when people come to see her and she has to go to the bathroom every two minutes. She needed the preacher, but he's up here all the time. It just ain't right."

Shirley accelerated the car along as they neared the driveway of Oliver Paxton. Turning in, they saw him walking from the barn back toward the house. He stopped and waved as they approached. The two plump ladies slid out of their seats like Weeble toys, rocking back and forth and laboring to stand and turn. Somewhat stiff from their ride in the car, they needed to take a moment to stand fully erect.

"Oh, I can hardly wait for our classes to take effect and get this stiffness out of our joints," Bea said as she turned to the back seat to retrieve the lemon pound cake she had made the previous morning. "I hope you enjoy lemon pound cake, Oliver; it is my specialty. It's a prize-winning recipe, you know."

"Really, Ms. Kirtland, it is so kind of you to bring us one of your prize-winning cakes. Let's take it inside." They moved toward the screen door, and Paxton held the cake in one hand and the door in the other as the two ladies trudged up the steps to the porch.

"I think I am still a little sore from our last class, Oliver, but I do enjoy the exercise."

"Anna, Willow," Oliver called. "Look what these lovely ladies have brought for us today. It's a prize-winning pound cake Bea made herself."

Anna walked into the kitchen as the ladies were making their way to the table to sit.

"Well, that really looks special, Ms. Kirtland. Oliver and I love pound cake, and you say you have won prizes with this recipe? You must share it with me." Anna Paxton's words were as sweet as the cake she was eyeing.

"Actually, I didn't win the prize; I just got the recipe out of my *Ladies' Monthly*," Bea explained, trying to correct the misunderstanding. "I've never won anything, really." Bea turned her head with a blush.

Shirley spoke up, however. "We did win that Charleston contest at the senior adult dinner one year, Bea, remember. It was ages ago, but we did win; I still have that ribbon they gave us. Our husbands wouldn't go, so Bea and I went over and danced together and showed them old ladies how to cut a rug. Most of 'em are too old to dance anyway; they were easy to beat."

"Yes … well, I'm sure you're boring our host with that silly old story, Shirley. You should have some cake, Oliver, and your lovely wife too.

"Nonsense, I bet you're just being modest, and as for this prize-winning cake, I can't wait to try a piece." Oliver was in his glory. He saw these ladies as his devoted disciples bringing him his deserved homage.

"And what about that little girl of yours—is it Hanna or something like that? Does she like cake?" Bea asked.

"No, Ms. Kirtland, I am Anna," she spoke with a bit of agitation. "My daughter's name is Willow."

"Willow—isn't that pretty, Shirley? What a pretty name. Where is the little darling?"

"She's in her room, doing her schoolwork."

Bea was scanning the kitchen like an army ranger on a scouting trip, and she saw two small dolls and moved over to the counter to pick them up. "Oh, I see her little dolls; I used to love to play with dolls when I was a little girl. I'd rock them and dress them and do them up so nice—" Bea stopped and looked down at the dolls in her hands. She tried to hide her concern, but Oliver heard the words coming out of her mouth as if she were unable to stop them. "Oh dear! Where are their little fingers? All their fingers have been cut off!" She sat the dolls back down on the counter.

Anna and Oliver Paxton exchanged glares as Oliver sliced into the moist cake. "Mmm, this sure looks good, ladies. Would you like some milk with your cake?" Oliver asked with a smile that tried to hide his embarrassment.

"No, but some coffee would be nice," Bea suggested, trying not to look back at the dolls on the counter. Anna caught her looking, and when Bea turned her head, she slid the dolls into a silverware drawer.

"I'm sorry, ladies, but there is no caffeine in this house. It poisons the body, you know, and we must purge the body of all but the most natural of foods." Oliver was speaking, and Anna was turning away so that no one could see her roll her eyes. She also made sure that the jar of instant coffee was not sitting out on the counter where she had left it that morning.

Shirley was looking down at her slice of the cake and softly said, "Peaches."

"Oliver turned to the demure little lady with the heavy southern accent and said, "I beg your pardon? Did you say something?"

Shirley looked up almost sheepishly and said, "Peaches. I usually like peaches with my pound cake."

Bea shot her a glance, but Shirley just shrugged her shoulders as if to say, "Well, I do."

Oliver said, "Mmm, that does sound good. I think I'd like some peaches as well. Anna, do we have any peaches in the cupboard for our guests' pound cake?

Her answer was quick and cold. "No, dear, they have too much processed sugar. Remember, we must watch our sugar; the body must be pure." She spoke in a tone that was obviously meant to mock her husband. But before Oliver could reply, Bea spoke up to say that her cake was better plain. With that, Anna made her way toward the door. She turned to excuse herself; she had to check on Willow.

As she walked out the door, Oliver tried to start up some small talk. "Ladies, what have you been up to today?"

"We went for a ride today. We wanted to bring you this cake and to look at the flowers up at the Methodist church, and then we came back by the battlefield."

Bea was trying to remember the events of the day when Oliver interrupted. "Oh yes, I was by the battlefield myself today, and I could have sworn I saw the Reverend Strong there with that young Indian girl."

Shirley spoke first, saying, "Yes, Bea saw them there together also. But she isn't an Indian; she's a negress. They are quite the item, I hear."

"Oh, Shirley, she may not be a negress; she may be Puerto Rican. And it's none of my business, you know, who the preacher is seeing, but I do think he should use a little better judgment, a man in his position and all."

Oliver was fuming but trying to contain his anger. He blurted out, "She is not a negress or a Puerto Rican—she is Indian. I just wasn't aware that they were actually seeing one another." His voice trailed off, and he was finding it hard to hide his feelings. Then he began to breathe slowly, silently, in a barely audible rhythm. He felt the warm sense of calm come over him, and he looked back up at the ladies with that odd serpentine smile and asked, "And how were the flowers at the Methodist church today? I must get by there myself and see them. Willow and Anna love flowers, you know."

The sudden change in personality caught the ladies off guard, and they weren't sure how to respond. Finally, Shirley spoke up, saying, "Maybe you could show us your flowers sometime?"

Oliver's face flushed for a moment when he realized they had no flowers growing in the yard, but he was quick to tell them that most of his plants were spring flowers, and the bulbs were in the ground. Bea and Shirley just looked at one another, and Bea was the first to speak. "We must be going now, and I do hope you like the cake. Come along, Shirley. You've got to get back before it's too late, ya know."

"Don't rush off, ladies, Willow will join us soon, and I know she'd like to thank you for the wonderful cake." Oliver was herding the ladies toward the door as he spoke.

When they were on the porch and Bea was making her way down

the stairs, Shirley turned back to Oliver and, in a whisper, said, "You may want to toss out that cake; it's full of sugar. I told her not to put so much in, but she likes a little extra. That thing is sugar, sugar, and sugar! She just didn't know about the pure body and all that."

Oliver smiled, thanked her, and then waved as they waddled toward the car. He watched the old car's springs creak under the ladies' weight. He turned his gaze back inside to see Willow and Anna coming to the kitchen door. The ladies waved, and Anna put on her best fake smile.

When Anna and Willow reached the door, Paxton was stepping out toward the barn with an angry gait. "Throw that cake out," he shouted angrily at Anna as he walked away from them.

"Why? I thought it was a gift from your disciples."

Oliver slowed and started to turn; then he puffed some words under his breath and started back to the barn. "It's full of sugar, sugar, sugar," he finally said as he disappeared into the barn.

Anna turned to Willow, who had silently watched the exchange between her parents, and said, "Ya want some cake, baby?"

Willow followed her mom into the kitchen and saw the cake sitting on the table. She looked up with a question is her eyes. "But Daddy said it was full of sugar, sugar, sugar."

"Yeah, well, I'm gonna eat it, eat it, eat it. Now, do you want a piece before I get mine and throw it out?" Anna gruffly said. She jerked the plate around to slice from the uncut side of the cake.

"Okay," Willow said with a smile. "I guess I can eat it, eat it, eat it too.

Out in the barn, Oliver was trying to center himself and stretch into a difficult position, but his concentration was off. All he could think of was Sanchari sitting with that cleric and the ladies with their "negress" and "Puerto Rican" comments. She was more like a goddess than a negress. They knew nothing! Perhaps he was wasting his time here. He moved his head down toward the floor and felt himself getting a little dizzy as the blood flow slowed. Sometimes he felt it would just be better to slip into that state of being at one with the great Brahma; nirvana would be his. But obviously it would not be anytime soon. What could Sanchari see in someone like Strong?

On the highway, heading for home, Shirley and Bea sat silently for a few moments, until Shirley turned to Bea and said, "An Indian? I would never have thought that the preacher would take up with an Indian. What tribe do you think she is, Lumbee or Catawba?"

"Don't be silly, Shirley. Haven't you seen her? She is obviously Cherokee. Whatever she is, she gets around, first Mr. Paxton and now the preacher. She is definitely on the warpath." With that, both ladies burst into laughter at their private joke—which wouldn't stay private for very long.

Chapter 5

The new battle of Buford

The evening was coming on, and Topper and Cedric had opted to skip the mess tent for supper and go over to the store for some wholesome microwave delights. When they arrived, there were the usual guys hanging out and talking. When Leon saw the two, he said something to the group, who all burst into laughter and then began to mumble something about Topper and Cedric. In a few moments, most of the boys were walking out the door. Four of the boys got in their car, drove to the light, and made right turn. They drove to the old white house near the battleground and stopped. Only Leon and two of his friends were left in the store, and as Topper walked back toward the microwave counter, Leon moved up beside him.

"How's things going over at the battlefield? Find anything interesting over there?"

Topper looked at Cedric, and Cedric said, "Not really. All is pretty much what we expected."

Leon pressed on with more questions, seeming to be genuinely interested. "What were you guys looking for, anyway? Some said it was bodies; others said it was proof that the grave was a real grave and that the battle actually happened here. What was it really?"

Cedric was cautious but felt at ease to tell him a little bit about the work, since they were almost finished anyway. "It was a little of both, but mostly it was the experience of working a dig site. It's sort of a classroom for us. In case we want to be a historian or anthropologist or archaeologist, that sort of thing, ya know?"

"No, not really; I'm more into sports and stuff." Leon could be charming when he wanted to be, and now he was at his best. "What about you—what was your name? Uh, Topper or something like that? Sounds a little gay, don't it?" Leon laughed sheepishly, as if embarrassed by his own comment. Topper bit his lip the way his mom used to when she was about to cry, but he said nothing.

Leon smiled and said, "What are you gonna do with all that education you're getting? Will it get you a better job or just make you feel like you're better than everybody else?" This comment was followed by an evil grin.

Topper was uneasy and intimidated by Leon, and he was still suffering from worry over Criton, but he managed to mumble out, "Teacher, probably be a teacher."

"Teacher, yeah, that's a pretty steady job these days. They're always looking for teachers is what my mom would say. Pretty good pay and benefits for only nine months' work. Sure beats diggin' ditches. So, are you guys almost finished with all your research and stuff?"

"Yes, we'll be wrapping things up in a couple of days, and then it's back to school for some real classwork. This has been fun, though; I wouldn't mind doin' it again in some place like Mexico or Central America."

Cedric spoke up, trying to take over the conversation. "They say there are places there that have never been touched, they're just waiting for a team of researchers to dig in. Man, that would be a great trip."

Topper was through heating up his nachos and cheese and was headed for the counter to pay when Leon yelled, "What's the rush? You guys aren't leaving tonight? I've really enjoyed hearing about that anthropology stuff."

"Yeah, it's been cool, but we gotta' get back. Good talkin' with ya." Cedric was still trying to be as cordial as he could as they paid their bill and walked out into the parking lot. The sky was dark with an occasional flash of what the locals called heat lightning. A flash across the sky was usually a precursor for rain, but with heat lightning the rain was slow in coming. The air was starting to cool down, and the clouds were closing in, making things seem even darker outside. The lights from the store shone like a pathway toward the battlefield, disappearing into the darkness near the old house between the road and the campsite. Just a quick trip across the highway, behind the empty white house, and then across the field, and they would be back in the world of research. Back at the station, Leon's two friends walked out after Topper and Cedric, hopped into their car, drove through the stoplight, and turned down toward the battlefield.

"Not goin' with your buddies, Leon?" the little guy behind the counter asked.

"Nope, not tonight. I thought I'd just hang here for a while and keep you company. Maybe even tell you all about anthropology and stuff like that." The two men laughed at the idea of Leon Courtney being an anthropologist.

"You'd spend the first year of college learning how to spell it, Leon." The man behind the counter laughed to himself.

"Yeah, you're right, I'd be too dumb for that, but thank God I'm not so dumb that all I can do is run some cash register in a two-bit convenience store. What are you makin' now, half of the minimum wage? Yeah, I sure am glad I missed that career." The little man realized that the nice side of Leon had walked out that door with the two boys, and now the mean Leon was standing right in front of him.

As Leon stood looking out the window, behind the big empty house another argument was about to begin, but this one would go way beyond sharing quips and insults. While Leon was talking to the man behind the counter, his friends had quickly pulled into the drive at the old house and cut their lights, setting up positions to ambush Topper and Cedric. They had made their way over behind the house before Cedric and Topper could get across the road and were now just out of sight of the encampment.

When Cedric and Topper came around the corner to cut across the field, two of the boys stepped out from behind the corner, startling them. They surprised the two by saying, "We wanted to apologize for Leon. He was sort of rude back at the store, and he wanted us to come and give you guys that message."

Topper and Cedric looked at each other and then at the boys. They gave half smiles and mumbled, "Okay, whatever."

They started to step around the two, when the boy who had been speaking looked down at the ground and said, "Well, they ain't no reason to be rude." Topper was in front of Cedric, and just as Cedric moved past the boy, he said, "Oh yeah, Leon said to tell ya this, too," and with a quick twist of his body, he came around sharply. He gave Cedric a right to the temple as hard as he could, and Cedric went down to one knee as Topper stood there, momentarily frozen with fear.

Another boy came up from behind Topper and said, "What's the matter, freak? Never been in a fistfight?" Before Topper could turn completely around, he was hit just behind the ear. The knuckles made a sound like someone slapping cold meat on a counter as Topper twisted to try and raise his arm in defense. As he turned, he was met with another punch, this one flush on his jaw, and he crumpled to the ground. Cedric was trying to stand and reach toward Topper when his assailant landed a kick to his kidney. Cedric's body was jerked upright with his arms reaching to soothe the aching spot. By this time, two other boys had come out from their hiding and stood over the two wounded students.

"This is too easy," one said with a laugh. His tone was laced with anger like a glass of iced tea laced with arsenic. "Get the fags on their feet and see if they can do something."

Cedric managed to mumble something about leaving them alone, but a quick backhanded slap ripped across his lips and sent him back to the ground. By now Topper had regained his feet, and with courage he never dreamed he had, or perhaps it was a mix of anger and fear, he flung his body and arms at one of the attackers. His attack was clumsy and caused one of the boys to laugh as he sidestepped the attack. But Topper did manage to hit a mark. He struck Jake, who was standing over Cedric, hard on the back of the head. This sent him toppling to the ground with a barrage of curses flowing from his lips. He was unhurt but knocked off balance, and now he was embarrassed that he had been caught off guard. His friends were laughing at him, and this fueled his rage. He jumped to his feet, and for one of those moments that seemed like forever, the entire scene was displayed before their eyes as if in slow motion while the four boys stood over the beaten bodies of two frightened students. The moment's peace was a prelude to the chaos that was about to be unleashed. Amid the laughter of the others, Jake screamed a primal scream and blared with a deep southern accent, "You sumbitch! What do you think you're a doin', boy?" and with that he launched toward Topper with a fury, cursing and throwing a hail of lefts and rights, pummeling Topper to his knees. His rage was all-consuming, driving him to increase his intensity with every blow. He would not, or perhaps could not, stop.

Cedric was back up and stepping toward Topper to try to fend off his attacker, but the others were moving forward to block his attack. He managed a weak punch to the face of one of the boys, and a trickle of blood emerged, causing him to fall back and scream as if he'd been shot. Cedric then jerked Jake as he was hitting Topper and landed a solid punch to his face, but rather than hurt him, it spurred him to fight back harder. When Cedric didn't go down, he yelled for his friends to grab him. Two boys grabbed Cedric's arms, and the third stepped up to face him. Now his rancor turned toward Cedric, and as the others held his writhing body, the beating began. Bloody knuckles crashed into his face and head as Cedric fought against the hands restraining him, trying to dodge the punches. Soon his strength was worn, and he could no longer struggle or try to evade the onslaught. But there was no mercy to be had that day as the boy flailed at his helpless victim to the point of exhaustion. Behind them they heard the voice of Topper as he begged them to leave Cedric alone, but the smell of blood was in the air, and a spirit of rage had taken over the boys. In the darkness, occasional flashes of lightning illuminated the spot, seeming to silently orchestrate the scene. One boy was now holding Cedric up as another pummeled his near-unconscious body. The other turned back to Topper and began to unleash his barrage of hate on his helpless form. Three of the four were holding and hitting Cedric and Topper while another stood close by, holding a baseball bat. He had been the one most afraid to come with his friends and had grabbed a bat when he imagined himself trying to fight off these two college students. But he had done nothing except watch in stunned horror as his friends behaved like demons, punching and hitting at the other boys. He could not believe his eyes as he watched his friends transform into animals driven by bloodlust. But the worst was yet to come. The virtue of humanity was about to be lost once more near the Buford battleground.

Cedric was almost unconscious, being held up and beaten, the two boys coaxing Jake to hit him harder and knock him out with one punch. Topper was back on his feet, trying to evade his attacker but not fighting back. Now he was begging and crying for them to please stop. Topper reached for Jake's shoulder to try and turn him away from his carnage, but just as his fingers stretched toward Jake's face, Jake turned toward Topper, and one of Topper's outstretched fingers stabbed him in the eye. Jake recoiled in pain and grabbed at his face. The pain was far worse than the damage, and again it was the pain that drove the boy further into murderous rage. His words were barely audible as he unleashed a series of screams and curses. Topper stepped back, surprised and shocked at what had just happened. He began to mouth his pleadings, but his own pain and tears were blurring everything. The boy holding Cedric let him drop to the ground. Cedric was barely conscious; he spat blood and began to throw up blood from the blows to his stomach. The scene was getting uglier by the moment. Topper was staggering and rubbing his eyes, trying to see what had happened. Jake was holding his eye, cursing and becoming more infuriated.

Everything seemed to happen in an instant. Jake, still holding his eye, stumbled away. With his good eye, he saw the bat in his friend's hand, and in a lightning-quick move, he grabbed the bat, tightened his grip, and then looked back at Topper, who was standing there crying and pleading, his lips silently forming the words "Please, no." But Jake swung the bat, and it landed squarely on Topper's temple. The weeping face was instantly replaced with an emotionless look of peace as his entire body went limp and began to topple to the ground like a tree in the forest. He landed with a muffled thud, his head making one small bounce off the cool green grass, now moist from the evening dew. He lay there looking as restful as if he were taking a peaceful afternoon nap.

"Home run," one of the boys laughingly yelled, but the other was running to grab the bat from the hand of the near-blinded attacker— who was raising it into the air as if to come down on Topper with a final, killing blow.

"Hold it, man, hold it!" he yelled, trying to wrest the bat from the hands of his friend. "You trying to kill somebody?"

Jake struggled for a moment, and then he stopped, with a mumbled "Huh, what?" as if waking up from a dream. "Well, the bastard tried to blind me; you saw it. Serves him right if he is dead, dumb little prick!"

Julian, the boy who had held the bat but not taken part in the attack, walked over to Topper's motionless body and knelt down. He looked at Topper lying there and wanted to touch him, but he couldn't bring himself to do it. Was he breathing? He wasn't sure; he was so still. His face held no expression, and one eye was partially open. Julian softly spoke as he turned to the other three boys. "I think he's hurt really bad." Cedric was trying to get on his knees and crawl toward his friend, when the boy who had yelled "home run" kicked him in the rib cage, sending him curling into a fetal position.

"Where you goin' boy?" His words were followed by silence as the four boys exchanged glances at one another. In a few short minutes, they had achieved a victory over two unsuspecting and almost defenseless students. Having done what they'd set out to do, they were now confused and at a loss. Their instructions had been to jump them and rough them up a little, but there had been no exit strategy. What were they to do when they finished? They looked at each other again and slowly moved away from the bodies on the ground.

Julian was still kneeling near Topper. He turned when he heard the thud of the bat hitting the ground beside him. "Don't forget your bat, man. You brought it." The tone had a hint of accusation, as if he were responsible for the carnage and the injuries to the now-motionless body before him. The others were walking away as Cedric crawled over to Topper. The boy with the bat moved away in fear, as if he was concerned Cedric would come at him now that his friends were leaving.

"Get away from him," Cedric mumbled through lips that were bleeding and beginning to swell. He had to turn his head up to see the boy's face, because his eyes were beginning to swell shut. "Just get away from him."

The "batboy", as Julian would soon come to be called, stepped back and began to mumble to Cedric, "I'm sorry, man, I'm sorry. I didn't know they were going to do this. It was just supposed to be for fun, just to scare you guys a little. I didn't know, man; really, I didn't know." His words grew fainter as he backed away from Topper and Cedric. Suddenly, out of the corner of his eye, he saw a flash of lightning and the shape of someone standing near the corner of the old house nearest the battlefield. He heard the sound of voices coming closer from the battlefield. He didn't look twice but instead turned and ran after his friends, yelling that someone was coming and that someone else was right there at the house. With that, the others ran quickly toward the car. One boy slowed and turned back toward the scene to see who, if anyone, was at the house, but no one was there.

"I don't see nobody, dip wad." He spat the words at the "batboy."

"Well, he was there all right. He had on a green coat and was coming around the corner. Now, come on!" With that, they jumped into their car and sped away.

The lightning flashed again, and a few drops of rain began to fall on Cedric's face. Cedric brushed the moisture away and began to weep. He looked around for someone to show mercy on his friend, but there was no one near. A few minutes that seemed like forever passed, until Brad and Oscar came running up. They had heard a commotion from the campsite and were making their way toward the backyard.

Cedric heard their approach and, still leaning over Topper, drew a deep breath. With all his strength and ignoring the pain in his mouth, he cried out," Over here ... come over here!" Then he collapsed on the stomach of his friend, with one hand reaching toward his bruised head.

When Brad and Oscar arrived, they were horror-struck by the scene. Brad said, "Get back to camp, Oscar, and get Alan over here right away!" Oscar was moving as soon as Brad started to speak, and Brad yelled after him, "Tell him to bring a car! We need to get these guys to a hospital."

Back at camp, Oscar had barely told them what he'd found before Alan was on his cell phone calling 911. He barked at one of the boys to drive his truck around to the back of the house, and he started to run toward the backyard.

When Alan arrived, he had to struggle to hold back his anger at what he saw. He dropped to one knee and began to check for a pulse on Cedric. His touch roused Cedric, who said, "I'm okay. Check Topper."

Alan smiled and said, "You're not exactly okay, Cedric. Somebody beat the hell out of ya." Cedric rolled over beside Topper and tried to speak again, but his lips were caked with blood and his eyes almost completely swollen shut. Alan moved to the other side of Topper and began to feel for a pulse. *Thank God*, he thought as he felt the faint rhythm of the young boy's heart. "Ya had me scared there for a minute, Topper. Now just hang in there; help is coming."

"Shouldn't we put him in the car and take him on to the hospital, Alan," Brad said in a tone of deep concern.

"No, he's hurt pretty bad, and I'm not sure if we should try to move him. He may have a concussion or neck injury. Go get some ice and a rag, and we'll try to keep the swelling down until the ambulance gets here." Brad was off like a track star out of the starting blocks. By now the whole camp was buzzing, and Sandy and some of the other kids were hurrying across the field. They arrived to see Cedric trying to sit up and Alan holding him down. Sandy was like Florence Nightingale on the battlefield. She moved to help Alan and soothe Cedric, and then she asked about Topper. Alan just raised his eyebrows and shook his head, not wanting to alarm Cedric. Brad was back in a flash with an ice-filled towel, and Sandy gently held it against the bulging bruise rising from the side of Topper's head.

"What's happened, Alan?" one of the kids asked.

"I'm not sure yet, but I've got a pretty good idea. The guys said they had words with some locals at the store a few nights ago, and that would be my first guess." Alan couldn't hide his agitation. "Whoever they were, they did a hell of job on Cedric and Topper, and for what reason? They weren't doing anything to anybody! What kind of people are these that would do something like this? I just don't get it!"

Riley Jackson was the first law officer on the scene. When they saw the blue lights of his cruiser pulling into the camp, Alan sent Oscar to bring him over to the yard. The ambulance drivers saw the cruiser and followed him into the backyard of the old Victorian home. It only took a few moments for the paramedics to get the two boys stabilized and loaded in the back of the vehicle. Riley asked whether they had been able to say anything or give any details about what had happened, and Alan told him that they knew nothing. The two men walked toward the sheriffs' cruiser as the ambulance pulled out onto the highway. Alan shouted back to Sandy, Oscar, and Brad to watch the camp while he went to the hospital. "No one is to leave camp" were his last instructions.

Across the road, the store clerk was standing on tiptoes, staring out the window. "I wonder what happened at the old Hartley place."

"Beats me. Maybe somebody fell in a well or something," Leon said as he slurped the empty slushy cup. The clerk noted the odd, almost sarcastic, tone in Leon's voice. He turned to see a wry smile creeping across his face.

"Do you know what happened over there, Leon?" the clerk asked.

Leon raised his hands with an exaggerated gesture and anger in his voice, yelling to intimidate the shy clerk. "What you asking me for, man! I been standing right here with you all evening, haven't I? Well, haven't I?"

The clerk dropped his head to avoid eye contact with Leon, who was now leaning over the counter and wagging his head back and forth like one of those little head-bobbing dolls in the back windows of old cars. "Yeah, yeah, you were here all right. Now back up."

"What's the frickin' magic word, ma-a-a-n?" Leon stretched the last word out in a whiny singsong tone as irritating as fingernails on a chalkboard. "Well, what is it?" he demanded, leaning even closer to the clerk's face.

"The word is, get outta his face, boy! I wanna get my doughnut." It was Buck. In the excitement, they had forgotten that he would come in for his nightly cream-filled doughnut. Leon leaned back quickly, and his tone of voice suddenly changed to that of a child playing a game. Leon stumbled back away from the counter and mumbled to Buck, but Buck wasn't paying him any attention. His focus was now on his friend behind the counter as he rang up the cost of the doughnut. The clerk smiled at Buck. "Take two, Buck. One's on me," he said, grinning back at the big man with the sweet tooth.

Leon moved to the door and slipped out as if trying not to be noticed. He had an appointment to keep down the road. His tires squealed a little as he gunned the engine and headed away from the store and the gathering crowd across the way. He was going to a friend's house to get a report on the evening's activities.

Chapter 6

Scene 26

At the hospital

The ambulance was parked in the ER bay of the local hospital. Inside, a group of people sat and paced around a small waiting room. Riley was still trying to put together a time line of events, but no one could add anything to the story. They would have to wait for the boys to come out of the examining room. Alan watched Riley talking softly to a couple of students and couldn't stand it any longer. He moved across the floor and stood, trembling with anger, behind Riley.

"Why are you wasting time here, Deputy? You and I both know who is responsible for this." Alan was on the verge of tears in his rage.

"Take it easy, Alan. I've got procedures to follow, and I was hoping to hear from the boys before we run off." Riley was trying to be as patient as he could, but Alan was swaying nervously back and forth.

Alan began to wring his hands. "You know who's behind this, Deputy, and he's sitting his old butt at home right now, probably celebrating his handiwork. Arthur Kirtland wanted us out at any cost. That old fart would do anything to get rid of us, and now we see that includes trying to kill us."

"Wait a minute, Alan. There's no way an old man could have done this, and no one saw him anywhere near the scene."

"Come on, Deputy, he may have not been there, but he was the power behind this. He's like Charlie Manson, sending people out to do his dirty work. His hands are just as bloody as the ones who did the beating." Alan was still shaking when Riley sat him down and tried to calm him a little.

The group sat around for about a couple of hours, but it seemed like a whole day. Riley was about to ask whether Alan had called the boys' families, but before he could say anything, all eyes moved toward the door, where an older couple was making their way in, followed by a slightly younger couple. These were Cedric and Topper's parents. Alan got up and moved over to meet them at the door, but Mrs. Owens wasn't wanting to be consoled by this young professor who had convinced Topper to come on this trip and to stay when he had called and told his mom he was coming home after the sighting. She was biting her lip when her husband touched her arm with a look that seemed to say, "We have already discussed this." She turned and walked back out of the waiting room. The Harris family just watched the drama unfold and then finally asked whether they had heard from the doctors yet.

Alan was about to say no when the doctor walked in and asked for the families of Cedric Harris and Terri Owens.

"We're here," they spoke almost in unison. Mr. Owens called to his wife, who came jogging around the corner.

"Mr. and Mrs. Harris, Cedric is stable and doing fine right now. We'll have you back to see him in a moment. Mr. and Mrs. Owens, I'd like for you to step in here with me to see some x-rays of Terry."

Mrs. Owens let out a barely audible sigh and began to moan slowly under her breath. The doctor led them away to the conference room. It seemed like an eternity before they emerged from the darkened room. Mrs. Owens was crying, and a nurse came to lead them down the hallway toward the ICU. Alan and Riley were anxiously waiting to hear the prognosis, but the Owens walked on through without stopping.

Riley stepped over to the doctor and said, "I'll need some info for my report, Doc. Have you got a minute?" The doctor nodded and led Riley into the back near the nurses' station. Riley would not be able to tell Topper's friends what he learned, but perhaps the parents would share some information when they had settled down. The doctor informed

Riley that Topper was in a coma and had some swelling around his brain, which might require surgery to relieve the pressure, but they were observing him right now. For now, all they could do was sit and wait.

Sandy came in and told Alan that things were quiet at the camp. Another deputy had arrived to watch over the scene. She'd felt it was safe to leave the kids, and she wanted a report on things. Alan nodded his approval but could tell her very little. As they sat there, Reverend Strong came into the room; he had heard there had been a problem at the battlefield. Sandy met him in the hallway and told him what they knew. Brad saw that the folks were anxious, and so he explained the HIPAA regulations of privacy to the group and asked them to be patient; they would get some information as soon as possible. Bruce sat with the students for an hour or so and continued to talk with them to help calm their worries. Meanwhile, Sandy was moving around the room like an associate pastor talking and just spending time with the kids who had accompanied Alan to the hospital. She showed remarkable poise under the strain. They spent the next hour sitting quietly in the waiting room doing just what the sign on the door said—waiting. The kids didn't want to leave until they knew the condition of their friends.

Scene 27

The aftermath

A mile or so from the crossroads, a group of boys sat breathlessly in the room of Batboy. They were still running on adrenalin and excitement. "Did you see that dude hit the ground? It was a like a movie, man! His eyes rolled back, and he just leaned over." The boys laughed and fell onto the bed, mimicking Topper's fall to the ground.

"Oh yeah, it was sweet, man! One whack and he was out like a light," another boy spoke, and the group erupted into laughter, all except for one.

Batboy sat in the corner near his desk and watched his friends' revelry. He had a curious look on his face, as if he were realizing that these were his friends, but they seemed so distant now, like people he didn't know.

One of the group looked at him and, frowning, asked, "What's up with you man? You look white as a sheet. Come on, dude, man up! We scored a win for the home team tonight." The others joined in with shouts of approval as if it were a Friday night football game.

"What is the big deal? You jumped a couple of guys and beat 'em up. They didn't do nothin' to us, and they didn't even see it coming." Batboy was surprised at his own courage, because he usually was the quiet one in the group.

The boy who'd wielded the bat was called TJ by the gang, and he was quick to respond. "Hey, back up. dude! What's all this *you* crap? Don't you mean *we*? You were there, and it was your bat; you even brought it, man—or should I say 'Batman'?"

The other boys, Jake and Spud, laughed, and then Spud said, "Don't you mean *batboy*? He ain't lookin' like no man to me." The room burst into laughter again as the boys began to chant "Batboy, batboy," over and over.

Suddenly the door opened, and Leon stepped in. "What's up with the noise? I could hear you guys from outside, hollerin' and laughin'. Who's Batboy?" The laughter began to subside as all eyes turned toward the corner. Leon didn't pay attention to the batboy question as things got quiet in the room, and he turned his attention to the group. "So, how'd it go, guys?" he asked with the same playful tone in his voice that the others had used moments before. The room erupted in the sound of voices as each boy tried to tell his version of the assault, each one shouting louder to drown out the competing voices. Batboy just sat there looking at his friends and silently shaking his head. What had he gotten himself involved with this day?

A few moments later the door opened. Batboy's mom knocked once and stepped in, as she normally did before entering. "What is all this ruckus, boys? I can hear you all the way in the kitchen. Who got hit with a bat?"

"Oh, it wasn't a who; it was a *what*, ma'am. We were practicing ball earlier, and your Julian there tagged one over the fence, and we may have found a future star!" Leon was all smiles as he looked around for approval and support from the others. The boys all mumbled their agreement with their perfect southern gentlemen's accents and appropriate "yes, ma'ams."

"Is that so? Well, your dad will be so proud of you." Julian's mom was completely taken in by the story, and Julian just gave her a half smile as she backed out of the room and closed the door behind her.

Leon turned and looked at Batboy. "That's right, 'Batboy'—you hit a home run today, and that better be all you tell them got hit today, you understand? You're in this up to your elbows, man. You brought the weapon, and you may have even been the one who used it, if anybody finds out it was you guys. It's our word against yours, and just remember that." The others understood what Leon was talking about, and they began to see the weakness in Batboy. The idea of being caught now entered their minds in place of celebrating a job well done. Batboy might be the weak link in their alibi. They would tell everyone that they had left the store to go practice ball at the park and had been nowhere near the battlefield when the attack took place. This was their pact, and only one person had the potential to ruin it for them.

"Time to ride, guys. Y'all must be tired from all that batting practice." Leon laughed as Spud, TJ, and Jake made their way to the door, each one looking back at Batboy as if to say, "Remember to keep to the story." Julian sat there in silence for a few moments, thinking of what had just happened. A sick feeling began to rise in his stomach. Guilt and fear can make for a terrible taste in the mouth. He replayed the attack over and over in his head and kept thinking of all the things he could have done. Why had he taken his bat with him? Why had he even been there in the first place? He didn't care about that battlefield or the people there; he'd just wanted to hang out with his friends. Some friends! That group of angry, threatening strangers who had just left his house didn't seem so friendly anymore, and he began to question his desire to even know them, let alone call them friends. The sun was setting, and the light was fading in his room, but he was in no hurry to turn on the lights. He just wanted to close his eyes and try not to see that boy falling to the ground. Then, for some reason, he sat up and looked over his shoulder, recalling the person he thought he had seen. A cold fear gripped him as he thought about the guy in the green coat. What if it had been someone who had seen the whole thing and could identify them? Where had he gone, and who was he? No one else had seen him, but Julian was sure he had seen a guy standing there, if only for a split second. Now his dread over the event was replaced with the fear of being found out.

Later that evening, when Julian's' dad came home and heard about the big hit at practice, he went right up to Julian's room to congratulate his son and hear all about it. Julian sat up and began to create a story about a hit that hadn't happened. With each detail, his father was more and more excited. He had never thought his son would be knocking them out if the park like that. He could hardly wait for the next day, when the two could go back out and he could see his son's new batting power firsthand. At that, his son began to rearrange the details of the story and add a strong wind that may have helped the ball out of the park. He doubted he would ever be able to hit another one like that. His father just passed it off as modesty.

Now a new pressure and problem arose; he would have to replicate something that had not really occurred. He had never come close to hitting the ball out of the park! As a matter of fact, he was the weakest hitter of all the boys who played together. This was the weak brick that could bring their wall of lies tumbling down. When his dad left, he got on the phone to Leon to report what had happened and get some advice. Leon just laughed, but then he began to take it more seriously when he realized that it was his lie, and he had placed himself at the ballpark with the boys and witnessed the hit. He told Batboy to fake an illness or pretend to sprain his wrist to buy some time before going out to the ball field. It would give Leon some time to think. He would need more lies to cover these lies; this could get complicated.

Scene 28

The investigation begins

Early the next morning, Sheriff Croften met with Riley as he laid out his plan of investigation and questions. They spoke of possible suspects and what they would be charging the assailants with once they were arrested. They just hoped it wouldn't be murder, but Topper was still unconscious in ICU. Riley told him he had gone by the store and gotten the names of the boys that had been there. The clerk had told him he didn't know where they had gone but that Leon had stayed behind. Sheriff Croften said to talk with Leon anyway. Riley closed his notebook and walked out of the room, heading for his cruiser. All he could think about was how stupid and pointless this was.

Out near the battlefield, another meeting was beginning. Leon had just pulled up to Arthur Kirtland's house and was walking up to the house, full of pride.

"What brings you out this way, Leon?" Arthur said, smiling at the young boy who he admired so much. In many ways Leon made him think of himself at that age—or how he envisioned he'd been at that age. Leon was tall and strong, with a firm jaw and handsome features; he was as all-American as apple pie.

Leon grinned and said, "Nothin' much, Mr. Kirtland. I just wanted see if you had heard what happened yesterday at the battlefield."

"No, can't say I have, Leon. I hope them folks have packed up and gone."

"Well, I don't know if they're gone, but I bet they're thinking hard about it today, after what happened to that one fella." Leon was fighting his desire to burst out with a confession of his plan and how it had worked.

"What happened, Leon? One of them get snake bit or something?'"

"No, Mr. Kirtland, nothin' like that. It seems that somebody got in a fight with a couple of the college kids and put one in the hospital." Leon paused to gauge Arthur s reaction but couldn't restrain his enthusiasm.

"I guess that'll teach 'em to mess around here!" Leon let a small laugh slip past his smirking lips.

There was a brief pause as Leon looked at the face of his imagined old mentor, but the reaction was not what he had anticipated. Instead he saw a look of curiosity, coupled with an odd frown. "What is it, Mr. Kirtland? Of all the folks around, I figured you would be happy to hear that these smart alecks got what they deserved."

Arthur was still processing the thoughts, but he could tell that Leon was expecting some sort of pat on the back. "Leon, I don't know what to say. I told them folks that they shouldn't be around here, but I didn't mean for anybody to get hurt." Arthur paused to choose his words but finally blurted out, "You didn't have anything to do with this, did you, boy?"

Leon was surprised by the response but was quick to go into defensive mode. "No way, sir; I just heard about it today. I agree with you that it's bad, but they really brought it on themselves, don't ya think?"

Arthur sat there for a moment and tried to take in all this new information. Then a scowl crossed his brow like an earth tremor, as he began to consider his role in the protest. He had appeared to be a community leader against the team, and that could make him a suspect in any actions taken toward the group. He would need to prepare a story in the event anyone came to ask him any questions. His mind was racing, and he forgot that Leon was sitting on the porch beside him. Then, as if he were reading through a script and had come to his lines, he looked up at Leon and stared into the boy's eyes. "Leon, why did you come out here to tell me this today?"

Leon was caught off guard by the question and was confused about any possible implications. It was time to choose his words carefully again. "Well, I just thought that you and me were sort of on the same wavelength about this whole battlefield thing, and I really respect your opinion and stuff, and the way you've handled these folks the other day was really cool." The flattery was flowing, and for a moment it seemed to be working.

Arthur was quick to burst his bubble. "I appreciate your admiration,

Leon, but I think you came out here today to brag about what you had done. You had something to do with this attack, didn't ya, boy?"

"No way, sir, I was nowhere near that house. I was at the store the whole time, and then I went out to the ball field with the other guys who were practicing." Leon blurted out his memorized speech.

"That was really good Leon; it hardly seemed rehearsed. But when you mention that part about being at the store the whole time, just how did you know what time the attack took place, and why did you stay at the store during the attack instead of going to the ball field with your friends?"

Leon just sat there with a curious look on his face. He started to speak, but Arthur waved him to be silent. "Don't say anything, Leon. That's just some of the stuff you're gonna hear when the police get a hold of you guys. You know that you're the first ones they'll come to, and besides, you said that a couple of boys were beat up but only one is in the hospital. That means that one is out there telling the police who jumped 'em; that boy can recognize you guys. If I were you, I'd be trying to find someone else to blame. Juvenile hall ain't no fun, from what I hear. What got into you kids, anyway? There was no reason to go and do a thing like this. Them folks were leaving in the next couple of days. We won, son. It's over."

Leon stood there in stunned silence; all his plans and emotions now seemed pointless. He had acted in a way that he'd thought would please all the locals. From all they had said, that had seemed to be what they wanted. But now he saw that all he had accomplished was to possibly get himself in trouble. That comment about juvenile hall had come like a slap in the face. It had just been a fight, not a crime. Suddenly the idea of a boy lying comatose in the hospital took on a new reality. Why had they hit him with that bat? What had they been thinking? They hadn't planned to try and kill somebody. Leon looked up at Arthur Kirtland and mumbled good-bye; then he went back and started to his car. He needed to make a new plan. The threat of going to jail was looming large in his head. He would get the boys together, talk it over, and try to figure out what to do. Mr. Kirtland was right about being identified.

That other boy might not know their names, but he could remember faces and where they had been seen. It wouldn't take long to connect the dots that led right back to his friends, and they led to him, especially the one who seemed a little shaky already. He got on his cell phone and started calling the guys to meet at the ball field right away.

Arthur Kirtland watched as Leon drove away. He shook his head. These kids today were going to mess up everything. As Arthur stood there watching the car disappear down the drive, his houseguest stepped out onto the porch behind him. It was John Criton, sipping a cup of tea. He had been in the parlor with the window open, so he had heard the conversation, but he tried to pretend that he had just walked out from the back of the house. He said nothing as he walked to the edge of the porch.

"Well, sleepyhead, I see you're awake," Kirtland said.

"Yes, Arthur, I have been up for a while. What do you have planned for the day? I would sort of like to visit the gravesite again." Criton spoke in a soft, effeminate voice.

"Really—what for? The folks will be leaving today or tomorrow—or at least I hope they will. I'm not so sure now." Criton's voice faded away as if he were talking to himself.

Criton knew what he was talking about, but he wanted to see how much Kirtland would tell him. "Why would they not be leaving, Arthur?"

"Oh, no reason I guess. They have a lot of packing and stuff." There was a pause. Arthur looked up at Criton and said, "I guess you'll be leaving soon, now that the hoopla has settled down?"

"I don't really know just yet, Arthur. I received some very odd thoughts at the gravesite, and I would like to go back and see if I can discern what the spirits are saying." Criton was looking off toward the highway as he spoke and did not notice the look that Arthur had on his face. It was a mixture of disdain and disbelief.

Bringing John Criton in had not had the effect Arthur had anticipated in his battle against the college folks. There had been no press; the celebrity had not really drawn the attention he had hoped for. Now he was stuck with this weird-acting houseguest. To top it all off, he was beginning to think that Criton might be gay, and that was something he could not tolerate or accept. He was worried what his friends would say, so he had tried to keep this houseguest and his friends as far apart from one another as possible. The whole Buford battleground affair had gotten bothersome, and nothing had seemed to work out the way he'd planned. Now, with that bunch of hotheads beating up those boys, things were looking even worse. Arthur wanted to disassociate himself from the battleground, but now he had this weirdo wanting to start his own investigation. He would have to put his foot down and get this guy out of his house.

He had been standing there in silence, just thinking. When he looked up as if waking from a nap, he spoke with his gruffest voice. "I'm not sure going to the battleground today, or for a while, would be such a good idea, not with them folks packing up and moving and all. I don't want to seem inhospitable, but I really can't see any reason for you to waste any more of your time in this little old place. I'm sure you've got a lot of things going on." He forced a smile and a hint at laughter.

The not-so-subtle hint was not lost on Criton, but he chose to ignore it. He was deep in thought about the battleground and the sensation he had felt there. But now he must deal with the matter at hand. "I have appreciated your warm hospitality, Arthur, and I do not wish to impose on you any longer, but I do wish to do a little more study at the battlefield. I have checked in to some living arrangements nearby. I will be leaving soon."

While this was welcome news to Arthur, it was not entirely what he had hoped for. He wanted to clear the area of all things that could possibly connect him to the battleground. He had a bad feeling about what might happen if that young boy didn't pull through. "Well, I hate to see you go, but I knew that you were a busy man. I still don't see what could be so important about that old battleground over there, however." Arthur was grinning but feeling some trepidation. He knew that he was contradictory in his attitude about the battleground. The thought of Criton leaving was good, but the fact that he wasn't going very far was troubling.

Criton just smiled at Arthur as he walked past him back into the house and up to his room. He nodded and spoke to Bea as he passed her in the hall. She made her way onto the porch and smiled at her husband.

"Would you like some coffee, sugar-bugger?" She wrinkled her nose as she spoke.

Arthur did not smile; he just grunted a negative response and stepped down off the porch. He did not wish to spend any more time than he had to with his wife. She was getting more and more annoying.

"Well, if you don't want anything, I'm gonna ride into town and go by the battlefield to see if the preacher is there again. I may stop by the Paxtons' to see about our next yoga thingy. Do you want anything from town?" She was still talking as Arthur moved around the side of the house. She was getting used to being ignored; she just smiled and turned back to the house.

Rounding the house, Arthur was trying to come up with some plan to distance himself from the events of the past few days. He stopped and thought about what Bea had said. Why distance himself, when a distraction would work just as well? All he had to do was redirect people's thoughts away from the battlefield. There was another problem looming on his horizon that might be more serious than some dead bodies. This involved some very real, living bodies.

Riley was leaving the store; he wanted to visit the homes of the boys that the storekeeper had told him were there on the night of the attack. He was surprised to find that Leon had been in the store the whole time. Riley thought for sure that he would have been in on something like this. The other names on his list were not a surprise—all except Julian. He was not the type to be involved in a fight. Riley thought he would save him for last, to see what the other boys had to say. He rode around the neighborhood until he had met with all the boys except Leon and Julian. It was remarkable how similar Spud, Jake, and TJ's stories had been. Right now it was getting late, and he thought he would catch the other two the next day or maybe even on Monday, just to let 'em sweat a little.

Meanwhile, Leon was busy making his own calls, and it was just luck that he had not met Riley at one of the houses. He had spoken with everyone except Julian, and he was now pulling up at Julian's house again.

"Good evening, ma'am. Is Julian here?" Leon was sweet as sugar as he met Julian's mom at the door.

"Sure, Leon, He's back in his room. I don't think he's left since you were here before." She had a faint tone of concern in her voice.

Leon made his way through the house and back to Julian's room. He found the boy sitting there with partially swollen eyes; it was obvious he had been crying. "Dude, what is up with you? You can't sit around cryin' all the time. Someone's gonna want to know what's going on, and what are you gonna tell em? Look, Julian, you gotta' get it together, man, or you're gonna find yourself in Columbia with a sore butt, cause them guys in juvie don't kid around. You're either doing or getting done, so suck it up."

Julian held his head up for a moment and seemed to acknowledge Leon's comments as he envisioned the horrors of juvenile hall in Columbia. How had it come to this? Was he going to go to jail? He had only been there. He hadn't done anything, and now he was in the same trouble as the others. To top it all off, he had to find some way to lie to his dad.

"Spud, TJ, and Jake have already talked to the law, and you're probably next, so get it together." Leon's voice broke Julian's concentration. Leon waited for a response, but Julian just sat there, until Leon leaned back, grunted a noise, and walked out of the room. Julian began to think about what Leon had said. He envisioned the horrors of going to jail and what could happen there. Then he thought again of that boy falling, and he wondered if perhaps he didn't deserve to suffer. That boy had done nothing to deserve what had happened to him. Julian began to realize that he was more like those boys than he was his so-called friends. He kept thinking about his life and what would happen now; he had been a part of something that could change his life forever. Before the other day he'd been filled with thoughts of school, and the teachers, and classes he had. Now all he could see was shame and embarrassment for his family and the possibility of being brutalized in some detention facility. He had thought about being on the marching band or trying to run track in the spring, anything to make his parents proud. But now, what would they have to be proud of—a "batboy" with a criminal record? It was getting late, and the deputy hadn't come by, so maybe it would wait until Monday. Tomorrow was Saturday. On Sunday he would go to church and pray like never before.

Reverend Strong was making his rounds as well. He'd gone by the store and spoken with Lester, the store clerk. Lester had told him plenty and informed him that he had told the deputy the same stuff. He had no proof, but he felt that Leon had had a hand in the whole affair. As Reverend Strong left the store, he turned toward the battlefield, where he saw the group packing up. He decided to pull in and bid farewell to the kids whom he had come to know and enjoy. He saw the truck had been loaded and most of the tents were down, except for Sandy's and Alan's and those of a couple of grad students. He was going toward Alan's tent when he saw him coming from the field pit area where they had been digging for artifacts. As he waved his hand, Alan smiled and walked more quickly toward where Reverend Strong stood.

"What's up, Bruce? What brings you out this way?" Alan was in a better mood than Bruce had expected; he barked a couple of commands at the kids as he walked past.

"Oh, I wanted see how things were going with you folks. I knew you would be leaving sometime his weekend."

"Yeah, the kids are pulling out in an hour or so. Their parents will meet them in Columbia. The next session starts soon, so they won't have much down time. I think I'll hang here and put the last touches on this site and clean up a little." Alan looked back toward his tent. Reverend Strong turned and looked around the campground. "And what about our friend there, is she leaving today?"

They both looked toward Sandy's tent, and Alan said, "I'm not sure what she plans to do, but I guess we could ask her." Alan smiled, and he and Bruce walked toward her tent. "Hello in there, anybody home?" he called.

"No, I'm not here. This is a recording. Leave a message at the beep.

Be-e-e-p." The flap swished back, and Sandy poked her head out of the tent. "Oh, my goodness! It's missionaries or something, come to tell me about their church! I gave at the office, guys." After a hint of laughter and a smile from the guys, she asked, "To what do I owe the honor of this visit, gents?"

Bruce looked to Alan to speak, but he said nothing; he stood there smiling at Sandy and looking at the ground like a shy schoolboy. Then he spoke up. "We were just wondering what you were going to be doing, now that the camp is breaking down and we are moving on. Have you got any plans?"

Sandy stepped out of her tent and stood tall, stretching as if she had been asleep. "Well, I guess I'll be heading for home sometime this week. I hadn't really thought about it much till just now. But I guess you're right; I can't stay here. Are you all going to be gone today?"

"No. I'll be hanging around till Monday morning," Alan advised her. "I've got a few things to do, and I sort of wanted to wait and see what was going to happen with Topper. His parents said that they wanted to take him to their doctor and hospital in Columbia, and the doctor here said that he could probably be moved by the first of the week, even if he didn't snap out of this coma thing." Alan's voice began to trail off as he looked toward the ground.

The three stood there silently for a moment, thinking about Topper. The silence was broken by Bruce as he glanced up at the two. "Hey, guys, I've got a radical idea. Why don't you two stay with me at the parsonage? I've got a three-bedroom, two-bath house all to myself, and it's completely furnished. It seems a shame to sleep on the ground when there's a perfectly comfortable bed standing empty nearby."

The two looked at the preacher and then at each other. Alan was first to say that it sounded great to him. Sandy was a little hesitant. "Aren't you afraid of what your parishioners will say?"

"I don't think it will be a problem. I housed two boys and two girls last year when a college choir came through and sang a concert at the church. What's the difference?" Reverend Strong said with a convincing tone.

Sandy looked at Bruce and then at Alan. "Well, if you did it last year, I guess it would be all right. The thought of a nice hot shower instead of that camp shower and toilet sounds scrumptious. I'm in, fellas, and I call dibs on the bathroom!"

"Great. I'll tidy up a little and cook you guys one of my special bachelor dinners. You can come by any time after you break camp; I'll be waiting." Reverend Strong was excited about having guests in his home. It had been lonely living in that big, empty parsonage; having visitors would be a fun distraction.

After a big spaghetti dinner, they spent the evening sitting around the table, talking about the summer and the events of the past few days. Alan and Sandy were both impressed with Bruce's skill in the kitchen, but all three knew that spaghetti was the universal meal for single people to serve. Sandy offered to cook an authentic Indian meal for the Saturday night supper, and Bruce and Alan were quick to agree. After they'd eaten, they had coffee in the den, and then Sandy headed for that long soak in the tub she had been wanting. Alan and Bruce settled in for a night of that guilty pleasure called TV.

Riley Jackson was making his way home when he saw Leon pull into the gas station near his house. He thought that he might as well ask him a question or two. Of course, Leon had known nothing of the events and was saddened to hear that one of the boys had been hurt. Riley mentioned that the other boy might be able to ID the attackers, and after a brief conversation at the pumps, Leon told him that he was sort of in a hurry to get home, and so Riley let him go. His story was neat and supported what the others had said. He had been at the store, and when some of his friends had gone to play ball, he had hung around the store and then gone by the ball field on the way home—and that was it, all neat and tidy. Riley didn't mention that Cedric had told him that he had seen his attackers at the store before he and Topper had started back to the camp. So, if these boys that Leon had said were at the ball field had actually been beating up Topper and Cedric, then Leon was covering for them. That meant he knew what was going on, and that made him a part of this little drama. One more boy to talk to, and that would wrap this up. All that would be left was to find out who actually put Topper in the coma. He hoped Leon hadn't caught his slip of the lip and realize that he had talked with Cedric when he'd mentioned that one of the boys had been hit by a baseball bat.

Leon went straight home and got on the phone to Julian. He told Julian that he and the others had talked with the deputy, and they had all told the same story. It was up to him to stick to the alibi. Julian was slow to answer as he listened. There was a kind of numbness over his body and brain. The pause agitated Leon, who then added that Riley had said that whoever had done this was in big trouble, especially the one who had hit Topper with a bat—and all the others would be willing to tell Deputy Jackson that it was Julian who had brought the bat. Obviously, Leon hadn't realized that Riley knew about the bat and that meant he probably could ID the boys who had been involved.

As he hung the phone up, a new wave of fear gripped Julian when he imagined his so-called friends turning on him and placing the brunt of the blame on him. Julian thought of the bat and ran out to the garage where he had left it when they'd come back. He picked it up and looked for signs of blood or hair; he remembered watching a cop show on TV where they were able to find micro clues on everything and see blood under black lights or something like that. He rushed the bat into the backyard and started scrubbing it with a hose and brush, trying to get all the grass stains and scuff marks off.

"Hey, pal, what'cha doin'—cleanin' her up for another big blast? I used to do the same thing when I was hittin' good. Take care of your equipment, and it will serve you well." It was his dad coming home from work. "Ya wanna go blast a few in the morning?"

Julian held up his hand, wrapped sloppily in an Ace bandage. "I don't know, Dad; I think I sprained my wrist this afternoon."

"Sprained your wrist? What in the world were you doin' to do that, son?"

"Uh, I was just, uh ..." Julian froze; he couldn't remember what he was supposed to say. He turned away from his dad and mumbled something, but fortunately his dad was already turning to go into the house. Julian breathed a sigh of relief, but then realized that he couldn't lie very convincingly to his dad—or anyone else, for that matter. What would he do when the deputy started grilling him? He jumped a little when he heard his dad calling in to his mom, asking what had happened to Julian's wrist, and then hearing her say she didn't know it was hurt. That meant that he would have to explain everything at dinner. He finished scrubbing the bat and then tried to get his story straight about how he had hurt his wrist.

After dinner, his mom wrapped his wrist in an ice pack, and he sat in the den in silence as the family watched TV together. Julian alternated watching the television and the driveway to see if the sheriff was driving up. Finally, about nine o'clock, he relaxed a little. It was probably too late for the deputy to show up. That meant that he had until Monday to work on his alibi. He made his way to bed about nine thirty and sat there in bed, thinking about his options. The room seemed heavy with a feeling of doom. It was fear taking over his mind and his body, and he felt sick to his stomach. Images of Topper falling, Leon yelling at him, and then the inside of a jail cell rushed through his head. He shoved in his earphones and cranked his MP3 player up to drown out the thoughts, but the fear wouldn't go away. A tear began to slide off the side of his head into his hairline, and soon emotional fatigue weighed him down to exhaustion. Somewhere in his swirling thoughts, he slipped into the haven of sleep.

Scene 29

Mysteries

Saturday morning at the local hotel found John Criton sitting in a chair, looking at the blandly decorated room. It reminded him of his younger days of poverty and being alone and unknown. He had called his secretary and canceled most of his upcoming appointments and taping schedule. When the assistant had asked why, Criton had explained that he was involved in a very important project near Lancaster, South

Carolina, but he should tell no one where he would be for the next few days. Criton had been up all night, staring at the walls and trying to focus his thoughts, but nothing would come to him. He had not wanted to tell anyone, but he had not heard voices or felt the presence of Murmus since that day at the battleground. For the first time in his life, he felt truly alone. What had happened to him out there? He closed his eyes and continued to call upon Murmus, but his friend would not answer—and now all those voices that had controlled his life were missing. Criton was sinking into despair.

Outside of town, at the parsonage, Bruce Strong was mixing up his morning coffee as he looked out the window at the field behind his house. He and Alan were planning on going up to the hospital to check on Topper in a while, and Sandy had said she would stop by on her way to the store. He was trying to be quiet, when he realized that Alan and Sandy were sitting in the dining room, reading over notebooks. They were deep in thought when he asked if anyone wanted coffee. Both grunted yeses, and he started pouring two more cups. In a moment, he was sitting across from two people lost in thought; he wasn't sure whether he should interrupt.

"Cream and sugar, anyone?"

"Uh? Oh yes, please, extra cream for me," Sandy said.

"I'll skip the cream and add a little more sugar." Alan reached over for the cup, and there was a clamor for condiments and spoons. Alan looked different, and Bruce realized that it was the first time he had seen him out of his unofficial uniform of khaki pants and shirt, with a tan broad-brimmed fedora somewhere near. Oh, and there was also the worn leather bomber jacket that he wore even on the hot days. He definitely had an Indiana Jones complex, which Bruce had just shrugged off with a smile.

"So, what's so interesting? How long have you two been up?"

Alan looked down at his notes and then back at Sandy as if to say, "Me first or you?" Sandy nodded at Alan to go ahead, so he began. "I got up early this morning and started going over some notes, and then I started thinking about those notes you were getting in church, and it made me think of something I'd read in one of the diaries. I would show you, but oddly enough, the things I was thinking about were in the very notes that were stolen from me at the campsite. But I can tell you what was in it and some of the other resources I have read. I took your notes and started thinking about what they were saying. I realized that they could be threats, but from what I have read, they could also be descriptions of things that have already happened."

Sandy shifted in her seat and sipped her coffee, but Bruce was frozen in a look of confusion. He smiled a little and looked at Sandy, wondering what she thought of all this. Sandy smiled and said, "Just listen, and keep your mind open."

Alan continued, "I told you that I thought a lot of the stuff we have been experiencing was just some copycat historian playing pranks, but I kept thinking that it would take someone with an extensive background in history to make these connections. Do you have anybody in this area who was a history major or local history buff?"

"Not that I know of, Alan. I'm sure that some of the folks are familiar with local history, but I can't think of anyone who would do this."

Alan glanced over at Sandy and said, "Well, actually, I can think of someone, but I don't know if he's that smart." Everyone at the table gave a chuckle, because they knew he was thinking of Arthur Kirtland.

"I know that he's been a thorn in your side, Alan, but you gotta' believe me that before you came he really was just a nice old man sittin' on his porch most of the time. I don't know what has come over him." Even as Bruce was speaking, he was questioning himself and his opinion of Arthur Kirtland. Maybe he didn't really know this man at all; he had never really talked with him at length. Alan was forcing him to rethink his relationship with a church member. Bruce Looked up at Alan and said, "Okay, maybe he's behind some of this, but I don't get the connection with your notes."

"That may be where I come in, Bruce, Alan has made a historical connection with activity, and I am wondering if there could be a paranormal connection." Sandy had that serious tone in her voice, and Bruce knew that these two were not kidding around. "I think that we should combine Alan's historical evidence with what we know about the area and that incident with Topper and Cedric at camp the other night. Remember when they said that they saw a person in a dark-green coat, with a hat, and then they saw this same figure but smaller?"

"Whoa, maybe you better back up a little and let Alan tell me about the notes and what this historical connection is." Bruce was feeling the hair on his neck start to rise.

Alan went into the kitchen, refreshed his cup of coffee, and offered some to the others. "Here ya go, guys. You might need a little boost. The connection starts with our infamous Colonel Banastre Tarleton, one of the commanders of the British forces in this area. We know him for his exploits here at Buford and around the Camden area. He was attached to General Cornwallis, but from what we can tell, he did a lot of missions on his own initiative. He was definitely looking for recognition. He had fought against Washington in New England and came south when Cornwallis came to Charleston. Tarleton was a young man and eager to make a name for himself. When the British arrived in Charleston, he led a small cavalry detachment that destroyed the Continental supply line and hastened the fall of Charleston. As a reward, he was allowed to scour the coast road to forage for supplies. He proceeded to burn and pillage all along the coast. His knowledge of the area was probably the reason he was sent after Buford.

"Tarleton already had a reputation as one of the most hated British soldiers in the colonies. His brutal ways may have infected his officers as well, and that is where we get some interesting similarities with your church notes. The notes that were stolen from me spoke of an incident that involved the Wyly family. Samuel Wyly was a young Quaker boy from near Camden who had fought at the battle of Charleston. He was captured and paroled, and by the rules of war, he was to return home and fight no more against the British troops. Two days after the massacre at Buford, Tarleton came back through Camden, where Wyly was living up to his parole. When Tarleton came through looking for rebels, someone, possibly a local loyalist, gave them Wyly's name, or they gave the name of his brother, John Wyly. John Wyly was a local sheriff who had presided over the hanging of some Tories and, it would seem, more likely a target for Tarleton's' rage. Tarleton dispatched a detail to the Wyly farm to get John, but they found Samuel Wyly instead. The leader of the detail was a Captain Christopher Huck or Tuck; some records even say his name was Hutt. Hutt arrived and stationed two men to hide out by a fence post, and then he went in to arrest Wyly. Young Samuel presented him with his parole, but the captain rejected it and told him he was under arrest. Samuel resisted, and in a scuffle, the captain struck Sam Wyly in the head with his saber. Wyly tried to block the blow with his hand, but this cost him several fingers, and the blow went on to split his head open. Severely wounded and dazed, Wyly managed to run out toward the gate, where he was met by the hidden dragoons, who impaled him on their bayonets. Later, Wylys' body was drawn and quartered and set up on stakes along the road as a warning to others.

"Now, consider the notes you received in church, which said things like, 'Bust his head'; 'Cut 'em off'; 'Pieces'; and 'Gut him like a fish'—all of which sound like the work of Tarleton, or his officer Tuck, Huck, or Hutt, whatever his name." This may be a coincidence, but it seems like too many similarities to me."

"I'm sorry, Alan, but I don't see the connection. Exactly what we are connecting?" Bruce was beginning to understand, but he wanted to see where these two were going to take it.

Sandy spoke up. "Maybe I can be of some help to explain the hypothesis that Alan is suggesting. We have a couple of options here. One is that we have a historical copycat who is trying to reference the Wyly incident, and maybe even reenact it to some extent, especially considering the attack on Topper and Cedric the other day. Secondly, we may have some type of paranormal connection with a particularly vicious poltergeist that is trying to reveal itself to us. I say that because of Topper's description of what he saw that night. It was a figure in a long, green coat and a broad-brimmed hat. That could be a description of a member of the Tory light infantry that Tarleton commanded. If so, then we can connect the notes with a member of Tarleton's cavalry, and we see the potential for affixing an identity to this poltergeist. If that is the case, we could have a genuinely interesting phenomenon."

Bruce looked up at Sandy and back at Alan. "Sandy could this have anything to do with your research project?"

"Honestly, Bruce, I'm not sure yet, but I have given that some consideration. My father found something at that barn, and I have reason to think that there may be some sort of connection there as well."

"Well, in that case," Bruce paused a moment and took a deep breath, "there is one more bit of info to add to your list of evidence or coincidences. The deputy told me this, and I think he meant it to be confidential, because I never heard any talk of it. It makes the connection with the Paxton's' barn even stronger than either of you could be aware. The former residents of that place had a little girl who was attacked by her father in that barn. He was later found in North Carolina, dead from an overdose, with the family dog in the trunk, drawn and quartered. That gets you the drawn-and-quartered aspect from the Captain Huck story. But more directly, the deputy gave me a little detail that he had been mulling around in his head, because he didn't know what to do with it. It's like it was part of a puzzle, but he said he couldn't find the puzzle to put it in, but now, today, you two may have given a place to put that piece. You see, it seems that the mother of the little girl who was attacked told Deputy Jackson that on the night of the attack, when she found her daughter in the barn, she thought she saw someone in the corner—a thin man wearing a long, green coat and a broad-brimmed hat."

The three of them sat there silent for a moment, frozen in time. "I must tell you that I don't know what to do with this. I am more comfortable with blaming the whole thing on Arthur Kirtland than on some ghost of the Revolutionary War." Alan's voice broke the silence. "Suppose we do attribute this to the supernatural, who we gonna call—Sandy? She's the ghostbuster. I just don't know if I can tell the deputy that we are ready to blame this on a ghost."

Bruce sipped his coffee, swallowed hard, and then said, "Sandy gave us a couple of options, but she left out my preferred explanation." After another sip of coffee and a long pause, Bruce looked at Sandy. "I do not believe in the spirits of the dead coming back to haunt us. I do believe in spirits, but not the kind we are talking about here."

Sandy fidgeted and looked at Bruce. "What are you talking about then, Bruce? You are a man of God who preaches about the Holy Spirit all the time, and now you're telling me you don't believe in spiritual beings?"

"That's not exactly what I said, Sandy. I don't believe in spirits of the dead coming back to haunt; I do believe in spirits. The spirits I believe in are spoken of in the scriptures. They are beings that are almost ageless, and they have been here since before the dawn of time. They are liars and deceivers who impersonate the dead so that the living will listen and allow them a place to experience life. They're called angels or better known as demons. I believe that if we are dealing with the supernatural here, it is not the ghost of some dead Tory; it is a demonic spirit trying to get us to think it is a ghost of a dead soldier."

"Wow, just when I was about to accept the idea that there were ghosts, you want to take me into hell or heaven?" Alan was scratching his head and shaking it from side to side. "Let's just blame Arthur and leave it at that. It works for me and makes a lot more sense."

Sandy was sitting there lost in thought as she tried to comprehend all that Bruce was saying. She was a scientist and was somewhat uncomfortable with the idea of a poltergeist, and now Bruce was taking her into the world of religion. This was a world that she had avoided for most of her life; it seemed this man wanted to erase her world and replace it with his. He was so sure of himself; such confidence was hard to stand against, let alone overcome. "So, are you proposing an exorcism, Reverend Strong, or just how does the Church rid itself of demons these days?" There was a cynical tone to her voice. She'd thought she was just beginning to understand and appreciate this man's way of thinking, when suddenly he'd done an about-face and jumped back into the Church for answers. Was he just another religious nut?

Bruce just sat there, while Alan said, "Well, I guess that leaves me out. It seems you two have this all figured out: it's either a ghost or a demon. Did someone forget the other option that is not nearly as glamorous as yours but far more plausible? It's a guy doing all this? Mix that in with a big bag of Doritos before bed, and you got the potential for folks to see all kinds of things. Let's just go see what Arthur's been up to for the past couple of weeks. I bet we could get the truth out of the old geezer."

"I don't want to ruin your lynching there, Alan, but think about it. Arthur is too old to have been running around in the middle of the night scaring kids or even beating them up. He is all talk and maybe a little behind-the-scene action, like bringing in that Criton guy to catch some publicity." Bruce was using his most calming tone to try and persuade the excited historian.

Sandy looked at the two and said, "Hey, whatever happened to that guy, anyway? He makes one appearance, and *poof*, he's gone."

"Yeah, he sure spooked Topper that night with all that 'this-is-how-we-move' crap. I'll show him a few moves! I wonder why Arthur even brought that guy in on this. He was like a dud firecracker, all fizzle and no bang."

"There was no bang because there was nothing to go bang about, and I think Arthur knows that now. We haven't seen or heard from him in a few days, have we?" Bruce pointed out.

"It's just as well; I don't want to see him. It's guys like that that are just odd enough to get people's attention. They think that because they are bored and still alive they can sit around thinking up ways to cause trouble. By the way, Sandy, what is the deal with these guys like Criton and that other one on TV? I can't remember his name. Are they just sideshow freaks, or do they have some real ability for communicating with the dead?"

Sandy was uncomfortable with the question. "I don't want to close my mind to any possibilities in my field, but I don't like the idea of opening the field to just anyone who has the ability to imagine an interesting scenario. I can say that there are some paranormal investigators who trust and use these psychic mediums during investigations, but I prefer exhausting all possible empirical avenues before considering any one that relies so much on conditions that could only be considered questionable at best. My father has worked with a lady who never talked about spirits or voices, but she did think that she could sense energy fields. She did not try to interpret words or emotions within the energy; she simply suggested that she could sense an area where the fields might exist. That is hard to prove but seems more feasible to me. However, some of these people have shown a high level of accuracy in certain investigations. I think most of this can be attributed to chance. It still creates a very uncomfortable area for investigators of the paranormal. It falls under the heading of unexplained phenomena. If it would make you feel better, we could talk to him. If nothing else, he would be interesting."

"That sounded like one of the most ringing endorsements of *maybe* I have ever heard!" Bruce spoke with a laugh. "I have the luxury of dealing with the supernatural realm on a daily basis. If you choose to consider yourself a person of faith, and without sounding too spooky, I think that the Critons of this world are people who suffer from a delusional form of possession from these demonic spirits."

Alan jumped at the chance to get into the conversation. "I thought possession was where a demon takes over a person and makes them do all sorts of weird stuff, like in the movies."

Sandy rolled her eyes and said, "Well, as with psychics and mediums, I am rather skeptical on the subject of possession, as well."

"I'm afraid I don't have that luxury, Sandy. My faith is based primarily on the acceptance of a relationship with a spirit being that communicates most often through the written word, the Bible. So, whatever is in the Bible I take seriously and seek to understand, explain, and interpret in a relevant manner for the day. I must do this in a hermeneutical context, which I don't think everyone in my field always does, but I cannot simply ignore something because it causes me a cultural problem. You guys opened this supernatural doorway, and I can only step through based on what I believe. The Bible speaks of demons, and therefore I must account for them in some way. I have tried to pass them off as first-century neuroses, but that just doesn't fit with everything. That, coupled with human behavior today, leaves me more and more convinced that there is a real presence of evil—that presence can be, and often is, personified in the form of the demonic."

"Well, touché, Reverend Strong. If I gave a ringing endorsement of *maybe*, you have just given a masterful endorsement for the existence of demons, and I am sure that if any of them are listening at this very moment, they are very pleased." Sandy gave a warm smile, and Bruce responded with the same, while Alan eyed the two of them.

Bruce finally grinned and said, "Ya know, if we blame Arthur, we can cover all these topics in one person. He's a demon-possessed old fart. What do ya say?" The laughter circled the table like a wave running through the stands at a ball game. With that, the group seemed to breathe a collective sigh that signified it was time to take a break from thinking and get busy, before the day was gone. Sandy slid away from the table and headed for her room, while Bruce and Alan made plans for their trip to the hospital. Sandy would meet them there later. With that, the three were off.

At the hospital, Alan and Bruce spoke with Topper's family for a while. They found that he was still unconscious, but the doctor was very optimistic. The parents still wanted to take him to their own physician in Columbia, but at least they were in a better mood. Cedric's family had stayed until the morning, and even though Cedric wanted to stay with his friend, they convinced him to head for home. They could visit early in the week, perhaps, when he was stronger, and Topper was up and around. Sandy had arrived by that time, and when the three left the room, Bruce asked Alan to ride home with Sandy, because he had an errand he wanted to run. Alan was more than willing to do so. The two of them took off for the parsonage. Alan quipped that he could get used to the domestic life as he and Sandy headed for their temporary home.

Bruce wanted to make a side trip because he had been feeling a compelling desire to go out to the battlefield. It was so strong that he felt it was more than just a passing thought. Bruce had often attributed such feelings to the urging of God, and so he based his actions now on that possibility as he drove his car out to Buford.

When he arrived at the battlefield, he felt a sense of awe but not so much of surprise. There was a car sitting there, Criton's, just as Bruce had somehow expected. He knew then that this was one of those providential meetings that he had often experienced in his ministry. He only wished he knew what he was supposed to do at this meeting. Everyone always loved to quote the saying that the Lord works in mysterious ways, but he often found himself asking, would it hurt for the Lord to make things clear for the ones who were sharing in that work, just once in a while?

Bruce stepped out of his car and moved across the grass toward where he saw a man hunched over a table, looking deep in thought. Criton didn't seem to notice his approach until Bruce was very near, and then he only turned to acknowledge another presence. Bruce smiled and said, "Mr. Criton, I believe. We haven't really been introduced; I am Bruce Strong, Arthur Kirtland's pastor."

"Yes, Mr. Strong, I recall seeing you ... uh, well, actually it was here, I think, was it not?" Criton spoke with a hint of a smile, still trying to use his official voice, as if he were making a personal appearance on some talk show.

"Yes, I think it *was* here, as a matter of fact, Mr. Criton. I was just driving by and saw your car and thought I would stop and say hello." Bruce's comments were followed by a drawn-out pause as Criton just stared at the man.

"Yes, well. Hello, Mr. Strong, but something tells me that you stopped to say more than hello. Is there something I can help you with?" Criton spoke as if he were reading Bruce's mind, and Bruce wasn't sure how to respond.

"No, really, I was just ..." Bruce realized he was looking for something to say as a word of explanation, and nothing seemed to be coming to him. "Can I speak plainly, Mr. Criton, in a way that perhaps you can appreciate?"

"Certainly, Mr. Strong. I'd have it no other way. One human being to another, as it were." Criton's voice now took on a feminine nasality that surprised Bruce a bit, until he realized that Criton was dropping the pretense and speaking in his normal tone.

"I know that in your field you rely on intuition and a form of spiritual direction. Well, I rely on spiritual direction as well, and I'm here today because I felt directed to be here ..." Bruce slowed down, pausing to take a breath, and Criton interrupted.

"And just what did this spirit tell you is wrong with me that I would need a visit from you?" Criton spoke with a more serious tone.

"I didn't really say that I was told anything, Mr. Criton, and I am not sure if there is something wrong. I just felt that I should come, and here I am." Bruce was trying to be sensitive and not overly assertive, but now he felt that perhaps there *was* something wrong and that was why he was there. "I don't mean to seem rude, but if there is something you would like to talk about, I've been known to be a good listener."

Criton hesitated and fought back his discomfort, perhaps because he could realize that he had been one of the people who acted on spiritual urgings—until recently. Criton was at a loss for words. How could he know that this man's visit wasn't some part of the spirit's plan to reconnect with him? "So, what did your spirit tell you to say to me?"

"Well, it's not like I was given a message for you or even definite instructions. It was more of a sensation that perhaps you were here, and I could be of service to you in some way. I'm sorry to be vague, but that's how it works sometimes."

"My spiritual friend was a lot more precise in his instructions and relating information." Criton had an almost smugness to his voice.

"I have always been curious as to just how that worked, Mr. Criton. Do you like ... go into a trance or something?" Bruce was probing.

"No, no, nothing as boorish as that. I leave the trances for the charlatans and amateurs. I have a more directed line of communication through a spiritual liaison. He was sort of a traffic cop who directed the voices to me in an organized manner. There are so many people who have messages for loved ones. I am a bridge of communications between the dimensions, and as such I feel that I serve man in a sort of ministry, not unlike yourself."

"You said he *was* a traffic cop. Do you no longer use the spirit guide?" Bruce watched as Criton stiffened at the mention of his spirit guide in the past tense. "Did this spirit have a name, or was it a person who had lived recently? I don't mean to seem nosy, but I do find this subject sort of fascinating."

"I don't mind talking about it, but I'm not sure if you'll understand." Criton wanted to steer Bruce away from his mention of Murmus in the past tense. "Yes, my guide has a name. He was once known as Murmus, an ancient holy man and philosopher. He came to me when I was very young and first experiencing my gift. In the early days, there were so many voices that I could not understand all that was being said to me, but Murmus came and took a central role, siphoning all the voices and helping me to hear them one at time. Of course, you could have gotten all this information, and a little more, in my second book. I devoted an entire chapter to my personal history." Criton smiled at Bruce.

"Yes, perhaps I will check out your book. Did Murmus ever tell you when or where he lived before? You say ancient, I wonder just how ancient he was and how long he's been dead?"

"Actually, those who have passed on prefer to think of themselves as enjoying a new and better dimension of life rather than death. You, of all people, should understand the idea of the afterlife. They are merely in a state of continuance in a far better place."

Bruce thought for a moment and looked at Criton. "I do accept the concept of the afterlife, but I am not as clear as you are on what that life is, Mr. Criton. I always imagined heaven as being a wonderful experience, but I have never really felt that man could communicate with loved ones who had passed on. There is a story in the New Testament that mentions a great gulf between the two and that we should not try to cross that gulf or communicate with those who have gone on. But you and I both agree that it is a better dimension of life, so I wonder why they would trouble themselves with communication with this dimension." Bruce paused as he realized that he was doing more talking than listening.

"I think it has to do with the power of love, Mr. Strong, which is the most powerful force in any dimension. Love attempts to reach beyond all bounds, and I count it a type of blessing that I can be a part of that chain of love."

Criton's' voice began to trail off, and Bruce began to question his mood. Criton was talking about his ability with sadness and speaking of his friend Murmus in the past tense. Bruce felt he should push his probing questions a little further. "Mr. Criton, when the voices come to you, do you hear the individual voices now, or does Murmus relay their comments?"

"I use Murmus as a translator of the messages. You would not believe how many people have things they want to say; there are legions of people trying to communicate with their loved ones." Criton had spoken up with renewed energy, but Bruce was focused on the word *legions* that Criton used. Why had he used that term?

"Have they ever told you what it was like in heaven or where they are speaking to you from, Mr. Criton?"

"They have never really spoken of the place they are in. It's obviously not hell, but I think that it is more of a dimensional place. I felt that we were very close, as if we were sharing a space with them. Does that make any sense to you, Mr. Strong?"

"Yes, I think I understand what you're saying. It reminds me of something I read from a German theologian, I think it was Oscar Cullmann, who mentioned something like what you are saying. It's been a while since I read it. But do you still use Murmus as a conduit?"

At this Criton bristled. Bruce had brought the conversation back to the point that he was trying his best to avoid. How could he tell this man that he was no longer in communication with the spirit world? If word of this ever got out, he would be ruined. Criton felt sure that his ability would come back soon, and any mention of his current plight could destroy his credibility for the rest of his life. How could he avoid this question? The answer was simple; he would not answer this question, or he would simply lie. He looked at Bruce and smiled. "I'm afraid that the easiest way to answer that question would be to just say yes. However, the voice of Murmus is not like a light that one turns on or off; it does take some preparation." There, those were well chosen words, only involving a small bit of dishonesty laced with just enough tact and avoidance that perhaps this clever man would not notice.

"I understand, Mr. Criton, but you needn't work so hard to give answer. A simple 'none of your business' would have sufficed." Bruce smiled and nodded politely.

"You are either a very clever man or you possess some latent ability that you may not be aware of. Have you ever tried to communicate with the spirit realm? I sense a presence within you of great power." Criton was actually sensing nothing at the moment, but he remembered feeling something that first day at the battlefield. Now he was beginning to think that this man might have been the source. A bit of envy began to rise in his heart.

Well, if that's true, Mr. Criton, then I sense that you are not being completely forthcoming with me about something. However, I just want to say that should you have need of my services, or maybe just enjoy a good conversation, don't hesitate to call." Bruce knew that the seed had been sown, and whatever reason had brought him here to meet with this man had been fulfilled. Criton smiled, and Bruce turned to leave. Bruce took a few steps but then turned back. With a sincere smile, he invited Criton to come to church the next morning.

As Bruce left the area, he looked back in his mirror at Criton, who was still sitting on the bench, lost in thought. Meanwhile, Criton was turning to watch Bruce driving away. What was his role in this supernatural human drama being played out all around him? He had felt at peace talking to this man, and it was a peacefulness that he hadn't felt since Murmus had stopped communicating. Criton turned back toward the grave of the soldiers, just looking and listening. He sat there until the sun was going down, as if waiting for an old friend to come and call. He tried to think what to do, but the feeling of emptiness was a new sensation for him, and he didn't know where to turn for help. He had even considered a prayer, but the words were just stuck somewhere in his throat; he wasn't sure what to say. He wasn't even sure that God would listen if he tried to pray. As the sun silently fell behind the trees, Criton stood and stretched the stiffness from his knees. He hadn't eaten in a day or two, but the gnawing at his heart masked the gnawing in his belly. He drove toward the empty hotel room as the sun disappeared beyond Highway 9. Saturday night in a sleepy southern city meant everyone was either somewhere else having fun or sitting at home getting ready for Sunday morning.

At the parsonage, Reverend Bruce Strong had excused himself from his house guests to go over to his church office and look over his sermon for the following day. He also wanted to do a little research on the name that Criton had given him. Murmus sounded familiar, for some reason, but where would he start looking? After an hour or two of poring over books, he found it in what he thought was an unlikely place. It was in a list of names for angels. Initially this made him feel a little more at ease, but further research revealed a more disturbing tale. According to Jewish writings, Murmus was one of the fallen angels. Specifically, Murmus was the fallen angel who had led thirty legions of infernal spirits or lesser fallen angels—demons. He was often seen as a warrior riding a gryphon, with a dual crown on his head. He was a philosopher and held the spirits of dead prisoners.

Bruce leaned away from the text and began to think about the implications of Criton's description compared to what was written there. It could be just a coincidence that he'd used that name, or it could mean that Criton was in league with a demon—and not just any demon but a commanding demon. But if what he suspected was true, Criton was no longer in touch with Murmus. What could that mean? Was Murmus loose around the area, or had Criton just done some research and made the whole thing up? Bruce was being forced to ask himself some tough questions about his beliefs. He had always preached the Bible and believed it all, but that had been easy when he was teaching about the things of scripture. Now it was possible he was dealing with a real manifestation, and he wasn't sure if that was bothering him as much as the feeling that he was seeing it as reality. Had he become an armchair Christian who sat around talking all about the battle between good and evil but not really accepting it or being a real part of it? The darkness outside his window suddenly seemed almost pregnant with an ominous presence. Had evil come to the little community, or was it that it had it always been here and he had just chosen not to notice?

Scene 30

Sunday morning

Sunday morning came quietly. Outside people's homes the land was at rest, and a gentle breeze blew across the fields, moving the grass as if in slow motion. The fields looked like plush green velvet being brushed by an invisible hand. The scene was similar in many homes as folks sat at small tables sipping coffee and juice and reading the paper. Women were choosing Sunday dresses and trying to remember the last time they had been worn, hoping no one would remember. Some looked for hats or gloves, and when entire outfits had been chosen, they were laid out across beds, looking like lifeless skin waiting to be filled.

Sunday morning in a small community often centered on the local church service. Everyone attended church for various reasons. The teens came to see the other teens; boys and girls too young to date used church as the informal meeting ground, where they could usually get the Sunday schoolteacher distracted long enough to sit and tell tales of the previous Saturday night's excitement. The parents would congregate in classrooms based on their age, or age they would be willing to admit, and plan their social calendars. Occasionally they would get around to Bible study, but mostly it was a time to see their neighbors. For the ladies it was a time to discuss the problems of child-rearing, and for the men it was a time for shared stories of deer hunting and car building as they all planned class parties.

Then there were the senior adults, who gathered in two classes, one for the men and one for the women, while down the hall was a mixed group that refused to admit they were over sixty. They would often quip about how they would not move up to the senior class because the next stop after that class was the cemetery. So, there they sat, living the life of eternal middle age. Behind these closed doors of senior adults sat the informal power structure of the church, where all conversations were of a serious nature. Today's topic was very serious. In the men's class, the teacher was assigning passages for each person to read from their quarterly lesson book, when Arthur Kirtland spoke up.

"This may be the wrong time, fellas, but it's the only time that we can get together." All the men looked up at Arthur to hear what he had to say. "We got a real problem in our church, and I don't know what we should do about it."

"What's up, Arthur? I thought that now them folks was gone from the battlefield everything would be okay." It was the voice of Ralph Barnes, one of Arthur's high school buddies.

"It's a matter of propriety. We all know what's right and wrong, and there's something going on right here in our backyard that has the potential to make us the laughingstock of the whole county, or worse."

The class teacher, Jake Walters, spoke up next. "Just what are you talking about, Arthur? We don't know of anything going on around here."

"Just look out that window toward the parsonage and tell me what you see."

A couple of the guys rose and moved to the window to look out but turned back with looks of confusion.

"Do y'all recognize that car over there?" Arthur was getting perturbed and trying not to show it, but it became harder when the others said they had no idea who the car belonged to. "Well, what would you fellows say if our unmarried preacher had a woman spend the night with him at the parsonage?" There was a small gasp from a couple of the men, while others just looked bewildered.

"I don't think the preacher would do such a thing, Arthur. Are you sure that's not just a friend or family down for a visit?"

"No, it's not family, but it's a friend—his new friends from up at the battlefield. You thought they were gone, but it looks like a one of them stayed behind right here in our parsonage the past couple of nights." Arthur was getting more adamant with each word, and the class began to mumble disbelief and frustration.

The teacher leaned over his lectern and said, "Hey, wait one minute, men. Let's not go jumping in the pond before we see how cold the water is. Arthur, you said he spent the night with a woman, and now you're saying 'they'. Does that mean that there's more than one person over there? That don't exactly sound like anything bad to me. He could have been—"

Arthur interrupted Jake and cut him off. "It don't matter how many, Jake. You don't know about the preacher and that little girl that was running around in short shorts up there and how the preacher went to her see almost every day. I think she was the only female in that house with the preacher and that Alan fellow. Men, I don't know about the rest of you, but that just don't look right to me, and I have spoken with others that agree with me." Arthur had played the trump card for arguments like this. He had called in the nebulous "they"—those people who are always referred to but seem to remain nameless. But "they" can sway any argument, like the cavalry coming to the rescue of an old-west wagon train. When Arthur made it seem that there were others who agreed with him, his argument took on daunting power. There would be no way of rebutting him now, even though his "they" referred only to his wife, Bea, and her friend. The room was a buzz of conversation as small groups broke off to debate the situation that Arthur had brought to their attention. Jake was trying to keep the men from blowing things out of proportion or adding details from imagination, but the air was ripe, juicy, and messy with gossip, like a peeled peach.

Meanwhile, across the hall, a similar scene was being played out in the senior women's class, led by Bea Kirtland. Arthur had given her some talking points at breakfast that morning, and all she had to do was start the conversation. The women seemed more open to the worst possible scenario and seemed to enjoy fleshing out their fantasies. The hope for a Sunday school lesson was lost in these two classes.

Up in his study sat the Reverend Bruce Strong, the spiritual leader of this congregation. He was unaware of the topic of discussion in the classrooms below. He was busy looking over his sermon notes, interspersed with moments of prayer, as was his custom. He always hoped that he could deliver a sermon that would be the message people needed to hear that day. He looked at the window of his office and remembered his personal philosophy of ministry. He had been asked to write a paper about his idea of ministry, and he could still see the odd smile on his professor's face when he'd read the title, *Ouris*, Greek for window. He wanted his ministry to be a window that, when polished and clean, would allow the light to shine through so well that no one would see the window, only the light. God was the light, and he just wanted to be the window. That was his prayer again this morning: "Make me a window of God's word."

Bruce's concentration was broken by the sound of the organist warming up in the sanctuary and the choir members walking toward the choir room to practice their song for the service. Every week it was the same, just the way these folks wanted. The same routine each week was the way they thought church should be. The hallways began to buzz with the sound of feet clopping down the tile and wood floors, and then the sound was muffled as they reached the carpeted area. Ladies balanced precariously in high-heeled shoes that were only worn once a week. Then there were the sounds of the nursery kids zooming toward the children's church class and the occasional little bundle of energy who would run into his office to show Preacher Bruce the imprint of his hand in pastel chalk or a Bible verse framed in fresh-glued macaroni shells. They would beam as if each piece was a priceless work of art, and with their parents, these art works might survive until these children grew to have their own children. Bruce would muster his best look of awe at these offerings, trying to match the look he knew the parents would have on their faces when they saw the same works. Then, as quickly as they'd entered, the fruit-punched, cookie-filled dynamos would run out to create their next masterpieces. There were always some who worried that it annoyed him, but the truth was that he loved those moments most of all.

Outside the church, the lot began to fill with those who had skipped Sunday school and were just arriving. In a minivan across the lot, Julian was getting out of the back seat and walking away from his parents. His Mom and Dad walked briskly to the sanctuary to make sure they got their favorite pew, and his mom shot a glance back and a terse smile as she shouted some inaudible last-minute instructions. Julian nodded as if he had heard her; then he turned his head to look for some of his friends. Suddenly Leon and Jake came out of a side door, giving Julian a look and a nod. Julian nodded back and turned for the main entrance. These were not the friends he was looking for. He walked into the sanctuary and made his way to sit beside his parents.

The room was filling up with people all talking and smiling, but Julian still had a shiver of fear running through him. He looked around and then quickly turned his head away when he saw Deputy Jackson come into the room. He did not want to make eye contact, but he felt that Riley was staring a hole through the back of his head. But Riley was not paying Julian any attention; instead he was focused on Leon and Jake, coming into the sanctuary from one of the side entrances. Julian slid down a little in his seat and pulled the hymnal out of the rack.

The organ began to play softly, but the conversations going on around the room didn't abate. If anything, the people began to talk louder to overcome the volume of the prelude. These moments designed for meditation and preparation for worship had lost the battle with gossip, recipe sharing, and the swapping of Saturday fish tales.

The preacher entered and took his seat, and then came the choir, led by their volunteer director, all of them wearing their beautiful red-and-white robes. The first hymn was followed by the children's sermon and then scripture reading. Next came a second hymn, designed to accompany the giving of tithes. The service was moving along as usual, quickly to some and dragging on for eternity to others, like Julian. Julian felt as though the walls would close in on him at any moment. He had a nagging fear that pulled at his stomach and tied it in knots. Finally, the choir sang its anthem, and Reverend Strong prepared to take to the pulpit. Everyone knew that they were only thirty minutes away from a big meal and a lazy Sunday afternoon. But then something odd happened. Just as Bruce stepped into the pulpit, several senior adults got up from their seats within the congregation and moved toward the door. Bruce paused as they exited, to allow the people to turn away from the distraction. Bruce was caught off guard and very curious, but he regained his composure, even while noticing the whispers drifting across the room. He wasn't the only curious person in the congregation.

Arthur looked around at the people leaving, but he did not move. He was finding it hard not to smile. In his mind, he had proven his power.

Scene 31

The sermon

Bruce stood in the pulpit and opened His bible, but before he started, he bowed his head and began a prayer. The people all bowed their heads, and when he said amen, everyone looked up. "In your bibles, you will find the story of Daniel in the book that bears his name. Daniel chapter one tells of Daniel as a young teenager resisting peer pressure. Later in the book, we see three of Daniel's contemporaries, possibly his friends, Shadrach, Meshach, and Abednego. They withstand the pressure of the king and people around them; they do not give in to the pressure of worshipping false gods. In the latter chapters, we see Daniel as an old man, still consistent in his faith. When Darius becomes king, Darius likes Daniel, but Daniel is surrounded by jealous men who plot to get rid of him. This leads to the story of Daniel in the lion's den, where he would rather be eaten alive than forsake his faith. But Daniel was spared, miraculously, and went on to be one of the most influential leaders in the land. If we look carefully, we will see ourselves in the various stages of life. Teenagers look at Daniel and learn a lesson in how to deal with, and show no fear to, peer pressure. Young adults look in Daniel at the story of his three faithful friends, who were miraculously spared from a fiery furnace. Senior adults, look at Daniel in his old age, standing firm for God in the face of the lion's jaws. Do we model consistency of faith like this in our lives?"

When Bruce mentioned fear and peer pressure, Julian looked up. His attention had been shifting back and forth from Riley Jackson to the cute little blonde classmate sitting near the front, and then occasionally to the preacher's message. But now the sermon had touched on two subjects that were at the heart of his concerns. Fear and friends had been rattling around his brain for days now. He turned full attention to Bruce.

Across the aisle from him sat Arthur Kirtland, whose mind had also been wandering until he heard the comment about influential leaders. Both Julian and Arthur were looking closely at the preacher and waiting to see what he had to say. Each hoped that the preacher was about to offer them some way to find the peace and respect for which they longed. Instead, the preacher began to speak of the peace that God offers.

"The peace of Christ is what the Hebrews called shalom. A peace that is more than merely finding solace in our troubled lives, it's the finding of wholeness. The peace I speak of is a sense of fulfillment in our lives, a feeling that we are happy with our actions and that we have been true to God in all that we do. It is a peace that does not come from personal satisfaction; it comes from knowing that we have satisfied God. It comes when we look at how we have lived and how we have interacted with all living things and are able to say it was good. In the book of Genesis, God looks at each phase of creation, and after each he says, 'It is good.' But he wasn't speaking out of pride in his accomplishments. God was stating the fact that what he had done was perfectly in harmony with all and that it was a perfect place for humanity. In this we see the love of God in creation; we see that even in the beginning God was acting in a way beneficial to his creation. We have lost that desire to do good for all people. It has been lost in the mental maze of selfish pride. When we work for our own sense of worth, we venture into the maze of selfishness, where we begin to justify and rationalize every deed as a good deed for others, when in fact we are seeking to gain notoriety, power, and acceptance in the community. This community we create is not a true community based on love and fellowship. We are creating our personal kingdom and then firmly placing ourselves on the throne. In this kingdom, there will be no peace, only the continual lust for satisfaction that is always elusive. We cannot make enough money or control enough lives to find the peace we seek. Here is a riddle for you. The true shalom style of peace, or wholeness, is a free gift that comes with a great price, a price many are not willing to pay. The price for this essence of shalom is not paid in what we do or what we give up. The cost of this free gift is measured not in physical wealth but in the willingness to give. Give away the treasure of our man-made kingdom, and most importantly, give the love that has been given to them. Jesus taught many things, but when it came to the crux of his ministry, it could be summed up in two commands. When they are met, true peace will result. They are love God with all your heart and love your neighbor. He said that if you do these two you will keep all the Ten Commandments, and you will find the peace that surpasses understanding."

Arthur and Julian both had a feeling of disappointment in their hearts. They were looking for something simpler in the sermon. The preacher was right about one thing: the price for the free gift of peace was very high. How could they love the people that had caused them such distress? The preacher was still speaking, but they had tuned him out as they both started back on their mental journeys, wandering in their minds down different pathways of crisis.

Julian was lost, trying to figure out a way to show love to friends who had dragged him into a web of violence and lies. And how could he show love to the ones he had already hurt without destroying his own credibility with his parents, teachers, and even the boys they had attacked?

Arthur was lost in another maze of questions, concerning how he could maintain his role in the community as a leader and director of community energies. He wanted to lead people in what he considered the best way for the community. These people needed a firm hand, not a hug, and he was the only one qualified to take the lead.

Normally the sermon would be coming to a close by this time, but something happened that even Bruce could not explain. He was usually a very controlled pulpiteer who delivered his sermons using the principles of simplicity and brevity, with emphasis on the brevity. He had stated the scriptural principles and planted the seeds for thought; now it was time for a conclusion and invitation to join the church. But then it happened. He found himself almost uncontrollably launching into a scathing stream of conscious on the presence of evil.

"We call ourselves Christians, which means to be like Christ, but how like Christ are we? Do the actions we take and words we say reflect Christ? In the hospital today there lies a young man in a coma. His injuries were possibly inflicted by members of this community. But that is just the end product of an attitude of evil that has begun to leach its way into our homes and even into our church. The police look for guilty people, but I think that anyone who harbors anger and hatred in their hearts is as guilty as the ones who attacked this young man. The gossips and the instigators have as much blood on their hands as the attacker.

"We love to quote John 3:16, but John 3:19 says this: 'And this is the condemnation, that light is come into the world, and men loved darkness rather than light, because their deeds were evil.' We love to smile and claim Christ in our hearts, but we need to realize that our deeds condemn us as evil.

"We seek power and position, and this, too, is an act of evil. Keep reading in John's gospel in chapter 7 verse 18, where we find these words: 'He that speaketh of himself seeketh his own glory.'

"We have shed humility and become glory-seekers, desiring the praise of men. This rejection of Christ love is reflected in acts of kindness, but the actions of evil are just as evident and carry a horrible cost. The scriptures tell us that we will 'die in our sins' if we deny Christ, and we can deny Christ by taking part in evil deeds.

"Who are we really? That is the question we need to ask ourselves today. Stop playing a role and pretending that we are children of God, when all that we say and do tells us just the opposite. Listen to the words of Christ when he was confronted with people that were just as sure that they were good people. In John chapter 8 we read the following:

"'They answered him, we be Abraham's seed, and were never in bondage to any man: how sayest thou, ye shall be made free? Jesus answered them, Verily, verily, I say unto you, whosoever committeth sin is the servant of sin. And the servant abideth not in the house for ever: but the Son abideth ever. If the Son therefore shall make you free, ye shall be free indeed. I know that ye are Abraham's seed; but ye seek to kill me, because my word hath no place in you. I speak that which I have seen with my Father: and ye do that which ye have seen with your father. They answered and said unto him, Abraham is our father. Jesus saith unto them, if ye were Abraham's children, ye would do the works of Abraham. Jesus said unto them, If God were your Father, ye would love me: for I proceeded forth and came from God; neither came I of myself, but he sent me. Why do ye not understand my speech? Even because ye cannot hear my word. Ye are of your father the devil, and the lusts of your father ye will do. He was a murderer from the beginning, and abode not in the truth, because there is no truth in him.'"

Bruce stopped for what appeared to be a dramatic pause, but he felt as if he had just run a race—his heart was pounding in his chest. What was he saying and doing? The congregation sat there and stared for a moment. Some looked back at their bibles as if to verify what he was saying, and the others just looked at Bruce, dumbfounded by the boldness and pointed nature of his comments. Was he accusing them all of being evil people? Some began to look down and feel a sense of shame as they realized that these verbal missiles had struck them right between the eyes. In these same eyes, there were the hints of tears as they read the section at the end of the chapter, which Bruce had left out, but Bruce wasn't finished yet.

Bruce looked down at his bible and quietly said, "But there is hope in realizing the truth, for the truth will make us free. If we will open our eyes and our hearts to the truth, we will see the will of God. Sadly, the Bible tells us that many will have eyes and not see and ears and not hear. What I am asking of you today is more than just an altar call or a call for repentance. I am asking you to be one of the ones to strike a blow against the evil that has invaded our community by making sure you are not harboring some of that evil in your own heart. Let us pray that we can hear and see the truth for ourselves and for God's sake. Let us pray."

With that it was over, no song, no impassioned plea to come forward and make the walk of shame or put on some emotional show in front of everyone. Bruce had given the easiest and hardest of invitations. It required the person to take actual stock of themselves and react to God as opposed to confessing to Bruce or in front of all those in church. As the prayer ended, the people were surprised to see Bruce still standing at the front of the church instead of at the door to shake everyone's hand as they left. But Bruce was not in a handshaking mood, nor was he in any hurry to hear people tell him what a great sermon that was when he knew they were really thinking what a long sermon it had been. There were some folks who would be genuinely appreciative of his efforts and comments, but these people didn't need to say a word. Bruce knew them well enough to know their hearts by just a glance and a smile. The organist paused awkwardly for a moment. Then Bruce looked over and gave her a nod to start playing, and everything went back to normal. But things were far from normal. That last bit of scathing truth would not sit well with some and, coupled with the rumor that was seeping its way through the community even now as church members were standing around outside and talking, would create a dark shadow over the sunny Sunday afternoon. Bruce made his way back to the office, being stopped by a few on the way to exchange pleasantries, but he noticed the odd looks from others. He felt that his sermon might have had a greater impact than even he could imagine.

Scene 32

The meeting

As he sank into his high-back desk chair, he felt the cool of his dark office and sighed. He felt as if he had just run a marathon. He was emotionally drained, but it was a good sensation. Bruce liked to keep his office dark, with the exception of a small desk lamp illuminating his work area. Some thought it was strange, but it kept down the glare, and it was very relaxing for moments like this. He felt his body begin to ease from his neck down as if someone was loosening a wrestling grip from his head. He was so relaxed that he did not hear the man step into his office.

"That was a courageous sermon, Mr. Strong. Not many preachers have the nerve to say things like that to their congregation these days."

Bruce was startled. He turned in his chair to see a tall man standing in the doorway. He was half in and half out of his office, with a glare coming over his shoulders. Bruce tried to see his face, but the facial features were in shadow from the harsh fluorescent hallway light. He squinted and rubbed his eyes to try to get a better glimpse of the man, but this just made it more difficult for his eyes to adjust to the glare and the shadow of his own office. All he saw was the green of his sport coat and tie.

"I hope you mean that as a compliment, sir." Bruce smiled as he spoke and started to get up to greet the man properly.

"Oh, I did, Reverend, but please don't get up. I can't stay. I just wanted you to know that I heard your words and accept the challenge you offered today in that sermon. It moved me a great deal."

Bruce thought he heard a hint of sarcasm in his tone, but he thanked the man for coming by to tell him. "Are you a visitor with us today?" Bruce asked, still not seeing the man clearly as the figure turned his back to walk out into the hall. Bruce noticed that he turned away from the light and that his face was still not clear. But he heard the man's voice trail off as he walked around the corner and toward the outside door.

"I am not a faithful member, but I've been here several times before, and I will see you again. Have a good day, Reverend Bruce Strong. I wish you well in the days to come. You may need it with these folks around here." The voice was barely audible now, and Bruce heard the side door open and close before he could walk across his office. Bruce stepped out into the hall and right into the path of Jake Walters. They made a *humph* sound as they bumped into one another.

"Well, Preacher, I was hoping to run into you before you went home, but not quite this way." Jake had a warm country smile that Norman Rockwell would have willingly immortalized.

"I'm sorry, Jake. I wasn't looking where I was going; I was trying to get a look at this fella who was visiting with us today. Did you see him? He just walked out the side door there." Bruce was talking as he stepped over to the door as if to show Jake, the door that he had been using most of his life. Bruce pushed on the door, but it wouldn't open, and so he put his shoulder against it and shoved until it popped open like a soda pop bottle on a hot day, and Bruce almost fell onto the portico porch. He looked out at the nearly empty parking lot but couldn't see anyone he didn't know. He stood for a moment, staring at everyone in the lot, but there were no tall, thin strangers.

"Do ya see him anywhere, Preacher?" Jake asked as he slowly stepped up behind Bruce.

"No, Jake, he must have been parked right by the door, 'cause he sure disappeared in a hurry," Bruce said as he brushed the dust from the door off his shoulder. Do you have the visitor cards for today, Jake? I would like to see if there is a man alone whose name I don't recognize." Bruce held out his hand, expecting Jake to drop the cards in his hand, as he always did on Sunday after the service.

"No, I don't have any cards, Bruce. We didn't have any visitors that I could see, or at least they didn't fill out no card and drop it in the plate." Jake spoke with an almost apologetic tone that betrayed his gentle nature. "But we did have this." And with that Jake extended his hand, which held a small, folded piece of paper.

Bruce turned with a questioning look on his face that turned into a muted look of fear when he saw the paper.

"It's another one of them notes, Preacher." Jake handed it to Bruce. "Maybe you better read this one, Preacher. It's a little different."

Bruce opened the note with hesitation and dread at what it might contain, but his look quickly turned to confusion as he read the words scribbled on the page: "Paramahamsa Samhita," of the Vayu Purana, "Sri Gauranga Candra Udaya," the prayer to Sri Hari.

"What the heck is that all about, Preacher?" Jake asked, scratching his head.

"I'm afraid you got me on this one, Jake. I am not real familiar with these words, but I've got an idea who might be able to help me. I will check it out today. Let's not tell anyone about this one until I can get a little more information, okay?" Bruce knew he could trust Jake, but he still wanted to curb any curiosity.

"Don't worry, Preacher, I don't think I could tell anybody what I just read anyway! That looks like gibberish to me." Jake laughed but then quickly stopped and took on a more sombre look.

"What is it, Jake? You got that I'm-about-to-bust-to-tell-you-somethin' look on your face." Bruce smiled at Jake, but he soon realized that Jake had something serious on his mind.

"Well, I don't know where to begin with this, but Arthur Kirtland sort of stirred up the class this morning, and I couldn't get control after he gave another one of his little speeches." Jake paused.

"Oh no! What is it now? I thought we would be finished with that now that the team has left the battlefield." Bruce couldn't help sounding disgusted at such news, but the disgust was going to get deeper and hotter.

"Well, that's just it. He said that this wasn't over yet, and then he mentioned the fact that the pretty little Indian girl from up there was staying at the parsonage unsupervised and all. It really got some of the guys hot under the collar, if ya know what I mean." Jake sank back as if he'd just thrown a rock through the church window, and in a way he had.

Bruce had a look of incredulity on his face; he was at a loss for words. He hung his head and clapped his hands together. "I don't suppose he mentioned that there was another man in the house as well all weekend?" Bruce was fighting back the rage.

"He sort of tried later, but he had already planted a pretty ugly seed in them fellas' heads. I think that's why some of them walked out this morning; it was like a sort of protest or something, except nobody knew what they were protesting." Jake smiled at that, thinking that it might help ease Bruce's ire.

"If I know Arthur, the whole community knows by now what they're protesting. I am probably the topic of every lunch conversation in the area. You know the old saying, Jake: 'When it rains it pours.' I think we are about to get a gully buster." At that, the two broke into laughter.

Bruce advised Jake to go home and not worry about it just then. Jake left by the side door, and Bruce stepped into his office. He was stopped by the sound of the door opening and closing smoothly. How odd that it had stuck only moments before. He walked over to the door, pushed the crash bar, and felt the door open with ease. Bruce stuck his head out, examined the locking mechanism, and then shrugged. It was just another one of those weird things that seemed to be happening around him lately.

Bruce returned to the comfort of his office. He wished he could hide there all day, but he knew what was going on in the community. Arthur would be watering the seed of gossip he had planted that morning, with phone calls and visits. What could Bruce do about something like this? He felt sure that not everyone would pay attention to it, but it only took a handful of the disgruntled to disrupt the fellowship. He smiled as a sardonic thought crossed his mind—what fellowship? It was a group of people who were connected by bloodlines, past events, and geography, but that was about all there was bringing them together. He could preach all year for hours at a time to a room filled with nodding heads and padded pews and not be as effective as one little old man with fifteen minutes of dirty thoughts and insinuations.

Then it hit him. *Why should I sit here and let Arthur control the dialogue? I can go and confront him. I'll tell him the whole situation and then ask him to call off his gossip dogs. I will give him time to eat his lunch, and then I'll pay a little visit to good ole Arthur Kirtland and pull a few of that old tiger's teeth.* Bruce was feeling confident and a touch belligerent, for good measure. Maybe that sermon this morning had pumped him up a bit also.

Bruce pushed back from his desk and remembered that he had guests at home who would be hungry about now, and so he headed for home. He was about to enter the parsonage when that same feeling of belligerence hit him, and he thought, *why should I give him a peaceful lunch? I'll go see him now before the phone starts ringing.* Bruce turned, hopped back into his car, and started off.

Arthur's house was only a few minutes from church, and as he slowed to turn into the drive, he saw a familiar face entering the house. It was Oliver Paxton. Bruce put his foot back on the accelerator and turned his head, hoping no one would notice him driving by. Bruce was perplexed as he tried to put the pieces of the puzzle together. Why would Paxton and Kirtland be meeting today, of all days? What did those two have in common, other than a dislike for Bruce? Then it hit him like a slap in the face with a cold towel, and it caused him to shudder. Oliver Paxton was into this whole yoga thing, and that last note had looked like a reference to Vedic scripture. Could he be the mystery note writer? It didn't explain the other notes, unless he was angry at the team for some reason, but it could explain the last note, which was out of sync with the others. It was time to call on some help from his new friends.

Bruce hurried back to the house, unaware that the meeting taking place at the Kirtland house was merely about the yoga class that Bea Kirtland was involved with. Of course, Arthur didn't waste any time filling Oliver in on the latest gossip about the preacher. He told him enough to cause Oliver to stomp out in a controlled rage. His envy and jealousy were getting the best of him, and his attraction to Sandy was verging on an obsession. He wished that he hadn't told her she could not take the yoga class, but he didn't want to deal with his wife's jealousy.

Back at the parsonage, Bruce got out of his car and practically ran in to talk with Alan and Sandy. When he walked in, he was met with the succulent smell of chicken and rice being cooked with saffron. It stopped him dead in his tracks. "What is that wonderful smell?" he asked.

"Have you ever had paella? It's a little Spanish dish that really feels like it's from India, but I thought you guys would like it. Have a seat; it's almost done." Sandy was looking very domestic, and Alan was sitting in the den watching the sports news.

"Can you look at this and tell me what it is while you're cooking, Sandy?" Bruce said. He heard Alan yelling from the next room to make sure it didn't interrupt the cooking. Sandy's hands were a little sticky, so Bruce held the note up to her face and watched as her eyes grew larger as she read.

"Do you recognize any of these references?" he asked her.

"Not exactly, but by the look of it, I would say it is definitely Vedic. I must confess that I am probably more familiar with Christian literature than I am with Hindu writings." Sandy swiped her hair back with her forearm and said that after lunch she would call home and see if her dad could tell her anything. She needed to check up on in him anyway; it had been a while she'd talked with her folks.

The three sat at the table, eating and talking about the events of the day, Bruce told them of the note and how he'd seen Paxton going into Arthur's house. It seemed to make sense that the two of them were working together, but why was still a mystery. Sandy suggested that Kirtland wanted to get rid of Alan, and Paxton had shown some interest in her.

"Well, if you got Kirtland, and you've got Paxton, that leaves me without a nemesis," Bruce said with a chuckle. Even as he spoke, the image of Murmus jumped into his head. He hadn't told the others everything about the meeting with Criton and his spirit friend, Murmus.

"Arthur Kirtland is behind all of this—you know he is." Alan was getting angry again just thinking about Kirtland. "He set the kids on us at the campsite, and he's probably behind the attack on Topper, and don't forget he called in that psychic guy. Now he's getting Paxton to drop little notes in the church box. Am I the only one that sees this, that it's all Kirtland?" Alan sounded frustrated again.

"I hadn't really thought about that, Alan. I suppose Arthur could have told Paxton about the notes and put him up to this one, but I don't see the point."

"Unless he's going to try to drag me into his rumor mill. Having a note with ties to Hinduism might be the angle he's trying to play." Sandy was becoming a little angry herself.

Bruce sat for a moment and thought about what they were saying. What could move a man to such hatred? "I'd still like to know what that note is all about, Sandy, when you get the time to call your folks."

Sandy got up to use the phone while Alan and Bruce continued trying to decipher the clues before them. Both men were still perplexed about Arthur's motives. They tossed idea after idea across the table, from frustrated old man fighting the onset of age to disgruntled community leader who feels power slipping away. They even suggested marital problems after Bruce related the story of Arthur's first wife. None of the theories seemed to be enough to elicit such hatred, until Alan finally said that perhaps Bruce was being a bit naïve about these good country folks.

"I am not saying that I'm not naïve, Alan. It just seems that things have erupted in the past few months, and I can't see what has sparked this." Bruce tried not to seem too defensive.

"I'd say that things have been festering for a while around here, and maybe no one noticed. People in a community like this don't seem to be in a hurry for confrontation. Look at this morning. Nobody spoke up in that class to defend you; they just went along with ole Arthur there. He's a bully, plain and simple!" Alan had cut right to the point. Like it or not, everything did seem to center around Arthur Kirtland.

"Arthur is a key player, but I can't shake this feeling that he's not at the center of this, maybe just to the right of center. I keep sensing something else, like a man-behind-the-man scenario. I just can't imagine who or why." Bruce looked up at Alan with a sheepish grin. The two men sat quietly for a while, and Bruce's mind wandered back to his visitor again. Who had that stranger been? As Bruce thought about the brief conversation, he tried to play the dialogue over in his head. "He said that he was accepting my challenge and that the sermon had moved him." Bruce paused and looked at Alan.

"Who said that, Bruce, and what was the challenge?" Alan asked.

"That's just it; he didn't really say what challenge he was accepting. I'd asked the people to do some soul searching to see whether they were part of the evil in this community. He said it as if he were mocking me. The guy was just sort of creepy, but I can't put a finger on why."

"What did he look like, Bruce? Didn't you say that you'd never seen him before?" Alan asked.

"I didn't get a clear look, but I'm sure I've never seen him before. He said that he had been here before and that he would be coming back. As far as what he looked like, all I saw was this tall, thin guy in a green sport coat, with a glare behind his face."

Bruce was trying to remember details when Alan interrupted. "What did you say, Bruce? Are you kidding?" Alan had a strange smile on his face.

"Uh, kidding about what?" Bruce said.

"Think about what you just said—tall, thin, green coat. You just described the ghost from the battleground that Topper saw and what I think was seen at the barn. Could it be a coincidence? Maybe you just had a sighting!" Alan was almost laughing, but Bruce wasn't smiling. He had turned toward the window and was lost in thought.

"I was just kiddin', Bruce—ya know, the ghost. Bruce, hey, Bruce." Alan was trying to get Bruce's attention, but Bruce wasn't listening. Alan had stumbled onto something that was resonating in Bruce's head. His mind ran back to the previous weeks and all that had happened at church and up at the battlefield.

Bruce was just turning back to Alan when Sandy walked into the room and sat down with a long sigh. Bruce was most eager to hear what she had found out, so eager that he didn't even ask about her dad. "Did the words mean anything to your dad?" he asked her excitedly.

"Yeah, how is your dad, by the way?" Alan asked, and when Bruce heard the question he was embarrassed at his lack of sensitivity.

"He's doing well; he sounded better than he has in months—until I mentioned the note. He didn't like the text reference I gave him, and he made an instant connection to the Paxton place," Sandy said with an ominous tone.

"You're kidding! What did he say, and what has it got to do with Paxton? This is getting better and better." Alan sounded like a kid getting ready for a scary story around a campfire.

"Let me back up and start at the beginning. I called, and Mom answered. I told her what we were dealing with and that I wanted to ask Dad about some text. That's when she said Dad was doing so well, and then she put him on the phone. I told Dad what we were doing, in a brief version, and then I said that I had a scripture passage to test on him. When I finished, he was silent, and I thought he was looking it up somewhere, but then I realized he was still on the phone. I asked him again. That's when he said that it was a well-known section of a prayer, and it dealt with the time of Kali Yuga. He began to explain the whole passage and implications that it might have, and he said he could send me some notes, but would rather I forget it and come home. He was getting more and more agitated on the phone, and then, just out of the blue, he said, 'Stay clear of the barn at the Paxton house.' I asked him why, but he was silent again. Mom got back on the phone and spent the next ten minutes scolding me for asking disturbing questions. But I'd had no way of knowing that it would upset him." Sandy seemed guilty, as if she were responsible for her dad relapsing into whatever world he had been in for the past year.

Then Sandy slowly opened her laptop, looked at the two men, and said, "Dad just emailed me this as an explanation of the prayer that the phrase comes from." Sandy placed her laptop on the table, so all could see the email, and the two men began to read.

> In the age of Kali, people are spontaneously attracted to sinful activities and are devoid of the regulations of the scriptures. The so-called "twice-born" are degraded by their low-class activities, and those who are born in low-class families are always hostile to Brahmanical culture. The twice-born are low class by quality and do business by selling mantras. These so-called learned men are engrossed by their intestines and genitals, and their only identification is the thread they wear. Indulging in overeating, absorbed by bodily consciousness, lazy, intellectually dull, and greedy for others' properties, they are consistently against God-consciousness. Due to being overly inclined toward false paths without essence, they manufacture their own processes for self-realization. Neglecting their actual duties, they are expert in blaspheming the Supreme Personality of Godhead and the saintly persons; hence again, Mother Earth is in tears due to this burden. Therefore, oh Lord

of the universe, destroyer of the miseries of the destitute,
please mercifully do what is befitting for the protection
of the Earth and the living entities.

The very day and moment the personality of Godhead,
Lord Sri Krishna, left this earth, the personality of Kali,
who promotes all kinds of irreligious activities, came
into this world.

"Sounds like today! What else you got on this Kali Yuga thing? It
sounds intriguing." Alan was pressing for info.

"Well, Kali was, or is, another incarnation of what you would call
God, but he is the bad side. He is like the devil to some in Hinduism,
but it's not quite that simple. As for the Yugas, they were time periods
based on the astrological calendar, and the Kali Yuga was, or is, the time
of Kali or of chaos and evil."

"When does this period begin, and what's with the 'was' and 'is'
stuff?" Alan probed.

"According to what Dad said, it depends on interpretation, as usually
happens with these sorts of things. It could coincide with our Iron Age or
go back about 2000 to 3000 BC. According to Dad, it can be based on
the Hindu Buddhist calendar, the Surya Siddhanta, which makes Kali
Yuga start at precisely midnight on February 18, 3102 BC."

"Okay, when did it end?" Bruce asked.

Sandy gave an uncomfortable smile and said, "Well that's the *was*
and *is* of it. It didn't end. According to Dad, we're still in it. The day
is specific, but the year is up for interpretation. It doesn't end until
sometime within the next decade."

Alan said, "I've never heard of this Kali Yuga thing, but this is a
little creepy. It may make some sense based on what I have read in the
archeological periodicals."

"How's that, Alan?"

"If we take Sandy's older date, it could coincide with recent
discoveries. In archeology, ancient cultures were always seen as nomadic
cultures, moving from place to place. Then they became agrarian

cultures, and next came the city dwellers. Their behavior was always marked by warlike behavior and struggles for power. War and fighting had been the accepted pattern until a city was found in Peru. This city is old, as in one of the oldest in human history. It's called Caral. The unusual thing about it is that it seems to have been built when people were still hunter-gatherers or early stages of an agrarian civilization, and it has forced scientists to rethink the behavior patterns of early man. You see, Caral had no signs of fortifications or even a military complex—no weapons or stories of war. The evidence in Caral suggests that humanity may have been more peaceful in its earliest age. But suddenly humanity entered an age of increased violence and warfare, complete with human sacrifice. Some suggest that it may have begun about 3000 BCE. But that's not the creepy part. That date just so happens to coincide with the end of the other calendars. Remember all the fuss about the Mayan calendar? According to Mayan prophets, the end of the age will be a time of unprecedented evil and then—*boom!* —it all ends in a bang. The Chinese had prophecies like that, and other cultures seem to point to this century as a climax. Maybe we could blame the age of Kali for the evil behavior of mankind." Alan smiled as if he didn't really believe his comments.

Bruce then leaned back from the table and said, "I guess this is my cue to relate some apocalyptic biblical revelation about the end times that coincides with all this. I think I will pass on the end of time and just focus on current time. We have gone from kooks in the county, to ghosts from the revolution and now an ancient Peruvian city, an ancient Hindu god, and a Mayan prophecy. All I wanted was to know why someone keeps putting these notes in the offering plate. Can anyone tell me the connection?"

The three sat staring at one another until Alan broke the silence. "I don't know about all this other stuff, but I'm still banking on the number-one county kook, Mr. Arthur Kirtland. I think he's the Pandora who opened the box of bad behavior around here, and he's the one that needs to be stopped."

Sandy spoke up. "That may be true, Alan, but it doesn't explain the evil occurrences before you and your team arrived. Things haven't exactly been rosy around here for some time. You are forgetting the guy who decapitated his dog and attacked his own little girl. I think that the source may go beyond just some geriatric old grump. There's a lot of evidence to suggest paranormal behavior here, which could also explain Mr. Kirtland's sudden turn toward the dark side."

Bruce sat there listening to the two. He felt it was his turn to offer a solution, but he sat silent. None of the theories put forth explained the local behavior, and they were offering no comfort to him. Something was nagging at him, like something pulling at him from a dark well. He didn't know what it was, but it was disturbing to him. The three sat at the table for a few more minutes and then adjourned their conference and went into the den, where Alan turned on the sports news and Sandy read the paper. Bruce had planned to visit Arthur, but now it seemed useless. If he confronted him now, it would just be seen as some sort of attack, and Bruce would be the bad guy again. It was a no-win situation for Bruce.

Scene 33

The wages of sin

Not far from the church, in the Hopkins house, another person was thinking about the sermon and replaying words over and over in his head. The preacher had said something about being "condemned because our deeds are evil; we are servants of sin and murderers from the beginning." Julian wanted to turn back the clock. He was a part of this now, all because he'd wanted to fit in with a bunch of guys that it had turned out were just losers. But who was the real loser? Julian was almost shivering with fear. He couldn't make it stop; all he could think about was the wages of sin being death. Then he had his visions of hell, images that he had been taught as a child, filled with lakes of fire and people screaming in pain for eternity. All he wanted was for it to go away.

In another part of the house sat his parents. His dad was watching TV and mom was talking on the phone. His dad was lost in the tube, and his mom was getting the latest scoop about the preacher on the local gossip hotline. Her conversation was broken only by the occasional gasp of disbelief. When she got off the phone, she immediately began telling the story to her husband who sat there in a state of tingling disbelief. It was like seeing an accident in the road. He didn't really believe what he was hearing, but the story was just too interesting to stop listening. Julian walked by the den but didn't stop. He wandered into the kitchen and looked in the fridge for something to drink, more out of habit than need. He breathed a shivery sigh and then stared toward the den. He couldn't bring himself to go in and talk with his folks about the things that were bothering him. He didn't know what he could say that would explain the past few days.

He took a quick side step into his parent's bedroom when he thought he heard his mom coming down the hall. He stepped back toward his parents' closet, and his hand slid into the closet, where he felt the cool barrel of his dad's shotgun. In an instant he felt a sense of calm. He waited to see if his mom was actually coming down the hall but realized that she was just changing her chair to get closer to his dad to tell the story. He took the barrel of the gun in his hand and pulled it carefully out of the closet. He moved his hands down to the stock to caress the grip. His feeling of fear was gone. He had found his talisman of protection against the torment in his mind. He took the gun and hurried back to his room.

Once behind his closed door, he sat on the bed and held the gun out before him. He sighted down the barrel at imaginary enemies and saw himself killing all the things that were tearing at his mind. For the first time in days, he felt a sense of ease. He lay back on his bed, with the gun beside him like a tall thin lover. The sun had gone down, and long shadows had filled his room. At last he rested.

The house was silent, and the last thing Julian did was to pull the bedspread up to cover the shotgun before he fell asleep. In a while his mom came back to check on him, only to find him sound asleep. She didn't want to wake him, so she softly closed the door. By ten o'clock everyone was in bed and Julian was dreaming, but his dreams were not peaceful ones.

Somewhere in the deep recesses of his subconscious, Julian began to see images. They were images of a grassy yard and a ball bat, then a boy falling, and a figure nearby in a green coat. Then he saw Leon and TJ, and suddenly he was back at the store, looking at doughnuts and sodas. The man behind the counter was offering him sweets and candy, but it wasn't the right person behind the counter. It was the man in the green coat with a long, thin face, and he was frowning. "Here ya go, batboy," he said with a frown. "That poor college boy isn't going to eat any candy, so you can have his. Did you hear that he died in the hospital?" Then suddenly, in his dream world, Julian was standing over the body of a young college boy. He was in that yard again, with a doughnut in one hand and bite of chocolate in his mouth. The candy tasted dry and caused him to cough, but he couldn't get it out of his mouth. He began to choke and gag on the sawdust taste in his mouth.

Julian woke up almost gagging on the dry feeling in his mouth. He tried to swallow, but he had no spit. His head was hurting. He reached for the gun beside him and quickly felt a little better, but he needed water. Julian sat on the side of his bed for moment, trying to separate dream from reality, until he realized he was in his room. Quietly he slipped into the bathroom and began to drink cup after cup of tap water. His stomach began to ache from the lukewarm water and the imagined feeling of indigestion from his dream candy.

As he stepped into the dark hallway, he saw what looked like the shape of a man down the hall near the living room door. Julian was startled and felt his chest tighten. He froze in fear, not taking his eyes off the figure. For an instant, he blinked, and the figure was gone. Julian backed into his room and grabbed the gun, watching the door all the while. He aimed the gun toward the dark opening and moved slowly and quietly back out into the hall. With gun in hand, he felt secure and determined to see who was in his house. When he reached the front door, all he saw was the hat rack behind the door, and for a moment he wondered if that was what he had seen earlier. But just about the time he was convinced it had been a trick of the shadows, another dark shadow moved across the porch window. Someone was outside on the porch. Julian froze in place and again felt his chest tighten. Should he call his dad? How could he explain having the gun?

He slowly opened the door and stepped out onto the porch. There was no one around, so he stepped out into the yard. Barefoot and in his pajamas, he felt the evening chill and moisture of the grass against his feet. He walked toward the side of his house, and just before going around the corner, he heard a sound. He stepped back between two of the bushes that lined the front of his house. They were as high as his waist, so he had to drop down into a squat position to hide behind them. He leaned his back against the house's exterior wall. He felt a hint of warmth from the brick foundation and then the cool clapboard siding as it pushed its imprint into his back.

The sky was dark, with only a few stars and a distant streetlight near the drive that spread shadows toward his feet. He tried to hide the sound of his breathing, waiting to see whether someone would come around the corner. He felt his body begin to shiver in the cold night air. Soon it began to feel numb from the cool air, and he pulled the gun close as he waited and waited. He was too scared to move; he kept hearing a faint sound from around the corner. At some point his legs began to fall asleep, and soon his body relaxed. Tension and fear had exhausted him, and soon he was slipping into the unconsciousness of sleep.

Once Julian was asleep, the dreams came again. He was back at the yard, seeing the boy on the ground, and then standing at the counter of the store with the green-coated clerk frowning and offering him sweets and drinks. In the dream, the clerk reached under the counter, pulled out an extra-long chocolate bar, and handed it to Julian with a promise that it would not taste like dust. Julian took the candy and put it in his mouth. It was warm and moist and tasted sweet, and the green-coated clerk's frown turned into a smile as he said everything would be fine now.

The sudden sound woke Julian's' parents. His dad looked over at the clock and read the numbers—3:00 a.m. What had made that noise?

It sounded like a giant firecracker had been thrown into the yard. He stumbled to the closet and reached for his gun but couldn't find it.

His wife whispered her protest. "Thomas Hopkins, don't get that gun! You will shoot somebody or yourself." His wife was doing that whispering yell that marked her own level of fear. "Just go outside and see if there's anyone out there."

Mr. Hopkins moved cautiously out into the hall and made his way to the front of the house. He jumped only once when he realized that Edna, his wife, was right behind him. The two of them began to look out the windows but saw nothing. There was no movement in the yard and not even a barking dog could be heard. They kept looking out the windows all around the house and finally came to Julian's' room. Mrs. Hopkins went in quietly but quickly she was speaking full voiced as she called for her husband to tell him that Julian wasn't there.

Now they were no longer concerned with silence or intruders. The instincts of parents took over, and they began to shout for Julian. Edna was on the front porch, calling for Julian, while Thomas was in the backyard. They met at the side of the house after walking around in opposite directions. Edna was almost frantic as she pleaded with her husband to call the police. She ran back inside, and Thomas walked out further into the yard. Inside, she sat chewing her sleeve and fighting back tears, staring at the phone. Thomas came in and wiped his moist feet on the mat. He sank into his easy chair and picked up the phone. His hand was shaking as he dialed 911 and tried to maintain his composure when he spoke to the officer on the other end of the line.

"This is Thomas Hopkins, 622 at East Harris. We just heard something that sounded like a gunshot out in our yard, and we can't find our boy, Julian." There was a pause and then Thomas mumbled, "Yes" and "Okay." He hung up the phone and said that someone would be there as soon as possible.

Not far from the church, Riley Jackson received the call of a disturbance and possible missing persons at the Hopkins residence. Before the dispatcher could tell him the address, he told her he knew the family and was en route. Riley left his blue lights off but pushed his engine to the limit and arrived in three minutes.

Thomas met him in the yard, and the two walked into the house. Riley heard their story while looking around inside the house and in Julian's room. Riley then told the couple to sit back and try to relax; he would take a look outside. The night air was cool and damp, and there was a strange quiet. He stopped for a moment and realized that the crickets weren't chirping and there was no wind at all. Riley went out to his car and pulled out his oversized flashlight. He began shining it around, holding it up next to his head. He walked around and shone the light back and forth; then he stopped. Something was on the siding behind the bushes. Riley saw what looked like paint stains on the siding. He stepped over to get a better look and began to feel tightness in his gut when he saw that the stain began to look ominously familiar. He pushed the bush aside and followed the stain down the wall to the still form of Julian Hopkins there on the ground.

The body was in a fetal position, with one leg extended, and could have been asleep if not for the mangled mass of flesh that had been his face. Blood pooled around the shoulders where half of his face had been blown off. It looked like he had put the barrel in his mouth and pulled the trigger. Riley had seen suicides before and was trying to put the scene together in his mind, but already he had a problem with what he was seeing. How had the boy pulled the trigger? Riley looked at his arms and determined that they were too short to reach the trigger, and he didn't see his feet anywhere near the trigger to suggest that he'd used his toe to push it. Riley pulled himself away from the scene and got on the radio, asking for an ambulance and a counselor or chaplain. He asked the dispatcher to also call Reverend Bruce Strong and tell him that he had a potential suicide at the Hopkins' and that it was their son, Julian. Riley told them to come in quietly; he wanted someone to help break the news to the parents.

He moved away from the scene in case Thomas or Edna came back out. Then he walked over to his cruiser and watched the front door from there. The ambulance arrived at about the same time as the sheriff's chaplain. There were no sirens, but the additional lights in the drive prompted the Hopkins to come out on the porch. Thomas ran off the porch to Riley and frantically confronted him. "What's the ambulance for, Riley?"

The chaplain stepped up as Riley took Thomas by the arm. The medics stayed in the background, waiting for Riley to point out the location of the body.

"Thomas, now get a hold of yourself, there's been an accident involving Julian, and I have found him, but I'm afraid he's, he's …" Riley paused, trying to find the words. "He's dead, Thomas, and it's not a pretty sight. I need for you to get hold of yourself, for Edna's sake. I don't think she should see him. As a matter of fact, I don't think you should see him either, Thomas."

Thomas was shaking and trying to speak, and then when he heard what Riley said, he stared at Riley with a questioning frown. "I want to see my baby, Riley. What are you talking about? Where is Julian?"

When she heard that, Edna launched herself from the porch to where the men were standing. "Where is Julian, Thomas? Riley Jackson, what is that ambulance for! Where is our baby? The chaplain stepped over to Edna and Thomas as they clung to each other.

"Look, folks, there ain't no easy way to say this except to tell you that Julian is dead in what looks like an apparent suicide. The scene is pretty gruesome, and I just don't want you two to get that image in your head. Give us a chance to try and fix things up a little."

The chaplain was still speaking when Edna began to wail over and over to herself, "Lordy, Lordy! Tommy, Tommy—what are we to do! What are we to do? Where's my baby, my baby, my baby!" As she sank to her knees, repeating the same thing over and over, Thomas began to sob and fell beside his wife. Edna broke into hysterical screaming and made a move toward the body. The two men grabbed her, struggling to keep her from the scene.

She was frantic, and in a rage of fear and anger, she cried out, "He's my baby!" She kept saying over and over, "I want my baby!" Finally, her struggling began to weaken, and her sobs and anger began to quiet as shock set into her mind.

Riley knelt down beside her and quietly whispered, "Can we go back in the house and let the boys do their job?" Edna just looked up with a look of confusion. He continued, "Don't worry, Edna, you'll get to see him soon. Just let us clean him up a little, please. Won't you just come back inside?"

Another car pulled up in the yard. It was Reverend Strong, who jogged over to the couple on the ground. Edna reached up and put her arms around Bruce as Thomas tried to tell him what had happened, but Bruce said not to worry right then. Riley told Bruce that they were trying to get the couple to step into the house. Riley needed to take a couple of the pictures before the paramedics did their job; he wanted to treat this as a crime scene and not just a suicide, because something didn't feel right to Riley. Bruce and Thomas lifted Edna up and held her close; both were doing their best to keep her from looking toward her son's body.

"C'mon, folks. Let's go inside and sit down for a bit," Bruce urged. The group walked across the yard and back into the house. As Bruce and the chaplain flanked the Hopkins, Riley dropped back and motioned for the medics to come up with a body bag. After Riley took a few pictures, he asked the medics to work quickly and put the body in the ambulance as soon as possible. They were pulling out of the yard when Riley stepped back up onto the porch. He stood at the door and motioned for Bruce to come over.

"Do you happen to know what funeral home they would use, Bruce? I think that some of their people used Martin's up town, but I don't know who they would want us to call. I just want somebody to try and fix that little fella's face up, if they can. It wouldn't do for his folks to see him like he is right now," Riley said in a whisper.

"I'll see what I can find out, Riley," Bruce replied, echoing Riley's tone.

"Oh yeah, Bruce, see if y'all can keep them in the house for a while. The sun will be up in a bit, and I'd like to wipe some of this blood off the side of the house and clean up the spot. But I gotta' take some pictures first and call the forensic boys; there's somethin' odd about this, so I can't mess with the scene a lot." Riley was showing why he was more than just a good officer; he was a good friend.

"You do that, Riley, and I'll get the funeral home information and give 'em a call. Will the ambulance take the body to the hospital?"

"Yeah, probably. Bruce, if you can get the funeral home, tell 'em the name and they'll find the body. I'll get busy out here."

Scene 34

Buford's play

The next two days were a horrible blur to everyone connected with Julian and the funeral. Bruce sat in his study most of the next day, trying to write a sermon for the funeral, but he was too shocked by the death. He could not get the picture out of his mind of the Hopkins crying on the ground. Thomas and Edna were both in a state of mild shock, which was only to be expected. Bruce had stayed with them on the Monday night, talking a little and sitting quietly for most of the evening.

The funeral was Tuesday afternoon at 3:00. The church was full of weeping teens and parents stunned into silence. Try as he could, Bruce could not separate his own feelings from the moment. It all seemed surreal, until the graveside service was ending, when Edna lost all control and went into hysterics. Thomas could hardly restrain her, and Bruce could see that he was nearing his own emotional breaking point. They took her home, and Bruce found out later that she eventually went to the emergency room, where they sedated her.

Bruce stood by the graveside for a long time. He spoke with the few family members that were present. He shook the hands of the young pallbearers and thanked them for their help. Bruce noted all the people and watched the young girls crying crocodile tears. He wondered how many of them had really known Julian. How well had *he* known Julian? He had baptized him and counseled him for a few hours. The night of the youth lock-in, Julian had spent a long time sitting with a few adult chaperones. Bruce had noticed that Julian wanted to stay with the adults. He had been a quiet guy and only recently had shown signs of coming out of his shell by hanging around with a few of the guys up at the store.

As Bruce was thinking about the boys who had become Julian's new friends, he noticed Deputy Riley had pulled a couple of the boys aside and was talking to them. Leon and Jake had been pallbearers and seemed to take a certain pride in being selected. Bruce watched the group for a moment and thought that he would like to be a cricket at their feet, listening to that conversation. It was probably good that Bruce could not hear what was being said. He might have screamed out in anger if he had witnessed the ultimate evil and betrayal that was facing Riley Jackson.

"Deputy, we need to talk to you about that fight up at the battlefield." It was Leon, using his sweetest voice. Riley just stood there but finally nodded for the boys to move over, away from the graveside.

"What's up, Leon? Have you boys got some new information that you might have left out when I spoke to you the other day?" Riley was irritated, because he felt that this was not the time or the place for a conversation about his investigation.

"Yeah, we do, Riley. Ya see, we weren't exactly ..." Leon paused as if trying to avoid saying that they had lied. "Well, we didn't tell you everything, because ... we were scared and didn't know what to do. Things happened up there that was not supposed to happen. Nobody meant anyone any harm, and it just got out of hand." Leon was stumbling with his explanation.

"Wait a minute, Leon. You're talking like you were there?" Riley stated in a questioning tone.

Leon responded quickly. "No, I wasn't there. I just found out what had happened afterwards, and the fellas here asked me to help them out. So, I am trying to tell their story for them."

Now Riley was irritated. "Why don't you let them speak for themselves? Maybe you boys need to grow a backbone. If you got something to tell me, say it yourselves." Riley moved closer to Jake and

TJ, who had joined the group after the funeral. "Let's start with you, TJ. What do you need to tell me that you couldn't tell me a few days ago?"

"I … I don't know, Deputy. I was just there, and we got in a fight with them guys, and I I … I …" TJ froze up and couldn't say anything.

"We didn't go over there looking for trouble, Deputy. We went to tell them fellas that we were sorry for making fun and laughing at them at the store. Then they got up in our face and stuff." Jake was more confident in his speech.

"What happened at the store, and why didn't Lester or Buck mention any problem?"

"Well, we were at the back of the store, just kiddin' them, and when they left, Leon said that we should apologize for giving them a hard time." Jake looked over at Leon, who smiled and nodded as if to say, "You got the story straight, now stick with it."

"Okay, so you were just being courteous kids. Then how did one kid end up with his head busted open and laying in a coma?" Riley's voice was getting a little louder, but most of the people had moved away from the gravesite.

Jake continued, with a little more confidence. "Well, after Leon told us to apologize, we took off to follow the boys, and we caught up with 'em at the old house. When we tried to apologize, one of the boys got an attitude and was dissin' me and TJ and then he shoved me, and when I wasn't lookin' one of them stuck a finger in my eye and just about put my eye out. It was on after that, but we were trying to back away from them, and then it just happened sort of from out of the blue. We don't know why he did it. It surprised—no, it shocked us."

"Yeah, it was a shock." TJ had found his voice again, even if for only a moment.

"What was so shocking, boys? And just who all was with you guys?" Riley was impatient.

"It was just me, TJ, Spud, and uh …" Jake now started to freeze up. He didn't want to say the last name.

"Okay, so it was you, TJ, Spud, and who else? Who else was out there? Was it Leon?" Riley looked at Leon, and Leon responded with a strange look as he gestured toward his chest and mouthed the word *me?*

"No, no it wasn't Leon, it was …" Once again Jake stalled, and then he looked over at Leon.

Leon stepped closer to Riley and said, "It was Julian, Deputy, Julian Hopkins. He had his ball bat with him, and for some reason he just went off on that one boy and busted him in the side of the head. That's what they don't want to say. They didn't want to snitch on Julian, but now it doesn't seem to matter, him being dead and all." Leon sounded like an FM disc jockey with his low mellow voice and serious tone.

Riley snorted and looked at the boys. He took a couple of steps away from them. His chest began to tighten up as if it would burst with anger, and he moved away further, because he felt as if he might do something he would regret. He turned quickly, moved back toward the boys, and gazed at each of them square in the eyes as he spoke. "So that's the way you wanna play it? You gonna stand there and blame it on a little fella that probably never swatted a fly? He ain't even in his grave, and you three skunks come stinkin' up his grave with that pack of lies? TJ, I thought a little better of you, boy! Your daddy ain't gonna be real proud of you when I talk to him. And Jake, I thought you were more man than to blame somebody else with your crime. But I guess you had a good teacher, didn't ya?" Riley looked at Leon. "I smell your dirty little hands in this, Leon. Did you work all this out for these boys and decide to take advantage of a dead friend?"

"I don't appreciate that, Deputy. You ain't got no proof that what we said isn't the truth. These boys were there, and they saw the whole thing and you ain't got anybody to say different. Even that other guy that was there will tell you that's how it happened." Leon was trying to intimidate Riley.

"Shut up! All of you, just shut up! You're making me sick, just lookin' at ya! I will talk to them two boys, if the one of them ever comes out of his coma—and if it sounds like there was one blade of grass growing different in their story, I will run you all in, including you, Mr. Leon Courtney. Now get out of my sight, and get away from this grave, you bunch of skunks." Riley was almost trembling with anger, because he realized that Leon was right about the story. If those three stuck to the same story and let Julian take the blame, they would walk. He had already talked with Cedric, who couldn't remember who had swung the bat and wasn't sure whether he could ID the boys. Now the culprits had someone to blame who could neither confirm nor deny what his friends were saying about him. He looked back at the grave, with the coffin still sitting on the vault, and felt a tear slip out of the corner of his eye. "You rest in peace, little fella. I ain't gonna let 'em do this to ya." Riley walked straight to his car and drove away; he was in no mood to talk with anyone after that conversation.

When Bruce got home, he found Sandy sitting at her computer, reading notes and email, and Alan sitting quietly in the den. "I thought you might like a little good news after that one, Bruce," Alan said.

"I sure could, Alan. What have you got for me?" Bruce sat down hard in his chair.

"I was thinkin' about the kids while you were at the funeral. I called Topper's folks to see how he was doin', and they said he had come out of the coma Monday about three in the morning."

Bruce looked up with a half-smile. "That is good news, but are you sure about that time?"

"Yeah, I know. Pretty weird, isn't it? That was about the time the Hopkins boy shot himself, wasn't it? Alan spoke more softly, as if not wanting to disturb Bruce.

"That's just too strange, Alan. What in the world is going on around here?" Bruce just hung his head. They sat there for the rest of the evening, just reading and occasionally passing a word or so in casual conversation. Early in the evening Sandy had informed Bruce that she was going home the next day to check on her dad. She felt that it might take some pressure off Bruce for a while. Alan said that he was thinking the same thing; he needed to get back to his office and get ready for his classes.

By the next day, Bruce was alone in his house, and it seemed very quiet and empty. He had never realized how lonely his life had become until he had shared his space with others, even for just a couple of days.

Thursday, Friday, and Saturday passed uneventfully, with the exception of the occasional visitor who dropped by unannounced. This led Bruce to believe that they were checking to see whether he still had house guests. None of the visitors stayed long, and the reasons for coming all seemed a little trumped up. Bruce felt resentment welling up inside as the week came to an end. He needed to focus on the Sunday sermon, but he didn't know what he was going to say. His first impulse was to repeat the previous Sunday's message on evil. He wondered whether anyone would notice.

Sunday morning service came and went, leaving Bruce to feel that he had delivered a lackluster sermon. It was hard to praise and worship while knowing that a young boy was lying out in that fresh grave. The question on everyone's mind was what happened to people who committed suicide. Bruce had spoken on the subject on a couple of occasions. He felt that only God, in his final judgment, would determine humanity's fate, no matter what the cause of death. But this protestant congregation still held to the Roman Catholic belief that a suicide victim was automatically condemned to hell. To Bruce it further reflected a general lack of compassion, wisdom, or both by the membership.

Bruce was sitting in the office again, as was his custom. The room was cooler than the rest of the church, and the cool air helped relax him after a service. Then Jake showed up at the door with the visitor cards. "We got another one here, Preacher," Jake said.

"Another what, Jake?" Bruce smiled but then realized what Jake had in his hand as soon as he had asked the question. "What's this one have to say?"

"It's another weird one, Preacher, but not as weird as last week's."

Bruce took the note and opened it slowly. He read, "Buford's play yet again."

"Got any ideas on that one, Preacher?" Jake asked.

"No, it's just more of the mystery, Jake. Uh, were there any visitors here today, like that guy from last week, or Oliver Paxton?" Bruce was rubbing his temples. He could feel the start of a headache.

"No, Preacher, but I think I did see Mr. Paxton's wife and little girl, but I'm not really sure if that was them." Jake smiled and moved down the hallway, leaving the preacher resting his head. Bruce sat there mulling the words over and over in his mind: "Buford's play yet again."

Scene 35

What to do?

Bruce was still deep in thought when he heard a familiar voice at the door. "Gotta minute preacher—maybe two or three, come to think of it?" Riley spoke with a half laugh and a grin.

"Always have time for the local constable, Riley. What can I do for you today? Was it something I said in today's sermon?" Bruce gave a slight chuckle.

"No … well, in a way, yeah, it was something you said." Riley's voice took a more serious tone, and Bruce turned in his chair as if bracing for an impact.

"What's on your mind, Riley?"

"Well, it's not just something you said today, Bruce; it's what you talk about a lot these days. All that stuff about evil and sin and what we can do to fight it or overcome it; I can't remember exactly how you put it sometimes." Riley looked and sounded as if he were searching for the right words to say, and Bruce was getting worried that he had said something to offend his friend.

"What I have been trying to say is that evil exists, and we need to see what part we play in it and try to stop ourselves from being the instruments of evil." Bruce was trying to sum up several sermons in a brief statement.

"Ah … yeah, that's it, Bruce. But ya see, I … sort of … have a different role than a lot of folks around here. I have to watch myself, and in the course of my job I come face to face with what we consider evil several times a day, and it sort of wears a guy down, I guess. I hope that's all it is. I was hopin' you could help me figure some things out." Riley was stuttering slightly and was wringing his hands. Bruce could see the signs of tension and concern in his face and body language.

"Is there any one thing that you can point to, Riley, that's causing most of your concern?" Bruce was probing and hoping to give Riley the opportunity to open up even more, but Riley didn't need much help getting started.

"You want to know what's really eatin' at me, Preacher? I can tell ya, but I just can't figure what to do about it. I'm about as mad and frustrated as you'll ever see me. I have seen a lot of things with these ole eyes. The world out there is a sewer sometimes, and I feel like I walk in it all day and at night until I can't get clean from it. I feel like the stink of crime is on me all the time. I deal with some of the worst situations around this county, and I don't know if I am just full up to here and need a break or if this latest case just hit too close to home." Riley had dropped his head and was shaking it from side to side.

"Which case is that, Riley … if you can tell me? It will stay as our confidence."

"Oh, I can tell you. You know as much as I do, since you were there." Riley was on the verge of showing his emotions.

Bruce knew now what he meant. He lowered his voice and said, "You mean Julian, don't you, Riley?"

"Yeah, that's it, Bruce. I keep seeing that little fella's body lying there beside that house in his little pajamas and that gun and blood. It's hard enough anytime you come on somethin' like that, but when you know the person it makes it extra rough. But that's just the half of it, Bruce. Did you see me the day of the funeral, talking to them boys after the service, out there in the graveyard?"

Bruce just nodded an affirmative nod. "I just glanced over at the group for a moment, Riley. I didn't really pay attention. What was going on?"

Oh, them three wanted to talk to me about the incident up at the battlefield. Seems they want to come clean now and tell the whole story. They were staying quiet to protect a friend who had been there and put that boy in the hospital. It seems, according to those three, that they were at the fight and that they had tried to apologize to the boys for something being said at the store, and things got out of hand and one thing led to another and they had a fight." Riley was getting visibly upset; he was almost shaking.

"You sort of figured they had something to do with it, didn't you, Riley?"

Bruce couldn't finish his thought before Riley interrupted. "Oh yeah, I figured they were in on it, but that's not the part that's botherin' me, Bruce. Ya see, they say that it was Julian who did the hittin' ... he used a ball bat and cracked that kid in the skull." Riley was visibly shaking now.

Bruce leaned forward in his chair, instantly outraged. "They said *what?* Of all the ... those ... what the ..." Bruce's voice was rising in inflection, and at the end it took on extra volume. He stammered in trying to say something without losing control.

"Now you see what's got me all tore up inside, Preacher. I told them little scoundrels what I thought about blaming a dead friend, but they just stood there, cool as cucumbers." Riley sat back with a bit of relief at being able to get some of his frustration off his chest. But his frustration shared was not cut in half. Now the preacher was welling up with rage at the situation.

"I'd run 'em in so fast it would make their heads swim if I were you, Riley. What's stopping you? They practically confessed to the assault, didn't they?" Bruce was still fighting to contain his anger.

"That's the other thing that's got me all tied up Bruce. They didn't confess to their part—they confessed that they were there and trying to cover up for a friend. If I take them in, they'll just tell that story again and get slapped on the wrist for withholding evidence, maybe obstruction or conspiracy. The DA could make a good case. But if I do that, look what happens to Julian's name. These guys are gonna make him take the biggest part of the blame and drag his name all through the mud. I just hate the thought of doing that to Julian's folks right now and to the memory of that little fella. I'm gonna talk to the sheriff about it, but I don't know what to do. I got evidence, and might nail them guys, but they've got a plausible story. To beat it all, Julian's parents would have to get a good lawyer and sit there and listen to those boys lie about Julian, all to save the little guy's reputation. They are skunks of the worst kind; they don't care about nobody but their own worthless hides. I'm mad, Bruce, and I gotta make some decisions, and none of them are easy. I was hopin' you could help me see this one through and figure out the best thing for everybody. Should I just drop the whole thing and let it go? Let these punks get away with it?"

"No, Riley, there's got to be some way to see justice done here. Have you tried talking to them individually and finding a break in their story?" Bruce was still infuriated about what he had just heard and getting angrier when he thought about the perpetrators going free.

"I see evil all the time, Bruce, and this is one of the worst cases of pure evil you'll ever see, when friends use a dead child to save their own scrawny necks." Riley sat quiet for a moment.

"I now its sounds hard, but if that kid hadn't come out of that coma, I could have locked those jokers up on the spot. But it would have had to be for accessory to murder, and Julian would still get drug through the mire and the mud. What can I do, Bruce? Every option is bad. It's like playing cards, and every play you make just gives something to your opponent." Riley paused for moment.

"What did you just say, Riley? Something about playing cards?" Bruce was pulled away from the present by the reference to making a play. He turned back to the note on his desk and read it slowly. "Buford's play yet again."

"I was just comparing things to a card game, Bruce. Ya know when you're stuck, and everything you do is gonna lead to disaster. Seems like everything ya do helps the other guy win. That's how I feel right now, all tied up and about to lose. Surrounded by evil and just waiting for the final assault to come."

Bruce listened, focusing on Riley's words, and then he thought about Colonel Buford and the battle that day at the crossroads. Surrounded and knowing that he couldn't win, he had hoped to surrender and save his men, but Tarleton had wanted blood and death, and that's what he'd gotten. And now, here at the church, evil had gotten the blood and death it wanted. Julian was one of the best and most innocent of kids; he'd just wanted to fit in. Now he was dead, and his so-called friends were more than willing to bury their sins in his grave. It was Buford's play all over again!

Chapter 7

Scene 36

The lull

Weeks passed, and the days were quiet around the community, as if everything was taking a holiday. Bruce was catching up on his sermon preparation. There was no one in hospital, so he could just visit around the community. School was in full swing, and the kids weren't burning up the highways. In the evenings, Bruce sat quietly in the parsonage, thinking about the events of the past month or so. So much of it still made no sense, and there was a sort of pregnant feeling in the community, as if something were about to happen but no one knew what or where. When faced with that feeling of uncertainty, Bruce would think about Sandy and Alan and how he had felt close to them in such a short period of time. He wasn't one to make friends quickly and let people into his life. This had always been his big weakness in ministry; it made him seem standoffish and aloof; some just called him arrogant and left it at that. But he really did care about people. He liked to think that he loved people but hated their ignorance. He preached how fear was fed by ignorance and the new great sin in the world was presumption. Most problems, he felt, came from people who presumed to know the thoughts of others and then based their own actions on that assumption. The problem was that nine times out of ten the assumption was based on a negative, and the actions were even more negative. He was convinced that's what had happened to Arthur Kirtland. An old man with too much time on his hands had let his mind wander into a thicket of barbed negativity, and it had spread like a disease through the community. Now that the battlefield protests were over, Arthur would have to find some new field of confrontation. Bruce was sure that Kirtland was behind the rumors about him entertaining single women overnight at the parsonage, but what good would it do to confront him? Arthur would just assume that sensitivity to accusation was a sign of guilt, and so Bruce had let it all drop, or so he thought. Others in the community were not so willing to leave things alone, as he would soon find out. But for now, everything seemed quiet.

The phone rang, and Bruce heard the familiar voice of Alan saying hello. He was surprised and a little excited to hear from Alan. After exchanging a few pleasantries about how his classes were going and how things were at church, Alan got to the point of his call. Alan had applied for another permit to do some research at the battlefield during fall break in October. He was surprised to find out that it would all depend on how fast the workers were going to get started on the building project near the battlefield. Alan had been surprised to hear of a building project, and Bruce told him that he had read in the paper that they were planning to build a recreation center near the battlefield, but he didn't think it was that close to the gravesite. Alan was livid as he told Bruce that the area where he wanted to investigate and look for artifacts was at the same place as the complex. Alan wanted to go over the actual battleground and see if he could pinpoint the exact location, and all speculation and descriptions pointed to an area southwest of the gravesite—exactly where the sports complex was being sited. Everyone knew it was somewhere to the southwest of the grave, but no one had ever marked off an actual battlefield. Alan was screaming about how business and development were robbing people of their heritage and this was just the latest example. Something had to be done; those people must stop what they were planning to do. Alan was coming up to talk with the developers and county manager and see what could be done. Bruce welcomed the chance to see Alan again and offered him a place to stay, which Alan had been hoping he would do. Alan would be up in a couple of weeks to get things ready.

As their conversation ended, Bruce thought of the great irony unfolding before him. Alan was coming to protest about digging at the battlefield, and that could mean that he and Arthur would be on the same side in this struggle. Talk about your strange bedfellows! Then it struck Bruce as odd that Arthur had said nothing about that latest encroachment on the hallowed ground he'd been so eager to defend earlier. News of the complex had been out for two weeks or more, but not a peep had come out of Arthur. Surely, he'd seen the story and knew what was going on. Why no protest? Bruce decided he would take a drive up toward the battlefield; it had been a few weeks since he had been by there.

The next morning brought a perfect day. The sky seemed extra blue, and there was a cool breeze blowing to remind him that fall was almost there. Was this Indian summer or blackberry summer? He was trying to remember what his grandmother used to call late August and early September. He turned off the car AC and rolled down the window to let the breeze blow in. He was reminded of his childhood days and the car rides with the windows down. Air conditioning was a luxury his parents had not been able to afford on their cars when he was young. He was still lost in remembrance as he arrived near the battlefield. He turned left on a road just before the gravesite to see if they had started on the construction. There he saw stakes with red flags sticking up all around, marking off invisible ball fields and tennis courts and a gymnasium building. He sat looking for a few moments and then began to drive back toward the gravesite.

Scene 37

Demons among us

John Criton spent much of his time either sitting in his room or at the battlefield, locked in deep concentration and meditation. He was opening his mind to his spirit guide, but Murmus and the other voices had been silent since that day at the graveyard. He felt alone and helpless. He was afraid to do anything, to leave or go back to his home. The many years of dependence on his spirit guide had made him weak and powerless to act on his own. He had no contact with Kirtland anymore; he realized that he had been used as a pawn in the old man's game. That was just as well, since Criton had his own worries now. Some days he would drive out to the battlefield and sit there reaching out with his mind into the invisible world, but there was just darkness and silence.

He thought of the afternoon he had spoken with Reverend Strong. The reverend's words had been the last kind ones he had heard in this place. He had decided that maybe he would drive back out and try again. The Friday morning was cool and clear, and Criton drove the familiar road toward Buford crossing. A right turn, and he headed down to the battlefield. He pulled his car into the gravel drive, looking toward the grave area as if expecting to see an old friend waiting for him. As he turned off the ignition, he was struck by the sudden silence, except for the distance sound of a passing car. After a slow walk up the small hill and over to the picnic table nearest the grave, he sat down in his usual place.

But this day would be different than the ones he'd spent sitting here alone, because today he would have a visitor. It just wasn't the one he wanted. He heard the car coming up the road but didn't give it another thought until he heard it slowing and turning into the rough gravel drive. He hated it when others came to this place while he was there. He turned toward the sound and immediately recognized Reverend Strong sitting behind the steering wheel. A slight feeling of confusion came over him as he wondered whether God had sent him here again. The last time they had talked, he had been cordial and kind, even if he did seem a little too perceptive for Criton's liking.

The two men exchanged greetings, and Bruce sat down across from Criton. "How have you been, Mr. Criton?" Bruce spoke with a large smile on his face. "It's been a while since I talked with you."

"Well, things have actually been rather quiet around here since the team left." Criton spoke warmly in a low tone, and when he said *quiet*, he may have subconsciously been telling more than he intended, since it was doubly quiet for him, with no voices speaking to him. "What brings you out this way?"

"Well, I could ask you the same, Mr. Criton, since things here have died down—oh, no pun intended." The two men shared an uncomfortable chuckle.

"I find this place is very restful and interesting. Perhaps it is the energy of the spirits here that attracts me." Criton used his more professional-sounding voice now, which did not go unnoticed by Bruce.

"Has Murmus been relaying messages from the dead lately about the plans for building a recreation center here at the battlefield?" Bruce asked. Criton was shocked by the directness of his question and wasn't sure how to respond. Should he say no, or should he try to make up something to assuage Reverend Strong? His hesitancy did not go unnoticed by Bruce; this might be the opening in the conversation that he wanted.

"I don't want to seem rude, Mr. Criton, but I have wanted to talk with about your gift and its possible implications. Since our last conversation, I have done some research, and I wanted to share some findings with you, if you were interested."

"What's on your mind, Reverend?" Criton seemed defensive.

Bruce looked down at the table and spoke softly. "I do not wish to offend you, but there was something you said last time that aroused my curiosity and caused me some concern for your safety."

Criton smiled and sort of laughed. "I thought you were very perceptive, but I can't imagine what I said that could be a concern to you, Reverend." Criton was leaning back away from the meeting, and Bruce was reading his body language as defensive.

"Uh, well, the last time we spoke you said you were in contact with a spirit called Murmus and that he was an ancient philosopher or something."

"Yes, Murmus has always been my companion," Criton said confidently.

Bruce leaned forward and said, "Are you aware that in some ancient texts Murmus was the name of a ..." Bruce paused and swallowed, "a demon being who commands legions of demons?"

Criton's smile left his face, and a more serious one stared back at Bruce. He had again been caught off guard, but he tried to recover himself without revealing his discomfort. "I am not familiar with the name being related to demons, Reverend. Surely you aren't suggesting that my spirit guide is actually a force of evil, are you?"

Bruce was trying to choose his words carefully. "It's just that when we last spoke, you mentioned Murmus and said that he spoke on behalf of "legions" of people, as you put it. That word *legion* is what caught my attention."

"I understand your curiosity, Reverend Strong, but doesn't it seem odd that a demonic being would be helping me do good and positive things for people all my life? I assure you that Murmus has always been a force for good." Criton was defensive and insistent.

Reverend Strong didn't want to get into a deep theological argument; he had hoped that Criton would be more open. He decided to try another tactic. "Another thing I noticed during our last conversation was how you referred to Murmus in the past tense. Have you not been in contact with Murmus?"

A conflict began to arise in Criton's mind. Part of him wanted to confide in this man who seemed genuine in his intentions, but his practical nature was screaming that no one must know that he was no longer in contact with the spirit world. If that knowledge were to be made public, he would be ruined financially and professionally. He sat there, locked in his internal struggle, and suddenly he looked up and spoke in a detached tone. "I think you are being a bit presumptuous, Reverend Stone, and I am not sure if I wish to discuss such intimate information with you. I can't be sure that you are not simply another person seeking to discredit my gift. There have been many others, and while I do not wish to sound rude, you must understand my position." With that Criton closed his lips into a rigid smile.

It was now Bruce's turn to speak or change the subject, but it seemed clear that if he pursued this topic there would be no further conversation.

Bruce looked sincerely into Criton's eyes and tried to reassure him that he was genuinely concerned with the spiritual implications and not with debunking him as some sort of fraud. "I was not sure of what you knew or believed about spirituality from the religious perspective. We both deal in the spirit world, and we both presume to have a certain level of expertise. I feel that I am as much an expert as you feel you are. You feel that you are helping, and I feel that I might be helping you, because if I am right, you are subject to a very powerful and deceptive being. With regards to the fact that you have known this spirit all your life, I can only refer to the historical records of human and demonic activity that suggest that spirits will stay with people for decades to create a relationship."

"Are you suggesting that I am demon possessed, Reverend?"

"No, I am suggesting that you may have a relationship as a familiar with a demonic spirit. People in this type of relationship are often hurt and disappointed when they find that they have been used or duped." Bruce was in full preacher mode now as he made his compassionate declaration.

"So now I am a dupe? I really feel you are overstepping your bounds here, Reverend, and—"

But Bruce interrupted him before he could finish. "Perhaps I am, but at this point I am not concerned with our relationship as friends as much as I am concerned for you and the harm that you may be unwittingly doing or have done. Has Murmus finished with you and left you here alone with no more communication?"

The sudden silence was thick as a fog rising between the two. Criton was angry, but Bruce had hit a nerve, and Criton was falling into thought as he tried to balance what had just been said with what he was experiencing. Criton regained his composure and his cool demeanor and eyed Bruce with a look of smug arrogance. "Let's say that I have been duped with my work. What harm have I done by bringing comfort to the relatives of the deceased? It seems a strange tactic for the devil if he wants to bring sorrow to the world. Can you explain that to me, Reverend?"

"Actually, John, I think I can. Demonic possession is not about Hollywood movie effects and taking over the world. It's a personal situation. Look at the people that Jesus dealt with who were possessed. They were lonely individuals, and he could have easily left them in their state of being, because freeing them from their tormentors was not a high priority for many; it was an individual and family thing. He took compassion on them and set them free so that they could be in control of their lives again. Consider the story of Paul, who freed a young slave girl from demonic possession. He was hated by her owners because they had been getting rich from her possession.

"Look at you sitting here—you're lost without that spirit guide, aren't you? You have no life without it, and you don't know what to do. You have surrendered yourself to Murmus, and you're not aware of the life you lost. As for the damage to others, you have people believing that your messages from Murmus are from dead relatives, but I suggest that these messages are designed to get people to trust you and your spirit guides so that it will be easier for other spirits to approach and dupe them. I believe that a demon will tell ten truths to get you to that one lie that will destroy a person. It is the same tactic con men use, and the guys who play three-card monte, or the shell game off the street. They let you win, and you keep doubling your bet until they get you to bet it all, and then they show you that they were in charge all along. You have a national following of your TV shows and books, people who have turned their backs on reality and on the only real spirit that can help them—and that is the Holy Spirit of God."

Bruce paused to take a breath. He had hit Criton right between the eyes, but he'd decided he might as well tell him all he could, since this could be their last conversation.

Criton was stunned and momentarily speechless. "Well, that was quite a speech, and I don't know just what to say, Reverend Strong. You obviously are very passionate about your beliefs, and I must tell you, so am I. And as for the past life I supposedly lost, I am aware each day of my past life and very happy to leave it all behind. Perhaps you are a little jealous of my sure spiritual direction because you lack such certainty in your spiritual life. Remember the day you came here and said that you felt you should be here, but God was noticeably silent as to what you were to do or even expect? When Murmus speaks to me, he is very clear." Criton stood up and took one look at the gravesite and then back at Bruce. He politely nodded and said, "Excuse me, Reverend, I must be going." And that was it. Their meeting was over, and Bruce found himself sitting alone again at the battlefield.

As Criton pulled his car back onto the road and headed for town, the words of Reverend Strong were echoing in his mind. He had made a strong speech with regards to his own faith, but now, without Murmus, he feared he had lost the object of his faith, and he had no explanation for the loss. The young preacher had had an explanation, and it had even had some logic to it. Criton knew he had another sleepless night ahead of him. The new question for him was not where Murmus was but what if Murmus was not what he had believed him to be? Now he had to deal with his doubts.

Scene 38

Justice and God time

In a small house down the road from the battlefield, another battle was raging, in the mind of Deputy Riley Jackson. What should he do about the boys and their graveside accusation of Julian as the one who had hit Topper? *If I pursue it and they stick to their stories, it will be like Julian was dug up and killed again.* Riley had put the scene together in his mind, and he felt sure that someone else had done the swinging of the bat and that Julian had been told to keep quiet. The guilt had probably driven him to suicide, so in Riley's mind those boys had killed Julian. But with no solid testimony, it would become their word against an unsure witness. He believed in justice, but where was justice now? It seemed absent, and Riley needed justice to show up and make things right again, so that these punks did not get away with assault and murder.

In his office, Bruce Strong sat trying to write a sermon, but his mind was juggling and struggling with events of the previous weeks. It seemed as if a tapestry of evil had been tossed over the area. The events of the battlefield had indirectly left one child dead and had caused tensions in the church as people began to take sides in the argument. As well, there was the tension between Bruce and Arthur Kirtland, who had made it a point not to speak to Bruce in a few weeks. This anger had carried over into the senior men's Sunday school class, as the older folks were still angry about Alan and Sandy staying in the parsonage. The rumor had been started, and even after they realized that Alan had also been there and that the two had only stayed a couple of nights, some continued to talk about it as if it had been some wild party. It angered Bruce, but he had decided that the only way he could make people happy would be to stand up and tell them that there had been no wild parties and then yes, there had been wild parties! In that way, everybody would be happy and could believe whatever they wanted. He was pretty sure it didn't matter what he said; their minds were already made up. He felt anger and pity at the same time. He felt sorrow that people could take joy in rumors and still call themselves Christians, but human nature was what it was, he thought. Why did evil seem so easy and kindness so hard for some people?

Bruce was not having a true crisis of faith, but he could feel the depression creeping in as if someone had draped a blanket over his shoulders on a hot day. He wanted to shrug it off, and he even moved his shoulders as if shaking something to the floor. He didn't realize how tense his muscles had gotten just sitting in his chair. He turned to his bible and began to read through the Psalms. Psalm 34 came to mind at times like this. He began to write out selected verses from Psalm 34 that seemed to speak to his heart.

1. I will bless the LORD at all times: his praise *shall* continually *be* in my mouth.
4. I sought the LORD, and he heard me, and delivered me from all my fears.

6. This poor man cried, and the LORD heard *him*, and saved him out of all his troubles.

7. The angel of the LORD encampeth round about them that fear him, and delivereth them.

8. O taste and see that the LORD *is* good: blessed *is* the man *that* trusteth in him.

11. Come, ye children, hearken unto me: I will teach you the fear of the LORD.

13. Keep thy tongue from evil, and thy lips from speaking guile.

14. Depart from evil, and do good; seek peace, and pursue it.

17. *The righteous* cry, and the LORD heareth, and delivereth them out of all their troubles.

18. The LORD *is* nigh unto them that are of a broken heart; and saveth such as be of a contrite spirit.

19. Many *are* the afflictions of the righteous: but the LORD delivereth him out of them all.

He read for a while and softly spoke a prayer, and then that sensation of calm came over him, and he began to smile. "I sought the Lord, and he heard me and delivered me from all my fears," he mumbled to himself and then sighed. "That is so cool how he does that."

Scene 39

The visitation

Bruce's mind shifted back to his work. He needed to visit the Hopkins family; maybe he could be of some comfort to them. He had been by to see them each week since the funeral and had noticed Edna falling deeper and deeper into depression. He understood the grieving process and how a person goes through various stages, but she was like a woman lost in a dark forest. Thomas Hopkins was delaying his grief because he thought she needed him, and Bruce wondered how long it would be before he snapped. Thomas had let him know that he had taken Edna to a doctor, who had prescribed a sedative, but she wouldn't take them. She'd just gotten angry and said there wasn't anything wrong with her and then started pacing and crying again. Thomas didn't like to leave her alone, but he had to go to work.

Bruce felt he should be there with them, but it was challenging. Edna needed rest and time to heal, but she wouldn't take it. In her mind, sleep was a betrayal to Julian, because she'd been sleeping when he'd needed her; she hadn't been there. If she had been awake, she could have stopped him, but she'd been asleep. Now she didn't sleep, except for naps in the living room chair by the door, as if she were guarding the doorway.

He did not look forward to these types of visits, because his sense of empathy pulled him deep into people's grief, and it was hard to not be overwhelmed by their sorrow. Words sometimes came in an awkward way; platitudes just sounded hollow coming from his mouth. He actually needed to enter their grief with them, and it was just so exhausting.

"I sought the Lord ... he delivers me from my fears," Bruce mumbled as he turned in his chair and started to rise. But then he started with a jerk and let out a quiet "Oh."

"Sorry, Reverend Strong, I didn't mean to startle you." It was that man again, and he was wearing that same green sport coat but with an open-collared shirt this time. He stood in the doorway just as before, and Bruce could still not get a clear look at his face. "Were you going somewhere? Because I can come back another time rather than inconvenience you."

"Oh no, I can take care of my work later. What I can do for you, Mr. ..." Bruce paused and realized he didn't know this man's name. "I'm sorry, I don't think I ever got your name." Bruce waited for a response.

"My apologies. My name is Lerajie, Marcus Lerajie. I live in the community and come to church here on occasion. I am not originally from around here, but of course no one can be from around here, unless

you are of one of the few families that seem to have lived here forever."
He laughed softly.

"Lerajie, that is unusual. Is it French?" Bruce asked.

"No, actually it is Eastern European. My family was from Poland and Czechoslovakia, and so I'm not sure who gets the most credit for me. I consider myself all-American."

"Come in and have a seat, and tell me what brings you in today, Mr. Lerajie." Bruce sat back down.

Lerajie shifted his weight and slowly moved to the small loveseat across from Bruce's desk. "I really can't stay, but I was thinking of your sermon again and how you were focused on fighting the evil in man and in our community. Then, when I saw your car, I felt compelled to stop by and just give you a friendly word of warning. A sort of heads-up, you might say. I am not especially close to the folks in the community, but I see and speak to various ones on occasion. I've heard a few comments that I thought were a little over the top, shall we say. I think you are doing a bang-up job here and that the things people are saying are just unfair. I try not to let on or take sides, and I think that this allows me to be objective."

"I appreciate your concern, Mr. Lerajie. But I doubt that there is anything you have heard that I haven't already heard, and I can probably tell you who said it, as well. But I feel that it is best if I just pray for these folks and try to win them over with kindness." Bruce was getting uncomfortable with Mr. Lerajie, and a bit curious about what he had heard, but he wasn't going to fall into the gossip pit.

"Please call me Marcus." Lerajie spoke with a definite effeminate quality in his voice. "Don't you want to know what these people are saying about you? I know I would. I would want to confront their slander to their faces. The only way to stop it is to shame them into submission. Trust me; I know these people, and they can be live, ravenous wolves, or lions, and such. You are a strong man, Reverend Strong—no pun intended—and I think you are just what this community has needed: a strong leader who can keep these loudmouths in line. Think about it, because there are a lot of people like me that have a great interest and concern for the status of this church. We are fighters when we think the cause is the right one. I am just doing what you said in that sermon; I am accepting the challenge to confront evil. You think about what I said. I have to run along now, but I'll be in touch."

"Thank you, Mr. ... I mean Marcus. I appreciate your support," Bruce said almost hypnotically. This man's concern had been comforting. With that, Lerajie was up and out the door before Bruce could so much as see him out.

Bruce sat there for a minute, going over the conversation. This man made him feel very comfortable and yet somehow uncomfortable, and his voice and mannerisms seemed so kind, almost feminine, and yet slimy at the same time. He was glad to see him go. Bruce suddenly realized that he had sat right in front of him and he still could not get a clear mental image of the man's face. If he saw him on the street, he probably wouldn't recognize him. But he would know that voice. Bruce was so lost in thought that he forgot all about going over to the Hopkins'. Later that night, as he lay in bed, he remembered that he had wanted to visit with them in the hopes of helping them feel a little relief from their sadness, but he had let that man distract him from that work. Everything about this guy felt wrong. He couldn't explain it; it just felt wrong. He would visit the Hopkins first thing in the morning.

The next day he went into his office and checked his mail. Then, just as he grabbed his bible and started out the door, the phone rang. Bruce decided to ignore it; he was going to the Hopkins', and nothing would stop him. He hurried to the door—but ran into it with a thud. The door was stuck. He shoved and shoved, and it still wouldn't open. It was the same as that first day that Lerajie had been there, when it had mysteriously jammed and then opened. Today he would not play the game and let things stand in his way. He stepped back to take a running go at the door, but then he stopped, smiled, and turned to walk down the hall and out the other side of the church. He laughed and told himself it was a nice day for a stroll. He would visit the Hopkins even if he had to walk to their house.

Fortunately, his car was in fine working order and after a short ride from the church, he was driving up in the yard of the Hopkins' house. He couldn't help but glance over to the bushes and the spot where Julian had been found. There was a faint discoloration from the bloodstains on the siding. As he stepped onto the porch, Thomas met him at the door and stepped out of the house.

"Boy, am I glad to see you, Preacher; it has been a rough night. I tried to call your office, but your phone just rang and rang. I wish you could have been here yesterday. Edna is having a time with everything. She's about cried herself out and been hysterical at times. I have held her and tried to get her to take one of those pills the doctor gave her, but all she does is walk from the front of the house to Julian's bedroom, saying she wants to be with him and she wants to die. She keeps praying that the Lord will let her die, or saying she is going to follow Julian, so she can be with him. I just don't know what to do. I loved that boy with all my heart, and I don't know what to do." Before he could say any more, Thomas Hopkins began to sob almost uncontrollably.

The sound of his tears brought Edna in from the next room. Her eyes were swollen, and she could not speak for sobbing. She saw Bruce holding her husband's head to his chest. She fell into his arms, and the three of them sat embracing on the couch. Bruce said nothing; he just held these two adults as if they were his children, and his tears fell down upon their heads. They sat there for about an hour, crying and just holding one another. Soon Edna rose and asked if she could get Bruce some coffee. He nodded yes. Thomas got up and went into the bathroom to wash his face, and he brought a cool cloth for his wife.

They drank some coffee and washed the tears from their eyes. Then Bruce, Thomas, and Edna sat there in silence for a long time. It was amazing how quiet the house was in those hours of grief. You could hear each person breathing and sighing. Bruce had no words of wisdom or devotional platitudes. Instead, he began to share memories of funny moments he'd had with Julian in bible school and on youth trips. And amid the tears there were moments of laughter, as they all realized that Julian was dead in the physical, earthly sense, but in these memories and in their faith and hope he was just as alive as ever. Death could not rob them of the love they had for their son. Bruce suggested they both take one of the sedatives the doctor had given them and try to rest. He instructed them to feel free to call him or come by if they needed a friend to share tears or laughter with.

When he left, he realized that, as usual, he'd had no super ministerial game plan. He'd come to share his love for them as family and his love for their son. In this God was free to act, and God had ministered to these people's hearts. It was another of those things that he could not explain very well. His ministering didn't come from a textbook or how-to manual. It was just what he was led to do, and he said a prayer of thanks as he drove back to the church. As much as he always dreaded visits like this, he remembered that afterward there was always a feeling of peace and joy in knowing that he had been allowed to be in the presence of God as God brought healing to grieving people.

Scene 40

Revelation

Spiritual forces were working at another place in the county that day. In a small hotel room in Lancaster, John Criton sat at a desk, staring out the window. After a moment, he stood up, closed the drape, and began to focus on Murmus. He did something he had never done; he actually prayed to Murmus to come to him and speak with him again. He needed to hear from his spirit friend one more time, just to be sure that what Reverend Strong had said was all a lie. His brow began to furrow, and sweat drops formed on his forehead. He was praying audibly now, calling on Murmus to speak to his mind again, as he had so many times in the past. It was midday, but the room seemed to be getting darker, and as the intensity of his prayer rose, it seemed the temperature in the room rose. And then, like the soft touch of a cool hand on the back of his neck, he sensed the voice.

"My friend, you are troubled. What worries you so? Don't you know I am here?" It was Murmus.

Criton felt an almost euphoric relaxation come over his body, and he sat back in the chair. "Where have you been, old friend? I have needed to hear from you for these past weeks, and you were not there, and now when I pray to you, you come. Is that what you have wanted—my prayers?"

Murmus was silent for a moment and then spoke to Criton's mind. "I have always been here, John, I didn't leave you; I have watched you and heard your cries for help."

"But then why didn't you respond, my old friend?"

"Because of your doubts, John. You have doubted my presence and been unsure of me, and it has changed you, John, I can tell. As you change, so does our relationship. I wish it were not so, but there are many who seek my guidance and council, and I must attend to the needs of others. You have made new friends, and so have I. All your life you have felt that I belonged to you in some way, but it has always been my power that made you strong. I am the source, and you are the instrument of my goodness. Now, along with my other friends, we will spread the goodness from the afterlife with many more. You will be my strong right arm, if you so wish it. I have a special place reserved in the work for you, my old friend. You will lead others to me, and together we will share the gift of knowledge."

As Murmus spoke, Criton was realizing that their relationship was taking a new shape, and it wasn't until he said the word *strong* that his mind almost snapped awake. *Strong right arm, share* with others—this was a new relationship. When Murmus had said "strong" all he'd been able to see in his mind was Reverend Strong. Reverend Strong spoke of God the way Murmus was speaking of himself, and Murmus wanted him to serve him now, almost like a high priest. This was not what he was accustomed to, and now he was thinking that maybe Reverend Strong had told him the truth. As soon as he had this thought, his mind went silent again.

Then, slowly, like the rumbling of an earthquake, a voice rose up in his head. It was Murmus, but it was different—deeper, echoing, and ominous.

"Your thoughts betray you again and again, Criton, and I will not tolerate it any longer. Choose your allegiance and make your choice now. You are getting weaker by the hour and becoming unworthy of this great work we perform. You have let outside voices infect your mind with their superstitions and doubts. Now choose! Follow me or suffer the emptiness and loneliness of a dull existence. Do you want to go back to your life of mediocre invisibility or rise higher than ever before and bring peace and hope to more people all over the world? Choose, Criton. This is your moment, and it will not come again. If you have no faith in me, then I will put no faith in you. Now choose!"

Criton's head was spinning, and he saw his life from his early struggles as a child to his successful life as a seer. What was he to do? And then a new feeling came over him, a new sensation of knowledge and with it a sense of calm. He opened his eyes, raised his head, and spoke as if Murmus were standing in front of him. "It wasn't me who doubted or abandoned anyone. It was you; you left me long before I spoke with Reverend Strong. I was trying to help these people, as I always have, but then you betrayed me and left me alone out there on that battlefield. Now you want me to worship you and serve you like a high priest. Answer one question: Are you an ancient man or are you a demon leader of legions?"

There was a moment of quiet and then a rumbling sensation, and Criton wasn't sure whether it was real or imagined. He felt a rush of cold air and then a gut-wrenching ache which bent him over toward the floor, as if someone were pushing him down. "Why won't you answer me? Who are you?" he demanded. Still it was quiet in his mind.

"You're no holy man or philosopher, are you? You are Murmus the fallen one, just as Strong said, and you have duped me and used me all my life, waiting for this moment to turn me into your puppet."

Criton was almost shouting now, shouting at the walls like a crazy man. And then, in the sudden silence, Criton realized that he was talking to an empty room. Criton began to ask himself what he was doing. Did he really believe what he had just said? Was this all some sort of dream? As the question came, so did the sound in his head, like a million birds in flight coming out of the darkness right at him. There was a stabbing pain in the back of his neck, and he collapsed on the floor.

The maid found him the next morning when she came to change the bedding. He was quivering and unconscious, and she called 911. Criton was taken to the hospital and treated for a seizure. It was days before he could speak again, and when he could, he said, "Get me Reverend Strong ... please."

When Bruce arrived at the hospital, he found Criton sitting up in a chair, staring out the window. A smile moved across his face when Bruce entered the room.

"I'm happy to see you, Reverend Strong, it's been a rough ..." He stopped and asked, "What day is it, anyway?"

"It's Tuesday, Mr. Criton."

"Three days. The last thing I remember was Saturday afternoon, and then it all went black. Well, that's not exactly true. I remember a lot before the blackout. Whoa, have I a story to tell to you." Criton looked funny, like a little boy, grinning, with mussed hair and a twinkle in his eye. Except for the three-day growth of beard and the deep voice, he was quite boyish. Bruce pulled the other chair over to him, and Criton began to relate all that had happened. The hair on Bruce's arms began to stand up, but Criton was just smiling and talking a mile a minute.

"And here I am." Criton said, taking a deep breath as if exhausted. "By the way, where am I? I assume it's the Lancaster hospital. The doctors and nurses haven't told me. They said I had a seizure, but they don't know how wrong they are. It wasn't a seizure; it was more like a release." Criton laughed at his own play on words. "It is amazing how free I feel! I never realized how under Murmus's control I was. Even when I wasn't in communication with him, I was thinking of him. I know I shouldn't say this, but in a strange way it's almost like I miss his presence—but then I recall that deafening darkness, and I snap back into reality. Is that how it is with people who have had these kinds of experiences? Murmus said that I would be alone and powerless, in darkness and a dull existence. But what a lie! I feel clean and lighter than air, as if a burden and a sorrow have been removed. It is an amazing sensation!"

Bruce looked at him and gave a laughing sigh. He spoke deliberately and with detachment. "I confess I do not know, Mr. Criton, how one feels after struggling with a demon." Then he paused, laughed, and said, "What am I saying? I know exactly how you feel. I would say you have had a salvation experience! I get so used to thinking that it can only occur in church after a sermon that I forget that God can act anywhere and in any way he chooses. I think you have had an encounter with God, Mr. Criton. When you made your choice, it wasn't a choice between Murmus and emptiness. It was a choice between light and dark, and the darkness has lost. Your story is incredible! From what little I have read about possession, I believe parts of your story are not unique. I just don't remember reading about anybody being as happy as you." And with that they both laughed out loud like crazy men.

"It has given me a new perspective on life and a new mission as well, Reverend ... Can I call you Bruce?" Criton asked.

"Only if I can call you John, Mr. Criton." Bruce seemed a bit apprehensive to be calling this celebrity by his first name, but Criton assured him that they were definitely on a first-name basis.

"Why, if it weren't for you, I wouldn't have understood what was happening in my room the other day. It was as if you were sent to me that very day to prepare me for what was about to happen. But it's something more than fate or luck. I sense a presence of goodness such as I never knew with Murmus. He seems like a cheap imitation to me now. Have you ever felt that way, Bruce?"

Bruce smiled and admitted, "Well, actually, I have—on several occasions, as a matter of fact. But it is so refreshing to see it in someone for the first time."

"Refreshing, yes, that is a good word for it. It is refreshing, like a cool shower after a hot day's work. You must tell me more about what I can expect from now on. I am like a new person, a blank slate to be written on. But it's not totally blank, because I used to wonder what I would do without Murmus, and now I know. I have a whole new focus in life and a new mission. I need to tell everyone what has happened, my experience with God and the devil."

"I am really glad for you, John, but I feel I must warn you that the world may not be as receptive to your new message as they were to your old one. At least that has been my experience." Bruce heard himself speak and couldn't believe that he was throwing water on this man's enthusiasm.

"I don't expect they will like it, Bruce, but it is a story that must be told, for the sake of the few if not the many. And if the many listen, all the better. Murmus said he had others out there, and I was to be their high priest. We live in a very spiritual age; even though on the surface most people are trying to deny their spiritual side, they are more receptive to it than ever before. I know I made millions of dollars off them. It's time to use their own money for their own good. I tell you, Bruce, it is *refreshing* to think about the future and my coming opportunities."

Bruce and John Criton sat there for hours, talking about the events of the past three days. They discussed how Criton could become more familiar with God and scriptures. They talked until the sun slipped below the window and the evening moon began to rise, and then they talked well into the night. About midnight, Criton said, "I think I have a new book to write, and I will do book signings all over the place to present it to the world. I must contact my assistant in the morning and start making preparations. Mind if I mention your name in the book, Bruce?"

"No, go right ahead, as long as I get a signed copy."

"Deal," Criton agreed with a laugh. "Now I must make arrangements for a home while I am here. I will rent a house and write the book right here in the place where it all happened. Oh, and when can I get baptized?"

Bruce head came up, and he spoke with a tone of surprise. "Well, anytime you want, I suppose. Any place in particular you'd like to be baptized? We can do it at church or at the river, whichever."

"Great, let's do it in a river. That seems more natural, doesn't it!"

Scene 41

The battle plan

Bruce walked silently out of the hospital room and down the hall and made his way home. It had been quite the eventful past few days. It was the kind of week that seemed to energize him for his work. He had seen sorrow turned into smiles a few days earlier and a potential adversary become a new friend and convert today. At home, he sat in his favorite chair and pondered it all in silence. Life seemed filled with purpose.

The next morning, he sat sipping coffee that the part-time secretary had made, reading, and jotting down ideas for sermons. He barely noticed the sound of the side door opening. He looked up and started to say, "Mr.—"

But the figure in the doorway said, "It's Marcus, remember? No need for formalities between us. Have you a moment for a little light conversation?"

"Sure. Come in, Marcus. What seems to be on your mind?" Bruce was still feeling the euphoria from the previous day and was anxious to be of service to someone again. Marcus came in, and this time Bruce was able to see him better. It was a tall, gaunt man but with a warm smile and a sort of grandfatherly look of wisdom who sat across from him. Bruce got up and stepped down the hall to tell the secretary he would be in a conference and not to disturb him. When he came back, he pulled the door almost closed and sat back down.

"Now we won't be disturbed. What's on your mind, Mr. ... I mean, Marcus?"

"Well, it goes back to that discussion we were having about evil in our midst, and I wanted to sort of pick your brain on that topic a little more. I was wondering about things like how do you know you are dealing with evil, and if there were different kinds of evil, that sort of thing. What is your experience in these things?"

Bruce smiled like a child at play and began to recount the events of the past few weeks, leaving out the names, of course. He tried to put them into context of actual demonic evil, and evil inspired by demonic activities, and man's role as agent of evil. He quoted some scriptures, but Marcus said that he'd always found the Bible a bit confusing and was amazed at how well Bruce could interpret it and make sense of things. They spoke for the better part of the morning, and Bruce didn't even notice when the secretary left down the hall.

Around lunchtime, Marcus suddenly looked at his watch and said, "Oh my, I have taken up your whole morning, and I have a lunch engagement. Can I come again and discuss this further?"

"Certainly," Bruce said, smiling. "I love talking theology with an interested person."

"I am that, Bruce. I have never fully understood it, but I do feel that theology is one of the most important subjects we can study. I was more into philosophy in college, and you know how that can be sometimes. They say politics and religion don't mix, and it seems that today philosophy and religion aren't as close friends as they used to be. I think that is a shame, though. Both have much wisdom in common, wouldn't you agree?"

"Yes, I would agree, Marcus. I just don't get the opportunity to express such deep thoughts in my day-to-day work. This has been refreshing!"

"Then we must do it again, and soon. It has been an honor to sit with you and listen to your wisdom. You truly have a gift of reason and expression. Have you considered writing a book? I think I could read your thoughts over and over. You know, you should share that gift with the world. There are a lot of people who need your keen wit and ability to clarify things. I have learned a lot in just the past few hours. But I must go. I will drop in again soon, if you don't mind, Bruce. I have a ton of questions."

"Come by anytime, please, Marcus. It has been invigorating." And with that their meeting was over. Marcus made his way out the side door and Bruce sat there thinking that perhaps he had misjudged this man. He seemed to be out of place in this quiet farming community, but it was nice to meet someone with such a keen intellect and a hunger to learn. It was another moment of purpose for Bruce. He felt as if he had helped someone else on a whole different level. But now it was after lunchtime, and he not finished his midweek study for tonight. No problem; he would just grab something out of the file and go over it again. Perhaps something on wisdom would be good.

Scene 42

The magician's secret of distraction

Over the next few weeks, Marcus came by more and more. Bruce began to look forward to his visits, as the two of them contemplated the theological and philosophical ramifications of all sorts of things. As Marcus had suggested, Bruce began to write down many of their thoughts and ideas and shape them into a manuscript. It could be a whole new theological treatise that reflected some deep philosophical undertones. Bruce would stay up late at night writing and putting things on paper, and he enjoyed this very much. It was as if someone had set his mind on fire with ideas.

Bruce was staying in his office more and more, researching topics for his writing, and his sermons began to reflect his research. It was not that they were bad sermons, but for the congregation they became more and more theological and less practical for their lives. He spoke of the battles between good and evil and how one must always be on guard against satanic deception. He spoke of complacency in the Church and marginal Christians who were more prone to creating a God centered on moral relevance than truly understanding God as revealed in scripture. All of it was accurate and passionate, but the congregation began to sense that they were being attacked and accused of these behaviors. And in some way, they were correct. Bruce was on the attack; he was railing out against the unseen evil in their midst and pointing out how evil was working in the community. On Mondays, almost like clockwork, Marcus would arrive at his office and tell him what an excellent sermon he had preached and how effective his messages were. Whenever Bruce would question him about not seeing him in church, he would always remark that he sat in the back area, where he could be indiscreet, and that he usually slipped right out the door during the invitation prayer. Marcus confided that he knew many of the people in the church but had never really had such an interest in coming until he had heard Bruce speak. This story seemed to go along with what some had said when he'd asked about Marcus. A few said they knew *of* him but didn't really know him, and none had really noticed him in church. Usually the conversations quickly shifted to questions about Bruce and what he was doing.

Some people remarked that they missed seeing him out in the community, and Bruce knew that they were hinting in their less-than-subtle way that he needed to visit more. Bruce always made a mental note to get around to seeing the sick and elderly, but he couldn't avoid the feeling that he was involved in some important work with his writing. He didn't realize it at the time, but he was rationalizing that his writing was more important than the needs of the congregation. He was here to share God's word, he reasoned, not to be a paid friend or babysitter for someone whose own family should visit more often. He was going to the hospitals regularly and often, and that, along with the occasional visit to the rest homes, should have been enough to satisfy. He needed time to study and prepare. Some could understand that, but many were traditional. They felt that the preacher should spend all his time in the community and then just get up and say what God put on his heart.

It wasn't long before the critics saw their opportunity to strike, and it began in the same place as before. Arthur Kirtland was using each Sunday-morning class time to report that the preacher had not been to see him in weeks. One Sunday a gentle old man spoke up and said that he thought Arthur didn't like the preacher, so why would he want him to come visit him? This was quickly met with a scathing rebuff. Arthur laid out all the expectations of a pastor as if reading from an official job description, which actually did not exist. After that, everyone just mumbled their quiet acceptance of Arthur's accusations, and on and on it went, week after week, like a slow-growing cancer.

Meanwhile, Marcus was still stopping by weekly and sometimes twice a week. The meetings were some of Bruce's favorite times. He looked forward to the stimulating conversation, and the constant praise was a welcome change from the criticism he sensed from the congregation. When he spoke of his critics with Marcus, Marcus would smile and relate how the Church had a history of negative treatment of leaders. He advised Bruce not to worry, because the enlightened people coming to church were very supportive. They understood and were pleased with what he was doing.

Bruce did make a point to go by Arthur's home one afternoon, and it was one of the coldest visits he had ever experienced, even though the weather was a little on the warm side. The atmosphere in the house was chilly, and Bruce found himself talking more to Mrs. Kirtland as she went about her daily activities. Whenever he tried to engage Arthur in conversation, he was met with short answers, given more in grunts than with words. He was ever so happy to leave, and once he was outside the house, it was as if a boulder had been lifted from his shoulders. Later that week, he would find that Arthur had had much more to say to his friends about how the preacher had stopped by for a few minutes, spoken to his wife, and almost totally ignored him, leaving him out of the conversations. He accused Bruce of being a flirt with the ladies and suggested he must have impure thoughts. Then he started digging back up all the gossip of how he had let that girl stay at the parsonage. Arthur was very busy after that visit, and he had a captive audience, as men began to mention how they had not received a visit, and they wondered why Arthur had been visited. Speculation ran rampant as each person began to more freely voice his concerns about the preacher, who was not doing his job and was always pointing out sins as if was sitting in judgment of the whole congregation. The spiral effect of gossip and complaint was in full swing.

One Sunday, after another sermon on the dangers of sin, a seemingly well-intentioned member actually stopped in Bruce's office. She was a kindly woman who was known for speaking her mind about any subject. She came in but would not sit down. Instead, she stood by the door and said, "Preacher, let me give you a little advice. If you want to stay at this church for a good long time, you need to stop making folks feel bad about themselves and instead tell them that you love them and they are all going to heaven. If they hear you say it enough, they will believe it and be less likely to fire you. Now, I know you can't win everybody's hearts, but you will impress a lot of us older folks. Just think about what I'm saying."

Bruce thanked her for her advice, while at the same time he wanted to kick her out of his office. He was out there telling the truth to people, and she was back here telling him to go out and lie just to keep his job. He thought she might be a demon in disguise, and then it occurred to him, *Well, at least she told me to my face instead of running it through the rumor mill.* He should appreciate that much at least. But everything in him said that to sugar-coat the message would be as sinful as not saying it at all. People needed to be convicted of their sins and warned of eternal punishment. He felt responsible for the eternal life of every person who heard him speak, so he must be honest, even brutally honest, if need be.

When Marcus came the next day, he was in complete agreement with Bruce; these people were in need of revival. Oddly, he usually didn't like revival speakers, who would come in and preach fire and brimstone, scaring children to the altar, and then in a few days collect their checks and be on their way, leaving the preacher to follow up and explain heaven and hell to people only interested in avoiding hell rather than learning anything about God. No—he would be their revival preacher and at the same time stress the importance of knowing God's will for their lives. And so, day after day and week after week, it continued. The deep chasm between preacher and people began to grow wider and wider.

Chapter 8

Encircle and attack

In her home in North Carolina, Sandy had been doing her research for her degree and trying to spend more time with her family. Most of the time things were great and very normal, but on occasion it was as if someone else had come into the house and was creating tension. Her father was himself most of the time, but then, when you least expected it, he would change and be angry and argumentative. Or he would just sit quietly for hours and avoid everyone. He would be reading ancient text, always looking for something, and then he would stop. But if Sandy asked if he needed help, he would say, "Help with what?" It was if he didn't remember what he had been doing.

One evening when Sandy and her father were alone in the house, she caught him staring at her, and she asked if there was something he wanted. His smile was odd, and he said that he just enjoyed watching her work. The next day he was acting as he had when she was a child, loving and playful. In the evenings he would become quiet, and more and more she would feel his eyes following her around the room. One evening when Sandy was doing the dishes, her father came up behind her, put his hands on her waist, and said. "We have noticed what a beautiful young woman you have become." Sandy turned quickly and stepped to one side.

"You startled me, Dad!" There was a long pause as her father stared at her with a drunken look in his eyes. "Have you been drinking, Daddy?"

Her father stepped back and blinked. In a different tone of voice, he said, "What are you talking about? I don't drink! Why would you suggest such a thing?" Her father looked around, and Sandy could sense that he was disoriented.

"What were you just saying, Daddy?"

Her father paused and looked confusedly at his daughter. "Uh, I'm not sure now ... must not have been too important. What were we talking about? Let me get back to helping you with the dishes." Her father smiled and gave her an uncertain look.

"Daddy, you weren't helping me with the dishes. You came up behind me and was grabbing my waist. Now do you remember what you said?"

The look on her father's face was one of shock and confusion, and he turned and walked toward his chair in the den. He looked away as if trying to avoid her eyes, but Sandy followed and sat down in the chair beside his desk.

"Talk to me, Dad. What do you remember about the last few minutes?"

He sat with his head down for a few moments, and Sandy was about to speak again when he spoke. "I'm not sure. I thought I was talking to you, but I can't remember." He paused and looked at her; his face began to pale. "What did I do? Did I hurt you in some way?" His voice was shaking, and he seemed almost on the verge of tears.

"You put your hands on my waist and said, 'We've noticed what a beautiful young woman you have become.' There was a long pause, during which her father looked embarrassed and seemed to be trying to form words in his mind. Then Sandy said, "Who is the *we* you mentioned, Dad? Why did you say *we*?"

Her father shook his head and mumbled, "I ... I'm not sure. I don't remember saying that." After a long pause, he pleaded, "Please don't mention this to your mother."

Sandy sat back and looked at her father. "Dad let's talk about what's been going on for the past few months. Mom doesn't want to talk, and I have noticed you acting different. When I suggested leaving to do some research, you didn't want me to go, but Mom seemed insistent that I leave. Now, why would she do that?"

Her father had regained his composure but kept looking down. "I'm not sure how to answer you. I was concerned with you going back to that site in South Carolina, and yet at the same time, part of me wanted you to go. Your mother wanted you out of the house because, she said, I was acting strange, and she did not want you to see how I was. The problem was that I didn't know what she was talking about. It was like I had blank spots in my memory, and then she would tell me some of the things that I had said or done. I did not believe her, but more and more friends and colleagues began to confirm what she was saying. But then it just stopped happening. I have been feeling fine and was thinking about going back to work."

Sandy sat listening to her father's comprehension of the situation he was describing. "What sort of things did Mom say you had done or said?"

Her father looked at her with shame in his eyes. He shook his head and said that he had been very rude and had made crude remarks to friends and even students. Sandy sat there listening, incredulously trying to imagine her father acting in such a way. Suddenly she heard her mother's voice behind her.

"What has happened? What did he do?" Her voice was a mix of concern and anger.

Sandy turned and saw a look of fear and disgust on her face. "It's okay, Mom. Dad just had a sort of blackout spell, and he can't remember speaking to me."

Sandy was trying to water down the incident, but her mother was not consoled. She moved over, knelt in front of her husband, and said, "You must send her away until we can fix this. It is not good that she is here now." Her voice was filled with concern, but now the anger was replaced with love as she pleaded with her husband.

Sandy spoke up strongly. "No! I'm not running away from home and leaving you two to wrestle with a problem that I may be able to help with. Besides, I deserve to know what's going on. We are going to talk this out, and you are going to tell me everything.

"You don't understand, daughter. It is a very embarrassing thing, and I am trying to save your father's honor—"

Suddenly her husband cut her off. "No! Sanchari is right. She has a right to know, and she may be able to help." Her mother stood, stepped over to the small couch, and sat down. The man of the house had spoken, and his will would be obeyed. Sandy had seen this before in her parents. Even though they had lived in the United States for better than two decades, the old patriarchal habits still surfaced from time to time.

Sandy turned to her father, and he began to relate the chain of events that had taken place since he had completed his work in South Carolina. Her mother sat quietly, except to fill in the gaps concerning incidents that her father couldn't remember. The story that began to unfold was hard to believe, and yet to Sandy it did begin to make some sense. Her father spoke of the investigation in South Carolina and what had happened when he returned. Her mother told her that he had skipped classes and had been accused of making sexual innuendos to students. Some had been laughed off as jokes, but a couple of students had complained to the dean about what they thought was behavior bordering on sexual harassment. That is when the administrators had suggested a sabbatical. They had been able to fend off any lawsuits, and after speaking with others on the faculty who supported Dr. Prasad, the dean had allowed him to take a break. The details her mother provided were not pretty, and she could not believe her father would act in such a way. She realized that her mother had taken more abuse than anyone else, and that was why she had wanted Sandy to leave.

Just when she thought the story was over, Sandy saw her father look down at the floor and almost whisper, "There is more ... some things that I have spoken about to no one. Perhaps, Sanchari, you can help." Dr. Prasad looked at his wife and said, "I didn't tell you all that had happened at the barn, because there is nothing that you could have done or probably understood. But Sanchari may understand and have a more objective viewpoint. I did not mean you any disrespect, my dear."

Sandy looked at her father with confusion, trying to piece the story together. Tilting her head and looking at her father, she said, "I am a little confused about the faculty support. When I spoke with an assistant, he said that there had been arguments at the site between you and the faculty. He said you shut them out and then suddenly stopped the investigation."

"He's right. There were arguments, and I did do much of the work on my own, but only because I was concerned about the effect it was having on the others. After a while I would not allow them back into the barn, and they protested."

Sandy looked perplexed. "Why? What would make you restrict your staff, and what do you mean 'the effect it was having on the others'?"

"There was more than energy in that place, but I do not know what to call it. It defies scientific explanation, and so I tried to discount it and insisted we focus only on measurable empirical evidence for physical activity and not some sort of psychic energy. The others agreed at first, but eventually they were becoming less involved with a scientific examination and more ... personally involved. The faculty is supporting me because they feared I would tell what I am about to tell you, but you must say nothing of this to anyone. I am still unsure why they just didn't insist I be removed; it seems it would have been easier for all of them. But I have a theory on that, too."

Sandy was confused and wanted clarification, when she asked, "Dad, what do you mean they were 'personally involved'?"

"Well, Sanchari, I am not sure how to describe it. I began to observe inconsistencies in their professional demeanor. They were short tempered and frustrated with the investigation. We started with electromagnetic readings, but soon they dissipated, and yet there were incidents of what can only be described as psychokinetic events. It was nothing big, and much could be dismissed as rats or pests in the barn. There were things like straw on the floor moving and making a brushing sound when there was no wind or evidence of an animal present. We had unusual sounds, which could also be explained as wind whipping around an old wooden structure, except that when we stepped outside there would be no breeze.

It was all very confusing. Then we had one member report a visual phenomenon. She insisted she briefly saw a figure in a darkened corner. Each member, it appeared, had some sort of experience, and then there was the group behavior. One evening we were in the barn, discussing these events and trying to determine a valid scientific explanation, when something happened to the group. It is hard to describe, but it started with heat. It became so hot in the barn, but no one suggested leaving. We sat there, and soon one of the females just unbuttoned her blouse a few buttons, and Dr. … well, never mind who it was, but he made the crudest remark about not stopping there, and he added some other words, which I will omit. Rather than be shocked, she unbuttoned another button, and everyone began to laugh. At that point I suggested we stay focused, when another member responded by suggesting I go to hell. At that I got up and called the meeting to a close for the evening. The late hour and the heat had obviously put a strain on everyone. We had our two campers set up, and everyone went back to their quarters.

"Later that evening, I awoke to the sound of an altercation. I ran out and found a fight going on between two team members. The female professor was coming out of the barn, and she was not fully dressed. I asked what had happened, but no one wanted to talk about the events. In the morning, we called a meeting, and I insisted we discuss the previous evening's events. To my shock, no one could remember anything except that I had canceled the meeting abruptly. I won't go into great detail, but we had a similar incident that next night and again the following morning. No one seemed to know what I was talking about, and when I tried to tell them, they questioned my veracity.

"You must remember that these are professionals, married men and women. We had two other men and women and two assistants who were not in on our evening meetings, so I think they had no idea of what was going on. On the first night, when the fight occurred, they were fortunately at the local club and knew nothing of the behavior. After the second night, I closed myself in the barn one evening and locked the door. I wanted to run more magnetic field tests and record for sound phenomena. All I recorded was the team members banging on the door and cursing me loudly enough to disturb the assistants. The next morning, we packed up and left."

Sandy sat for a moment and then asked her father, "How long were you in the barn alone?"

"Maybe an hour or so," her father replied.

Mark, the grad assistant, said you were in the barn all evening and wouldn't let the others in. He said that some left that night." Sandy had a suspicious tone in her voice when she asked, "What else happened in the barn that night when you were alone?"

Her father spoke slowly, as if trying to force a memory, "Mark may be right about some people leaving, but I don't think I was in there that long," He paused as if reconstructing the evening. "I went in after supper, I think, and then I ran a test … it was an … uh … I'm not sure what test I ran, but then the others were outside."

"Dad, did you run a recording test?"

"Yes, I know I ran the digital recorder, but I can't remember when I started it."

"Do you have that recorder or the data from the recorder?" Sandy asked quickly.

"I have it on my computer, in the sound file folder." He stepped over to his desk, opened the laptop, and pulled up the file. He pushed Play, and they sat there for a few moments in silence. After a long wait, Sandy suggested he look under Properties on that file and check the date and length. She was already at the desk standing over her father before she finished speaking. She reached over his shoulder and clicked the button to open the file and check its properties. Her eyes grew large, and she leaned back.

"How long were you in the barn alone, Dad?"

I don't know exactly. I went in sometime after supper and ran few tests, and then the others were banging on the door. It was only an hour or so."

"But you don't know which test you ran first. Was it this one, Dad? When did you start the recorder? Do you at least remember that?" Her tone was growing intense.

"I ... I don't remember for sure. Maybe I did it first ... I'm just not sure. Why? What does it matter?"

Sandy voice was firm and almost angry. "Dad, you say you were in there alone for one hour or so but look at the size of this file!"

Her father turned back to the computer and looked down at the file size, two hundred megabytes.

"So, what does that mean?" her father asked; he sounded close to tears.

Sandy looked at her father and said accusingly, "Dad, that is about five hours of recording!"

There was a pregnant pause and ominous silence until Sandy's mother said, almost in a whisper, "You were alone in there for over five hours, and you can't remember anything."

Dr. Prasad sat there for a moment, and then he looked at his wife, and his face seemed to change into a smirking smile. "She is a clever little bitch, isn't she?" he pronounced.

Sandy and her mother looked at one another with shock and fear as Dr. Prasad pushed his chair back, rose, and walked out of the room. Sandy ran to her mother, and they embraced one another. They looked toward the door that Dr. Prasad had just walked out of.

Sandy started to speak, but her mother said, "No, no, just wait. I have seen this many times in the past few months. He will probably be okay in a few moments, and I doubt he will remember what he said. Just wait, my dear."

As surely as if she had seen the future, Dr. Prasad walked back into the room, holding a cup of tea.

Innocently he looked at Sandy. "Did you hear anything on the recording yet? You should have gotten to the part where everyone was yelling by now."

"Yes, Father, we did find out something that is interesting and disturbing. It appears you were in the barn for longer than you can remember. But I have a question, Dad. When we were talking about why the rest of the faculty did not move to have you dismissed, you said you had a theory. Why do you think they did not move against you? It seems that they were all angry with you after what happened at the barn."

"It is because I know what they did with all their unprofessional behavior."

"But Dad, it would be their word against yours, and coupled with your behavior here, it seems to me they could have gotten rid of you. I think it must be something else." Her logic was clear, and Dr. Prasad sat looking at the computer screen, realizing that his daughter was probably right. In a moment, he looked up at her almost sheepishly.

"What else could be the reason, Sandy?"

Sandy walked over to her mother, sat beside her, and took her hand. She said, "Dad, this will be hard for you, and maybe even more so for Mom, but I want you to just consider it." Sandy paused and then gripped her mother's hand. "Dad, what if they see you as one of them, and they are trying to protect you?"

Her father was stunned. "One of them! What do you mean, one of them? We are colleagues, and still friends on some level, but I can't forget what happened in that barn—"

Sandy interrupted, "But Dad, you don't remember what happened in that barn! You know some of what they did but none of what happened to you. So how do you know that you are not experiencing the same thing they are? Based on your forgetfulness and your recent behavior, wouldn't you say you are acting more like them and not yourself?" Sandy stopped and held her breath, waiting to see how her father would receive her comments.

Dr. Prasad sat for a moment and then said, "Sanchari, you are suggesting some type of conspiracy, but for what reason? What are they conspiring to accomplish?"

Sandy hung her head. "I don't really know. I may have a theory, but I don't like my own theory."

"Okay, what is your theory? Let's reason through it." Dr. Prasad spoke lovingly, but Sandy was playing a game that neither he nor her mother were aware of. It was like fishing, and she was trying to get a bite. Now was the time to throw the bait into the water. If she got what she was expecting, she should elicit another outburst from her father or bring forth whatever it was that was causing the outburst. But now was the time.

Sandy looked at her father and quietly said, "What if it is a case of multiple demonic possessions?"

"Sanchari!" It was her mother and not her father who lashed out. "What are you saying? This is still your father, not some demon!"

Dr. Prasad just sat there, but Sandy thought she could see the change in his eyes; his glance seemed cold and emotionless, non-responsive. He watched her as she moved around the room and listened to his wife chiding her for her disrespect. Sandy realized she was playing a dangerous game; her opponent was letting someone else do the fighting. He had decided to hold his tongue. She had to do something.

"Still think I am a clever little bitch, Daddy?" Her words were loaded with disdain, and there it was, the response that could not be hidden. A slow smile eased across his lips, and he mouthed almost inaudibly the word *clever*.

Sandy's mother was quiet, stunned by her daughter's profanity. But now, out of the corner of her eye, she noticed her husband's response, and it began to make sense. Both women were staring at Dr. Prasad now, and he realized that he had given away his identity.

Her mother broke the silence by calmly asking him, "Why are you smiling? Did you hear what she said? She has accused you of being a demon."

Dr. Prasad turned to her and asked, "And what do *you* think, my dear? Am I not your loving husband—or do you think I am some creature that copulates with goats and she-devils?"

His tone was sarcastic and venomous, and his smile was like none ever seen on the Dr. Prasad that Sandy called father and her mother called husband. Mrs. Prasad turned her head away as if she could not bear his gaze, and Sandy asked again, "Are you my father, or are you something else?"

"Oh, I am your father—can't you see? What do your eyes tell you, and your ears? Use your reason, child. What you are proposing is purely illogical and cannot be proven by any form of empirical evidence. What is a demon? Wouldn't it be some invisible spiritual being, so we would not be able to trust our five senses? It would be out of the reach and realm of logic. You and I are scientists, my daughter, and as such, are we not bound by logic and reason? Are you willing to cast that aside for a ridiculous belief in myth and magic? Perhaps I am having some problems, but wouldn't a diagnosis of schizophrenia fit better than some witch doctor's rants? I fear you have spent too much time with your new friend, Bruce Strong. His delusion is rubbing off on you."

"You're right, it is very illogical and outside the realm of scientific logic. But in our field, we always knew that while investigating the supernatural we might have to deal with something like this. We always expected to find the logical explanation for superstitions. But what happens when we have evidence that moves beyond our natural realm? For instance, I told you that I was talking with and even stayed with Reverend Strong, but I never told you his first name was Bruce, now did I?"

Her father chuckled. "Touché," he said, in the same tone and almost an exact imitation of Reverend Strong's voice from the day they'd sat and spoken at the battlefield.

"Perhaps you didn't, but are you so sure you didn't mention it in passing? Can you say for certain that you did not tell me his name? How else would I know it? Can we stop this foolishness and get back to trying to help me get better? I am aware that I have been under stress and have done and said some odd things, but it's not really me. I am convinced that I need to see someone, a counselor or doctor. Won't you stay and help your old dad? We are a family, and a family sticks together, don't we?"

Mrs. Prasad stood up and said, "Yes, that is what a family does, and we do want to see you better my husband but—"

She was cut off by Dr. Prasad's angry snarl; it was almost like an animal's growl. "I wasn't talking to you, old woman! I am talking to this charming young lady who is sitting in judgment of her own father. She who is so willing to toss out all reason and sanity to pursue these fables and stories of ghosts, she is the one I want an answer from."

Sandy smiled and said, "Who called you a ghost? I said demon, and there is a difference, as you should know full well. I am not sure how to cure something like you, because you are a new experience for me."

As they stood there, the doorbell rang, and her father smiled. "Was anyone expecting company tonight? Sandy, would you get that? I am really getting tired."

Sandy moved curiously to the door and pulled it open. She could barely hide her gasp of surprise when she saw the members of the team that had been with her father at the barn. They were all pleasant as they walked in and asked whether her father was at home. She directed them to the den. While they came in and were exchanging pleasantries, Sandy stood at the door and motioned for her mother to join her in the hall. Her mother greeted her guests and offered refreshments but scurried out before anyone could answer. As she left the room, she noted the silence behind her. Everyone in the room had fallen quiet and gathered around Dr. Prasad's desk.

Sandy grabbed her mother's hand and pulled her toward the door. In a moment they were outside. Her mother pulled against her hand, but Sandy pulled all the harder and said that they were getting out of there. Sandy literally shoved her mother into the car and looked back toward the windows of the den. She paused when she saw five blank, emotionless faces staring out at the two of them. She felt a chill, and she was trembling as she put the key in the ignition. She turned the key, and it felt like it was moving through stone, but the engine fired up. The two of them drove away into the night.

After a moment, her mother turned to Sandy and said, "What just happened back there?"

"Well, Mom, I'm not sure if I know, because whoever that was speaking through Dad was right—it is totally illogical. I am moving out of my field into something new for me."

"Me too," her mom softly added. "What about your father?"

Sandy just looked at her mother silently as the grey highway melted into the falling darkness.

Chapter 9

Scene 44

A barn is not a home

While all this was going on in North Carolina, the barn that had been at the center of discussions sat like a theater awaiting an audience. Oliver Paxton sat in the barn, meditating and pushing his stretches to new limits. Deep in his concentrated state, he did not feel the pain that he was putting his body through. Sweat ran down his body as his mind neared a new level of emptiness. When the door to the barn crashed open, Oliver was startled out of his mental state, and the pain rushed to his limbs. It was Willow, home from school and excited to tell her father all about her day. But her father was filled with anger and fed by pain. Before she could say a word, her father was screaming almost hysterically. She froze in fear as the rant continued, until Anna ran in to rescue her daughter. She said nothing, just grabbed her little girl and ran out toward the house, leaving Oliver panting as his rage abated. Almost as quickly as his anger had flared, he realized that he had overreacted. He took a few deep breaths and jogged to the house. Inside he found his wife and daughter sitting on the couch in a tight hug. He started to speak, but his wife gave him a cold stare. He looked at her and whispered softly how sorry he was. Then he spoke to his daughter. He was overly apologetic, but it did seem sincere.

In a moment, Willow looked up and him and said, "What did your friend say about all that yelling?"

Oliver looked at her with confusion on his face. "What friend, Willow?"

"That man in the corner, in the green coat."

Oliver looked up at his wife and shrugged as if to say he didn't know what she was talking about. Anna looked into Willow's eyes and asked, "What man did you see?"

Willow pulled her doll close and began to describe the man she'd seen. "He was a tall soldier or something, in a green coat and a funny hat. He may play piano, because he had those long fingers that you said would be good for playing the piano. He didn't say anything; he just smiled when I came in, and then you started yelling. I didn't pay attention to him after that."

Oliver stood up and went into the bedroom; he returned with a small revolver in his hand. He motioned for Anna to distract Willow while he went out to see if in fact there was someone in the barn. He walked slowly across the yard and crept to the barn like a kid playing soldier. He stood in the doorway and looked all around, but he saw no one nor anything out of the ordinary. He jumped into the barn and turned to look up into the loft. For the first time, his yoga sanctuary felt threatening. After searching the loft and the lower level, he'd found nothing. He closed the doors to the barn and walked back to the house. Anna and Willow were sitting at the table, looking at her schoolwork. When Oliver walked in, he moved to the bedroom, and Anna followed to ask if he'd seen someone or something. The two were in the bedroom when they heard Willow call out, "There he goes, Daddy!" The two ran back to the kitchen and found Willow looking toward the barn.

"There *who* goes, Willow?" asked Anna.

"That soldier just went into the barn," Willow said, smiling.

Oliver looked to the open barn doors and then back to his wife, with fear in his eyes. "I closed those doors. I know I did!" He ran back, grabbed his revolver, and started out the door.

Anna grabbed his arm and said, "Wait! Let me call the sheriff."

Oliver shook free, saying, "I can take care of our home," and then out the door he ran. The two women sat for what seemed like an eternity, watching the barn with intensity. There was no movement nor sound, just the open doorway that seemed to get darker inside with each passing moment. Finally, Oliver walked out into the yard, and looking to the two faces on the porch, he just shrugged his shoulders. Once they were inside, he told them that he had seen no one. He sat down at the table. He didn't bother taking his gun to the bedroom.

In the days that followed, he was more apprehensive about working out in the barn. He felt there were eyes on him every time he went in there. He noticed that his class participants were now absent more and more often, and it frustrated him deeply that no one was taking his class seriously. He was seeing his dreams and aspirations evaporate before his eyes, and he felt less and less relevant. All his mental discipline could not hold off the growing depression and complete feeling of insignificance, until at last he closed his classes and shrank back into himself.

Scene 45

Gathering the troops

Sandy and her mother drove into the night and eventually stopped at a hotel to spend the night. They were both exhausted and fell asleep almost as soon as their heads hit the pillows. They had driven south for two hours and stopped in Charlotte. When the morning came, they got back on the road, and Sandy's mother wanted to know where they were going. Sandy told her that they were going back to the source. About mid-morning Sandy pulled her car into the parsonage drive. She was hoping that Reverend Strong could put things into some understandable context.

Bruce welcomed the two women, and Sandy and her mother sat telling him their tale, while he listened incredulously. He tried to stay focused, but he was feeling a certain excitement about having Sandy back in his home. After an hour or two of listening, Bruce offered the ladies a sandwich lunch, and they moved to the kitchen to prepare their meal. As they ate, the topic changed to some small talk, as Bruce took a moment to fill her in on all that had transpired since she had been gone. Bruce then began to discuss his feelings about demonic possession.

"I must admit that I didn't think I would be having this discussion with you, of all people. You have been the bastion of logic and reason. What you tell me is intriguing. As you know, I don't believe in ghosts, but I do believe in demons. If not for the visit from the other staff, I would have suggested that you were dealing with schizophrenia."

"Just like my father said," Sandy put in.

Bruce looked up with a concerned scowl. "I do not claim expertise in the field of psychiatry, but I do seem to remember something to the effect that when a mental patient diagnoses himself, that person may not be mentally ill at all. It must be something else."

"Are you saying that the something else is demonic possession?" asked Sandy.

"I think that could be one answer, but all the others may be, in a way, worse. Because at least with demonic possession you can blame it on the demon; otherwise, the only one left to blame is yourself.

"That was not my husband speaking all those times, it was another consciousness. I don't know about demonic possession, but I do believe that sometimes a man may have a demon. We have ways of dealing with this in India, but I don't know what happens here in the United States." Mrs. Prasad spoke with confusion in her voice. "How could this happen to such a good man as my husband?"

"There are rituals in the Catholic Church, as I am sure there are rituals in Hinduism, but I find them to be more for the observer than for the possessed. I have never exorcised a demon, but I don't believe that scriptures put forth any ritual for us to follow other than prayer and fasting. I do believe that possession does not occur unless the possessed is in some way willing to be possessed."

Sandy's head jerked up. "Are you suggesting that my father wanted this evil spirit?"

No, not exactly, but I do believe that if a person does not allow possession, then that person may be overcome, because they have no protection against the demonic spirit. You say that your father's behavior was sporadically bad, like a disease, that the demon was getting stronger and your father's will was getting weaker. Your father was not a religious man, was he?"

Sandy looked at her mother and said, "Not particularly. He was a good and kind man, however."

"Well, I don't mean to offend, but I think goodness is fine when men deal with one another, but it takes the goodness of God and His Holy Spirit to deal with spiritual beings such as demons. Would you consider your father someone who was possessing of the Holy Spirit?"

Sandy and her mother looked a little perturbed at Bruce's comments. "That depends on what you mean by Holy Spirit, Bruce. Considering Dad's religious background was closer to universalism, I doubt he would meet your criteria," Sandy said sarcastically.

"Maybe Criton could give us an idea or two?"

Sandy again gave Bruce a skeptical look and asked, "John Criton, the man who speaks to the dead, is still around here? I thought you two were on opposite sides of the local problems."

Bruce sheepishly shrugged and said, "A lot of things have changed, and one of the biggest changes is John Criton." Bruce explained what had happened to Criton after his run-in with Murmus. "Perhaps he can help us, or ..." Bruce paused. "I have another friend who may be able to help us figure things out. I'll talk to him in the morning." Bruce told Sandy to fix up the spare room and let her mom get some rest. Sandy and Bruce sat up a little longer, talking about the events of the past few days, until they were both exhausted.

In the morning, Bruce went to his office and was preparing to visit John Criton, when in walked Marcus. "Going somewhere, Bruce?"

"Why yes, Marcus. I was going into town to visit a friend, and then, actually, I was thinking you might come by later, and we could have a word."

"I noticed you have visitors at your house and wasn't sure if you would be in your office. But here I am. Maybe we could talk. Why rush off? Let's sit down and have that word now."

"My visitors are part of what I wanted talk about. They are friends from North Carolina who worked on a project recently, and they're down for a visit."

"Ah, it must be that lovely young girl that almost caused you problems before. I hope she's not alone—that would set the tongues to wagging again." Marcus spoke with a smooth tone that was almost offensive.

"Well yes, it is her, and she is chaperoned by her mother." Bruce was abrupt, but then he thought about the fact that Marcus was here. He had been hoping to speak with Criton that morning, but Marcus was here now, so maybe he could just stay a few minutes. He sat down at his desk, and Marcus sat down on the small love seat across from him.

"What's on your mind, Bruce?" Marcus asked.

"Well, we have had some great conversations but never spoken much about demons, and I wanted to get your opinion on the demonic," Bruce said, pausing to give Marcus a chance to respond. But the response was slow. Marcus just looked at him with a strange smile, which seemed to convey a sense of confusion.

Finally Marcus spoke, but slowly. "I don't know if I understand the question. What do you mean when you say demonic? Are you referring to evil again?"

Bruce shook his head and looked bewildered. "No, Marcus, I mean the source of evil—you know, demon spirits."

At this Marcus laughed and then suppressed his laughter. "Oh, forgive me, Bruce, but I am a little surprised to hear that coming from you, seeing how we usually dig into theological matters as opposed to ghost stories." He turned his head to mask his slight chuckle.

Bruce was confused and looked at Marcus. "You mean you don't believe in demons as mentioned in the Bible? That does sort of surprise me, especially since we have spoken so much about the spirit of evil in our discussions."

Marcus regained his composure and said, "I thought you shared the opinion that evil was from man and that man was the source of true rebellion against authority. It seems that is what is presented in scriptures, with possession used as more of an analogy."

"Then you don't believe in demonic involvement at all, or spirits such as fallen angels inhabiting, influencing, and deceiving mankind?"

"I guess I would have to say no when you use those terms, Bruce. I am surprised that you take such a literal stance on such myths. Demons and fallen angels influencing and deceiving men is a bit of a theological stretch for an intellectual such as yourself." Again, Marcus seemed to chuckle, but his laughter carried an undercurrent of agitation. "Why not put aside this topic and focus on more pragmatic areas of theology?"

Bruce looked at him and said, "No, Marcus, I am dealing with situations that cannot be explained away with simple intellectual debates. Scripture often speaks of demons, and not as analogies or metaphors but as real beings that cause real problems. I was hoping that you might add some insights to the topic. I guess we never have spoken of real spiritual matters such as the Holy Spirit, God, and Jesus." Bruce noticed a pained frown at the mention of Jesus.

"Oh, I'm sure we mentioned those things at some point in our conversations." Marcus smiled and began to edge up in his seat as if he were getting ready to leave.

"What are your feelings toward God, the Holy Spirit, and particularly the person of Jesus? Start with God, Marcus. What are feelings about God?" Bruce leaned back and waited for a response.

Marcus paused and looked uncomfortably around the room for a moment before he spoke. "Well, I suppose I hold the Nameless One in such high regard that I often fail to mention him."

Bruce jerked his head up at the reference to "nameless one"; it echoed in his memory from conversations with Criton, who had said that Murmus had referred to the term *nameless one* on occasion. Then he asked, "Marcus, do you mean God?"

"Yes, of course, Bruce. You know the Nameless One. I was just holding with the Old Testament practice of keeping the holy name silent. I simply say, 'the Nameless One,' just like they did in the Old Testament."

"I'm still a little curious. Why use that term rather than just say God, since God isn't actually the name of God—unless, of course, you happen to know the true name of God. It just caught me a little off guard." Bruce smiled and quickly asked, "Well, what about Jesus? What are your thoughts on Jesus the Christ?"

Marcus scowled in a way that almost looked painful. He cleared his throat and slid forward on his seat. "That's one topic that may take more time than I have today. I must be on my way; I have several appointments. I will be back later this week, and we can discuss this topic in depth." Marcus was up and moving for the door before Bruce could say a word.

"Don't rush off, Marcus." But it was too late; the side door was already closing. Bruce was left to try and understand what he had said that had caused Marcus to leave, especially since he had wanted Bruce to stay and talk—until he had mentioned demons. No, it wasn't just demons; he had dismissed that topic. It was God, and especially Jesus, that bothered him. He definitely didn't want to discuss Jesus. As a matter of fact, he hadn't wanted to say God or Jesus. How odd. Bruce was filled with even more questions now, and he felt an even more urgent need to speak with Criton. Bruce went back to the house to get his keys, only to see another familiar face.

"Alan, what are you doing here? I thought you were coming up in a couple of weeks."

"Well, I was, but I was in town, so I thought I would drop by. Hey, is that Sandy's car?"

Bruce smiled and said, "Yeah, but hop in my car. I'll fill you in on the way into town."

"What's going on, Bruce?"

"Plenty, Alan! Just hop in. You may find this interesting—that is, if you've got the time."

"Are you kiddin'? This sounds pretty good." The two jumped into Bruce's car and headed for Criton's apartment in town.

When they arrived, Criton was sitting at his computer, working on his book, but he was all too willing to take a break for a conversation with a friend. Bruce reintroduced Alan to Criton, and the three men sat down. Bruce began to tell Criton what was going on and what he suspected.

Criton was especially interested in Marcus and his apprehension over speaking of demons and Jesus, as well as his referring to the nameless one in the same way that Murmus had. It didn't seem like a coincidence to him, and the situation involving Sandy and her father just added more intrigue.

Criton sat for a moment and then asked, "Are the Prasad's still at your home? I would like to speak with them."

"Yes, Sandy and her mom are still here."

"Good, I'll get my notepad. I would like to hear more about Dr. Prasad senior's behavior. Let's go." With that, Criton was up and walking out the door. He paused, turned, and looked at the two visitors. "Well, what are you waiting for? Let's go talk to them—now!"

Bruce looked at Alan and smiled. "Yeah, what are we waiting for?"

When they reached the car, Criton was sitting in the front passenger seat, staring out at the road as if seeing the future. "I hope you don't mind me sitting up front, Alan. I get a little carsick."

"No prob', John." Alan smiled as he looked across the top of the car at Bruce with a quirky smile and rolled his eyes.

When they reached the house and all the pleasantries of introduction were over, the group assembled in the den. Bruce began by asking what everyone's opinion was on what they had seen or experienced. Sandy and her mom were first. They described what Mr. Prasad had been like over the past few weeks. Mrs. Prasad had more to add, speaking of her husband's blackouts and lapses of memory. She added that he had met with the team at their home several times but been forbidden to tell anyone, and afterwards he'd claimed he had no memory of the meetings. Sandy spoke of the things she'd found in her dad's notes, and they compared the information with her mom's story.

Alan then spoke of some of the information he had come across while doing more research. He'd been reading letters and official communications from British war records about the battle; mainly he just pointed out the inconsistencies of the stories about the battle. He said that it was to be expected that colonials would remember things as atrocities that British historians would just attribute to acts of war.

Criton said he wanted to just listen for a while. He asked Bruce to tell of his recent experience with Murmus and subsequent salvation, and then about Lerajie.

Bruce began by telling about what had happened to Criton's abilities and how it had led to his revelation about Murmus, his supposed spirit guide. Bruce told about the demonic connection for Alan's sake, since the others had already heard the story. Alan was still having problems accepting the spiritual element. Then, to Bruce's' surprise, Sandy began to take Alan's side in the discussion.

"What if we are dealing with some sort of projected schizophrenia that somehow causes others to experience the feelings and behavior of the schizophrenic?"

Alan sat up and said, "I think Sandy may be right. That would explain things in a more scientific way. Sandy, tell us more about this projected schizophrenia."

"Well, it is more scientific sounding, but I was just thinking out loud. I've never really heard of projected schizophrenia. But, as a scientist, I must consider all the alternatives. I admit that my father's behavior caught me off guard and was frightening, but now I think that we need to consider all explanations before we jump back to the dark ages and religious extremes. What I observed was my father suffering from some sort of psychotic hysteria or full-blown schizophrenia. It could be some sort of manic disorder as well."

Bruce was a little perplexed but willing to go along with the scientific possibilities. Criton sat quietly observing the group, especially Mrs. Prasad. She seemed detached—and was he reading frustration of some sort? Bruce suggested they run through the possibilities and see which could be a more likely diagnosis.

Sandy spoke up. "I think we should look at psychotic hysteria or some sort of manic disorder first, since both could have been triggered by what happened at the barn. If Dad had been overcome with the emotion of failure, or some sort of group hysteria, it could have triggered a mental break."

"Maybe, but what was the source of the hysteria? Disappointment doesn't seem like a good reason to have a breakdown. I would suspect that scientists, more than other professionals, would be used to disappointment, since experimentation requires a lot of trial and error." Bruce was trying to join in the analysis.

Then Alan spoke up. "I agree with Bruce. Something would have had to trigger such a mental reaction, and disappointment doesn't fit the bill. Could it have been an external source?"

The three kept tossing ideas back and forth, but two members just sat and listened. Criton was listening with frustration as they worked through the scientific options. He felt that it was a waste of time. He watched Bruce and wondered how long he, of all people, would let this farce continue. He knew where it would end—it was the only possible explanation. He knew because it had happened to him, and the sooner they realized it the sooner they could do something. But for now, let them chase their scientific ideas. The three kept at it with theories and possibilities until Bruce looked at Criton and Mrs. Prasad and said, "You two are being awfully quiet. Do you have anything you would like to add?"

Criton looked at Mrs. Prasad and said, "Have you anything for this group of scientists, Mrs. Prasad?" His voice had a slight chuckle, which brought an unusual frown from Bruce and Alan.

"I don't know what I can add or even how I can help you. You all talk as if my husband is some sort of insane monster. All I know is that at times he is not the man I have known for thirty years. First you talk of demons and then of mental illness, and I just don't know what to think. Sanchari, you saw him and heard how he acted! What can we do? Does he need a doctor or a holy man?"

"And there it is, ladies and gentlemen!" Criton spoke in almost a yell, startling those around him. "*That* is the question," he pronounced. Criton had waited long enough, and he had heard more than enough, to his way of thinking.

Everyone reacted with a blend of shock and anger at the sudden explosion of sound. It rippled around the room amid comments of exasperation.

Alan spoke up first. "All right, Mr. Criton, what do you mean? We are trying to work thr—"

But Criton stopped him before he could finish. "What you have been doing is trying to assuage your own beliefs in the power of science and the natural world, while we are clearly not dealing with a singular scientific occurrence. I am amazed at how far you'll stretch your theories to fit your desired scenario. Mass hysteria and multiple or projected schizophrenia—really! Even I know what a stretch that is. Why are you wasting so much time trying to figure out what is so obvious? Your father, and your husband, madam, is under the influence of some sort of demonic force, and the sooner we realize that and deal with it, the sooner the two of you will get your husband and father back."

The room was silent as the group sat there trying to take in all that had been said. The silence was broken by sound of a hard knock at the door, and everyone in the group jumped. Bruce leaped up and opened the door, but he did not know the man standing there. He was about to ask if he could help him, when he heard Sandy's voice, almost in a gasp, say, "Father!"

Scene 46

The first battle

Bruce looked back into the room and then turned again to Dr. Prasad standing there. Dr. Prasad smiled and said, "May I come in, Reverend Strong."

"Yes! Yes, sir. Please come in. We were just ..." and Bruce stopped awkwardly.

"Just speaking of me, Reverend? That is understandable, and I apologize if my actions of late have inconvenienced you with my family, but I appreciate you showing them hospitality, as you obviously have been doing. I am here to hopefully put an end to this confusion. I do apologize again for bringing you into our family difficulty." Dr. Prasad looked around the room and said, "That includes you all as well. If I could just have a little time with my family, I think we can resolve this misunderstanding."

The room fell silent at that, and once again it was Criton who spoke up. "Dr. Prasad, I think I can speak for all of us when I say that this has not been a problem, because we all wish to be of assistance. Since we are involved, perhaps we can be of aid in some way. May I ask you a few questions?"

Dr. Prasad was struggling to maintain a civil composure, but he was obviously perturbed. "Mr. Criton, you do realize that these matters are rather personal?"

"Yes, I know, but just for instance, how did you know your family was here, and how did you know that I was Mr. Criton?" Criton smiled, knowing that this information was easy to figure out, but he was trying to prompt a change in Dr. Prasad's demeanor.

"Well, there's nothing mystical or supernatural about that, Mr. Criton. You are a well-known TV personality, and Sanchari had spoken of Reverend Strong and Alan in her correspondences, so you see it was easy to assume that the person opening the door was Reverend Strong and that this young man must be Alan." He smiled a calm smile.

"Of course, you're right, doctor, but I didn't say anything about this being a supernatural inquiry. We were just trying to see if there was a physiological connection with your actions, this area, and your research that may have triggered your recent erratic behavior."

Dr. Prasad was becoming more aggravated, especially with the last comment about his behavior. "Do you or any of your friends here feel qualified to make some sort of a psychological diagnosis?" he queried. "I must say that I do not appreciate my family business being aired in a group of strangers." He shot a harsh glance over at his wife.

Criton smiled and forged ahead, ignoring the glance Dr. Prasad had given his wife. "I understand that, but we aren't exactly strangers to Sandy any more than the team you had over to your house a few nights ago are strangers to you." That comment really made Dr. Prasad bristle;

he realized that his wife and daughter had obviously told this group more than he would have liked them to know.

"I am not sure I agree or appreciate your comparison of my colleagues with your little …" Dr. Prasad paused, seeming to struggle to control his anger, and then finished his sentence, "uh, your little group here."

"Do you enjoy the voices that direct you, Doctor? Do they seem like old friends, or are you even aware of them when they take control? My own experience was one of being deceived over an entire lifetime.

Dr. Prasad was getting angrier by the moment. He almost barked at Criton. "What are you talking about—voices giving direction and old friends! You're being ridiculous, you and your little new friends here."

The others were stunned to silence as they watched the drama play out before them. Criton turned to Bruce as if asking for help, and Bruce finally realized what Criton was doing.

"I think what Mr. Criton is trying to ascertain is whether or not you are aware that you may be under the influence of a demonic spirit, and whether you are or are not a willing participant."

Dr. Prasad was tense, and he looked down when his daughter's voice joined the questioning. "Dad, what really happened in that barn? What are you not telling us? We only want to help!"

With that Dr. Prasad jerked his head up. With a red face and beads of sweat starting on his forehead, he shouted, "You would not understand! I can't say anything. Even my own team is still struggling with full comprehension. It takes a special ability and mental capabilities; we may be dealing with a new level of man's evolution. You ghost hunters sit here like children in a sandbox, playing with things you can never comprehend. I am speaking of a truly cross-dimensional line of communication with beings of extreme intelligence and abilities, which even I do not fully understand. Perhaps I have been affected somewhat, and it has caused some odd behavior, but I am gaining more control each day."

Criton looked at Bruce and said, "Tell him, Bruce, like you told me."

"Tell me what? What could you possibly have that I would want to know! You are nothing more than a tribal priest or witch doctor." Dr.

Prasad spoke with venom in his voice but still with some control. Criton and Sandy were looking at one another; they almost seemed to know one another's thoughts. This was her father, not a possessing spirit, and he really believed what he was saying.

"Perhaps I am little more than a witch doctor or spreader of myths and know-nothing. Tell me, is that what your friend is telling you right now?"

"Yes, he is a pure wisdom—far greater than you, or I, or anyone on this dimensional plane."

"Sandy told me that you were once a respecter of all beliefs, that in your Hindu tradition you were tolerant of all religions. Do you still feel that we should be tolerant of others' faith?"   Bruce was speaking softly and in a nonthreatening way, trying to touch the human side of Dr. Prasad.

"Tolerance is a virtue but also a flaw—no, not a flaw, I mean ... a weakness ... no, I ..." Dr. Prasad was struggling to answer, and the dual nature of his personality was being revealed.

"Isn't tolerance a trait of an advanced mind? And if that is true, why does your new friend have such a problem with tolerance and compassion? It seems he would rather belittle us, which would be a trait of a more aggressive and primitive mind. I think that maybe you are more advanced than your new friend from the barn. Besides, why a barn and not a lecture hall for all the brightest people in the world to hear him and meet him?"

The questions came at Prasad like machine-gun fire, ripping holes in his arguments and logic. Try as he could, he could not deny that what the reverend was saying was true. He had been so caught up in the excitement of his discovery that maybe he was not seeing things clearly.

"Dad, do you love me?" Sandy asked as she moved closer to her father.

He looked at her incredulously. "Of course I do, my child."

"Then why did you say those things to me at home? Why did you mention my beauty in the way you did? Was that you or someone else talking through you?"

Dr. Prasad shook his head and mumbled, "I don't know what you are talking about."

"Are you saying that I am making these things up and that Mom is making things up when she tells me about how you have been acting the past few weeks? How do you explain this behavior, Dad? It is primal behavior, not advanced."

Dr. Prasad was now bending and slumping into a nearby chair, the sweat gathering on his forehead and hands. He rubbed his hands and his head, pushing his hair back in silence. He was trying to process his thoughts, and then suddenly he sat up, and an almost different person raised his head.

"I am impressed at how quickly you were able to weaken my resolve, but your feeble attempts at emotionalism are not enough to make me turn away from this opportunity. Family and religion are chains connecting me to an ignorant past. Perhaps someday you will understand. Mrs. Prasad, my dear, and Sanchari, are you two coming with me?" He rose and walked toward the door.

"Dr. Prasad! Wait, please. Before you go, just tell me one more thing." It was Bruce. "Can Dr. Prasad tell me one thing before you go?"

Dr. Prasad turned and looked at Bruce with contempt and frustration. "What is it now! You have wasted a great deal of my time, and I have a long drive home."

"Your friend's name. Did he tell you his name?"

Dr. Prasad stopped and said, "Do you expect that by knowing my name you can control me, as your ancient rituals suggest? You really are nothing more than monkeys standing erect, aren't you Bruce?"

"Perhaps, but I like to think that of all the virtues of humanity, love is the greatest. I fail to see or sense any love in you at all—you, whoever you are possessing the form of Dr. Prasad, for now I am sure that you are not Dr. Prasad. The Dr. Prasad that I was told of is a man who had the virtue of love for his wife and daughter and was a tolerant, peace-loving man. So, whoever you are, I know now what you are, and I have no fear of you. I just find it hard to believe that Dr. Prasad would want you to inhabit him and destroy all that he loves. Is that what you want, Doctor?"

"*No.*" The voice was almost a whisper, but once the word was spoken, it began to grow in strength, and again they heard, "No!"

What happened next was a bizarre scene to everyone except Criton. This was what he had been waiting for, the moment when Bruce could get through to Dr. Prasad and have him realize the truth. Dr. Prasad suddenly stood up and then suddenly, as if shoved, he was bent down, as if he were retching and heaving. He had a look of pain on his face, and he began to thrash around the room. But unlike Criton, he had friends and family there. They all gathered round him and tried to prevent him from hurting himself or any of them with his violent movements. Then he suddenly fell to floor, convulsing all the while and saying "No, no, no!" He was rejecting the spirit that he had accepted in the barn that night, but the battle was hard fought, because part of him did not want to relinquish this opportunity to gain new knowledge and power. He looked up at his wife and daughter, smiled, and said, "I do love you both." Then he fell to the floor, unconscious.

The battle was over. Criton was the first to celebrate the victory. "I knew you would know what to do and say, Bruce—I knew it. Congratulations!"

Bruce smiled and said, "Thanks, John, but it would have helped if I had known just what you were doing. Now, if you and Alan will give me a hand, we can put Dr. Prasad to bed. I think he's going to need some sleep and some answers when he wakes up."

"Shouldn't we call a doctor or take him to the ER or something?" Alan spoke up. "I mean, weren't you in a coma for days, John?"

Criton smiled and said, "Well, yes, but my problem was that I was alone and almost beat myself to death during my struggle in the hotel. Your father has just fought a major mental battle, even more mental than physical, and he is tired, so let him sleep."

Scene 47

A new battle line

Everyone was exhausted after the tense scene they had witnessed. Night had fallen, and the time for questions had passed. Sleeping arrangements had been made, and Criton had gone back to his rental home in town. After Sandy, Mrs. Prasad, and Alan had gone to asleep, Bruce was still restless. He sat up, reading and thinking about what had happened. As he sat with his laptop before him, he began to grow tired, and somewhere between sleep and waking he heard a sound. It was a low cry like that of a cat, but it kept getting louder. He decided to see what was wrong and made his way outside. The night was cool, and the sound grew louder; it sounded as if it were coming from inside the church. He moved up the stairs and unlocked the door to the church. As he opened the door, the sound changed, and he realized that it was no cat. It was the cry of a person, perhaps a child.

Bruce called out, "Who's there? Where are you?" and the sound stopped. He moved into the dark hallway to stand at the foot of the stairs outside his office. He was looking toward the sanctuary with a patch of light from the moon shining behind him. "Where are you? Who are you? Let me help you!"

Then a voice spoke, with a bitter tone that was no longer that of a weeping child. "Help me? It was your words that caused this pain."

Bruce turned to see a small figure coming toward him out of the shadows into the light. But then he froze in terror at the sight of a child with half its face missing yet speaking through a disfigured jaw and mouth that could not fully close. It was Julian! Bruce could not move, and Julian moved slowly toward him with his ghastly grimace. All Bruce could say was "Julian, Julian," and just as Julian reached to touch him, he felt a softer hand shaking him and a voice calling his name.

"Bruce, Bruce. What is it? You were crying out a name." Sandy spoke almost in a whisper. "What's wrong? What were you dreaming?"

Bruce was groggy and sweating. There was a trembling sensation in his chest; he could still see the image of Julian coming toward him in the shadows. What had Julian meant when he said that Bruce's words had cased his pain?

"Bruce are you okay?"

"I just had a terrible dream—it seemed so real." Bruce paused, not wanting to share the dream with anyone. "But why are you up? Did I wake the house with my mumbling?"

"Well, I would hardly call it mumbling, but I don't think anyone else heard. I was already awake. It seems you're not the only one dreaming tonight. My father was crying out in his sleep."

"What did he say, Sandy?"

"He was crying out a name or something. I am not sure; it may have been garbled nonsense. It sounded like Bara quel or something like that. I couldn't make out what he was saying. I touched his arm, and it seemed to quiet him, because he began to rest easier. That's when you started up." Sandy was smiling, and her voice was a soothing as a cool breeze.

She turned to go back to bed, but Bruce asked, "What did you say your dad said?"

Sandy looked at him curiously and repeated, "I think he said Bara quel. Why, have you heard that name?"

"I'm not sure, but it does seem to remind me of something. I think I will dig around on some of my research sites for a while now that I am awake. You go on and get some sleep. Thanks for waking me up; I wouldn't want to go back to that dream." As Bruce watched her leave the room, he was thinking, *There goes a very special girl.*

Bruce turned back to his computer and went directly to a site that spoke of angels. It was the same place where he had learned the name and attributes of Murmus. He typed in Bara quel, but nothing came up, and so he began to try various spellings, until at last he found one that was a close phonetic match: Baraqyal. This was a watcher who cohabited with women, one of two hundred fallen angels; he was able to teach astrology to those who summoned him. Bruce sat there and began to consider the description and compare it to what Sandy and Dr. Prasad had said. She had mentioned her father's sexual innuendos and aggressive behavior. And then Bruce thought of what the doctor had said about the being who was so wise and would teach him. Here was a spirit that consorted with women and taught those who summoned him. It all fit, but now Bruce was thinking about the fact that first there had been the discovery of Murmus with Criton and now there was Baraqyal, who seemed to be a spirit that had been there for some time. If what he read was true, then Baraqyal would be a subordinate of Murmus. Two demonic spirits in one place! Even though Bruce had been able to free Criton and Dr. Prasad from demonic possession, he had not been able to drive these spirits away. Then his mind went back to the dream of Julian. Could there be a connection? Bruce was drifting off to sleep again, but this time it was peaceful and uninterrupted, until he heard a voice talking softly in his ear.

"Wake up, princess. Sun's up, day's begun." Alan was waving a cup of aromatic coffee under his nose. "Up late, Bruce. Why did you sleep out here? Was I snoring?"

Bruce rubbed the sleep from his eyes, stood up, and was sipping the coffee before he could really see it. He looked at Alan and said, "You would not believe my night, dude!"

"What's up, man?"

"Well, it started with nightmares and ended with some interesting revelations about our unwelcome guest, which I discovered online last night. But let me wait until everyone is up and see if Dr. Prasad comes around. I would like to get his input," Bruce said as he buttered some toast.

Scene 48

"Coming for you by going to them"

An hour or so later, the kitchen was buzzing with laughter and conversation, as the four spoke of the evening's activities and tossed ideas back and forth. The conversation only lagged while they were gathered around the table for breakfast. Thoughts were mumbled between bites of toast and eggs and warm, cheesy grits and bacon. The smells of southern cooking circled the room, along with a hint of sweet-flavored coffee.

"Mmm, that coffee smells wonderful! I could use a big cup right now." It was Dr. Prasad, standing at the kitchen door, looking tired but wearing a loving smile. His wife was on her feet like a shot, pouring her husband a cup of coffee and offering her seat at the table. When he sat down, she gave him a gentle kiss on the forehead, and he held her arm to his chest. They had a moment of intimacy that had been missing for a long while. Sandy just watched and smiled. It was a scene she remembered from her childhood, and she felt a warm sense of nostalgia. Things were going to be all right now, she was sure.

Bruce broke the silence. "How do you feel this morning, sir? That was quite an evening we had."

"Yes, Reverend Strong. I confess some parts are a little vague, but it was like something I have never seen or experienced on any level. I am thinking that perhaps I need to speak with someone for a little counseling or therapy. I felt like I was somehow out of my body, watching from a distance, and yet it was me speaking and thinking those thoughts. What's worse is I remember other instances over the past few weeks that I cannot believe I was involved with. Yet they are my memories, and I am deeply ashamed. I must apologize to you, my dear, and to our daughter. I have no explanation that makes any sense to me."

Sandy spoke up. "There is no need to apologize, Father, because I believe that what we have been seeing was not your personality. I confess it makes no sense to me from a scientific point of view. But I think we must agree that we may be treading on new ground of understanding. We are dealing with the paranormal and trying to explain things in a more normal way, but what you experienced last night, and what Mr. Criton has experienced, is something very new."

There was a voice from the back door a few feet away from the kitchen table. "Did I hear my name?" It was John Criton. "Knock, knock! Everybody decent?"

"Come in, John, you're just in time for breakfast." Bruce was already up and getting another chair.

"I was hoping you would say that. I am famished and this place smells delicious! Oh, Dr. Prasad, I was hoping you would be awake. How do you feel?"

Dr. Prasad stood and reached out his hand to Criton. "Yes, Mr. Criton. I feel much better this morning; thank you so much for asking."

"I think we have some notes to share. I am anxious to hear of your experiences and compare them to mine. Your confrontation last light looked very similar to what happened to me when I broke free from Murmus."

At the mention of Murmus's name, Criton noticed Dr. Prasad's head jerk slightly, as if he had been slapped, and he could not let it pass. "Does that name mean something to you, Dr. Prasad? Have you heard it before? Perhaps somewhere back in your memories?"

"Hold on, John. Let the man have his coffee before we try to autopsy his brain." Bruce chuckled softly, but Dr. Prasad stopped him.

"No, no, it is okay, Reverend. I am anxious to try to explain these things myself, and he's right. That name did hit me with a slight jolt. It was like a slight electrical shock, but I do not recall ever hearing that name. And yet it seems somehow familiar now that we have said it out loud. Who is this Murmus?"

And with that said, it began. Criton took the lead and told his life's story to the group, how he had come to know and accept Murmus as a friend and guide for the better part of his life. He spoke of how he'd had a confrontation, during which the deception had been revealed. He described how, when he knew the truth, the rejection had become an escape route from a horrible influence as opposed to a friendly spirit guide.

At that moment Dr. Prasad softly mumbled, "The truth shall set you free." He looked at Bruce. "Isn't that how it goes, Reverend Strong?"

"Yes, Dr. Prasad. It's in the Gospel of John; I think it's somewhere in chapter 8. It's a very fitting verse for the two of you."

"Yes, it is, because I feel that I have been set free from something that I was unaware had enslaved me. I was a victim to my own pride and desire, so much so that I could not see clearly what evil I was dealing with."

Dr. Prasad was now lost in thought, and Criton picked up with the explanation. "It is the nature of deception, Doctor. We have had a very special experience, one that I think many people experience, and are experiencing, but never realize. I know that as a man of science, you must be wrestling with the term *possession*, but I can't think of any term to better describe what happened to me."

Dr. Prasad lifted his head and said, "Yes, it is difficult to accept the spiritual aspect. I want to think in terms of the being as a dimensional one; perhaps what we are dealing with is beings with superior abilities that can transcend special dimensions. These beings encountered early man and were seen as Gods and angels rather than aliens. They have been the basis of man's religions all over the earth, somehow invading through our minds instead of through space." Both men turned and looked to get Bruce's response.

Bruce grinned at the men and looked around the table. "Well, I guess the pressure is on me to give a spiritual explanation." He paused and then said, "I know you expect a sermon, but I must be honest. Whether I say a spirit, demon, or trans-dimensional being, it appears we are describing a distinct personality that has abilities in this world or realm to influence people to act in ways that are both comfortable and sometimes out of character—and that is a frightening power. But the odd thing to me is, if we are dealing with some being from another dimension, how is it that truth is our most effective weapon? That seems to make me think it has more to do with spiritual and moral dimensions than alien fourth-dimensional beings."

Criton looked across at Dr. Prasad. "I have to agree with Bruce, Doctor. *Demon* is the word that I feel best describes what I felt."

"Yes, I understand, Mr. Criton, and I may come to agree with you, but I am still trying to parse out the experience more than the terminology we use. *Demon* or *alien* may be of little consequence as we come to understand these events, so for now I think I will just consider the aspect of what these actions are all about rather than who is behind them."

Criton gave an understanding smile, but Bruce was not ready to move on. "I understand what you're saying gentlemen, but could we go back to the question of *who* for just a moment, since this discussion started with your reaction to the name Murmus. John dealt with Murmus as a guide. Was there a name attached to your entity?"

Dr. Prasad paused, seeming to be deep in thought, and then looked up. He said, "It's very odd, but I cannot think of a name associated with the being. But I do think he or it had a name; it just seems to be lost in a shadowy place in my memory."

Bruce looked at Sandy questioningly, and she smiled and nodded her head. "Does the name Baraqyal mean anything to you?"

The words had barely been spoken when Dr. Prasad sat back in his chair as if suddenly frightened. With a grimace of pain on his face and teeth gritted, he whispered, "Yes—that's it!" His body seemed laced with pain, and then as suddenly as it started, Dr. Prasad began to relax and breathe deeply.

"Wow, where did that come from? It was like someone reached into my chest and grabbed my heart!"

Mrs. Prasad and Sandy were up and leaning over to Dr. Prasad, but he reassured them that he was all right. "Just hearing that name again seemed to trigger some sort of myoclonic reaction." The sudden seizure-like response had passed quickly, and Dr. Prasad looked at the others with a knowing look. "A myoclonic reaction like that could suggest that whatever we've experienced has had an effect on our brains, creating some type of interference, like an epileptic symptom," he explained.

He looked at Criton, but Criton said, "Possibly, Doctor, but I haven't had any of those myoclonic things you're describing. As a matter of fact, I haven't had anything but a sense of relief since my rebuking of Murmus."

"Interesting. Perhaps it has something to do with the fact that I have only recently been freed from this influence." Dr. Prasad looked back at Bruce. "At any rate, Reverend Strong, what were you saying about this Baraqyal character?"

Bruce smiled and looked around the table. "Last night I fell asleep in my chair and was having a very disturbing dream. Sandy heard me and woke me up, but she said that I was not the only one talking in my sleep. It seems you were mentioning this name in your sleep last night, Dr. Prasad. When Sandy told this to me, I started doing some research on demonic angels. Murmus and Baraqyal are both names of demonic angels, as recorded in ancient church records. It seems that this Baraqyal is noted for behavior similar to that you have manifested and for being a teacher for those seeking to learn. He is also a subordinate of none other than Mr. Criton's ex-friend Murmus. A rather odd coincidence—or are we dealing with some intentional force at work? If it is an intentional force, then we need to know the intent. You three have asked the *who* and *what* questions, and I guess now we must ask the *why* question. Why is this happening? Why here, and why now?"

Then a voice that had not been heard—and was actually seldom heard—spoke. "You may all be wrong with your questions and seeking for reasons. You are trying to apply logic and common sense to that which for countless centuries has made no sense. Evil, anger, rage, and hatred make no sense and seek to follow no rule of law or logic. Evil is driven by a desire, and it is a desire to fulfill something within the very nature of evil that even evil itself cannot understand. In your bible, Reverend Strong, it speaks of a war in heaven because of Satan's desire to gain control of heaven—but no one ever asks why. What would or could that evil have done with control of the universe other than destroy it, and in doing so, destroy itself. There is no logic in this, no great cosmic plan. There is only destruction, and that is why evil cannot and will not ever win. Evil and good are just two forces working within the same existence. One creates, and the other destroys. In my belief, they will ultimately come together, because each one needs the other to exist. For how do we know evil if we have never known good, and vice versa? We all are born, and we live, and we die, and then we go back to the one who created us all. In your religion, evil is separated from the good and punished forever—but not destroyed. In my religion, evil is absorbed back into the good, until man makes his choice, and it is man who unleashes the evil, and we begin the cycle all over again.

"Now you are left with the realization that whatever you are dealing with will not be destroyed; it can only be overcome, and it can only be overcome when people turn from evil and choose to love one another. There now, I haven't said that much at one time in years, and now I am finished." With that she rose from the table and began to clear the dishes and put them in the sink.

The room was silent. All were left sitting with their mouths hanging open, oblivious to the little lady puttering around them and doing her self-designated chore. It was in what she was doing that Bruce saw something. A certain clarity came to his mind that comes only on occasions when learning has occurred. He began to watch her as she worked, and still no one spoke. Soon he was aware of the others watching him watch her. Still she worked on, content in her chores. She had chosen to do this thing for the others so that they could wrestle with the important aspect of seeking to understand the demonic assault they were all under. But she was under the same assault and yet seemed not to care. Bruce realized that she was at peace with herself and her surroundings, whether beset with demons or the duties of the day. Her only time of concern was when it was directed not at herself but at the ones she loved.

"What is it, Bruce?" It was that sweet melodic voice that he had first heard at the battlefield as Sandy spoke to him.

"It's your mom. She has reminded me of the simplest of truths in my faith. She isn't even a Christian, and yet she has revealed Christ to me in a way that was familiar to me as a child and in the years of training and education I guess I had forgotten. It is so beautifully simple; it is evil that complicates it and clutters our minds."

"What is it? What are you two talking about?" Criton was perplexed by the scene he had just experienced, and the way Bruce had just seemingly unplugged from the conversation and planning they'd been doing.

Bruce stood up and said, "I can't explain it all now, but just stop and think about it. Right now, I have a hunch that I need to resolve, just for my own peace of mind."

"Whatever do you mean?" It was Criton again. The others just sat there, as if critiquing a play.

"There is a third; I am almost certain of it. A third would make perfect sense in a twisted mind." Saying this, Bruce started for the door and out into the yard. He was walking toward the church and his office, with Criton on his heels, trying to keep up.

"A third *what*, Bruce? You're not making any sense, or else I missed something really big in there. What are we going to do about all this?" Criton's voice took on its tone of feminine exasperation as he followed up the steps.

Suddenly Bruce stopped and turned. He said, "That's just it, John; that's the beauty of it! We don't have to do anything about the situation. As a matter of fact, we have been doing the wrong thing all along. You don't defeat darkness with darkness but with light. Don't you see? We are attacking the wrong enemy with the wrong weapon." And with that, Bruce let out a loud belly laugh, and as if speaking to someone over their heads, said, "I'm coming for you by going to them," and he laughed again!

Criton stood on the step for a moment, trying to figure out what Bruce was talking about. Then he turned and walked back toward the house. Inside, everyone was still at the table, making small talk. They turned with questioning glances when Criton walked in.

"Will someone tell me what is going on and what just happened here? I thought we were trying to figure this out and plan our attack, and now he's over there laughing about 'going for them instead of coming for you' or something. I didn't get it at all, but he sure seems happy about it—he's downright ecstatic." Criton sat back down.

Dr. Prasad looked at his wife and warmly said, "I remember why I married you, my dear." There was a pause, while Mrs. Prasad slowly looked away from the sink and toward her husband. "It's because you have so much darned intelligence wrapped inside that beautiful head of yours."

Mrs. Prasad smiled at the compliment, and maybe there was a hint of a blush before she said, "Are you ready to go home, my love?"

"Yes, my dear, I think I am ready." The two turned to their daughter and asked whether she was coming with them, but Sandy smiled and told them she would be along later. There was a sense of peace in their voices and even in their steps as they quietly moved through the house. They stripped and made the beds and then silently walked out to the car, hand in hand, and left for home. Sandy stood on the porch and waved as they drove away, and Alan joined her there. They watched the car disappear around the corner and up the road before turning to go back inside.

Criton was still sitting there with a look of confusion. He again pleaded, "Would someone please fill me in on what we are doing?" Sandy and Alan looked at him and laughed; they shrugged their shoulders with inscrutable looks on their faces.

Scene 49

Demons speak

At the battlefield, the wind moved through the tall grass nearby, where two specters spoke to one another. It was Murmus and Lerajie, holding an unholy meeting to discuss the next move.

"He has almost put it all together in his head now and, unfortunately, I think he is slipping through our fingers." Murmus spoke with a smooth growl to his voice.

"What does it matter? He is one man in a remote place. I still don't see why he is of any importance at all, other than the joy of the game. I grow weary of this place and these people. They are so ordinary." Lerajie spoke in the tone of impatient that so often accompanied his comments.

"Oh, my dear Lerajie, you act as if you had some place to be. Am I keeping you from a pressing engagement elsewhere?" Murmus laughed a deep, guttural laugh. "Have you forgotten we are prisoners here, with only one purpose? It's in places like this that the battles need to be won.

Subvert the common man, and the theologians and prophets have no audience, and their whole system collapses from within."

"I prefer the cities and the large groups, where so many are willing to give in to my demands."

"Don't you mean *desires*?"

"Desires, demands—what difference does it make? It has become so easy."

With that, Murmus shuddered in agitation. "Yes, and that troubles me all the more. It has become easier, and for us that is a bad omen. It means that the day is drawing nearer. The greater our success, the sooner we usher in our own doom."

"Then why are we here, doing the things that we do? Why not just step back and let them destroy themselves? They seem very adept at self-destruction."

"It is our purpose, Lerajie. It's what we have become and what we are to do, according to the plan. Like it or not, we are all subjects to the One. You, of all beings, should realize that. I recall you were so zealous when Lucifer first called on our support. How were we to know that it was all part of his plan that we fail to fulfill our first estate? But the One knew, and that is why I hate him—and love him, as well."

There was a pause, and Lerajie broke the silence with a grunt of disgust. But before he could speak Murmus cut him off angrily, "Speak of this no more! It is time to close this door for Reverend Strong. Go and break him, destroy him—and then see what parts you can scoop up for us to use. Now go!"

Lerajie moved away quickly. He did not like to be around Murmus when he was like this. His rage could be fierce, and anyway, he was about to have some fun. It was the kind of action he enjoyed the most. It was time to end the games in this place and move on.

Scene 50

The third

Bruce entered his office and sat for a moment as if expecting someone, perhaps because in his mind he hoped he would have a visitor. His suspicions had been growing, and now he had a new vision and greater clarity. It came with a sense of shame. He had neglected his duties because he had fallen victim to his own pride. It had been so easy. All it had taken was some well-placed flattery that played to his own secret desires to be seen as more than just a country preacher. He had been told that he was smart and that his thoughts should be written down for posterity, as if he had a new and unique take on theology. How vain he was! He would not even have been aware now if not for the little Hindu woman who had brought him back from the heights of pride to the knees of humility. His prayers now would be for his own forgiveness and his weakness. He had thought that he could outsmart the trickster, who had centuries of experience. *Who did he think he was?* The question kept echoing in his mind. Still he was alone; the visitor had not come. And then the side door opened, and he jumped up with a start. Footsteps coming around the corner set his heart to racing. Was he ready or this confrontation? And then a figure came into view, and the figure jumped and let out a slight screech.

"Oh, Preacher, you scared me! I wasn't expecting you to be in this morning."

"I'm sorry! I thought you were someone else." It was his secretary. She usually didn't come in this early. Bruce realized that he had jumped in his seat also.

"Did you have a meeting this early?" she asked.

"No, no. I just thought that a certain person might come around today, but it looks like I may need to go and visit him. Could you check the membership role and find me the address to a Marcus Lerajie?"

"Lerajie? You may need to spell that one. I don't recall seeing that name on any of the church rolls. Are you sure he's a member?" she asked.

"Uh, well, now that you mention it, he may not be a member. I never really asked him if he had officially joined the church." The secretary made her way down the hall, and soon she was calling out, asking him to repeat the name and then requesting that he spell it.

Bruce walked down the hall and stood in the door, slowly spelling out, "L-E-R-A-J-I-E, I think? He said it was eastern European or something." Bruce waited as she typed the letters on her computer. She looked up and informed him that there was no match.

"What about Marcus? Try that; maybe it was entered backward."

Bruce moved around her desk, but by the time he was looking over her shoulder he could see there was no one with the last name of Marcus either. Bruce then asked her just to do a document search for the names. She quickly looked up and said, "Got one! A Marcus Larson; he's a member. I have an address that gets the newsletter, but I am not familiar with this guy. He's a member of the senior men's Sunday school class, but I don't see any record of him being here in a while." She turned and picked up the local phone book. But in a moment said was telling him that Marcus Larson wasn't listed in the phone book either.

Bruce instructed her, "Print out that address. Maybe I will give him a visit, if he hasn't been here in a while." Bruce went back to his office and thought about that name, Lerajie. He had not done a search on his friend's name. He typed it into his computer and hit Search. There it was, along with a lot of hits for Lear jet. But Bruce clicked on the first listing, and up popped a Wikipedia link—and what he saw caused a cold shudder to crawl up his back. It was what he'd suspected, but the description was so eerie. Lerajie, the Marquis of Hell, according to *The Key of Solomon*, could appear as male or female, handsome, clad in … Bruce was stunned when he read it and had to look again, clad in *green*! He corrupted wounds with gangrene and had thirty legions of demons at his call.

This was the third, as he had suspected! Why had he not searched this name sooner! The description fit so well. Bruce thought about the first few encounters, when he'd worn the green sport coat and had a feminine, almost seductive, quality in his voice. He thought about gangrene corrupting. Bruce felt he had been corrupted to neglect his duties. It seemed to fit. This was the third demon on the scene, a sort of unholy trinity. Bruce printed out the page and looked at the reference to *The Key of Solomon*. He was familiar with the text but didn't use it, because it had been discredited by bible scholars. It was a book on demonology, supposedly written by Solomon but obviously written by someone in the seventeenth century in France or Germany, as was obvious by the terms for royalty it used. He grabbed the paper and rushed back to the house to fill in the others.

Once back in the house, Bruce was talking a mile a minute. "This is the guy who has been visiting my office, and I am going to confront him."

"Do you know where he lives or where he is now? I don't know where demons hang out these days, but I could take a guess," Alan said with a smile.

Bruce paused. "Uh, come to think of it, I'm not sure where he lives either, but I have this address for a similar name. The name Lerajie isn't on the church role or even in the phone book."

Suddenly Sandy laughed. "Did you check the yellow pages under Satan's minions?" she asked cheekily.

Alan joined in the laughter. "Dude, you looked in the phone book for a demon?" Sandy and Alan were now laughing wildly, and Bruce was looking back and forth at the two with a sheepish look and an awkward smile on his face.

"Yeah, I guess that is sorta weird, isn't it?" Bruce felt a little silly as the laughter continued.

Alan, trying to catch his breath, said, "Bruce, Bruce, I got it! Call one of the staffing agencies and tell them you need a demon for a temporary job."

The crew lost it again with laughter, and all the tension of the past two nights melted away with the sound of the laughter. When the group had regained their composure, Bruce told them he was going to make a quick visit. If a man named Marcus Lerajie came by, they were to tie him up with garlic or something and call him.

Bruce still had a strange feeling about Marcus Larson. The similarity of the names was odd, but more than that, he just had a feeling that he should check out Mr. Larson. Besides, he was a church member whom Bruce had never met or even heard of before. He checked the address and drove out of the parking lot. Larson's home wasn't far away, and soon Bruce was pulling up in front of a small brick house that looked almost deserted. The yard needed mowing, and the trim was in need of a touch of paint. If he hadn't known that it was Larson's home, he would have thought it was deserted. He walked to the front door and pushed the bell. It didn't seem to be working, so he knocked. In a moment, he knocked again a little harder, but there was no answer.

He walked around the side of the house and into the empty carport. He noticed a few spider webs and an empty oil can sitting on the low brick wall. There was a greasy spot on the paint-speckled concrete floor, and the storage room door was slightly ajar, but the spider web across the top showed that it had not been opened in a while. But as he stepped up to the side door, he could see that it had been opened recently. As with many of the homes around the area, this was probably used as the main entrance. Bruce knocked again, but the house was dark and quiet. He reached into his shirt pocket, pulled out a business card, and slipped it in the crack of the door, just to let anyone who did live here know that he had been there to visit.

Bruce turned and began to walk away. Then he stopped. He had a sudden prickling sensation on his neck, as if he could feel eyes watching him from behind. As he stopped and started to turn, he realized that it was oddly quiet, with not even a cricket or bird call. It was if time had stopped, and now he noticed the musky smell of dead grass and heat and felt the weeds rising up around his feet, like fingers on his legs. He turned and stared at the windows of the house, and then he looked past the house to the wooded area. For a moment he thought he saw a form moving in the sea of green trees. He froze in his tracks and stared intently at the tree line. Then he felt a breeze and heard the birdsong, and the moment was over. The silence was replaced with all the sounds of nature. There was something here—he could feel it. He was sure there was a connection between Larson and Lerajie.

The next few days were like a family reunion, with daily visits from

Alan, Sandy, and Criton. He realized how empty the house had been and how much he enjoyed the company. He also was a man on a mission. He increased his visitations, making it a point to go and see all those whom he felt he had been at odds with over the past few weeks. He went by Arthur's twice, but he wasn't at home. He back to Mr. Larson's but missed him as well. Then he visited the homes of the boys whom Riley suspected had been involved in the fight at the crossroads. He had a chance to sit down with all of them except Jake. They were all anxious at the preacher's visit, but after a few moments of conversation the tension passed, and they spoke of school, church, and fun things they had done with the church youth group. Even Leon tempered his hard-tough act long enough to talk with Bruce. Bruce was doing just what he felt the Bible would require him to do. He was reaching out in love to everyone in the same way, going to places where he knew he might not be welcomed. But he was trusting in the power of love and kindness to tear down the new walls that had been built. His unspoken goal was to get back to the relationships he'd had before these demons had cast their seeds of discord. It seemed to be working. He just wished he could have seen a few more people, but Sunday was coming, and it would prove to be a very special day at the little country church.

Scene 51

Sunday

The day was bright and clear, and the sky was a deeper blue than anyone had seen in months. The haze of summer heat was gone, and a refreshing cool breeze brought calm to the morning. Sandy was up fixing breakfast, and Alan had grabbed the Sunday paper and looked as comfortable as an old pair of shoes as he sat in the den, with the morning sun lighting up the room. Alan was putting on a tie as he observed his friends and thinking what an odd group they were. They were only missing Criton to complete the group, but then, as if on cue, he heard a door opening at the back and that now-familiar voice.

"Knock, knock, everybody up? Did I miss breakfast?" He had a laugh in his voice.

"No, you're just in time. Come in and have a seat," Sandy said. Criton brushed by her with a Cheshire-cat grin and headed straight for the pantry to get a coffee cup. Everyone had become familiar with Bruce's home and, in a way, made it their home as well. As Bruce stepped into the room he was met by Sandy, who handed him his coffee cup.

"Two sugars and lots of cream, just the way you like it, *siddha*." Sandy spoke with a mischievous smile.

"Thank you—I think. Does anyone know what she just called me? You know cursing isn't allowed here on Sundays."

"Well, if you must know, it is a great compliment to one in your profession. It means an enlightened being, one who has achieved mastery over the senses and whose experience of the supreme Self is continuous." Sandy spoke as if reading from a dictionary.

Bruce looked at her and then at the others in the room. "Well, what can I say? If the shoe fits ... Now, what's for breakfast?"

The three sat around the table laughing and talking, until Bruce asked whether anyone was coming to hear his sermon that morning. Then everyone began to jokingly cough and tell of all they had to do that day.

Bruce just laughed and said in his best country twang, "Okay, you bunch of heathens, but don't say I didn't warn you. Y'all need to be in church and not just sittin' round here a-backslidin'." And with that he was up and off to get his coat. He bounded out the back door and headed for the church side door and his office to prepare for the day.

Once inside, Bruce saw the few early rising Sunday school teachers and deacons who were in charge of turning on lights and checking thermostats going about their work. He stepped into his office, where he would spend a few moments in prayer and looking over his sermon. He glanced up to see Jake Walters moving past his door, and he called out, "Excuse me, Jake. Have you got a minute?"

Jake turned and stuck his head in the door. "Sure, Preacher. I was just goin' down to my class and look over my lesson. Whatcha need?"

Bruce, turning in his chair, asked, "Is Marcus Larson in your class, Jake?"

"Uh, he is on the role, but we don't see much of him, as a matter of fact I can't remember the last time he came to Sunday school. Now, I did see him in worship service a couple of times here lately." Jake spoke as if trying to remember every bit of information.

"Really?" Bruce said with heightened curiosity, "Just where does he usually sit?"

Jake thought for a moment. "When I saw him, he was sittin' in the back, over close to the door. He usually slips out during the prayer to get a head start on the crowd; he doesn't like trying to maneuver in crowds, what with his bad back and all."

"You say he's got a bad back?"

"Yeah, he's got some sort of arthritis or something. It gives him fits and makes it hard for him to stand straight up. I guess that's why he don't come to church too much. And he's is a bit ... Jake paused, "Uh, you know, peculiar in a way."

At that Bruce perked up. "Peculiar, you say? Just what do you mean by peculiar?"

"Well, it ain't nothing real bad, not like he's retarded or nothing; he's just a little slow, if ya know what I mean. It keeps him from doing a few things, but he does drive a car and all, but just not as much since his back's been hurtin' him and makes him sit sort of stooped over. Why ya want to know, Preacher?"

"I just realized this week that I didn't even know the man and had never been to see him. When I did drop by, I could never catch him at home."

"I think he has to go to the doctor a lot, and his sister gives him a ride to town, 'cause he don't like drivin' in town. If she ain't around, he'll call somebody. Usually its Arthur Kirtland; they're sort of friends."

"Well, that would make sense," Bruce muttered under his breath.

"What was that, Preacher?" Jake asked.

"Ah, nothing, Jake. Thanks for the info. I'll try to run by Larson's house again this week." And with that the conversation was over, as Jake made his way down the hall and Bruce turned back to his review.

About twenty minutes later, Jake came to his door to tell him that Mr. Larson was there in class that day. Bruce realized that he had only a few moments before the class would start, but he had to see this mysterious Mr. Larson. He followed Jake down the hall and into the classroom. There sat the oldest men in the church, tightly crammed into the small space, shoulder to shoulder. As he swept his eyes around the room, Bruce noted all the familiar faces, and there beside Arthur Kirtland sat a figure slumped half over in his chair as if trying to touch the floor. Marcus Larson—but Bruce needed to see his face.

"Mr. Larson! I have been by to see you this week. I wanted to meet you and apologize for not coming sooner." Bruce spoke and leaned forward, trying to see the man's face, and them Mr. Larson slowly turned his head to one side and Bruce saw what he expected. It was Lerajie! But the light in his eyes was dull and the voice muffled as Mr. Larson spoke softly, with words that Bruce could not understand.

"He said, that's why he is here today. You invited him personally, so he wanted to be here out of a courtesy to you." Arthur almost spat the words out, with resentment. "He shouldn't be driving, but his sister lets him keep his car." He seemed to be almost blaming Bruce for the old man taking a chance on the highway.

Bruce turned his attention back to Mr. Larson and asked, "Mr. Larson, do you know a Mr. Lerajie?" Bruce repeated, "Lerajie, Marcus Lerajie."

Suddenly Mr. Larson jerked in his chair and spoke again in a barely audible tone. His head was shaking back and forth, and he was obviously agitated.

"What are you doing, Reverend Strong? Can't you see you've upset him somehow?" Kirtland protested.

"What did he say, Arthur?" Bruce looked at Arthur.

Nothing. It didn't make sense, but whatever you are talking about has him upset. Who is this Marcus Lerajie, anyway?"

Bruce turned back to Mr. Larson and asked again, "Mr. Larson, did you say you know Mr. Lerajie?"

Mr. Larson jerked again and mumbled something. Arthur began to protest once more, but Bruce didn't take his eyes off Larson, and briefly he saw Mr. Larson turn his head and smile. But the smile was from a face that had changed! In a flash, Bruce saw Lerajie—and then he was gone, and the simpleminded Mr. Larson had returned.

By now the entire class was looking at Bruce and murmuring. Bruce looked around and asked the men to forgive his intrusion. He turned to apologize to Mr. Larson for bothering him. As Bruce turned to leave, he was aware that Arthur Kirtland was on his heels.

"Please explain yourself, Reverend Strong. Did you invite him here just to give him the third degree? Can't you see that he's almost retarded and in pain, but he came here today because you left your card. He wanted to be courteous to you, and this is how you treat him—it's outrageous!" Arthur was trying to whisper, but he was livid with anger and his face was beet red.

Bruce was very apologetic, but he was also driven with curiosity. Even though Arthur was about to burst, Bruce asked, "What did he say in there the last time I asked about Lerajie, Arthur? You said it was nothing, but then you said it didn't make sense, so tell me. What did he say that didn't make sense?"

Arthur jerked his head up to look at Bruce and, still trying to whisper, spoke through his grimace. "Did you not hear a word I said? No, I guess you didn't; you don't pay attention to anyone except your friends you have over at the parsonage. I told you he said nothing that made sense." Arthur was trembling, and he continued, "I told you the man is a retard. Don't you get it!"

"But what did he say, Arthur?" Bruce was pushing the issue because he knew he couldn't make Arthur any madder than he already was.

"He said, 'I'm here'—but we all could see that he was here, so what's the big mystery there? You were mocking that old man and thank God he's too slow to realize the insult. But we know it; that whole class saw your little incident in there." Arthur turned back toward his class, and as he opened the door, Bruce could see the class was buzzing. He realized he had pushed the issue, but at least now he knew what he was up against. Lerajie was using Mr. Larson because of his weak mind.

Bruce sat down and tried to focus on the coming worship service, but it was difficult. The rest of the morning was a blur, and Bruce felt that his sermon was a garbled mess, because he kept watching the small green-coated man in the back.

Scene 52

The serpent strikes

After the sermon, Bruce stood at the back, shaking hands, and then finally he went back to his office. There he found Larson/Lerajie in his office, first bent like Larson and then rising to full height as Lerajie. Bruce moved toward his desk while Lerajie sat down on the couch, as he had done so many times before.

"I was not expecting you, especially after our encounter in the Sunday school class. Don't you think it a little risky coming to my office and standing straight and tall? Someone could walk in that door right now and see you sitting there, looking like a younger, stronger man," Bruce said with a hint of anger in his voice.

"Oh, I don't think they will be coming up here very soon. They are too busy trying to figure out just what's wrong with the preacher. They think I'm in the bathroom or just wandering around the halls like some dimwitted old man. It's easy to get around when no one notices you. I am just a comfortable figure that people pity and avoid. That is one of the reasons that I stopped coming to church. There is nothing wrong with this mind except that perhaps it's a little slow at times, but all that's changed now, one of the many gifts for my friend."

Suddenly the voice changed, and the figure before him slumped a little as Larson now spoke. "I don't think you'll ever understand what it's like to lose your life and then to get it all back—not just get it all back, but even better than it was! It's almost like I have invited the rich man into my home and he brought a chef and a banker and all, so that I could have all the things I always wanted. But most importantly, I would not be alone anymore. Your church and your good Christian folks could not, or just would not, ever do anything like that for me. I lived down there in that house for years, and no one came to see me. The only time I've had any human contact after my wife died was from a sister who sees me as an inconvenience. I get a patronizing visit at Christmastime or whenever they felt guilty about not visiting crazy old Mr. Larson. And then one day I had a visitor who showed me kindness such as I have never known from the good folks around here. He gave me back my life and asked very little in return. All they want is a place where they can experience life again, just like me. I have told you enough for now, and I guess I should say sorry. I'm sorry for what I'm going to do, but at the same time not really that sorry, because it's a small price to pay for the joy of living life the way I want for a change."

Mr. Larson was sitting there with an innocent look on his face. But as Bruce sat across from him, he seemed to change before his eyes, and he was looking at a younger man now sitting upright in the chair, with a sardonic grin.

Bruce did not smile but instead looked straight at Larson and said, "Lerajie, I command you to come out of that man. In the name of Jesus, the Christ, come out!"

Larson began to shudder and moan as if in pain. "Oh, oh!" and then the voice changed from a pained moan to a chuckle. "Oh really, Bruce, what are you doing? Did you read that in a book or see a movie about exorcism? I really gave you more credit than that. *Come out!*" Lerajie spoke in a mocking tone and laughed even harder.

Bruce sat there stunned. He had always understood that demons would obey when you knew their names and spoke in the name of Jesus, but now he was sitting across from a truly possessed man, and his statement had no effect.

"Leave this poor man alone, you beast." Bruce spoke again with anger.

"Well, I would, but Mr. Larson has no desire for me to leave. You see, our Mr. Larson benefits from our relationship. He gets clarity of thought and renewed energy of mind and body, and I get a vessel. It's a win-win situation! Why would anyone give up such a gift? I make him feel good about himself. You didn't seem to mind when I was complementing you."

Bruce looked up and realized it was true. He had been seduced by Lerajie's admiration, because he had wanted to be admired for his thoughts. He'd secretly felt that he was destined for more than a little country church. He realized it was his secret sin of vanity; Lerajie had exploited his weakness.

Bruce looked at Lerajie but seemed to look past him and somehow into him. He said, "I will still pray for you, Marcus, and I hope that you come to realize that this being is using you for evil."

"Very good, Bruce." Lerajie spoke softly but with a tone of hatred Bruce that had not heard in the old man's voice. "I'm glad you see that you are beaten. You cast down the gauntlet, and I took it up and defeated you, using your own pride. You are weak, and I have proven them wrong to think you were anything special. You have fallen, like the others and the ones who will come after you.

"After me?" Bruce looked at Lerajie curiously.

"Oh, I'm sorry, Bruce. I didn't mean to shock you, but you are done here. Even now they plan your dismissal." Lerajie smiled again with that evil grin.

"You're very sure of yourself, demon, but maybe these folks will surprise you. There's some good people here."

"Yes, there are some, as you say, 'good people,' but you and I both know that these good people always melt before the onslaught of the other good people, because they all cloak their actions with the label of goodness. You will either resign or be dismissed, 'for the good of the church,' and they will do it with a zealous righteousness, as they always do when carrying out what is best for the community. Your career as a minister may even be over, depending on how zealously they fire you." Lerajie spoke with a slight hint of joy in his voice.

Bruce sat silently, because he knew that what Lerajie was saying was potentially true. He looked at Lerajie and said, "So, why tell me so much, and why such efforts for a small country preacher like me?"

"But Bruce, it has always been about you. Even though you're not really that important, it's what you represent. You really need to get that pride in check; it will be your downfall—oops, I guess it already has been!" Lerajie laughed but quickly stopped and then continued, "That was really rude, by your standards. You may think I shouldn't gloat, but gloating is a virtue to us. I really enjoy tearing people like you down from your holy heights. You all are really disgusting, with your sanctimonious speeches and pseudo power. When you fail, you are like the first domino, as others who looked at you with admiration will become disillusioned, and even if they don't reject their belief, they will at the very least become marginal in their adherence to God. So, you see, I win. It's almost too easy these days. Now, go pack your bags; your time is almost up. I think just one more thing will seal your coffin, so to speak. Let's see!"

Lerajie jumped up quickly, considering the old body he was using, and stepped to the door. When he reached the door, he turned to Bruce and said, "Don't you want me out of this church and your life? All you have to do is order me out, but not in the name of Jesus. I will make a bargain with you. Tell me to get out ... on your own ... and I will leave Mr. Larson and your church. Show me that you can stand on your own two feet, and you will free this old man."

Bruce looked at Lerajie and then saw him bend over and become Larson again. Larson looked up and spoke softly: "Please help me, Preacher."

Then suddenly he stood up, and Lerajie was speaking again. "You see, he does want me to leave, but he is weak. You can free him, Bruce. No dramatic 'Come out!'—just say 'Get out.' Command it, and I will go. Just say it!"

Bruce looked as the old man reappeared. He heard Lerajie whisper, "I will give you this little victory, since I have won the war."

Bruce was confused, but his heart went out to Mr. Larson, and he wanted to help him. "Okay, demon, I'll play your little game. Get out." Bruce waited, but nothing happened.

"A little louder, please. You didn't think I would make it that easy, did you, Reverend?" Lerajie spoke with a guttural growl.

Bruce stepped closer and, almost shouting, said, "Get out!"

There a was a sound down the hallway like a person's gasp, and Larson stood in front of him, bent over and feeble, and then Lerajie's voice came out of the figure. "Oops, guess I lied." He snickered and launched himself out and onto the floor.

Bruce was just inside the doorway, and in anger he said, "Yes, you are an expert liar!"

But even before he could finish the statement, he heard Arthur Kirtland at the end of the hall. "What are you doing to that man? Did you push him down, and now you're calling him a liar?" Arthur was not alone; he was flanked by members of the deacon body, who were looking at the scene in astonishment. The men rushed forward, helped Mr. Larson up, and asked if he was okay.

Marcus could only say, "He pushed me down and told me to get out! I ... I don't know why—I just came by to see him. Did I tell you he pushed me down?"

Yes, you did, Mark, and don't worry. We'll deal with him. Oscar, will you help get Mr. Larson home?" Arthur was looking at one of the deacons and then back at Bruce. Oscar Smith stepped up, shot an angry look at Bruce, and then took Larson's arm and led him toward the parking lot.

"Well, we were coming to get you to and ask you to come into the called deacon meeting, but I don't know if we need to meet now, gentlemen. Not after what we've just seen. It's like I said—I believe that our preacher has a darker side that we don't have to tolerate anymore." Arthur spoke these words while looking around at the faces of the other deacons. "I think that, for the good of the people, action needs to be taken right away. Do we all agree?"

Bruce echoed softly, "'For the good of the people'? What have I done that makes me such a threat?"

Bruce was looking at Arthur as he spoke, and Arthur returned the glare. "How about shirking your duties, or your hard-to-understand and sometimes offensive sermon material, sermons which may have forced that young boy to shoot himself, driven by the guilt you put in his head? How about cohabiting with strange women in the parsonage, and now assaulting a senior adult and ordering him out of church, to name a few."

Bruce was so stunned he barely heard the voices suggesting they move to the boardroom to talk. Once in the boardroom, Bruce was asked to explain what the deacons had just witnessed. Bruce knew that if he told them he'd been trying to cast out a demon he would be laughed out of the church. Bruce was stuck. How could he explain what had happened without mentioning possession? So he sat there in silence. The men were talking among themselves, and even Bruce's supporters were confused.

Finally, Bruce said, "Gentlemen, I'm sorry I can't explain things fully, but there are certain things that must remain confidential when dealing with people in the church. The situation with Mr. Larson was a misunderstanding. He slipped and fell and thought that I had pushed him, but I assure you I didn't touch him. It was some of you that told me he had some mental difficulties. I really can't say any more than that, and for that I am truly sorry."

The room fell silent again, until Arthur spoke up. "I can't believe you men are gonna fall for that drivel. An explanation that explains nothing, and then he tries to blame the poor old simpleminded man that has never hurt a fly. That is low, and we all know it. And don't forget that little fellow that shot himself; I still think that Reverend Strong has some responsibility, for that sermon that drove him to suicide when he couldn't deal with his guilt. I move we remove Bruce Strong as pastor and make it effective immediately. Do I have a second?"

The room remained quiet, but after a few hard looks from Arthur, the sheepish voice of Ralph Barnes said, "I reckon I could second that motion."

Arthur called for a vote, and seven of the ten men raised their hands. Just like that, Bruce was no longer the pastor.

Bruce cleared his throat and asked quietly, "Gentlemen, I have told you as much as I can about Mr. Larson, and I resent Arthur's insinuation that I had anything to do with Julian's suicide. I can assure you it was not guilt that drove him to suicide. That being said, I will turn in my resignation this week and say my farewell to the church next Sunday, if that is acceptable."

Before the group could respond, Arthur spoke, "No, that's not acceptable. If you know something about that boy's death, you should tell us or at least tell the sheriff. And that's just another reason that I think we should take the resignation, and we'll read it to the church. I don't think it would be a good idea for you to come back to the church. You should vacate the parsonage as soon as possible."

The men were caught off guard and muttering to one another, when Jake Walters said, "Arthur, I think we're being a little hasty and even harsh. After all, this is Bruce, and we all know that he is no danger to anyone. I don't know or understand what happened with Mr. Larson, but I think we can show some Christian love to Bruce. He's always done the same for us."

There was a low rumble of approval around the room, but Arthur was fuming. "Christian love! You do realize that Marcus Larson could file charges, and the church would be liable! If he's hurt, he can sue, and we are responsible for the action of the pastor, because you guys didn't listen to me when I said we should incorporate. But now it's—"

Arthur was cut off by Bruce's voice, "He's right, gentlemen. Marcus could sue the church, and I wouldn't be surprised if he tried to take the church for all it's got, so you must show that you acted quickly and harshly. I don't want the church to be hurt, so we will do it Arthur's way. I will have my letter to you today, and I will leave the parsonage as quickly as I can. Thank you, fellows, for all you've done for me in the past, and best of luck for your future."

Bruce stood and walked out of the room, and a few men followed him out. Outside they questioned him about what he'd meant when he said he thought Marcus would sue, but Bruce avoided any detail. It was Jake who said that Bruce was not telling something that he felt they needed to know. But Bruce couldn't figure out how to tell these men that there was a monster in their midst.

Scene 53

The next step

That was it. In just a few moments his career, and maybe his life in the ministry, had come to an end. He felt a chill and a sick feeling in his stomach. He had not fought back; he had tried to do what was best for the church. Why didn't he go back and do something? He played the scene over in his head and realized that Lerajie was a master tactician. There was nothing he could do that wouldn't end in a church fight, and in the end Lerajie, as Larson, still had a lawsuit that could wreck the church—complete with witnesses that were on the same side as Lerajie. Bruce could only walk away defeated. It was Buford's play all over again, and he was Buford: outmanned, outflanked, and at the mercy of a ruthless enemy. He glanced up in the direction of the battlefield and wondered whether this was how Colonel Buford had felt as he fled the field, leaving dead and wounded friends and being chased by the enemy.

Bruce didn't want to go back and tell his friends, but he had been gone a long time, and they were sure to be wondering what was going on. He walked in and saw that they'd already had Sunday lunch. They were all in the den, relaxing. Sandy was the first to speak when they heard him come in, and then the questions started. Sandy started to fix Bruce a plate of lunch, but he said, "Let's sit down and have a talk first," and with that the story began. Bruce told them everything that had happened and the way he had even fallen into Lerajie's trap at the end. The group fell silent when he told them that he was being forced to resign and must leave the parsonage. Everyone was stunned and could only ask Bruce what he would do.

Bruce wasn't sure what to say, but Criton had no problem. "First of all, you will move in with me. I have plenty of room, and it will give you some breathing room to formulate a plan."

Bruce was quiet, but the others thought it was a great idea, and Bruce finally conceded that at the moment he didn't have many options.

"Then it's settled, and while you're there, we can start work on your book."

"Book? What book, John?" Bruce gave Criton an odd look.

"You must do something, Bruce, and it is obvious that you are not going to fight Lerajie with the church as a battlefield, so you must take all that you have learned and use it against him. Writing about it is your best weapon to expose what is going on around you. I have written several books, so I will be an invaluable asset. We may even tie the two books together and have a screenplay. The possibilities are limitless!"

"Whoa, John, slow down! I have a lot to consider here before launching into my writing career. I would still like to be a pastor."

"I think it's a great idea, Bruce, and I agree with John. You have a lot of information that not many people have been privy to, so don't waste it. You—"

Sandy was interrupted by Alan, who seemed to finish her sentence, "You need the time to process what has happened and incorporate it into your ministry."

Bruce was smiling and scratching his head. "You all make a lot of sense, especially at a time when things aren't making a lot of sense."

"There's one more thing, Bruce." Criton's voice took an ominously serious tone. "You have been given an opportunity that I think is unprecedented. I was involved with a demon for most of my life and had no idea until you revealed it to me, and it was traumatic. But look at you—you have just been speaking with a demon as if he were a long-lost cousin. He revealed a lot to you, and once you knew what he was, he still revealed information. I find this very unusual. You should be asking yourself why, and what does this mean to you? Have you been blessed or cursed, complimented or mocked? Why did Lerajie do this? Does he have no respect or fear of you, or does he see you as formidable in some way and is trying to weaken your resolve? You were writing with him, and now you are hesitant to write. Alan was right; you need some time to wrap your head around this event. I think I need to do the same."

Sandy interrupted and said, "Hey, wait a minute. We're so worried about you, but you've got a place to go. What about me and Alan? We're on the street again!"

They all began to laugh, and Bruce realized that what had been a major life tragedy for him a few moments ago had been be turned into a positive moment, thanks to good friends. Through the laughter, Bruce turned to Criton long enough to say that he would gratefully accept his invitation. Then his mind drifted to ministry again. What was he seeing here? Satan had attacked and, in a sense, had won the victory, as Lerajie had claimed, but here he was laughing with friends and feeling the warmth and love of friendship. Maybe Lerajie was wrong, or maybe he knew he had not won such a complete victory. That was it! Lerajie was a demon, and demons were basically liars. Bruce had fallen for the lie that his life and ministry were over, when in fact he was as strong as ever, because he had the love of others—he still had that same love in his heart! He hadn't lost; he had just changed battlefields. Criton was right; he must share this with any who would read his story.

As if reading his mind, Criton said, "You know, Bruce, if you doubt that people will believe you, just remember this. I have been telling people that I talk to dead relatives for years and made a good living. People believe what they want to believe."

Again, it was Sandy, with her pragmatic logic, who spoke up. "What are we waiting for? Let's start packing up your stuff, Bruce, and get you organized for the move. All Alan and I have to do is pack a bag and we're outa' here. I'm sure John has room for two more—don't you John?"

Criton stopped, looked around, and then burst into laughter, saying, "Well, of course I do! We can't break up the team, now can we? That is a marvelous idea. We've all been in this together, so now we can help each other in collecting and coordinating our data. Sandy, thank you so much for that excellent suggestion. Let's get started!"

Bruce was lost amid a whirlwind of activity. All the while they were working he kept thinking about how he had seen men destroyed by events like this, and yet his friends had turned it almost into a party. But Bruce was also thinking of others. He still had a lot of friends who would have many questions, and he hated leaving explanations in the hands of men like Arthur to twist and spin any way they wanted. He also knew that Lerajie would have a field day tearing this community apart, so he had to move the fight away from here. He would still like to say good-bye to a few friends, but he wasn't going far, so he hoped to see some of the folks around. Maybe they would understand—or at least be slow to judge.

Chapter 10

Scene 54

The end or just the beginning

The following Monday, Bruce was in his office, packing up his books and computer records. There had been a few people drop by to talk about the situation. Most were shocked and supportive; they were willing to fight the deacons on their decision, but Bruce explained that it had actually been his decision, and he felt it best if things were just left alone. This only caused more confusion, but those who loved and supported him trusted his judgment. Even though he could tell they wanted to ask more questions, they respected his decision. These were the people Bruce would miss the most; they were the ones he wanted to somehow warn. But he feared that if he said too much they, too, would think he had gone crazy. When the room was silent and empty, he thought about Lerajie and his mastery of manipulation, the way he had played on everyone's weaknesses. He was a master of deception, and Bruce realized that he was no match for a demon in this game of wits. The demon had been at this for a long time, and Bruce, who had always believed in the demonic forces, now realized that he had only given them passing thought and had not taken their influence seriously. That had been his greatest mistake. He'd spoken often of evil but had never really put a face on it. It had been easier just to say the devil or Satan and picture some creature rather than see evil in the face of the people around him.

As soon as he had the thought, he saw the face of Arthur Kirtland in his head. Was Arthur a demon, or was he just a pawn in Lerajie's plan, a totally unaware clown in this circus of evil intent? As Bruce finished packing boxes, his mind kept drifting back to the battlefield. Was this place the beginning point or just a staging area for an assault on ... he paused and wondered, *an assault on what?* Lerajie had made it seem that he had been the target all along, but Bruce could not accept that. He began to think about the church and its history, as faces and names began to scroll through his mind. This place, this quiet little community, had a history of negative action toward clergy and one another, and yet they always saw themselves as simple, good, hardworking, country folk. Bruce began to think about the nature of evil, and he wondered how much was demonically inspired and how much was motivated by the evil in peoples' hearts. Where did one evil stop and another begin? Was it "a curse on" this church and community to be constantly in turmoil?

As Bruce sat there, he suddenly realized that this community was not unique. Compared to other churches he had known and worked in, the pattern was similar. It seemed that very few churches were places of peace and love. Just as Buford's crossing had been one battle in a larger war, this battle for this church was just one of many battles in the spiritual war that was being waged daily in all churches.

Scene 55

A farewell

Bruce got a chance to say good-bye sooner than he'd expected. Deputy Riley came by later as he was finishing packing up his car. Riley and Bruce stood outside the parsonage, looking at the car. It looked like an overripe fruit just ready to burst. There wasn't room for anything else except one person in the driver's seat.

"Looks like you're pretty full, Preacher. I really hate to see you go like this. You know there are enough people who support you that we could have made a fight of this thing. I hate lettin' a few folks run the church and chase people off that don't dance in step with every tune they whistle. It ain't right, and I just hate that these people seem to always win. It will be the death of this church!" Riley was spitting fire with every word.

"They didn't win, Riley; they just think they won something. When all is said and done, they will have a hard time seeing what they really accomplished by asking me to step aside. It's just a game they play. I am convinced these are not bad people—"

But Bruce couldn't finish his sentence before Riley jumped in. "Well, let me help un-convince you before you leave, 'cause I see bad people all the time, and what they are doin' ain't much different than what I see out on the streets. It's one person hurtin' another, and usually for no good reason."

"You're right about that, Riley. There is no good reason, because good seems to have been perverted in their minds. I have learned a lot about evil in my years in the ministry, especially the past few weeks. The one thing I know is that when evil manifests itself in a person's life in obvious ways, that just means the devil isn't afraid of being seen. Most evil is hidden behind the guise of supposed good, and that's just how the devil likes it. He gets to hide behind the faces of deacons and Sunday school teachers and even preachers, sometimes. Matthew 7:21 to 23, Riley, says it all."

Riley smiled a kind of knowing grin. "You like that passage, don't ya, Bruce? I remember you mentioned it a lot in your sermons."

"Like it? Heck, no! I don't like it; it scares the bejeebers out of me! I am always afraid that I might say the wrong thing and lead people astray. As a pastor, I always felt a sense of responsibility, not only for the people but for what I try to teach them, and here lately I have found that the truth is not a high priority on their learning menu." Bruce's tone had gone from serious to calmer and kind.

"Well, say what ya will, I think there are some pretty mean-hearted Christians around here, and me and the wife are thinkin' about goin' over to Moriah Baptist Church and seein' what it's like."

"You do what you think is right for you and your family, Riley, but I will just about bet you that you will find the same thing over there sooner or later. Folks are pretty much the same in all churches, because a lot of them join the Church but never join God. It's that cart-before-the-horse sermon I preached once, remember?"

Riley looked down at the ground as if checking the records of sermons he remembered, and he stuttered a half truth. "Yeah, I think I remember that one … maybe …" As his voice trailed off toward the ground, the preacher just smiled a warm, understanding smile. "Ya know, Preacher," Riley continued, "I blame that whole battlefield ruckus. That's what started all this foolishness."

Bruce paused, seeming lost in thought for a moment. He looked up at the sky, and as his eyes came down, he was staring in the direction of the battlefield.

"Maybe in some ways, Riley. I think what we experienced wasn't *caused* by the battlefield, but I do think it was *like* that battle up there. Just like the battle between Tarleton and Buford, our battle was over before it ever began. Forces were at work that set things up for that confrontation and for ours. As a matter of fact, that might make a good sermon someday."

Riley cocked his head and looked at Bruce. "How do you figure to get a sermon out of this mess, Preacher?"

"Let's just say that Tarleton represents the devil, okay? And Buford and his boys, they represent the Church. Buford knows that the devil is after him, and he's thinking that by sending the governor off with someone else he's outsmarted that old Tarleton, and now he and his boys are just cruising along trying to get to where there are more colonial troops. But Tarleton, like the devil, has a plan too, and he's moving his troops fast to cut Buford off, and poor Buford never sees it coming until it's too late. He pays a hefty price for his lack of diligence, because the devil is smart like Tarleton, and he never hits us from where we expect to get hit. But when the battle was over, Tarleton, like the devil, thought he had won."

Riley suddenly interrupted, "Seems like they did win, Preacher. They just about wiped ole Buford and his boys out."

Bruce excitedly put in, "No, Riley, that's what's so cool about the whole thing! You see, the devil wins a lot of battles in our lives, and he celebrates and gloats, and we sit and mope and lick our wounds and run into our fortress we call the Church to hide out. But sometimes when the devil has a big win, like Tarleton did at the crossroads that day, some people don't get scared—they get inspired to fight all the harder. Alan and I were talking one night about how that little disastrous battle at the Buford's crossroads created a frenzy of anger at the next battles over in Kings Mountain and Cowpens, and the colonials beat the British so bad that they gave up their campaign in the south and moved north just in time to get trapped at Yorktown, where they had to surrender. Alan compared it to the Alamo out in Texas. It was one of those lost battles that inspire great victories. After Buford, the colonials were yelling, 'Remember Buford' and 'Give 'em Buford's play' as battle cries. Had Cornwallis won either of those, he might have stayed in the south, never moved north, and never got caught by Washington and the French fleet."

"Okay, I get the history lesson, but where's the sermon?" Riley asked, scratching his head.

"Well, the devil is out here racking up a lot of little victories and leaving a lot of casualties lying around, creating a lot of mean-spirited people along the way. But it only takes one person to show love to another, and Satan is reminded that his 'Yorktown battle' has already been fought. The crucifixion was his Battle of Buford, but the resurrection was his Yorktown, and he knows it too. He just hasn't had to surrender. But it's sad that so many people have to become victims, because they get sucked into evil. It's that whole 'powers and principalities' thing that Paul wrote about."

Riley just nodded his head as if he knew exactly what the preacher was talking about. "I guess when you look at it that way, all these people struttin' around thinking they have flexed their muscles and won a victory, they are actually the losers."

The two men looked at each other and spoke simultaneously, "And they don't even know it yet!"

They laughed and shook hands, and Bruce got that serious look on his face again. He said, "You're okay, and so am I, but they sure did hurt some good, innocent people along the way, and that's always the tragic part. Just remember, Riley, you can't always trust in the goodness of man, but you can trust in the goodness of God. Even when you feel like a victim, you're a future victor. Hey, I gotta' remember that—that'll preach."

"So, what's the plan now, Preacher? Where ya goin'?"

"Oh, don't worry about me. I got a little money saved, and Mr. Criton has invited me to stay at the house he's renting in town for a while, so I won't be too far away. I have a feeling there may be a few loose ends to tie up around here. I'll decide what to do after a while. Who knows? I may go work on that doctorate degree. I have been wanting to do that, ya know."

Riley smiled and said, "Dr. Strong ... it's got a nice ring to it. Maybe you could teach at the university and write a book or somethin'."

Riley was grinning, and Bruce wasn't sure whether he was serious or being just a little patronizing. "Ya know you're not the first person to suggest that, Deputy," he informed him. And with that, Bruce was climbing into the driver's seat and waving good-bye.

Riley smiled and waved as he watched Bruce pull his car out onto the road and disappear around the bend. He looked back up at the steeple of his church and then hopped into his cruiser to head up the highway. He drove back up past the barn and on past the battlefield, wondering whether he'd had his last encounter with Buford's play.

Scene 56

Loose ends

Bruce had thrown his belongings in a room at Criton's house, and the four friends had spent the evening talking and relaxing, but when the morning came, Bruce woke with a sudden sense of urgency. He had some loose ends he wanted to tie up that morning. He had thought about what Arthur and Lerajie had said the day before. He had been accused of having some part in Julian's suicide, so he decided that he must speak with Julian's family today, before anyone else could. Bruce arrived at their home, and as he had expected, they had already heard about his resignation. They met them at the door with odd looks on their faces, and Bruce wondered whether Arthur or someone else had already spoken with them. They asked him to come in and have a seat, and as usual, Julian's mom offered him some iced tea, which he gladly accepted. Their hospitality seemed a symbolic gesture that they still liked him and even supported him.

As they talked, he tried to tell them about all that had happened, without mentioning demonic activity and how he felt that evil had gripped the church and the community, and their son had been caught up in a wave of this evil and violence. He wanted them to know that no one could control or even fully comprehend what could have led to Julian's death, but that suicide was not an unpardonable sin, and that he felt assured that God's mercy would still apply to their son. Julian's mother then surprised him by asking if he thought that Julian had had anything to do with the attack on the boy who had been in a coma. Bruce wasn't sure whether they had heard a rumor to that effect or were simply looking for some explanation for Julian's suicide, but it didn't really matter. Bruce assured them that he felt Julian had had nothing to do with hitting the other boy, and they should disregard any thoughts to suggest otherwise. He was careful not to blame any of the other boys, but deep inside he wanted to shout out with anger over how they had been so eager to blame Julian at the funeral.

The subject changed back to Bruce and his resignation. They had heard all sorts of stories about him and had discounted them all; they did not tolerate gossips and were sad to hear that he had resigned. After another few moments of conversation, they offered their prayers of support for anything that he chose to do. Bruce told the folks that he had to leave and asked whether he could pray with them just once more. They took one another's hands and sat in a moment of silent prayer together, after which Bruce said a few words of prayer and offered a blessing on the family. After a round of good country hugs, he headed back to his car feeling confident that he had cut off any kind of attack from Lerajie.

Now Bruce decided that he was going to take a chance and make one more visit to Marcus Larson's house. He thought that now that he had resigned and was no longer a threat to Lerajie, perhaps he could talk some sense into Marcus and somehow help him realize that he had a better choice, that the spirit possessing him meant him no good. Bruce turned into Larson's driveway and noted how everything still seemed run down and the yard in need of mowing. The house looked empty and in need of repairs as well. It was the usual thing that happened to a house when there was no one there to manage the general maintenance. Bruce walked back toward the carport and knocked on the door. He didn't really expect anyone to answer, but he waited. After a moment or so, he knocked again. This time he felt a little bolder and reached up to turn the knob. He felt the door open. He gently leaned his head into the kitchen, where he detected the musty smell of dust and stale air as he shouted out for Mr. Larson.

He spoke with a soft rising inflection, his voice matching his mounting courage. "Mr. Larson are you here, it's Reverend—" Bruce suddenly paused and thought that he should not be called a reverend anymore, since he had just resigned. "It's Bruce Strong. I'd like have a word with you, if I could."

There was no sound in the house, but Bruce felt sure that Larson was there. He mustered a little more courage and stepped into the kitchen. Once again, he shouted out his name, but there was no response. Finally, after a moment of dead silence, Bruce heard a shuffling of feet down the hall, and slowly the old man appeared around the corner. His body was bent nearly to the waist as he looked down at the floor, moving slowly, his head bobbing up and down and cane pecking out in front of him like a blind man. Marcus Larson shuffled across the faded and broken linoleum floor in front of Bruce as if he didn't even see him standing there.

"I'm sorry to barge in like this, but I wasn't sure if you could hear me. Marcus are you entertaining anyone, or can I have a word with you?"

Marcus slowly lifted his head; there was a somewhat puzzled look in his eyes. He mumbled something, but Bruce couldn't quite understand. Bruce looked at him again, wondering where Lerajie was. Had the demon decided not to speak with him anymore and just continue this ruse of Marcus Larson, poor old man? Marcus sat down at a small dining table and motioned for Bruce to come sit down beside him. Bruce walked across the floor, took a seat, and again asked if there was anyone else there. Bruce was sure there were no other people in the house, but he was trying to goad Lerajie into an appearance. Marcus just nodded his head slowly and Bruce could hear him mumble, "No, no one here."

Bruce looked at Larson empathetically, thinking of the poor, lonely man who had become a willing participant in this demonic game of cat and mouse Bruce scowled and asked, "Do you remember what happened at the church, in my office, yesterday? We spoke for a few moments, and you told me that you had gotten your life back. Do you remember any of what you told me yesterday in my office?" There was a pause, while Larson just looked around as if deaf to any questions. "Do you still have your friend with you? Your friend Lerajie, is he here?"

Larson looked up at Bruce slowly again. His eyes seemed a bit watery and weak, and he did not respond. He just stared at Bruce as if he could not understand what he was saying.

Bruce tried again, "Mr. Larson I was wondering if I could speak with Lerajie, if he was here with us today."

The old man just looked at him. Bruce couldn't tell for sure whether the old man really couldn't understand or was just pretending he couldn't. He seemed to have a pained look on his face, and Bruce wondered whether he was battling the spirit within him. Bruce was getting a little frustrated. He had come here to try and get through to this man and speak about his soul's salvation. He wanted to try one more time to rid him of the demonic creature that had taken up residence in his body, but it was becoming more and more clear that the demon was either not going to make an appearance or not allow this man to understand what was being said.

Bruce sighed and looked around. Then he said softly, as if speaking to himself, "Sorry to bother you Mr. Larson. I just wanted to …" and Bruce paused, asked himself what *did* he want to accomplish here today—an exorcism or miraculous conversion? His frustration was building as he realized that like Jesus's disciples who could not cast out demons, he had failed this old man in his struggle with the forces of darkness. Bruce looked at the crippled body beside him and said, "I won't take up any more of your time today," the frustration audible in his voice. "Perhaps you wouldn't mind if I said a prayer for you."

Bruce placed his hand on the weak, bony hand of the old man lying limp across the table, squeezed it gently, and bowed his head. "Our heavenly Father, we come to you today on behalf of this one, this lonely soul, asking that you would enter into his heart—"

"Oh, please! I can't take any more of this! Just stop, Bruce—please stop, and I'll talk to you. This is really so ridiculous, but it's cute. I have to admit you have a loving heart, a foolish mind but a loving heart. What was it that you said?" The demon then spoke using Bruce's own voice: "On behalf of this one, this lonely soul." And then it was the voice of Lerajie, laughing and yet filled with bitterness and hate at the same time, a mocking wit overriding every tone.

Bruce looked across at what a moment before had been a decrepit old man and now saw a stronger man, sitting upright in his chair and squeezing Bruce's hand with renewed strength. He was lifting his cane as if he were about to use it as a club. Larson sprang to his feet and walked back toward the door, and Bruce wondered whether he was going to throw him out. He said, "For a moment I hoped that maybe you were gone, but our Mr. Larson couldn't be so lucky."

"Lucky? Oh, Bruce, you want to talk of luck? Let's talk about luck. Look at me. I told you yesterday, I've got my life back. I can enjoy life again. What you called demonic I call a second chance."

Bruce looked at him and then began to look around the dusty, dirty kitchen of the old house. "I'm not sure if I would call this exactly a great life, Mr. Larson. Are there no demons that do the simple housekeeping?"

Larson just looked at him and smiled. Then he turned and began to walk down the little hallway into a room on his right. He motioned for Bruce to follow, and when Bruce entered the room, he was struck by what he saw. There was a big-screen TV taking up most of one wall, with a smaller television on either side. These had various channels playing at same time, complete with an integrated stereo system and speakers in each corner. There was a large picture window in the back wall that looked out onto the pasture and woods. A comfortable-looking leather chair sat beside a small wine cooler filled with wine bottles cooling, and a decanter of whiskey was set near the chair. A half-smoked cigar sent curly smoke up and filled the air with the aroma of rich tobacco.

"See, Bruce, it's not as bad as you might think. From outside you would think this is just a three-bedroom brick ranch with one and a half baths, but as you see, I have made a few changes, purely for comfort. I have no real desire to travel the world, even though my body is feeling better than ever before, but I'm still a rather old man, and I wouldn't want to arouse anyone's suspicions. I now have the clarity of thought and vision to know what I want and how to enjoy it. As I told you yesterday, what else have I got to do? Why shouldn't I enjoy what's left of my life? No one else cares about me except this so-called demon you speak of. But it seems I remember the Bible says that demons were once angels, and this one's been an angel to me. He's asked very little and given a lot in return."

Bruce looked at the old man in this luxurious room and slowly shook his head. "I'm afraid I may understand it all too well. This demon has asked very little of you, that is true. All you had to do was put on one small show, tell one little lie, and in doing so end my career and confuse a lot of good people, bringing chaos to this place. That probably doesn't mean a whole lot to you, and maybe I'm partly to blame for that, since I haven't been the pastor you needed. For that I do apologize. The fact that your small contribution has created some pretty big problems, not just for me but for the church, doesn't matter either, I guess, since you don't really care about me, the church, or the people in this community, because they didn't care about you. You have built yourself a lovely tomb here, Mr. Larson. I suppose a brief sermon on the horrors of death and eternal damnation wouldn't really matter much either."

Marcus smiled. "I suppose it would matter a little if I could believe what you had to say, but the question is, why should I trust you? You're like a blind sightseeing guide trying to describe things he has never seen. Eternal damnation! Really! How do you know hell even exists? Have you been there? How do you know what heaven is like? I'm in communication with someone who's been there, someone who has seen and walked with God. He talks about God as a forgiving being. He's not worried about hell—why should I be? I think that this angel you call a demon probably knows more about the afterlife than you ever will. Why don't you take some time to get to know him? Listen to him; he is a great source of wisdom for young and old. You could do so much more with him than I can. Have you thought about all you could be learning from him?"

Bruce looked at him puzzled He wasn't quite sure whether this was Larson or Lerajie that was speaking. It seemed to be Larson, but it sounded like Lerajie was trying to bargain with him. "Are you making me an offer of some sort? Is that what this is about? You want me to join you, or perhaps I should say you want me to allow you to join with me, to be possessed by you and become your puppet."

"*Possessed* is such an ugly word when you say it, Bruce. Partnership, relationship, friendship—these words seem a little better to me. Remember what I told you yesterday? It's always been about you; you have talent, skill, and courage. I'm not asking you to rebel against God. I'm asking you to work for the good people, something you've always wanted to do. Larson is happy; you can be happy too. You might say there's a vacancy that's just come open, and we can use a man like you."

"A vacancy? Would that be that Murmus needs a new body?" Bruce dropped his head in disgust.

The sickening voice of the demon spoke again. "Just give it some consideration. No one is forcing you to do anything; there'll be no evil harpies flying down out of the sky, no dark angels creeping out of your closet. This is a love relationship. Criton remembers the beauty of it, but you came along, and he became confused. Dr. Prasad, he remembers; he was just misled. Let's meet tonight where this all began. Meet with me there, and we can discuss it further. Meet me at the battlefield around sunset."

With that, the meeting was over. Mr. Larson shuffled over and slumped into his leather chair. Leaning forward, he looked over at Bruce as if recognizing him for the first time. The old man smiled and pointed at the door, and Bruce knew that was his cue to exit. He backed out of the room, walked across the dirty kitchen floor, and went out the back door to his car. He had a lot of thinking to do, and he wanted to talk to his friends about meeting with the demon.

Scene 57

Meeting strategy

Bruce drove back to Criton's home, where his friends were waiting for him. He asked them to sit down, because he had a story to relate that he wasn't sure they were going to believe. He began to tell them about the visit to Marcus Larson's home, what had occurred there, the luxurious room, the conversation, and the invitation he'd gotten from Lerajie. As he was finishing his story, Sandy spoke up. "You're not going to the battlefield, are you? This meeting sounds incredibly dangerous. You have all admitted that we are dealing with powers or beings beyond our realm of comprehension, and I for one am not at all comfortable with this new friendly relationship you have developed with what you consider to be a demonic spirit. I am no theologian, but it seems only logical that you are doing something that your teachings forbid you to do, and that is to engage in a relationship with evil."

At that point Criton spoke up. "I must say that I agree with Sandy, and I think I have the background expertise to know what I'm saying. I have been in such a relationship, and ironically, it was you, Bruce, who got me out of it. I have a great deal of faith in you and your abilities, especially to reason truth, but sitting and talking with this being is dangerous."

As Criton was finishing his statement, he and Sandy both turned their heads toward Alan, as if expecting him to add his opinion. Alan leaned back and held his hands up, saying, "Don't look at me! As a scientist, I'm struggling with the whole demon thing and wondering if this is more of a mental-health issue than a supernatural event. But as a man who has seen what I have seen recently, my scientific curiosity makes me insist that you can't pass this up. Bruce, if you think you can handle this guy, I really think you should speak with him—or it, or whatever. Let's say this is not a demonic personality; let's say it actually is a being from the fourth dimension, not a spiritual being as we think of such things but just another life form that has crossed into our existence and now is offering us a glimpse into a reality that we have never even imagined. Our ideas of good and evil and right and wrong are completely based on our cultural norms, what we call natural law. Here we are dealing with someone of a totally different nature, and so it would only stand to reason that its concept of natural law could somehow be different from ours. I know that you are a Christian, and thus you base a lot of your thoughts on theology and spirituality, but I think we are faced with a new challenge here. The challenge to literally think outside of the box is one thing, but you are dealing with another box completely. This is way outside of our box.

"The greatest fear I have is what you may learn and the effect it could have on you. Are you ready for that scenario? This has the possibility of changing everything you have up to now seen as truth, fact, and normality, and that can be pretty devastating to someone who is not prepared to deal with it. Mr. Criton here started his relationship with these beings at a very early age, and they were there to help him shape a new reality throughout his life. These beings seem to understand us better than we understand ourselves. They used the concept of reincarnation or spirit guides, because they knew that this frame of reference could be understood. We are just now realizing that instead of three dimensions, or four, or even five, there may be multiple layers of dimensions in space and time, and new theories of creation are going beyond things like evolution into totally new realms of quantum physics. This may be a new kind of first contact with an alien life form. That is the invitation you have received—an invitation to step into a new realm of discovery. In the past they came as comforting or possessing spirits, but with you they have found someone who may be more open-minded, and so they have given you a new approach, one that is challenging everything you have been taught. Go back to what I said in the beginning and think about it. Their whole concept or idea of good and evil may be very different from ours."

"Wait! Wait just one minute, Alan." It was Criton speaking, and he seemed to be getting agitated. "As much as I appreciate your scientific mind, I must stop you and remind you of my experience regarding what you said about these beings being a part of my life from an early age. These beings which seemed so benevolent changed and became very hostile the moment I began to question them and their authority. It wasn't the kind of realization that you are talking about with Bruce that happened to me. I came to the realization that these beings were reflecting a pettiness and a simple lust for power. I rejected them and spent three days in the hospital because of my reaction to them. Their desire was no longer one of helping others; they made it clear to me their desire was one of conquest and control, and that they were willing to deal harshly with anyone who stood in their way. If we want to put this on a scientific level and reject any possibility of spirituality, then I would have to classify them as hostile aliens seeking to invade this planet and control it through the minds of the people. If we wish to reject that idea and consider them as spiritual beings, then I would have to say they fit the description of the demonic. The only consistent behavior they have displayed has been seduction toward their way of thinking and seeking to control. A being like the one that is speaking so kindly to Bruce also spoke kindly to me for the better part of my life, until that fateful moment when I rose up to express my own free will, and that's when things got pretty nasty. Based on my experience, I think we should rule out any hope for a first contact with some otherworldly creature and see these beings as what they have shown us they are—evil and demonic spirits."

Alan smiled and sheepishly nodded his head. "I can definitely see where you're both coming from. I guess I have let my scientific mind take over, but this is a tempting offer. Demon or alien just think of the possibility for gained information we have here! Yes, I realize that these beings are dangerous. But the information may be invaluable if they are *not* demons. Whatever the case, there is one thing I am most curious about, and that is why they are willing to reveal so much of themselves. What are they after? Bruce, it's my understanding that in exorcisms there are similar incidents of dialogues with demons, but the Church has always discouraged and even forbidden such interactions. Is that correct?"

Bruce nodded his head as Alan continued to speak. "Whether demon or alien, it seems apparent that they are here looking for something, and they are willing to expose themselves in an unusually open way."

"Well, if I may interject, I don't think they are here looking to conquer real estate." It was Bruce speaking up. "I think they are looking to conquer the minds of people. From what we've seen, they are willing to give gifts and special talents in order to have control of the individual, and at some point, in the relationship they ask that individual to do something that is out of the norm for him. From what I've seen, that request always takes the form of something negative, according to our morality and natural laws that you mentioned earlier. I agree with you on one point, though; it does seem they are looking for something. And if this *is* a demon, its willingness to be exposed seems unprecedented."

Bruce looked out the window and realized that it was getting late; the sun was setting. Bruce looked at his friends and smiled. "Pray for me. I'll be back later—at least I hope I will," he said and chuckled.

The others all stood up, and Sandy said, "Shouldn't we come with you?"

"Well, you didn't actually have an invitation; I wouldn't want to be rude to our host. But I won't deny that I would feel more comfortable if I had you guys backing me up. Don't worry too much, though. I have spoken with this being on several occasions, and for some reason I have not felt threatened. I'm not sure what he has planned for tonight, but something tells me that this may be a rather important meeting compared to the other times." And with that Bruce walked out the door.

Once outside, he felt the sudden chill of being alone. He looked to the east over the tops of the trees and saw darkening clouds. The cool breeze signaled that night was coming on as he began the drive toward the darkening horizon. He kept looking in his rearview mirror, watching the sun slip below the tree line. He was rushing toward what might be the most important meeting of his life. As he neared the crossroads, it suddenly struck him that he could be meeting the devil at the crossroads, and the songs of Robert Johnson began to play through his head. He wondered whether this was part of some plan or just a strange coincidence.

Scene 58

Dealing with the devil

As Bruce pulled his car into the crescent-shaped driveway, he was surprised to see other cars there and people milling around; it was unusually busy at the battlefield. Then he saw Marcus Larson sitting at a picnic table. Oddly, he was not hunched over. He sat up rather straight, and he had a big smile on his face as Bruce stepped out of his car. Bruce's brow furrowed as he looked at the people and back at Marcus. Marcus was not hiding himself, so either these people did not know him or he didn't care if they saw him. Perhaps they were with him. Bruce stepped up to the picnic table and sat down across from Marcus, who was smiling. Bruce looked around at the grounds and asked Marcus, "Are these some friends of yours?"

Marcus smile grew even broader. "Yes, as a matter of fact. They are just a few folks I brought along, most of whom I think you know, but I doubt if you know them in this capacity. Would you like to meet them?'

Before Bruce could answer and without a word being spoken to the people, they turned, one by one, to look toward the table. Bruce was surprised at some of the people he saw there but not so surprised by others. When Arthur Kirkland turned around, Bruce almost laughed to himself and thought Alan would be happy to know that he'd been right. Bruce was a bit surprised when he saw a couple of members of the senior men's Sunday school class. Probably the most surprising of all was when Paxton's wife and small child turned and stared at him. Behind them he saw Leon and then Jake. He thought to himself, *The mastermind and the executioner.* He had expected to see Paxton and was surprised that his family was present, but he was not. He saw two faces that he was not familiar with, a man and a woman, seemingly very ordinary but with attractive features. As each person made his or her presence known, they slowly began to move back to their cars and drive away.

When they were gone, Bruce turned and looked back to where the people had been standing. Now standing where the others had stood were beings. Each one was different in size and shape, but each appeared menacing and evil. The colors on and around them were all dark; he could see greens and purples and deep blues and black, but all were dark. Their faces were shadowy, making it hard to distinguish features, and he remembered that first day he had seen Lerajie at his door. They didn't move or make a sound, and yet he sensed motion as if they were moving their bodies but not their legs or hands. Then Bruce realized that the motion he sensed was reptilian, like a snake gliding along, as muscles moved in chorus in such a way as to appear to be almost standing still. Bruce felt a small rush of fear and the cold sensation that accompanied fear. His chest muscles tightened, and he could feel bumps rising on the skin on his arms. Each breath became a little harder to take in, and the air felt as if it were coming off a block of ice. He swallowed and tried to regain his composure, while Larson laughingly spoke.

"These are just a few of our friends, Bruce, and each one has a guide, or should I say influence? You're not afraid, are you? The only difference is that many of these people are not even aware that we direct their lives in many ways. Tomorrow, except for a few, none will remember being here tonight. They were all coming home from some meeting or event, or just a drive they thought they would take, and they happened to converge on this spot. But tomorrow this memory will be wiped away, and each will be rewarded in his or her own way. Their lives will be blessed in small ways, which will seem very natural. We may or may not ever communicate with them openly, as I'm doing with you."

Bruce swallowed hard and looked up. "That brings me to a very important question, Mr. Larson, or Lerajie, or whatever you are. Why are we conversing so openly? Why do you not hide yourself from me as you do with so many others?"

"Openness has actually always been our way; we do not hide like the One does. You know more about us than you do the One. Look at how you know our history and names. Can you tell me the history of the One—or even the name? No, you can't, because the One is mystery, the purest of mysteries, and that is the way and the truth of it. We are not secrets to mankind. Mankind has just chosen to ignore us and rename us as ghost, spirits, or demons—pick one. They are all right and they are all wrong. We are servants of the One; it's as simple as that. As for why you were chosen, that should be obvious to you by now, Bruce. They have seen potential in you and feel that it is a potential that is going to waste because of your limited information. They have decided to inform you and offer you a sort of membership in our group. You like to use the term *possession*, but that is not completely accurate, because to possess something one must completely control it. We prefer to think of partnerships. Partners are people who have some control of their lives, and they relinquish other parts of it to us. It is mutually beneficial. The only difference is that on rare occasions we seek to enlighten people who we see, like you, that have the potential to do great things. Remember how excited you were when we spoke of publishing a book? This is a desire that you have deep in your heart, and we can help fulfill the desire. Books have been one of our main ways of communicating with man down through the ages. You should not struggle with this concept, since even you have based your life on a book that was inspired by some of us. The Bible, as you like to say, is the word of God given to man through the inspiration of God. You call it 'scripture.' We inspire other men to write the information that we wish to share with them. We're not so egotistical as to call it scripture; we like to think of it merely as wisdom. So much of what you know today came to you not just through scripture but through the reasoned, logical thoughts of inspired men and women.

"The Bible is stories written by men, which carry the stamp of man's mental process as he has tried to explain things, the things that are beyond explanation. Man has always classified them as miracles and tried to relate them to others, often using metaphor. Let's look at the story of the Garden of Eden and the serpent; that's less about our work and more about man's work. It reveals the nature of man, the very natural law that you always talk about. Man was tempted, and since man hates to blame himself, he blamed two rather innocent creatures. First, he blamed the woman who was given to him as a gift, and then he blamed an innocent creature, the serpent, when in fact he should have blamed himself for his own curiosity. Man had a perfect existence of innocence in a perfect place; that was the place of the original natural law. Man, in the garden, could enjoy the pleasures of life. But then man screwed it up. He pushed the boundaries of natural law and order, and for that he was expelled into a harsher natural law. And throughout history, man has been seeking to regain the world of pleasure that he knew in the beginning. We are here trying to point man back to pleasure. The One is not a hateful god of judgment. The One is a loving god. He wants man to enjoy life. It was man who created religion, it was man who created the institutions, and it was man who created the rules. And why did he do all this? He wasn't obeying the One. He was seeking power for himself, power and control! It was man who wanted to be God. Now you see how you've got the story all wrong. We're not the ones who rebelled against the One! We serve the One. We have no power over that which has created us; we do the will of the creator. It was man who wanted to be God. It's man who exalts himself to the high places. Its man who puts a crown on his own head or a title plaque on his desk and seeks to control other people. It's man who perverts the pleasure of natural order. We simply are here to redirect and inform people, to lead them back to a pleasure-filled garden of Eden. But when we bring this good news, it's man's rulers, leaders, popes, preachers, and institutions that call us demons and devils.

"If you come with us, work with us, and let us teach you, we will give you wisdom to write and stories to tell that will make you rich and famous beyond your wildest belief. Then you will be doing a service for your fellow man. You see, I know your heart, and I know that you want to serve others. I share that desire; I was created to serve. Have you ever asked yourself why no one can explain why Satan rebelled? It's one of the main stories and theological points of Christianity—of almost all religions. And yet no religion can fully explain how that happened. Doesn't it seem like an accusation without any real evidence to support it? Doesn't logic suggest that a creature created for one purpose, and one purpose only, which is to serve, would continue to do what it was created to do? Do you have a can opener in your kitchen at home? Do you ever fear that it's going to rise up and rebel against you and try to take over the kitchen? Humanity was created to procreate. You are a born being. We were created, and we do not re-create ourselves. Our purpose is to serve, and that's what we do. Consider the writings of Job, wherein we see the one called Satan. He's not sneaking into heaven; he is reporting, as if reporting back to his boss on what he has found. And what he found was man constantly perverting the natural order of pleasure. So God sent him to tempt Job. And look at Job—he was not an evil man; he was happy and filled with pleasure in life. But when that order of pleasure was perverted, Job was unhappy. Lucifer was just following orders. Likewise, we have no malice in our hearts; we are servants, like you."

Bruce was listening intently, but Larson could tell he wasn't fully convinced. In a moment of silence, Bruce heard a car pull up behind them, and he saw Larson look intently at the people getting out of the car. Bruce turned his head and he saw that it was a young boy and a young girl. They seem to be average kids, and Bruce wondered if they were more of Larson's friends. The boy walked straight over to the large gray stone and began to read it. The girl just wandered around somewhat aimlessly, until the boy turned to go over to the gravesite. The boy had his back to the table as he looked over the wrought-iron fence into the grave area. Larson made a gesture with his hand, and the girl began to walk toward the table. As she drew closer Bruce could not help but notice that she was extremely beautiful and that the clothes she wore were tight fitting and very revealing. Bruce watched Larson's eyes move over the girl's form; they seemed to brighten as she drew near; Bruce couldn't help but notice the young girl seemed to exude sensuality. She stepped up to the side of the table, slightly pushing her hips against the edge. Larson looked back at Bruce, and almost ignoring the girls' presence, asked, "Do you like this creature? Do you want her? She could be yours. Her gift is her beauty, and as everyone has a purpose in life, her purpose could easily be your pleasure."

With that, Larson stood up stepped around the girl, who was staring down at Bruce. Her eyes were fixed on his, and she seemed to be in a trance-like state. Larson smiled as he pulled her hair back, kissed her on the neck, and squeezed her breast. Bruce turned his eyes away, but Larson just laughed. As he sat back down, the girl turned and walked back to rejoin her boyfriend. The two of them got into their car and drove away, seemingly oblivious to what had occurred.

Bruce looked back at Larson. "I guess she won't remember this tomorrow, will she? Like the others."

Larson smiled again and said, "No, probably not. You see she was a willing participant, but her mind is weak. She's not like you, Bruce. Her pleasure is in giving pleasure. Oh, someday she may grow and become wiser, but it's doubtful. Her future was set in motion by her environment; you can tell just by looking at the way she was dressed. She takes meaning in life by objectifying herself, and who's to say that perhaps she won't be happy as an object? That may be her source of pleasure."

Larson looked back at Bruce, smiling, and said, "It's getting late, and I wasn't sure if you would have had your supper, so I brought a few sandwiches. Are you hungry?"

At that Bruce almost laughed out loud. "I didn't see it before, but now I see you're going in reverse order! Am I supposed to say, 'Man does not live by bread alone' now?" Bruce chuckled and said, "No offense, but this is not the most original temptation I have ever seen, you know."

Larson laughed along with him. "You're right, Bruce; this was a bit clumsy. But you should take it as a compliment that I used the same model as was used on him. I should have realized you were too smart for that. You're so very perceptive, Bruce. You know that is one of the things that attracted us to you."

"Sorry, Lerajie, but as they say, flattery will get you nowhere. We've done the whole flattery ploy."

"Yes, Bruce, you're right. I told the others that you were far too smart for that. I just hope that you are smart enough to listen and believe that what I am saying is true. I realize that this is very difficult for you and that I am turning your world upside down, but I am offering you wisdom that the world is just beginning to see and understand. It's like an investment in a new stock that promises to really take off. More and more people are beginning to see and feel the truth. That truth is all over the world, as ancients have been given glimpses down through the ages. We have been working slowly, waiting for the day when man would come to realize the truth of his own past. I know that you are well read, so consider what other religions have said, and look at the similarities; these are not just coincidental. There is a thin strand of truth in all, and it leads to one conclusion. That conclusion is that the will of God is for his creation to enjoy pleasure. Religion has always been close, but its leaders drag you away into the world of suffering, whether it's the suffering servant, the suffering Buddha, the ascetic monks, or the brothers of poverty. How can you not see the futility of all this suffering? It hurts just to think about it!"

Bruce looked seriously at Lerajie. "You forget one thing, Marcus—or Lerajie. Suffering is not the goal; it's a path. You mention Buddha and the suffering servant, which I suppose is a reference to Jesus, but they were not suffering for the joy of pain. They were using it as a path to an inward look at life and to enable them to see life's priorities. All you have offered me tonight has been what you call pleasure, but from my perspective, it looks more like thoughtlessness and living on instinct and using others. It sounds more like being an animal that wanders the wilderness, preying on the weak and looking for food and comfort, and nothing more. I must believe that there is more to life than just rutting around seeking pleasure."

Lerajie/Larson sighed a heavy breath and looked across the table. "It's thinking like that which has led humanity into this darkness of pain and sorrow, and I was hoping that you, of all people, could realize that. It is a disappointment, Bruce. You do realize that if you are not part of the solution you become part of the problem."

"I suppose that is the threat, is it not?

"A threat? No, not a threat, just a statement of reality. All I offer you is a meaningful existence. If you choose to ignore, so be it. There will be others, but there have always been others."

Bruce looked around and realized that the other beings were around them again, closer this time. Bruce felt the fear again as they undulated ever nearer. He closed his eyes and whispered a prayer to overcome his fear. He felt a surge of peace, and he opened his eyes. They were alone again but sitting across from him was the bent body of the old Mr. Larson.

"No need for that, Bruce. We're not here to hurt you; we've already done that. I'm not sure if it has all sunk in yet, but this battle is over. I know it's a little anticlimactic, but that's how it goes, just a whimper, not a bang. You're not really that important. I will be leaving soon and some of my ... what did you call them? Legions? They will remain to continue the work. But let's get back to you. Do you want to spend your life rotting in some backwater town looking for a pulpit or trying to make enough money to survive on? No wife, no kids? Even your friends will desert you soon. I'm offering you a future with fame, wealth, and security—and even the desires of your heart." Lerajie had on that loving, seductive grin and Bruce felt a bit sick as he realized that a lot of what he was saying could well be true. But was that why he had entered the ministry? No! He had to remind himself that he was a servant and that that was enough.

"It is a great deal to think about and a great deal to consider. I admit this information is not at all what I expected. This challenges all the things I thought to be true, and yet in some ways you have confirmed many of my deepest beliefs. The face of evil isn't always monstrous. That smile of yours hides a darkness that I just can't accept. As for all the doom and gloom, you should know that real servants of God aren't in it for the glory or the money. I look forward to the day that I can lay a crown at the feet of my savior. You might want to read up on your scriptures; it seems you left that part out. This has all been very pleasant, Lerajie, and I admit I am, and have been, weak. But get this straight. We are on opposite sides; you know it and so do I. I may not be as smart as a timeless being, but I have a friend and an advocate, and I don't need much more. What if I just tell everyone what has happened here tonight and what is happening in this community?"

Larson sat up and smiled, "That's good, Bruce, I can sense your struggle. Go ahead and tell the world. We have plenty like you in nursing homes, institutions, and forced early retirement. You don't want to be considered crazy, now, do you? No, I don't think so. As a matter of fact, you're wondering right now how much of this is true and how much of it is lies. After all, you have been told that we are the fathers of all lies. But aren't lies relative to the situation? Here's something else to consider before you make your final decision. What will you do with the information you have gained tonight if you can't tell the world? If you choose not to accept my offer, then I assume you will seek to thwart my efforts. Am I correct, Bruce? Are you trying to figure out a way to defeat me and save all these unworthy people? You won't be the first or the last. I have been waging this battle since the dawn of time, and there is no weapon forged by man that can defeat me. As for your friend, you will soon realize there's no one you can really call upon, because this is his plan—the One set all of this in motion. We are just pieces of the cosmic game board. I have my role to play, and now you have yours, with the only difference being that you get a choice. My choice was made for me before time began, but you are special, so make your choice. Consider it, Bruce, but don't take too long. The invitation may expire. Oh, and if you are thinking of who you can tell, I'm sure your friends will be attentive, and if you wish to go door to door to warn the masses, be my guest. But I warn you, it may just add ridicule to your shame. I mean, really, Bruce, who will believe you when you tell them of speaking with demons and you make accusations toward all of these fine, upstanding people? It will be a little embarrassing, I promise you, as you stomp your sour grapes all over the community. Why not tell them we are fourth-dimension beings—what was it your friends said?"

Suddenly Bruce heard Alan's voice coming from Lerajie, repeating word for word what he had said earlier. *"Let's say this is not a demonic personality; let's say it actually is a being from the fourth dimension, not a spiritual being as we think of such things but just another life form that has crossed into our existence and now is offering us a glimpse into a reality that we have never even imagined."*

Bruce had a look of disbelief on his face as Lerajie broke into laughter. "Bruce, Bruce, why the surprise? We are everywhere, and we hear everything. Our legions, as you call them, are surrounding you day and night, watching, listening, and passing that information on to others.

Larson stood now and walked slowly to his car. He turned only to say, "Don't be stupid, Strong. You're good but not that good—accept it!" With that he got into his car and drove away.

Bruce was alone again, but he looked around to make sure. He was still feeling uneasy from seeing the others who had been there. It was then that he became aware of the sweat on his palms. He rubbed his hands across the surface of the table and then along the sides of his pants. He felt that tense fear in his stomach, and he felt embarrassment because he could not overcome the fear. He had just experienced a spiritual battle in the physical world. It was like nothing he had ever heard of or even read about, and he was feeling a little helpless. How was he supposed to fight against an evil like this? Who could he turn to? Almost as soon as he thought it he heard the word *prayer* in his mind, but then he remembered what Lerajie had said, that that was part of the plan. What if that were true? Didn't it fit with scripture? He was lost in thought, and then he pictured the faces of his newfound friends waiting for him, and he realized that the very thought of them was comforting. They would understand and believe him. He wanted to be with them and feel the strength of unity. Bruce quickly got into his car and headed back to tell his friends all he had experienced. As he drove, he thought of what Larson had said about a cosmic game board. Something about it kept rolling around inside his head. The idea of being a game piece, just a token or a chess piece in some spiritual game, was it just an analogy, or was Lerajie revealing something?

Scene 59

The devil's debriefing

As Bruce was driving away, invisible eyes were watching his car, and another meeting was convening. A ghostly mist began to swirl around the gravesite as forms began to take shape. The transparent beings began to blend with the environment, and bodies morphed into trees, and faces were blurred in the brush and leaves. No voices were audible, but the spiritual conversation began, with a rustle of many voices. Some were saying, "He said too much," while others seemed to laugh and suggest that it didn't matter. The more ominous sounds were questions like When do we start? Suddenly one voice dominated, and the others abruptly stood quiet.

"You may have spoken too long, my brother. Your revelry with Bruce Strong gave you too much pleasure."

"My apologies, Murmus. I did enjoy taunting the *good* reverend." Lerajie's stress on the word good brought a round of coarse laughter from the assembled council.

"Ah, speaking of pleasure, sire, is there a plan for this place now that we have removed their spiritual leader?" It was the voice of Baraqyal.

"Of course, my friend, there is always a plan. I see you have left our friend Dr. Prasad. Is he no longer susceptible to your charm? Perhaps you have lost your touch at seduction?" The others began to laugh as Murmus gave a guttural, mocking noise that could hardly be called a laugh.

Baraqyal turned away, wounded by the mockery. "He is a man who loves his wife again." Baraqyal almost spat the words out; his disdain for Prasad was obvious.

"Do not fret, Baraqyal, I know you wanted to taste the lovely daughter, but you still have the witch and her mother, enjoy them, I have others to deal with our traitorous Prasad." Murmus now moved through the black iron fence to hover over the grave of the patriots as he addressed the group. "My friends, I feel we shall make an example of our abilities here. Our friend Lerajie has given Reverend Strong a great deal of information." He cast a glance to Lerajie. "It was enough to make your good reverend feel empowered. I am not sure if that was intentional or just providential for us." The word *providential* drew another round of laughter as Murmus dragged out each syllable in a sickeningly sweet voice, followed by a sudden silence. Murmus smiled at Lerajie and spoke again. "Even now he is running to meet with his friends to plan their actions. He thinks the battle here is over, and his pride will tell him that he was the focus of everything." His words were followed by more laughter, and Murmus took a more ominous tone. "We will have our own battle to show this arrogant little band who is really in control here, and one more revelation for them to try and process in their monkey brains. They will see misery and feel they are to blame when all is done. Baraqyal, you ask for a plan; I give you a plan. The plan is pain and sorrow for some and reward for our servants. It will be the sweetest reward, for we will make them revel in their evil and think they are being blessed."

The eyes of all around began to burn a brighter red as Murmus related their instructions. As they received their directions one by one, they disappeared into the misty field, and the battlefield grew cold and silent once again.

Scene 60

The briefing

Back at house, everyone had been waiting anxiously for Bruce to return. There was an audible sigh as Sandy saw his car pull into the drive. And now the four them were together again, sitting around the table. Everyone listening intently to the most incredible story they had ever heard. They all had questions, questions about what the demons looked like and who all the people were that he had seen at the grave. Bruce answered their litany of questions, but his mind kept going back to the game-board comparison. For some reason, he felt that this comment was one of the most important things he had heard all night. Bruce felt that it might hold the key to fighting against this evil, but it was like a riddle, and he could not figure it out.

"Pieces on a game board ... that comment just keeps coming back, for some reason. What was he telling me? Was it intentional or just a slip of the lip? If we are all just pieces on a game board, like chess or checkers, how does that help us? If they are pieces also, how do we capture the enemy's pieces?"

Alan spoke up first. "Well, if it is like chess, the answer is obvious. It means you have to outthink your opponents and outmaneuver them."

"No, I don't think that would work. Lerajie all but told me that I was no match for him, that there was no weapon forged by man that could defeat him and no one who could match him in experience. He may have been lying, but I sense a certain amount of truth in what he says. I don't feel an equal to his cleverness, and besides, my Christian instincts tell me that this is not what I am supposed to do."

"Well, if it's not about strategy, like in chess, and it's not about overcoming someone, like in checkers, then you need to know just what game you are playing." Sandy spoke with a bit of frustration.

It was Criton's time to add something to the conversation. "Well, I guess you could say we are playing the game of life. But who knows how to play that game? I think we just live it as best we can. What do we do in life that makes life good? What do we do as pieces on the board game of life?"

"What do we do? What do pieces in a game do?" Bruce asked as if searching in his mind for an answer, and then he looked at the others. "What do the pieces in a board game actually do?" Bruce looked around at the faces of his friends, waiting for an answer.

Sandy was first to speak up. "They just stand there waiting to be moved."

"That's right, Sandy, they stand. Lerajie said that he was a servant of 'the One' and following 'the plan.' If I'm a piece in the game, and he's a piece in the game, and he moves at the command of 'the One,' then it stands to reason that we do the same thing. We stand until we are moved."

"Stand," Alan mumbled to himself. "Stand. Wasn't there a movie based on a book about just standing in the face of evil?"

"Yes, I know that novel! It was by Stephen King. I think it was called *The Stand*." Criton spoke up with a chuckle. "You don't think he was one of their writers, do you?"

"No—well, maybe not. It may be that this is what Christians have been doing since the beginning. We haven't been called to take up arms; we've been called to fight a spiritual war, to stand for what is right and, if needed, to die for what we believe in."

There was a hush over the room and, in a whisper, Criton spoke the word "Martyr!"

Bruce looked up at the crowd. "That is always a possibility for Christians. Jesus said, 'Take up your cross,' which has always been understood as a reference to martyrdom. To be willing to die for your faith is a real challenge for believers."

"Yeah, well imagine how hard it is for those of us who are still a little undecided," Alan offered; the others were not sure whether he were serious or just joking. "No, really, guys, I have never been much of a churchgoer and, frankly, hadn't given the spiritual world much thought until I started hanging around with the local ghostbusters club here. No offense, Bruce, but I'm not sure if I signed on for a fight to the death with anyone, especially someone or something I can't even see. You and Criton, here, are the only ones that have a lot of firsthand experience with these things. I know Sandy has done a lot of research, but I haven't heard talk like you two about possession and voices. What happened with Sandy's dad was weird, but as a scientist I can't rule out some form of schizophrenia. And now we are trying to develop a battle strategy against who-knows-what?"

"Point taken, Alan, and I must say that I agree in part." Sandy spoke with her authoritarian tone. "I'm not sure what we are to do with this fascinating information or even if action is up to us. As I see it, Bruce, we are out of our league when it comes to battling demons. We are doves trying to battle vultures."

"Yes, you're both right, I know. I think Lerajie may have played me again. It's like he taunts and challenges me to a duel and then doesn't tell me where to meet him. But I do think that the idea of standing is right if we interpret standing as simply being the best we can be in the face of evil. Christianity has always been more about being than doing. When we speak of martyrs, we must realize that the early martyrs didn't die in battle. They were the sheep who were slaughtered because they refused to be something they were not. So, Alan, you can breathe easy; we won't be suiting up for battle anytime soon. And Sandy, you're right as well; there is very little we can do against these forces. It seems we are left to stand on our faith and be willing to face what evil may come. One other thing Lerajie said was that this battle is over and he will be leaving soon. Some of his legions will remain, but my destruction seems to have been the focus of the battle, and they accomplished that, for sure."

Criton spoke up. "Bruce, forgive me, but that sounds a little arrogant, to think that all the suffering was just for you. What about that boy Julian and his parents, or Topper and Cedric?"

The word *arrogant* was like a slap in the face, and the others stared at Criton. But Bruce paused, hung his head, and then, looking right at Criton, he smiled and said, "You're right, John. I've let him do it again! I am just one big violin of ego, and he's playing me like a cheap fiddle. I'm sorry, guys. It's obvious that I can't tell the lies from the truth, so it's best to assume that everything may be a lie. I keep thinking of a battle and armies moving, but we are not fighting against an army; we are dealing with a disease. We don't need a strategy as much as we need a cure. We aren't going to stand *against* anything—we are going to stand *for* something. We need to stand for all the things that these fallen ones stand against: love, truth, peace, and justice. I accused Lerajie of not reading the scriptures, but I need to hold up a mirror and speak to myself. Ephesians 6:12 tells us, 'We wrestle not against flesh and blood, but against principalities, against powers, against the rulers of the darkness of this world, against spiritual wickedness in high places.' That verse says we wrestle, and so we imagine a physical battle, but the word there is more of a metaphor for holding our hands on the necks of our opponents, meaning that we immobilize them. It's just a fancy way of saying to be stronger than them. Our strength is not in beating them physically but in believing. It's all about faith. I realize that Lerajie was attacking my faith by trying to instill fear. He even told me he wasn't going to hurt me in a physical sense, but he was trying to destroy my faith in God. In an attempt to scare me, he said you guys would all desert me, but that may have been a little reverse psychology. I think he said that because he wanted me to urge you to stay here, when the truth is that you may need to leave. Sandy, I think you may want to go home and keep an eye on your dad. It seems odd for them to let him go that easily. Also, I'm not sure about his colleagues and what they may have planned for him."

Sandy nodded her agreement. "Yes, I was thinking about that myself—"

Bruce cut her off midsentence and turned to Alan. "Alan, I hate to say it, but you may need to think about getting back to your classes. I'm not sure that you will be able to stop the building project at the battlefield. All of that may have been just a tease to get you away from school and risk your job. They have already taken John and me out of commission by taking away our careers. That may be a tactic they like to use. There's no sense in adding your career to the list. John and I will keep an eye on things around here."

Sandy cut in, saying, "Slow down, Bruce! You're getting in that General Strong mode again. My parents aren't going straight home after all. They called and said they were going to take a side trip for a couple of days in the mountains, to rest and relax."

"And as for me," Alan spoke up, "I've got classes covered for a few more days, so don't be running me off—especially if Sandy's staying and going to be cooking that southern Indian cuisine."

They were all laughing again; it seemed no demon or devil could rob them of the moment. But Bruce was right. There was another battle to be waged, and they would have no control over the outcome.

Scene 61

What evil may come

Days passed, and all was quiet in the tiny farming community. Bruce Strong and his friends were living with John Criton in the home he had rented in town. The group had a few more days together before they split up. They decided to sit and wait and be patient until something happened. But there was no sign of anything out of the ordinary, and Bruce was beginning to think that his involvement in the community was truly over. He felt he had deserted his parish, but in truth it was his parish that had deserted him. He tried to write, and Criton attempted to help him take notes for a future book, but the days seemed to drag on, and his thoughts were always back at the small church and community.

Alan read the paper, but it only came out two days a week and on Sundays. The paper was filled with non-fascinating stories of local interest along with obituaries. It was a small-town paper with very little sensational news. Sunday morning came, and everyone seemed to be sitting around and waiting to see what Bruce was going to do. This would be one of the few Sundays when he would not be standing in a pulpit, and that seemed surreal. When Bruce came into the kitchen, looking for coffee, he was casually dressed, with unkempt hair and razor stubble. Everyone just stared for a moment as Bruce mixed the creamer and sugar into his coffee.

"I can feel you staring at me." Bruce spoke with his back to the three. "What's on your mind? Have you never seen a bum on Sunday?" Bruce queried as he turned to look at the group.

A chorus of voices mumbled, "Oh no, nothing, just ..." and their voices trailed off into silence as they spread out to their respective positions in the room.

"Guess you're not planning anything special today, are ya, Bruce?" Alan smiled a fake smile and then dropped his eyes back to his coffee cup.

"No, guess not, Alan. Was there something you wanted to do?" Bruce said.

"Oh no. I guess I'll just go get the paper and clip a few coupons." With that he headed out to find the Sunday paper; it was usually the largest of the week.

Alan was gone for a few minutes and Sandy and Criton were discussing some of his experiences with Murmus when Alan returned.

"I don't know if this means anything, but there is a really interesting story in the paper today."

Everyone stopped and looked at Alan. Like a speaker approaching a podium, he cleared his throat and began to read. "Local farmer and community leader arrested Friday night for alleged felony assault. Arthur Kirtland was taken into custody at his home late Friday evening after 911 operators say his wife made a cell phone call for help after locking herself in the cellar. She reported her husband had gone berserk and beat her, and she feared he would have killed her if she had not been able to run into the cellar and place the call. The motivation for the attack is as yet unknown. Kirtland has been confined in the psych ward of Cedar Hill Hospital for observation. Official charges are pending a psychiatric evaluation. Neighbors say they are shocked and surprised at these reports because the Kirtland's had always seemed to be the model couple."

Alan dropped the paper and sat down. They sat for a moment, and then Alan proudly spoke up. "May I be the first to say that I had this guy pegged all along?"

The others let out a collective sigh.

"Okay, okay—but I did say he was the root of the problem all along."

Bruce said, "Maybe so, Alan, but Lerajie spoke of rewards, and being locked up in a psych ward isn't my idea of a reward."

"And so it begins." Criton was looking out the window toward the sky.

Scene 62

The horror

Bruce and the team spent the rest of the day discussing possible reasons for Kirtland's apparent behavior. Bruce felt it was not in keeping with his previous actions to be so open. Perhaps the demonic presence felt it was no longer necessary to hide, or maybe Arthur had just had a breakdown. How would they ever know? Bruce considered trying to visit with Arthur but did not feel that it would be of any use. He had no official capacity, so it was unlikely they would even allow him access. His only other option would be to talk to the deputy; he felt Riley could give him better information. Bruce called Riley and asked if they could meet at the coffee shop uptown, just to catch up, and the deputy allowed that he would love to meet the next morning.

That evening, as they sat around talking, Bruce suggested again that Alan might need to go back early, and that Sandy should contact her parents and see if anything unusual was happening. When Sandy asked why, Bruce could only say that he was having a feeling. Sandy left the room with her cell phone to make the call. Alan questioned Bruce about the feelings he was having, but Bruce couldn't explain it. He said it was more like intuition, but he sensed some sort of connection with what had happened to Arthur Kirtland. Sandy came back into the room and stood silent for a moment before she said, "Your instincts are good, Bruce. Mom said that Dad was recalled to the university yesterday. It seems some of his colleagues have petitioned for him to be removed from the faculty, and I bet you can guess which members have signed the petition. I'll pack up and leave tonight; it's just a few hours' drive.

Alan spoke up and said, "Maybe she's right about leaving. I'll take off in the morning. I hope you don't get any feelings about my job." The group helped Sandy pack up, and when she had left, they turned their attention to getting Alan's gear ready for his morning departure.

Early the next morning Alan left for Columbia, and Criton and Bruce were alone. Bruce worked for a while that morning, but he was anxious to see Deputy Riley, so he headed for the coffee shop. He arrived early, only to find Oliver Paxton sitting at a table in the corner of the shop. He seemed to be hiding from people's view. Bruce sat down and watched him for a moment, trying to figure out why he was there. He had always espoused the evils of caffeine, so it seemed odd to see him sipping what looked to be coffee in the dark corner of the cafe. Bruce's curiosity could stand it no longer, and he decided to step over and speak to Oliver.

"Oliver Paxton, how are you? I haven't seen you in a while." Bruce used his old-friend tone of voice, even though he would hardly have considered them on friendly terms.

Paxton seemed almost startled, and Bruce thought he recoiled a little at the sound of his voice. It was then that Bruce also noticed a slight tremble in his hands.

"Oh, Reverend Stone, you startled me! I didn't expect to see anyone I knew here at this hour of the day." Paxton's voice had an edge of fear, and Bruce thought that perhaps he was just embarrassed about being caught drinking coffee. It was then that Bruce thought about the comment of 'this time of day.' Why was Paxton not at work, instead of sipping coffee in the middle of the morning?

"How've you been, Reverend? I heard about you leaving the church, and I ... uh ... uh, hoped you were doing okay. I ... uh, guess ... I guess you are, aren't you?" Paxton was stuttering through the sentences as if he couldn't put two words together.

"Oh yes, I'm fine. I like to think of it as just a career adjustment for the moment." They both shared a forced laugh, but Paxton's face still betrayed a sense of fear or anguish. There was an awkward silence until Bruce spoke again. "Are you still involved with yoga classes, Oliver?"

"Why yes, of course. Why wouldn't I be? I mean ... uh, yes ... but I am not doing as much with, uh, classes, mostly just me, working out ... uh, alone, uh ... out there. Ya know, out in the barn, at my house ..." Paxton's voice trailed off almost to a whisper, and his eyes stared blankly as if watching something intently. Then he asked, "Reverend Stone, may I ask you something?"

"But of course, ask away. I would be glad to be of any service—" But Bruce was cut off before he could say more.

"Fine, fine! I recall from one of our conversations that you possessed a great deal of knowledge on a variety of subjects, and I have a question concerning what one might say would be spiritual in nature."

"Yes, I definitely could say I have a background in spiritual subjects." Bruce chuckled and was about to say more, but once again Paxton cut him off abruptly.

"Yes, yes, I, uh, know. Perhaps our meeting today was destined, because I was ... uh, just wondering about this and ... uh, I wasn't sure who I could ask and ... uh, look, here you are." Paxton started to laugh quietly but somewhat uncontrollably. "You see, I have had this dream or vision, I'm not sure which, it seemed so real. It's happened several times recently, and then something happened one night at home. Oh, I ... uh, I'm not sure how to describe what I saw or what happened—"

Now it was Bruce doing the cutting off. "There, there, Oliver. Just take your time. It's obvious that there's something that is bothering you, or has upset you, so just slow down. Don't worry, it's just us, and I am here for you in whatever way I can be. Now, what happened at the house?"

"The house, did I say the house? I didn't mean to say that; you see, it was at the barn. I was alone and working out, and ... uh, well, maybe I was stressed. I was trying ... uh, very hard to ... uh, master a very challenging pose. I just haven't been limber enough to get it and ... uh, rather than relaxing me, it has ... uh, caused me a great deal of stress. Odd, isn't it? Yoga is about relaxation and feeling good, and ... uh, yet here I am stressing over it. Funny, isn't it? But that's not what I wanted to ask you; it was about something else. Something that happened, or I think it happened. Oh, I'm very confused about it, but—"

Bruce interrupted Paxton again. "Easy, friend. Don't get all worked up; just slow down and tell me what happened."

Paxton took a breath and sipped his coffee. "I'm sorry, Reverend, this is just not me, but I have been so on edge lately. It's probably nothing; I shouldn't have bothered you, but I—" and he stopped again and then looked up at Bruce. "I am not a superstitious man, but out there in the barn I began to get this feeling. I can't explain it; it was just a sort of feeling of dread, and it probably caused me to imagine things."

"What kind of things, Oliver?'

"Oh, just silly things, like sounds and that sort of stuff; it was most likely the sounds a building normally makes in different weather. You know, creaky boards and hay settling. It's just that on occasion things would be, uh ... moved. You know, I would look for something and it would be somewhere else, and I hadn't moved it. I even accused my daughter of moving things around. That didn't sit too well with her or her mom, I can tell you." And he laughed a sarcastic laugh. "But that wasn't the worst of it. I began to see things. I assume they were illusions brought on from stress, but ..." Paxton was starting to quiver a little in his hands and voice, and Bruce could sense that it was hard for him to speak about what he'd seen or thought he'd seen.

"Relax, Oliver. Tell me what you saw or thought you saw."

He sipped his coffee again and took a breath. "It was just something out of the corner of my eye at first, and when I turned there would be nothing there. I thought it was the old green horse blanket on the wall, but then it would be in different places, and I had that feeling, like someone was watching me."

Paxton began to shiver again, and he looked down at his cup. "I am sorry, Reverend. This is not me, and it all seems so strange. I have prided myself on self-control, and when I think about this, I get all weak and ..." Another pause, and suddenly Paxton's head jerked up and he said, "Are there such things as ghosts, Reverend Stone, or demons, or whatever you want to call it? I could swear I saw something or someone run from my barn into my house, and so I ran to the house, and when I looked in the back door, my wife was kissing this man, or letting him kiss her, and my daughter suddenly stuck her face up to the window and looked at me and said, 'Get out!' I was so startled that I fell back, and when I looked up there was my wife and daughter standing over me, angry, and asking why I was spying in them. The man was gone, and when I asked about him, they just laughed and said I was crazy. Maybe I am crazy, but it seemed so real. But then it seemed like a dream. I was confused, and now I am so nervous. My wife has told me that I must sleep in the barn and work it out with my yoga, but I can't hold my concentration long enough to relax, and I can't sleep at all. I just—" He stopped when he heard the sound of Deputy Riley's voice.

"Hey, fellers! Looks like old home week. Did you guys save me some of that fancy coffee they make here? Bruce, sorry I'm late. Oliver, it's been a while since I seen you two, especially together. How are things at the farmhouse, Oliver?"

"Oh, fine. I ... uh, didn't know you guys were meeting here. I was just ... uh, was having a word with Reverend Stone, here, sort of catching up, like you say. But I must be going, so you two can have your m-m-meeting. Enjoyed seeing you again, Reverend." Paxton was up and heading for the door, mumbling something about having a good day, before Bruce could say good-bye.

"Sorry, Bruce. Did I interrupt something there with you and Paxton?'

"I'm not sure, Riley. He was asking me a question about a problem he was having, but he didn't quite finish. I was a little shocked to see him."

"Is everything all right, or is it one of those preacher things you can't talk about?"

Bruce smiled and said, "Actually, I'm not sure. I guess about half and half."

"Speaking of half and half, hand me that creamer, so I can doctor up this here coffee. Stuff is awfully expensive to need so many chemicals to make it taste good." Riley smiled and stirred his coffee. "Now, what did you want to talk to me about, Preacher?"

"Well, that may be part of it walking out that door there. I didn't expect to see Mr. Paxton, but I had been thinking about him—or his wife and daughter, to be more specific. Have you noticed anything going on with them or around their place lately?"

"Are you asking officially or off the record?"

"I guess that depends on which gets me the most information." Bruce smiled a coy smile.

Riley chuckled and said, "Well, let's just say that if you were asking from a professional point of view, say after counseling with Oliver about, oh, I don't know, say it was marital difficulties, then I might be able to share some information from a collaborative point of view, if you know what I mean."

"I get your meaning perfectly, Deputy, and I do have some concerns over the marital difficulties expressed by Mr. Paxton, and I was wondering if you could give me any information that might help in the direction of my counseling with our Mr. Paxton."

"In that case, Bruce, I can tell you that I did get a disturbance call from a neighbor who said there was a whole lot of hollerin' and yellin' one night, and she was afraid somebody was gonna get hurt. I rode out there because, as you know, they must a' been makin' some noise to be heard. The nearest neighbor just ain't that near, if you know what I mean."

"I do know what you mean, and could I ask if there was any activity say, of a physical nature going on?"

Riley sat back, smiled, and said, "Oh yeah, they wuz some physical action, but it wasn't our Mr. Paxton. It was *Mrs.* Paxton. She got after him with a butcher knife, and he took off and locked himself in the barn, and she was a hollerin' to beat the band about what she would do if he ever yelled at that little girl again and threatened her. She was all up in a tizzy.'"

Bruce's eyes grew large. He smiled and said, "Really? How did that turn out, Riley? I didn't picture her as the violent type."

"Yep, it's always the quiet ones ya gotta' watch out for. But she settled down when I popped the light on her. That ole blue light has a way of helping folks to see reason, if ya—"

Bruce stopped him in mid phrase, "Yes, yes, Riley. I know what ya mean. So, it was Oliver who was being threatened and not the other way around? That makes sense now. He sort of hinted that he and his wife had had a bit of a tiff, but I didn't know it had weapons involved. But you say you sorted it out?"

"Oh yeah. She calmed down, and the two of them made up right there in the yard."

"What about the little girl?"

"Uh, well, come to think of it, I don't remember seeing her anywhere around until I was getting back in the car, and she met her mom on the back porch, just a smilin' pretty as you please."

"Interesting, Deputy. But actually, that's not what I wanted to ask you about. You may not be able to tell me much about this, but I was wondering about Arthur, and what happened there, and what you think will happen."

Riley shrugged and spoke with a tone of disgust. "Uh, that ole codger. Well, it's not much of a secret, 'cause I think a reporter is writing a story about it for tomorrow's paper. They say that he's doing fine and that the doctor told a reporter that he is responding well, and he doesn't think he had a permanent setback of any kind. Sounds to me like he's gonna get out of there in short order and probably won't even be charged with anything. His wife said she didn't want to press charges but that she was leaving the house. She'll probably file for divorce. I don't know how she stood him this long. A lot of folks don't know this, but that was not a happy home. I got it from a guy in his Sunday school class, who will remain nameless, but he said that Arthur was always cutting her down and slipping up and using his first wife's name, but everybody thought they were happy because she put up a good front. I guess she's had enough, though. You can't push a body but so far. I hope she gets a wad of alimony from him; she deserves it for puttin' up with him this long."

"So you might say he's getting rewarded for trying to kill her."

"Well, yes, in a way, 'cause he's gettin' what he wanted, and that was to get rid of her. Like I said, I hope she sticks it to him in the pocketbook.

He ain't got no heart, but he does have a wallet." Riley laughed at his own joke, but Bruce was lost in thought about rewards.

Bruce looked up and smiled. "Life can be pretty strange, all right. Good folks suffer and the bad come out smelling like roses."

Riley bristled and sat up. "Oh, that ain't nothing, Preacher. Ya wanna' hear somethin' that will burn you up? Speakin' of bad folks smellin' like roses, remember Leon and that Jake kid that set up poor little Julian for the assault?" Bruce nodded with a look of concern. "Well, I spoke with the parents of that other boy that got hit, and I even told them what information I had, and how they were gonna try and pin the assault on the little fellow who committed suicide. Turns out that neither boy can definitely identify Jake as the assailant, and the DA says that they may be successful in blaming Julian, so with the parent's consent, they dropped the investigation."

Bruce sat there with his mouth open and a look of amazement at the news. This quickly turned into a grimace of anger. But before he could speak, Riley held up his hand.

"Oh, but that ain't the half of it. You want to talk about evil people smelling like roses? Just up out of nowhere, a local businessman recommended Leon for a scholarship to a business school in Charlotte, with a part-time job at an accounting firm, so he gets paid while he's studying to be an accountant." Bruce tried to speak, but Riley stopped him. His voice came out almost as a snarl. "Oh, I ain't done yet! That Jake, the one who probably did the hittin',"—Riley's voice began to rise in pitch and volume— "he's getting a scholarship too, from over there at Gander College. But do you know what for? Take a guess. Just guess— no don't, I'll tell ya. It's a D-A-M-N *baseball* scholarship, because he was considered a power hitter in high school."

Riley was trembling now, as he spoke almost in a whisper to spell out the curse word, since he was in public. But it didn't matter; nearby heads were turning toward the two with concerned looks. Riley mumbled, "Sorry, folks" to the onlookers, and they all went back to their coffee and conversation. But it was hard to hide the anger the two men were sharing. Bruce hung his head and for a moment fought back tears of rage.

Bruce finally looked up at Riley and softly spoke. "I remember you once said I should ride with you sometime and see the evil and horror you face on a daily basis. Right now I think I have experienced all the horror I care to face for one day, from what you've just told me, Riley. I admire you and don't know how you can do it without just losing it sometimes."

"Oh, don't you worry, Preacher, there have been a few times I wanted to pull this revolver, and I don't mean in the line of duty. When I heard all that, I was ready to bust a cap all over the place, you better believe me. I just hope they get what they deserve someday; I just hope."

His voice trailed off to a mutter, and the two sat in silence for a long time, sipping their coffees. After a while they said their good-byes and left.

Scene 63

Rewards

In the weeks that followed, the small community was filled with actions that only Bruce and Criton could connect as being related. Seemingly random acts they saw as intentional, where no one else would have made the connection. To the rest of the world, it was just the evening news. Alan and Sandy had been in contact to say that things were not going so well for either of them. Sandy's father had learned he might be asked to take an extended sabbatical, and Alan said that the department head who once had been very supportive of his work would hardly speak to him anymore.

One evening, as Criton and Bruce were just sitting around the house, Bruce noticed an obituary in the paper that caught his eye. It was Larson. Mr. Larson had died from natural causes. It seems no one had known what a smoker and a drinker Larson was or how he had secluded himself in his own little world of gambling and pornography. No wonder his family had had so very little time for him. He was laid to rest in the cemetery with old friends and classmates. The director of missions had performed the service, and it appeared there had been very little to say about Mr. Larson, partly because his family was small and partly because no one had known the man very well. He had lived there all his life and been completely ignored. Even stranger was the fact that he had amassed a considerable amount of money from online gambling. This had financed his mail-order life, including ordering expensive whiskeys, cigars, and electronics. No one knew how he had assembled everything or who had done the renovations to his house—but Bruce knew. Bruce felt that within a few days the topic would be of no importance to anyone, and it would be as if Larson had never existed. That was Larson's reward for hosting evil in their midst. Bruce was now wondering where Lerajie would be and who would be his next host. The thought of not knowing bothered him somewhat.

Bruce was at the grocery store one afternoon when he saw some of the people from church, but their actions toward him were very strange. He tried to speak to the couple but was ignored; they walked right by him. Later that week he saw one of the deacons who he thought was a friend and asked him how things were going. The man nodded politely and mumbled that everything was all right, but he was in a hurry to leave. Now Bruce felt that something was going on, and he wanted to find out what it was. So, he called the only person he felt would be honest with him, Deputy Riley. What Bruce discovered cut like a knife. Riley had tried to avoid telling what he knew, but finally he came out and said that there was a rumor going around that, as Riley put it, seemed to have strong legs. He thought it had started in the senior Sunday school class, although he wasn't sure. But with rumors, it didn't matter where they came from; once spoken, a rumor had a life of its own. Since the rumor that Bruce was having a fling with Sandy hadn't worked out, the word now focused on the fact that Bruce had moved in with Criton and that the two were gay lovers. There was plenty of fuel for the fire when Kirtland got back to church and pointed out that he had asked Criton to leave his home because he'd thought he was too effeminate, a story that was totally fabricated. Then, the fact that Bruce wasn't married and had no female companions while he pastored the church looked suspicious. The final straw was when the two had moved in together in town. To the good people of the community the equation was simple. Two men, one effeminate and one with no girlfriend, equaled a gay couple. It was a neat little lie that many accepted without hesitation. Riley assured Bruce that the principle of threes was at work. He said one third believed it, one third did not, and one third couldn't care less. Still, it was disconcerting to Bruce. It appeared that the forces at work in the community would not let him off so simply. Now he wondered, should he tell Criton? He *would* tell him, because he had a right to know what was being said.

When Bruce told Criton, he was surprised at his response. Criton just laughed and told him that would not be the first time someone had started a rumor about him. As a public figure, Criton had a thick skin, and he encouraged Bruce to not let it bother him. Unfortunately, Bruce was a little more sensitive and would dwell on his ruined reputation for some time. Bruce had wanted to go and confront Kirtland, but Riley had advised that it would be pointless, especially since Kirtland had made a sudden decision to take a trip around the world and see all the places he had dreamed of—without his wife. She stayed home and spoke with divorce lawyers while Arthur was spending his fortune as fast as he could. It seemed Arthur Kirtland was getting his reward as well. For the next few weeks, Bruce watched and listened to see if more rewards would be handed out for service to the demons.

Bruce watched the papers and spoke with Riley. No one except Bruce would have noticed the names of the members of Arthur's Sunday school who were mentioned for receiving various awards and appointments to leadership positions in service clubs. Bruce could only shake his head at the idea of these men being considered leaders in service clubs when he remembered Lerajie talking of how they were just servants created to serve.

Scene 64

Death as a reward

At the Paxton's home, things were not going well for Mr. Paxton. He had once more been sent to the barn to sleep. His wife and daughter had become harder and harder to live with, and he had lost his role as head of the house. His wife would take the car and their daughter and disappear for hours at a time, and if he dared ask where they had been, he would be met with a barrage of insults and threats. He sat on the floor, trying to concentrate and practice his breathing exercises, but nothing seemed to help. He knew he would get no sleep in the barn because of his feelings of fear and dread. But it no longer mattered, because he didn't have to worry about getting up and going to work in the morning. That day he had lost his job, but he was too afraid to tell his wife. He would look for a new job the next day, and if he could find work, then he would tell her.

The evening shadows began to creep across the floor, and his feelings of dread began to rise. It was getting ever darker, so he moved to the door and flicked the light switch. The light was harsh in the old barn and filled every spot except the upper loft and one corner stall. It was impossible to sleep with such glaring illumination, but he felt more comfortable with the light on than off, especially since he had heard so many odd sounds in the barn. He often felt as if someone were in there with him. He went back to his lotus position and sat there trying to calm his restlessness. He heard the car pull up in the drive and the doors slam shut, but no one came to check on him, and he didn't get up to see whether it was his wife and daughter home from one of their trips.

He was sinking deeper into his concentration, and for the first time in weeks he felt the sensation of relaxation come over him. His concentration was broken by the flickering of the light, and suddenly he found himself engulfed in darkness. Determined not to surrender to his fear, he sat motionless until his eyes adjusted to the darkness. He could now see shafts of light coming in through the cracks in the walls and around the door. *There must be a bright moon tonight for the light to come in like that*, he thought to himself, but still he did not move. He must face his fears and overcome them. He slowly stood and began to move into a pose that had been especially hard to attain. The sweat began to bead on his forehead, and as he twisted his body, he took special care to match his breathing with his movements. In his mind, he repeated over and over that he was master of his body and his mind. From the corner came a slight rustle of hay on the floor, but he tried to ignore it; he would not be afraid. Then came another rustle from above. Still he did not stop his slow breathing, as he began to feel the strain of the stretch that his body was not able to perform. Another sound, and now he was in a battle with himself. He was determined to ignore his fear, no matter what sounds he heard, and to defeat fear with his power of concentration. Right when he thought he had it under control, something new occurred—he had the distinct feeling that someone was standing right behind him. The feeling was so strong that he began to imagine that he could feel breath on the back of his neck. As the sweat began to run down his body, he did feel a tremble in his muscles, as if they were tightening rather than relaxing. He was losing his concentration as the presence became more and more real. He closed his eyes and tried to regain his focus, but the air around him seemed to heat up and become thick. He could breathe, but he felt breath on his neck, a hot, moist breath. He collapsed on the floor, gasping for air and trying to move toward the door, but it was as if someone were standing on his body and pressing him into the floor. He had lost all concentration now; his body and mind had betrayed him to the fear. The sounds seemed to be all around him, getting closer, and that hot breath was smothering him as he struggled toward the door, using every ounce of strength he could muster. As he neared the door, the tightness in his chest had all but robbed him of air. As he reached for the handle, he saw the door swing open as if blown open by a tornado wind, and there stood a shape, the figure of a person. The last thing he saw before his eyes froze in death was that ghostly silhouette. He grabbed his chest, fell face down in the dirt, and with one last gasp he was gone.

A hand moved slowly over to the light switch and flicked it on. It was his wife, and then a small body stepped from behind her, his daughter. They stood staring down at his motionless body and slowly turned and

walked back toward the house. Once inside they called 911 to report that
Oliver had collapsed in the barn. An ambulance arrived and a deputy,
but it was too late for Oliver Paxton. His body lay there, twisted into
a hideous pose, with no sign of life. His death would be ruled a heart
attack, brought on by too strenuous a workout.

Everything was silent now, and the barn was peaceful. Outside there
was a breeze, birds were singing, and the yard went back to being just a
barnyard. With the exception of the faint sound of an approaching siren,
it was just a normal day at the Paxton's' home. Inside the house, Mrs.
Paxton was sipping a cold soda and eating a snack cake. She offered one
to her daughter, who sat next to her holding a small doll with no hair
or hands. Willow smiled and took two cakes. As the siren grew nearer,
Mrs. Paxton told Willow to help herself to the soda and cakes but to stay
inside until all the visitors were gone. There would be a lot of changes
in the Paxton family now that Oliver was out of the way. The two had
already planned their new indulgences, from the simple inclusion of
soda and snack cakes to entertainment systems and transportation. Mrs.
Paxton had made preparations for this moment, and all her plans were
coming to fruition.

The next few days were quiet. Bruce had read the obituary and
had contacted the deputy to get the details. Riley had told him that
Paxton's hair had whitened, and his face had been frozen in a horrible
grimace. Officially it was a heart attack, but Riley said it looked as if
he had been scared to death. He had done a little investigating and
found something he thought was odd. Mrs. Paxton had taken a life
insurance policy out on her husband just a few weeks earlier, and after
taxes, the insurance company's payoff would be $500,000. They'd also
had mortgage insurance, so their house would be paid off. Two people
living a modest lifestyle would be able to live very comfortably. Riley
mentioned this to the chief, but there was no evidence of foul play, so it
was just considered a coincidence.

Everything was falling into place, just as Bruce had been told it
would. All the people who had served Lerajie were being rewarded in
one way or another.

Scene 65

The last battle

Bruce was making mental notes of the people who had been rewarded for their unholy service. He wondered how many even knew that they were being rewarded or that they had been used by the forces and powers at work around them. He had seen people being used as puppets and pawns, and yet some seemed aware of what they were doing. He kept coming back to Larson, who had seemed to be the only one who really knew that he was host to a demonic spirit. The others were acting out of influence, but they really thought they were doing the right thing. How many knew? How many were willingly possessed? He was not welcomed by many, and he wasn't even sure who those people were. The powers had done the job well. He was broken and disgraced, and he and Criton were bunkered down, just sitting around watching events unfold, and now even that had slowed down. It seemed that the fallen ones had finished their work and were comfortable in their new positions. The feeling of insignificance was new to Bruce, and he was trying to adjust. Criton, on the other hand, was right at home spending his time writing and doing research on a book he was determined to write.

They had not heard from Sandy and Alan for some time, and Bruce had been thinking of giving them a call when his phone rang one evening. It was Sandy. They exchanged pleasantries, and she gave him an update on her father's situation. Then she was silent for a moment.

"Bruce, the reason I called was to warn you, but I am not sure of what. It may be nothing, but I was at my father's office the other day, and two of his ex-colleagues came in, talking. I was in the office and they were right outside the door. I heard them mention your name, but then one looked and saw me standing at the desk, and they got very quiet and walked away. I don't know what they were talking about or anything, other than they mentioned you." Sandy spoke almost apologetically.

"That is odd, especially since I have never met any of those folks, as far as I know—unless, of course, they were not speaking as actual people but as spiritual beings." Bruce said.

"Well, I was trying not to think like that, but it's hard not to reach that conclusion, since as you say, they should not know you at all. And yet ..." Her voice trailed off, sounding confused. "I just thought I should tell you so that you would be aware."

"Thanks, Sandy. I hoped they were going to leave your dad alone for a while, but I don't know why they would be interested in me. They have done a good job of neutralizing my voice around here."

"There's one more thing, Bruce, that my father did tell me about his research. I don't know how to interpret the information or if it means anything now, but remember I told you that in the barn I saw some new boards in the floor. It seems that my father had cut open the floor and dug down into the earth, where he found the skeleton of a colonial soldier. The bones were twisted and out of joint and the skull was mashed in on the side. The rest of the group wanted to study it further, but my father refused to allow them to even see it. He covered it up, replaced the boards, and then abruptly stopped the research. What is so odd is that he now says he doesn't know why he stopped the work. Do you think this is connected to all that is going on?"

Bruce paused and said, "No, I think that it may have something to do with the sanctity of a place or the possible ghost-story idea, but it is all part of a deeper deception to make us think that it is significant. Whoever that person was is no longer important. They are dead, and their spirit is gone, but the demons seem to enjoy making people think that dead bodies and ghosts are the source of all their problems. It's like they hide behind our superstition, but it's too late to hide from us now." Bruce then began to tell her of the events concerning Paxton and the others. After a few moments she hung up, and Bruce sat down to ask Criton his opinion of the situation.

"I must say I am not really surprised in the least, Bruce. I didn't want to say anything, because I know you think you have been squelched by these creatures but consider this: They wanted you on their team, and they didn't get what they wanted. I would find it highly irregular for them to just pack up and leave you alone. It's sort of one of those deals where If I can't have you, no one can have you. They have silenced you, but they haven't punished you personally, and after my run-in with Murmus, I think retribution is right up their alley. I'm not trying to scare you, but we must consider that you are still on their spiritual radar, it is as if they have cursed you." Criton had a tone of serious concern.

Bruce looked perplexed. "What else do they want from me—blood?"

"*Ahem.* You said it, not me. I'm just saying that some form of physical revenge would not be out of consideration, wouldn't you think?" Criton raised an eyebrow.

"I suppose you're right, John. I've been sitting here thinking how badly I have been treated and forgetting about Paxton lying dead in that barn, or Julian, or even Larson, not to mention Topper—and even you! All dead or injured, and I am alive and well. I guess we should keep our eyes open and be ready for anything."

"What do you mean *we*, kemo sabe? You're the Lone Ranger; I'm just Tonto." They both laughed at the reference and then looked at one another more seriously.

"How do you think they would do it?" Criton asked.

"I have no idea, John, but I doubt it would be very pleasant. How can we get out in front of this and be ready for them? Is there any way we can take the fight to them?

"Listen to yourself, Bruce. You're the one that said they were too smart and experienced, we are to stand, remember?"

"Yes, you're right, John. I guess that old spiritual warfare idea is creeping back in. Well, in that case, we do what I do best these days. We sit and wait until they make their play." Bruce stopped for a moment, frozen, and then he spoke the word again. "*Play*—as in Buford's play. There it is again, John! That word and that place just keep coming up in my mind. If I had just drove on by that day instead of stopping in to see what was going on at the battlefield, maybe I'd still be standing in a pulpit, blissfully ignorant of all that is going on around us."

"Think that if you wish, but it appears that you were a part of this all along, whether you like to admit it or not. This has been our destiny, or our providence, however you wish to see it. We came to a crossroads in our lives, and in this case, it was a literal crossroads, where we made our choices. We both have seen our lives turned inside out, and we are still standing, and that may be why they want to knock you down. I suppose I am a target just by my association with you. And you know what? I don't think I would have it any other way, knowing what I know now."

Criton was speaking, but Bruce's mind was wandering, still thinking about that word *play* and how all this was associated with the battlefield. He looked at Criton, saying, "John, let's consider this scenario. There is a barn where a demon passed himself off as a Tory ghost and has been doing it for some time. Then the activity at the battlefield was investigating the validity of the site being a revolutionary battlefield. It's a place that some see as insignificant, but when understood in the context of history, it is a very significant place; it is a place where unabated evil ran rampant for a day. What better place for the spirits of demons to hang around? A grave near where a church once stood, but which is no longer there. It was once hallowed ground but not anymore. It's a place where evil won a battle and has continued to win battles, when you think of the pain that community has suffered. It fits in with what we know of evil and how evil counterfeits and mocks the good. An old churchyard that is no longer a churchyard would be just the place for demons to congregate and mock the ground and defile it even more.

"That's where we need to be, John. If they intend to do us harm, let's take it to their own place of power. That's where the confrontation should occur!"

"Wait a minute, Bruce! I thought we were trying to avoid the bad stuff. Are you suggesting we go looking for demons? Didn't you say that was a bad idea just a moment ago?"

"Yes, I did, John. But, for some reason, I just feel that if we can face this thing at the source we can overcome it!"

"And how do we propose to do this overcoming then?"

"Well, I haven't quite figured that part out yet, but I just feel that Buford crossing is where we are to be."

"And when does this battle take place—and please don't say right now."

"Right now!"

"Oh, Brother Bruce—" But John was cut off.

"John, I have learned to trust my gut on some things, and this is one. You don't have to come with me. I'd totally understand, but I am going." And with that, Bruce headed for the door.

"Are you kidding? I have to be there so that someone can write about whatever it is that's about to happen. Wait for me." And with that, two were out the door and in the car, driving east along Highway 9 into the face of who-knows-what."

Not far away, the alarm had been sounded. "They are coming, Lord Murmus. They are coming here!"

"As I knew they would. I had hoped the good reverend would not let me down and bring himself to us. Summon the others but tell them to stay hidden. I want only Lerajie and Baraqyal by my side. This one's arrogance shall be his undoing, and what better place than here?"

Meanwhile, Bruce was looking out the window as Criton continued down Highway 9, nearing the crossroads.

"Bruce, what are we doing?"

"Really, John, I'm not sure, but I feel we need to be here, and we need to see this thing through to some sort of end."

"Well, it's that 'some sort of end' part that bothers me. I was thinking more of the happy ending sort of thing."

"Think about it, John. They have won every battle; they have been ahead of us at every turn, and we have just been reacting to their actions. I was thinking of the battle here that Alan told me about and how the British leader, Tarleton, set up the battle with Colonel Buford. Buford was beat before the battle began. He was surrounded and thought he was outnumbered, and Tarleton was just going through the forms by offering terms for surrender, and then he let loose his troops on Buford's men; it was like releasing the hounds of war."

"I think Shakespeare said *dogs* of war. 'Cry havoc and let slip the dogs of war!'" Criton spoke in a dramatic tone.

Bruce looked at him and said, "Are you sure of that dogs-of-war thing?"

"Uh, maybe. I think the 'release the hounds' was a reference from

Mr. Burns on *The Simpsons*. He always said, 'Release the hounds' and Shakespeare would say the 'dogs of war.' I don't like this analogy, Bruce, because we are Colonel Buford rushing into Tarleton's trap. Maybe we should turn around and go home, just to frustrate them."

"You can drop me off if you like, John and come back later.. There's no point in you walking into this; you've already fought your fight. I just feel that if I don't do this now it will just delay the inevitable." Bruce was speaking softly, almost as if talking only to himself.

They had stopped their conversation and were nearing the battlefield. They both scanned the area as they pulled into the parking lot, but it was deserted. When Criton turned off the car, there was an eerie silence. They stepped out of the car, and Criton looked over the hood at Bruce and noted, "Well, nobody here—guess we can leave!"

Bruce looked back at Criton with an odd smirk; the look said it all.

Criton smiled back and said, "Okay, okay, just trying to ease the tension."

The two moved up the low bank into the area where the church had once stood. They saw the tiny grave and the spiral of stones in the ground. Criton was staring through the trees down toward the larger mass grave as a cool breeze slid over him, causing little goosebumps to rise on his neck. Yet he felt a sense of comfort, as if a soft hand had brushed against his skin.

"Any other time and place, and I would say this was a very pleasant evening," he remarked to Bruce.

Bruce had walked back toward the picnic table, and at the sound of Criton's voice he turned to agree, when he suddenly froze as he looked toward his friend. But Bruce was not looking at Criton; he was looking beyond him and slightly above him in the trees.

"John, come here to me quickly, and don't turn around." But Criton gave an odd look and glanced over his shoulder. His knees began to buckle, and his own weight pulled him down as Bruce moved quickly to his side. The two were transfixed at what they saw, while Bruce tried to lift Criton from the ground, whispering into his ear to get up and move. Bruce was lifting and Criton was pushing at the ground, but everything was happening in slow motion. The two finally got to their feet and moved back to the table behind them. Criton, still weak, fell onto the seat, and Bruce turned to lean against the side of the table. He wasn't sure whether it was the chill in the air or the fear in his heart, but Bruce was rigid except for the quiver in his arms and chest. He was breathing fast and shallow, when the vision stopped its slow advance and hung there in the air just a few feet above the ground. Bruce felt his breathing slow, and he tried to get control, but his gaze was still locked onto the image that floated before him.

It was a swirling mass of dark colors, moving like a thin fabric, in and out of coherent shapes. Bruce was trying to grasp what he was seeing and staring at it as his mind attempted to process the imagery. A dress, a cloud, a cape or robe were all the relative forms his mind could think of, and at the same time, there was obviously some sort of life form encased. Appendages were running into the form at various levels, like abstract wings and arms and legs but not quite solid or regular. What appeared to be hair melted into the other shapes but was never fixed. As the feeling of horror began to subside, he couldn't help but realize that when there was no fear there was a strange sense of awe and affection at the beauty of the shape. The swirling mass was now adding color to its appearance. It was first a muted and then a deeper gold, unlike anything he had ever seen. Parts had an iridescent quality, and beneath there were various layers of colors, like light passing through jewels. It was almost mesmerizing to watch.

And then Bruce felt Criton's hand touching his arm as he rose and stood beside him. "What is that thing, Bruce?" came in a whispered tone. It was then that both realized how quiet things had become. Criton's whisper sounded like a broadcast through the trees.

"*Thing?*" It was a sound like a voice but with some sort of effect added, coming from the form, and the voice was oddly familiar. "Is that any way to refer to an old friend, John?"

Criton leaned back on the table as his knees grew weak once more, and his lips formed the words, "Murmus! It's you."

"Yes, John, I anticipated that you would come with the good

Reverend Strong. Good to see you again, old friend. Did you miss me?"
Murmus spoke with an almost mocking tone.

As the two spoke, there was movement in the air on either side of
Murmus, and two other shapes similar to Murmur's, began to materialize.
One appeared in various shades of green and the other in red.

"I think you two know my friends, don't you?" Murmus spoke
again, but his voice was different. It had a sound like static electricity.
"Reverend Strong, do you recognize your once friend and almost
companion, Lerajie?" he said, pointing at the green specter.

Bruce stared at the shape, thinking of the beauty it encompassed and
at the same time envisioning the body of the frail old Mr. Larson, who
now lay in the cemetery at the church.

Bruce moved his gaze back to Murmus and said, "Yes, I remember
the many faces of Lerajie. This face suits it best."

"You may be less familiar with Baraqyal, since I think you two have
had fewer dealings with this one of my most trusted companions. Yet
he is indispensable to my efforts."

Bruce was feeling less fear and more comfort knowing that these
beings were new, if more ominous, representations of the creatures that
he had had many conversations with before. Feeling a little braver, he
spoke up to Murmus. "Looks like we are all here now. What next?"

At that, Murmus reared up like a stallion rising into the air,
and Lerajie and Baraqyal drifted back as Murmus shouted out with
a deafening growl, "Do not get impudent with me, bone sack! Your
arrogance was once seen as a virtue to me, but your stupidity wiped
away any impressive qualities you may or may not possess. I can show
you things that will chill your blood in your veins or make your head
burst open like a melon from fear, so do not think you are here to impress
anyone! And by the way, we are not all here. That you putrid vomitus
animals think yourselves my equal in any way causes me disgust. You
are blind to the world around you and the powers that encircle you each
moment of each day. Look now upon your adversaries, and weep with
fear. Lerajie! Baraqyal! Summon my legions!"

Bruce was taken aback by the fury of the onslaught, and he did feel the fear rising in his chest once again. As he leaned back against the table, the sky around him began to change colors, and the clouds moved violently, as if pushed by a tornado. The wind began to spin and rustle the trees, and the two men had the sensation that they were being transported to another place, yet they could still see the ground beneath their feet. In the distance Bruce saw movement, and he realized it wasn't some single thing moving toward them but rather forms materializing in waves, getting closer and closer. Each contained a hideous visage, similar but still different from the three who stood before them. Criton gripped Bruce's hand and arm tightly but could not speak. As the legions appeared closer and closer, Bruce noticed something new. In this existence, or dimension, whatever it was, he was experiencing a new sense. It was the sense of smell; the creatures gave off the odor of rot and death. It was a sickening scent that caused the two to cover their mouths and noses to try to avoid vomiting. As the legions manifested all around them and they were being overcome with sights and smells, a feeling of loss and hopelessness filled the air, and they now found it hard to breathe. Bruce was bending his knees toward the ground as the weakness overcame him, and Criton was trying to bury his head in his arms at the table, but he had to lower his head to the side while he vomited at his feet. For a moment Bruce thought of the battle again and how Buford had been surrounded and seen his men die all around. The stink of battle could not be this bad, but the realization that death was closing in from all sides and would show no mercy would have been the same. Then his mind flashed to Paxton and his barn, the scene that Riley had described of a man, white haired from fear, dead on the floor. Is this what he had experienced? Bruce felt the air being sucked from his lungs by the stench, and all around him darkness was cloaking them like a blanket as the light of the sky disappeared. All his worst fears began to come to mind, and then he felt the pressure of Criton's hand squeezing his arm, and he grasped Criton's wrist in response. Suddenly and slowly Bruce began to feel something in his chest—it was like a warmth that was easing the tension and a sense of calm that was giving strength to his knees.

"Come, my children!" It was the voice of Murmus rising over the deafening din, calling his legions. A mixture of laughter and cursing could be heard.

Bruce leaned closer to Criton's ear and said, "John, don't be afraid. I think we're going to be all right!"

Criton's voice was shaking, and tears were running down his cheek, but he managed to speak. "Are you sure about that, Bruce?"

Now with a new-found confidence Bruce spoke softly to his friend, "Yes, never surer, John. Now close your eyes and hold on tight. We're gonna ride this storm out, I promise." And the two men gripped each other's arms tightly.

The display of force went on, as Bruce and Criton stood firm, but rather than becoming more and more afraid, the longer the barrage lasted the more confident the two became. They were like children cowering from a thunderstorm that never strikes their house. Soon Bruce began to lift his head up and peek out at the demonic display. Now both men were looking up, they noticed that the darkness was diminishing, and the legions were disappearing. The strength was returning to their legs, and they began to push their bodies erect. As the legions disappeared, the two men stood up beside the table, and soon it was just them and the three demons.

The air was still, and the clouds were moving slower again. Bruce and Criton were no longer in a different realm, but before they could speak, there was motion in the parking lot. A truck raced into the lot and slid to a stop; three men hopped out. They ran toward Bruce and Criton, oblivious to the three floating specters. Bruce and Criton were taken completely by surprise by this event and even more so when the first punch landed. The first man struck Criton in the face, sending him to the ground, and moved on to Bruce. He hit Bruce a glancing blow but still hard enough to make Bruce stagger to one knee. As Bruce tried to rise, the second man landed a strong punch, full in his face, and Bruce fell to his back. Before he could recover, the two men were pulling Bruce off the ground and swinging again. Bruce saw Criton getting pummeled from the third assailant until he rolled under the table, seeking shelter, but there was no shelter for Bruce. Bruce was nearing unconsciousness as he lifted his arms to block the incoming blows. One of the two men stepped away from Bruce and joined the other as he tried to pull Criton from beneath the table. When Criton had been pulled into the open, a merciless barrage of kicks and punches rained down on him. Bruce shoved his assailant back and made a dive at one of the men who was beating Criton, driving one into the other, and all three men rolled onto the ground.

Criton struggled to his feet and pulled at Bruce's hand; the two were now on their feet, facing their assailants. The fight began again, and the result was just as disastrous. Criton was quickly knocked down, and Bruce was set upon by two attackers, with similar results. Bruce and Criton were almost spent and nearing the point of losing consciousness. Bruce was looking to block a punch when the sunlight blinded him, and he turned his head and prepared himself for punches to the back of his head. But as he fell to the ground, he saw something odd out of the corner of his eye. One of the men fell beside him, and to Bruce's surprise, he lay there motionless. Bruce raised up to his knees and turned in time to see another assailant fall on top of the first. Then the third man fell like a rag doll onto the heap of flesh. Just as Bruce was trying to shake the confusion from his mind and see if Criton had suddenly become a master street fighter, he saw his friend crawling out from beneath the table again. The two looked at one another and the stack of bodies that had just been attacking them. They turned to see the silhouette of a huge figure; he was partially obscured by the light of the sun shining around him, as he now turned to face the three specters still floating in the air. The light seemed to come from the figure, and then the sound of a horn blasted in Bruce's ears. Bruce closed his eyes to a squint but couldn't look long at the light; it was like staring into the sun, and Bruce had to look away. But he seemed to see the shape expanding, like an eagle spreading its wings. For a moment it was as if the light were shining through their bodies, and then it softened, and Bruce peeked from behind his arm. He blinked at the still-shimmering figure; he could only glance for a second or two before looking away, but it appeared that as the figure faced the three demons they began to spin and shrink away. Only Murmus was still struggling to maintain a shape. Criton slumped over, semiconscious, and Bruce turned to support his head. When he turned his head back, the air was clear, and he was looking up into the face of his guardian angel.

"Hey, Preacher, you and this feller looked like y'all needed some help." It was Buck, the local truck driver and doughnut connoisseur.

"Buck, is that you? Are you alone?"

Bruce paused and then smiled up at the gentle giant, saying, "Buck, we were in a fix if you hadn't come along." Bruce was still dazed from the beating. He turned his attention back to Criton.

"That little guy gonna be all right?" Buck said with a tone of concern.

"Them boys looked like they wanted to beat the life out of him." Bruce glanced at the three men slowly trying to stand. He realized that Buck had just beaten the three guys who had almost killed him and Criton, and Buck looked as if he hadn't even broken a sweat or gotten winded.

"I think he'll be okay, Buck."

At that, Criton opened his eyes and looked up at Buck with a groan. "Is this our savior, Bruce?"

"Yep, this is Buck. He drives a truck around here and works as a part-time superhero, it appears." As Bruce was talking, the three attackers stood up. "You know these boys, Buck?"

"Yeah, I seen 'em around. They're troublemakers, but they don't fight real good."

Buck stepped over near the three men, who were still groggy from their beating. "Buck, where did you come from? And why'd you beat the hell out of us? We didn't do nothin' to you." The three stood up together and tried to look intimidating. "You done called down the thunder, Buck! You don't mess with us and git away with it—"

But before he could say any more, Buck reached over and grabbed the man's face in his massive hand. He squeezed the man's cheeks together and, smiling, said, "You'd look awful funny like this, ya know it? Y'all wanna dance with me some more, boys, ya better start the music now, while you can still sing."

The other two looked at Buck and then at their friend and shook their heads no. Buck released the man's face and shoved him toward their truck. The three staggered to the truck and drove away.

Buck watched them leave and then shouted, "Bye fellers! Don't hurry back." Buck softly chuckled at his own joke.

"Buck, what were you doing over here?" Bruce asked.

"I was coming from the store, and I saw them guys beating you up, and well, you know the rest. It just didn't seem right, three on two like that, so I made your third man."

"Well, Buck, I don't know how to thank you. I think we'd have been goners if it wasn't for you. Is there anything you need or want that I can do for you?"

"Nah, Preacher, it's like you said one morning in church: 'Kindness is its own reward' or something like that." Buck grinned a warm grin and told Bruce to get Criton home and put some ice on his head. Like a child taking orders from his parent, Bruce began to help Criton to his car.

As they were getting into the car, Bruce thought to ask, "Hey, Buck, when you were looking up at the sky after the fight, did you see those things floating in the sky?"

"You mean the clouds?" Buck asked.

"Clouds? No, it was three things floating in the sky, sort of different colors."

Buck smiled and said, "Those are clouds, Preacher, and the colors must be from you gettin' knocked in the head so hard." Buck chuckled again. "See ya later, Preacher. Oh, and ya better put some ice on your head too, okay?" With that he drove away. Bruce and Criton stumbled to their car and headed back toward town.

Scene 66

Making sense of it all

When Bruce and Criton arrived at home they did just as Buck

had advised and began to ice down their wounds. Sleep was out of the question. They sat, silently thinking about what they had just experienced. As darkness fell, they finally began to talk about it. Criton mentioned that he wasn't afraid but felt he should be after what had just happened. Bruce agreed, noting that he felt strangely confident. Once the silence was broken, the two began to share observations about what they could remember.

Bruce was first, pointing out how, in spite of all the lights, smoke, and mirrors, the demons had really done nothing physical to them. The other demons had been an assault on the senses but even they had not made a physical assault. It appeared their main weapon was fear and intimidation. Bruce and John both felt that if they had been alone they might have succumbed to their fear. They did not understand whether they'd been transported into another dimension during the demon assault or it had all been an illusion. What they both could agree on was that the physical assault from the three guys had been very real. If Buck had not shown up, they would be in the hospital, if not dead, by now.

"And what about the light, Bruce?" asked Criton. "What light? I was shaking from the noise. It must have been Buck's car horn announcing his arrival—I felt that vibration in my chest!"

"I didn't hear a horn at first, but I saw a blinding light. I guess it was the sun behind Buck, because it blinded me. I tried to look up, but the light was too bright. I think I saw Buck standing between us and the demons after he punched out those guys."

Bruce and Criton paused and sat silent for a few moments, until Criton asked, "What is it, Bruce? You've been silent for a while now."

"It's just that I didn't hear a horn when you did, and you didn't see a light. I feel sure that Buck was staring right at those demons, and yet he said he only saw the clouds. But why would he stop and stare at the clouds in the middle of a fist fight, and why did the demons shrink away from Buck when they had their guys there? Could they not call more helpers?" Bruce sat back, mumbling, "Heard a sound but didn't see a light." Where had he heard that before?

"Sorry I can't help you, except to say that maybe those demons were intimidated by Buck as much as their minions were. I mean, look at the man—he is massive! I'm just glad he was there. I guess Buck, you, and me make a majority of three." Criton was smiling, unaware of the significance of what he was saying.

Bruce realized then where he had heard the light and sound story before. It was the conversion of Saul on the Damascus road, where the travelers each had their own experience; some heard a sound, and some saw a light, as if each had their own epiphany.

"I'm still a little vague on why the demons didn't make sure they killed us, Bruce."

"I'm not sure, John. But I know that the Bible says that after the thousand-year reign of Christ, Satan will be set free and be given power to deceive even the elect. It makes me wonder if the demons' power is limited during this present time period. They seem to be able to do harm to those who are not believers, but to believers they are limited, unless the person allows them to have power."

"How does that work, Bruce?" Criton asked.

"It's all about the Holy Spirit, John, and I would say that is what got us through the day out there—that and Buck's strong right arm!"

The two laughed. They were ready to end an eventful day and feeling satisfied that they had learned a great deal about their enemy. They would figure more out in the future and maybe even realize what had really happened out there. There had been two simultaneous confrontations that day. They had seen what had been revealed to the physical world, but the spiritual battle had been something never before seen by human eyes. When the three men had come to beat up Bruce and Criton, the two had seen humans being used by demons. But, to even the odds, another spiritual being had joined the fight. This being had not only defeated the demons controlling the three men but had also faced down Murmus, Lerajie, and Baraqyal, forcing them to retreat. The horn heard by Criton might have been the battle horn of the archangel, leader of the host, and it was possible the light that Bruce saw was the Shekinah Glory of the presence of the Lord. Buck was the vessel for the human eyes, but the power driving the demons away was the power of God. It was the stuff of legend. Eventually Bruce would put all the pieces together and realize how blessed he and Criton had been. The last battle of Buford had been a victory for real freedom.

At the Paxton's' barn, there was a meeting of demons. They sat quietly, as if licking their wounds, but afraid to admit their defeat. Murmus spoke with a soft growl. "Nothing has changed. Our people are in place, and the work continues as before. We will—" Suddenly another voice interrupted.

It was not the volume but the tone. The words bored like leeches sucking into the flesh, permeating and burrowing deep into a body. A cold feeling paralyzed and sent shock waves of pain.

"You will do nothing but continue your mistakes and stupidity. Who authorized the sharing of information with Strong? What was served by unveiling some of the mystery of our being? I should banish you to some hole in the darkest part of this earth where no one lives and let you waste away." There was a pause and the voice came again. "But I will make you stay here, instead, and languish with these simpletons. They are all you deserve, and this is a gift instead of a punishment. I would expect this from Lerajie but not you, Murmus. You should have killed them when you had the chance."

"We did not expect the intervention from Michael. I allowed him knowledge because I knew that it would serve as temptation and desire for more, and then he would die in his despair, but then—"

"But then Michael came, and you were no match for his presence. What did you expect? Why waste my time? You expected nothing because you were enraptured with your host. As for Strong, I have a plan for him. He has tasted the fruit, and he wants more, and I have just the one that can satisfy his hunger. Enough! Take your legions and leave my presence."

A rustle of hay on the barn floor was followed by silence and then the creaking of the door and a small voice as Willow peeked into the barn.

"They're gone, Mommy. I wish I could have seen him, but I can feel where he has been. He has power and darkness all around. He is beautiful, so beautiful!"

Scene 67

The future

In the following days, Bruce and Criton spent a great deal of time sharing ideas and communicating with Sandy and Alan. The anticipated threat Sandy had warned of must have been the events at the battlefield, because nothing else happened. Bruce was no longer naïve enough to think that the demons were gone, but he understood better how they worked. Criton was determined to write a book about all that had happened, with or without or Bruce's permission. Criton still had connections and resources, and he finally convinced Bruce to join him in his search for more answers about the demons. Bruce considered his situation and, in the end, agreed to partner with Criton. He would work on his doctorate and, along with Criton, research the phenomenon known as demons. The unlikely pair would become their own dynamic duo of sorts. Criton asserted that, since he had experience and had been published, he would write the book based on their encounters. He would be Bruce Strong's amanuensis, and they would begin to write about *the curse of the Fallen and Battle at the Crossroads*. Of course, names would be changed, as would some locations, so as not to arouse suspicions of when and where these events had taken place. But Criton was sure that their stories needed to be told. And so it began.

Epilogue

Bruce was shopping for food one day when he saw a couple in the aisle ahead of him pushing their grocery buggy. They smiled as they approached, but Bruce stood frozen in dread and fear.

The two smiled and stopped beside Bruce's cart. They spoke as if they were old friends. "Bruce! Look, honey, it's Bruce. It's so good to see you again."

Bruce looked at the two and slowly said, "I'm sorry, but do we know each other?" But he felt sure that he recognized the faces.

"We weren't formally introduced, but surely you remember seeing us that night at the battlefield. We were standing down near the graveside as you spoke with dear Mr. Larson. Wasn't it sad that he passed on like that? But I believe he's in a better place, don't you?"

Bruce remembered the unknown faces he had seen that evening and here they were again, "I suppose that would depend on how you define *better place*, but his death was a tragedy in many ways."

"Yes, it's always about proper interpretation, now isn't it?"

"Forgive me for saying, but I don't get the feeling that it was a coincidence meeting you two here, was it?" Bruce said.

"There you go again, Bruce. Honey, you know Bruce here always was the sharp fellow. Why no, Bruce, this is not a mere serendipitous reunion. I have a message for you, a very simple sentiment from a mutual acquaintance. He says the offer is still open if you should wish to pursue it further. We would love to have you on our team. Folks like you and I are especially useful to the effort. It can be a blessing or a curse. He says to please give it careful consideration and contact him through channels, of course. I suppose I am that channel? You know where you can reach me anytime. Please come by. We can slice some of my wife's delicious pie. She makes a 'shell' of a pie, so they say. She flavors it with that old demon rum." The two erupted in forced and fake laughter at their not-so-clever comments. Then began to move on up the aisle.

Bruce waited and then turned, "Oh, by the way, you never did introduce yourself or tell me where I may find you."

The two stopped and turned, and with a putrid smile, the man said, "You are right, Bruce. How silly of me. I guess you would be the last to know. I am Reverend Mullin, and this is my wife, Lilith. I am the new pastor at … well, I suppose I am the pastor at your old church. You remember where that's at, now don't ya? Drop in anytime; we look forward to hearing from you. Have a blessed day!

When Bruce returned home, he went to his journal and began his writing.

Excerpt from Bruce Strong's journal

Hebrews 12 says there is a great cloud of witnesses around us, but there is another cloud, one less spoken of but just as real. It is a cloud of evil and terror that follows and watches every move we make, not for the sake of faith but for destruction.

How do I relate what I have learned and experienced? For even as I sit here I can sense their presence all around. It's like a sick feeling in the pit of my stomach that I have grown accustomed to. It is my troubling constant companion that I can never be rid of. I am not sure when it started or where, but as I look back on life, it seems that this feeling, which I have come to know as a presence, has been with me since my childhood. My grandmother used to say that some have the "witchy way," and she would look at me with a muted smile and a look of concern. My mother had it, and I suppose I share that ability to sense and hear the invisible and often inaudible sounds that most people just ignore.

I can only assume that this ability is what has brought me to this point. The greater mystery is why these others have decided to open themselves up to me. I assume it was with the intention of swaying me to their cause, or simply to have someone in human form to converse with and experience life. I have never felt close to being overcome by their spirit, and yet I have been seduced by their presence. Their methods are complex and deeply deceptive, and I realize that I should ignore any thought of them, but they persist in offering their unholy contract. I have made an ally in one who was once in their grasp completely. But he has now come to his mind and has rejected their presence in his life. For his help and information, I am eternally grateful. He often says I saved him from them, but from my perspective the rescue has been mutual, as he has kept me focused and centered on the task that we have had thrust upon us. Just what that task is has not yet become completely clear. As I look back on my life, I see that no matter what occupation I was involved in, the fallen ones were always present and reaching out to me. Even now I sense their existence.

I understand now why many who have had a similar experience don't like to discuss it openly, and yet they long to scream it out so that others will know. But that would only list me among the oddities of humanity, like those who see Bigfoot or are abducted by aliens. I must tell this story somewhere, and so writing it down is my outlet. Will anyone ever read my thoughts? I do not know, but it is therapeutic just putting them on paper. I know that when someone thinks of the word *demon*, they immediately have visions of Hollywood special effects and hideous monsters inhabiting the closets. I have come to understand what it means to be perfectly possessed, and partially possessed, or demonically influenced. These possessors are evil spirits with a knowledge base that is naive in some ways but in other ways is much deeper than our understanding. They have seen things and experienced things that we will never understand until we move from this life to the next. Yet they lack understanding of what we see as some of the simplest of emotions, like love, faith, and grace. They are frustrated to the point of rage at the concept of grace and forgiveness, and this more than anything fuels their actions. These actions take the form of so many plots and methods of subterfuge that it is nearly impossible to keep an accurate and comprehensive record. Theirs is an evil so complex that we mere mortals cannot stand against their wiles. We flatter ourselves for our knowledge and courage as warriors of God fighting evil on earth, and yet that is the first step toward our destruction, for it is the way of pride. Pride is the very path they wish us to take as they lead us deeper into their deception. There is only one spirit that can overcome the demonic spirit of the fallen ones, and that is the Holy Spirit. We can have that spirit, but we must never allow ourselves to trust our own power.

And so it begins. What have I learned so far? First, there are no such things as ghosts; there are only demons impersonating the dead. Second, these demons seem to have a limit to their power. They can influence, coerce, and deceive people into actions and manifest themselves into visual, but metaphysical, forms. Third, they communicate with one another across vast spaces so that what is heard in one place can be conveyed to another in a split second—which explains how mediums can seem to know details of actions and conversations that occurred between two people when they thought they were alone. The fact is that we are never alone. The fallen ones are always around us, watching and waiting for an opportunity to influence us into some action that fits their plan. And last, I've learned their plan. Their goals are destruction and lies. They will tell nine truths in order to gain trust for the moment they can tell the one lie that will lead to our destruction. Sadly, many people are duped into thinking they have friendships with dead relatives or ancient mystics, and it strokes their egos so that they become willing accomplices.

I will continue to chronicle my involvement with the "fallen ones" through various episodes and events in my life. I am beginning here with the revelation and curse I experienced at a battleground memorial outside Lancaster, South Carolina, called Buford's crossroads.

Bruce Strong

About the Author

Dr. L. Brooks Walker draws from personal experiences as a minister and teacher to offer a study on the supernatural and demonstrate how people become engaged with evil behavior either purposefully or without awareness. He holds masters degrees in music and in divinity as well as a doctorate in ministry and resides in Heath Springs, South Carolina. This is his first book.

Printed in the United States
By Bookmasters